SEVENTH EXTINCTION
THE GENESIS PROJECT

ERIC DONALDSON, PH.D.
AND TIM HARMON

SEVERED PRESS
HOBART TASMANIA

SEVENTH EXTINCTION
THE GENESIS PROJECT

ISBN: 978-1-925597-17-2

CHAPTER 1

To the outside observer, everything about Victor Kraus' childhood was strange. His father was a stoic academic type who had a full beard and always wore the same khaki safari outfit. Although he was recognized as a brilliant professor of evolutionary wildlife ecology at Frostburg State University, he was a quiet man who had few friends and always appeared to be lost in thought. Victor's mother was an adjunct professor at the same university where she taught molecular genetics, and while she generally received great evaluations for her teaching, she was frequently criticized for being too rigid and for requiring too much work of her students. These assessments did not bother her, however, as she always felt a little proud to be one of the tough professors.

When folks saw the Kraus family around the small mountain town of Frostburg, Maryland, they always thought they were strange. The image of the older father sitting quietly at a table at the local Wendy's, stoically eating his chili with his wife sitting across the table silently eating her burger, as a young Victor quietly ate his fries... it just seemed a little too orchestrated. It appeared as if the three of them were lifeless automatons only doing what was necessary to survive.

It was also confusing to folks who did not know this family, because Victor was their only child and he was born when his parents were well into their forties. So, by the time he was of grade school age, most folks assumed that he was their grandchild. Even more confusing to the town folks in this small mountain town, Victor did not play sports and was not involved in activities outside of school, therefore, most people only knew him from chance encounters around town. They pitied the poor boy that appeared to be trapped in a life of boring and meaningless privilege.

In fact, most everyone who thought about Victor assumed that the poor kid was being deprived of his youth by parents who were too stuffy and too emotionally unavailable. Many wondered if there was something going on behind the scenes at home. They assumed that this stoic family demeanor in public was a façade hiding the dysfunctions that were surely going behind closed doors. Speculations along these lines often floated around town in the form of rumors.

But Victor's life at home was anything but boring and glum. Despite the fact that both of his parents were introverts, in their home they often engaged in lively discussions about everything from religion and politics to the mating habits of the common prairie dog. As a result, Victor developed and honed an inquisitive imagination, an excellent vocabulary, and an insatiable curiosity that was fueled by scientific inquiry. In addition, Victor was exposed to many new ideas and developed many new skills through interactions with professors that his parents introduced him to, both permanent and visiting, at Frostburg State University. For example, Victor spent two years as a young boy studying Ninjutsu with private lessons from a visiting professor from Japan who specialized in Japanese feudal history and was an expert in Shuriken Jutsu and Kenjutsu, two martial art forms that honed skills for throwing and fighting with knives. The visiting professor taught Victor the basic techniques of these art forms, and then Victor spent hours on his own refining his skills in knife throwing.

Moreover, from the time he was ten years old, Victor spent his summers in the Dakotas with his father doing fieldwork that supported his father's research, studying the social behavior of prairie dogs. During those research trips, father and son spent every moment of daylight observing the behavior of these animals and recording information in their scientific journals. His father taught him the scientific method and set him up with his own journal, and Victor spent every summer with his father in the field until he went off to high school.

In Frostburg during the school year, Victor enjoyed observing wild animals in the area, and occasionally brought home hurt animals to take care of. Although most of the animals he tried to rescue died, he was successful at saving a few of them over the years.

His most successful rescue was of two baby opossums. One spring, he and his parents were driving down an old country road outside of Frostburg when they came upon a mother opossum that was hit by a car. Victor saw the opossum lying dead in the middle of the road and insisted that they stop the car to check the pouch for babies. Sure enough, there were two baby opossums in the pouch. Victor carefully removed the two tiny marsupials and placed them in a tissue box. The two baby opossums were so tiny their eyes were not yet opened.

When they got home, Victor built a nest for them in a small shoebox and fed them warmed milk from an eyedropper several times every day. To everyone's surprise, the two opossums not only survived, they thrived. Within weeks, they were big enough to move around the house, and Victor kept them alive by feeding them cat food.

After a few months, the family realized that they had a major dilemma on their hands. The opossums were nearly full-sized and they roamed around the house at night making strange clicking sounds, which Victor's father informed them were mating signals. They had many conversations about what to do with these creatures because his parents knew that they could not keep them, but they were also afraid to let them go because they feared they would not have the skills to survive in nature.

It was a sad day for the entire family when the two opossums escaped from the house and were never seen again. Victor's father took the loss of the opossums the hardest because, in retrospect, he felt that he should have stepped in and stopped Victor from raising them in the first place. Victor was surprised by his father's tears when the creatures were discovered to be missing because he was not typically an emotional man.

Victor's high school years were extraordinary. He did well at his Frostburg High School, taking as many science classes as he could, but the extraordinary part was that his father arranged for him to do very cool scientific internships during his summer vacations. He spent all four of his summer breaks in various programs around the world where he was able to study different animal species.

He spent one summer working with the Jane Goodall Institute studying chimpanzees in Tanzania. Another summer he spent at the Elephant Nature Park in Northern Thailand, an elephant rehabilitation center, where he helped take care of orphaned baby elephants. The third and fourth summers he spent on South Georgia Island in Antarctica studying the impact of climate change on seal populations. For his senior project, he wrote a scientific paper describing the impact of global warming on the animal species in areas where climate change was having the greatest impact on natural animal habitats. The project was awarded the grand prize in a national science competition, and Victor received a prestigious award and a check for $50,000.

By the time Victor was ready to apply to universities, he already had a handful of scientific publications, an excellent GPA, and SAT scores that were in the top 5%. Although he wasn't the brightest student to apply to some of the programs that he applied to, he strongly demonstrated that he already understood scientific principles and as a result, he was highly competitive. In fact, he applied to six universities and received admittance and scholarship offers from them all.

He accepted a full ride scholarship from the University of Wisconsin – Madison with the goal of studying Wildlife Ecology. At Madison, he was exposed to many areas of ecology, and ended up refining his major to graduate with a degree in Wildlife Ecology on the Natural Sciences tract. After completing his undergraduate studies, he attended the University of California – Davis to get his Ph.D. in Ecology, where he studied infectious disease ecology and took several environmental sciences classes focused on the impact of climate change on natural disease dynamics in animal populations.

Victor's training took him to many places that disturbed the young idealist that he had become. He attended conferences around the world, spending time in large cities where he was disgusted by the human waste and destruction that he witnessed in these cities. While in New York City to attend a conference at Columbia University, Victor was overwhelmed by the consumer-driven masses of people who appeared to mindlessly waste the earth's resources without any thought of the impact they were having on the environment. He was disgusted by the urban scrawl that seemed to encroach outward from the city, chewing up natural areas as it expanded.

While attending a conference in Cancun, Mexico, Victor was appalled by the island of high-end hotels and businesses that lined the beaches, and he did not miss the stark contrast between the luxury tourist area and the rest of the city that was devastated by poverty. It bothered him deeply that the privileged could so blindly carry on without any regard for the poor or the earth. He frequently dwelled on the devastating consequences that humans were having on the animal populations that they displaced and destroyed for their own pleasures.

Victor knew that the human population was over 6 billion with projections of it reaching over 10 billion by 2025. If left unchecked, humans would overpopulate the planet, destroying wildlife and consuming resources until there was nothing left. The scientific evidence was irrefutable. Climate change was being fueled by human activity, and it was costing all of the other species on the planet their habitats and their lives.

Victor decided early in his career that he would not, could not let that stand.

CHAPTER 2

Ethan Edwards sat on the corner at the end of the Antler Bar in Darby, Montana, with his back to the wall. It was the stool where Ethan always sat. On this late June Saturday afternoon, he nursed a beer and looked at his second shot of Wild Turkey. It was the 101 proof Wild Turkey, not the 86 proof. In fact, Ethan wasn't sure why they even made the 86 proof stuff.

There were a lot of things you could say about the Antler Bar. The walls were covered with the antlers of bull elk and trophy deer, thus the name. On the doors to the restrooms, one said Bucks, the other, Does. If you didn't know the difference, chances were you were a tourist. Moreover, the Antler Bar still had a wooden sidewalk out in front of it. In fact, all of the businesses on Main Street had wooden sidewalks.

As he kicked back the shot of Wild Turkey and followed it with a sip of beer, his attention turned to the other three patrons at the bar. They were looking at the TV, which was tuned to Fox News. It was always tuned to Fox News. He could hear their discussion on the situation in the Middle East. Apparently, the current number one terrorist organization had captured another city in Iraq.

Ethan had enough of the Middle East. In fact, he'd fought in the city they were discussing, along with several others in Afghanistan. Ethan served as a Marine, and once a Marine, always a Marine. He'd seen the men in his recon unit die and get maimed, and for what? The place they bled for was now in terrorist hands. The thought of it caused him to motion Vicki, the bartender, down to his end of the bar. He pointed at his empty shot glass. As he watched Vicki pour another shot, a mischievous grin crossed his lips.

"Hey, what's the chance of a guy getting lucky with you tonight?" he asked her.

Vicki took a step back, gave him a stern look, then broke into a smile of her own.

"I can remember when you used to come in here with your daddy and drink Shirley Temples, and you'd talk me out of an extra cherry. You were a cute kid then and now you're a smart ass! You going to order something to eat or what? I've got work to do," she said.

"Nah! Worst way to screw up a good start on a good drunk is food," he responded.

The conversation in the center of the bar was getting louder.

"Bomb the bastards back to the Stone Age!" exclaimed Burt Long. Burt was a local real estate broker. The sign on his office building read: *Your pick of a free gun with every property purchased.*

"Yeah, that's worked real well in the past, Burt."

"Well, what would you do, Phil, bake them a cake?" Phil, the local baker, went silent.

Carl, Phil's brother-in-law and local backyard mechanic, moved out from between the two men. Ethan slid off his bar stool. Burt and Phil had been friends since grade school, but Ethan could tell things were about to get out of hand. It seemed like everybody had been on edge lately because of what was going on in the world. There were reports of some kind of a new Ebola virus outbreak in China. The government had already set up the same precautions at airports they had during the last scare back in 2014.

The door to the Antler Bar opened, letting in sunlight, which stopped Burt and Phil, and everyone turned to see who was walking in. Bob Watkins entered the bar.

"Gentlemen and Lady!" Bob said, as he looked at Vicki. "How are we on this fine day?"

Bob walked over and sat next to Ethan. Bob looked exhausted, and there was clearly something on his mind. He did his best to keep it contained.

"The usual, if you please, Vicki. Include these other fellows and yourself, my dear."

"Won't do ya any good. I already tried to talk her into a night of fun," Ethan stated.

"My good lad, women like Vicki are not interested in a night of fun. A night of passion on the other hand..." Vicki shook her head and smiled.

"Perhaps, Bob, I'll give Fran a call so she can make sure you've taken your heart medications before this big night of passion! Just my luck! Kids and an old married man. Obviously, I'm losing my touch. That, and I forgot to wear my boots today and the bullshit is getting kinda deep on this end of the bar."

She turned and went about getting everyone their drinks.

Ethan threw back his shot. Bob gave him a glance over the rim of his glasses.

"Just making room for the one you ordered, Bob."

"Did I say anything, Ethan?"

"You didn't have to," replied Ethan.

"You want to go there? Because, I don't. I thought maybe we'd just have us a drink together."

"Sorry," replied Ethan. "Guess I'm a bit on edge here lately."

"Yeah, well you're not alone. Pretty much everybody seems to be, except perhaps that hunk of a woman behind the bar!"

They both laughed.

Bob had known Ethan's father, Clay Edwards, and thus Ethan from the time he was born. Watkins was born in Montana and lived there until he went off to college and then moved back to Montana when his education was completed to go to work at the Rocky Mountain Lab facility in Hamilton. Nobody was quite sure what Bob did there, but the consensus around town was that he was some kind of scientist and probably the smartest guy in the area. Ethan's father had helped Bob and his at-the-time new bride, Fran, move into their house. Bob was probably the closest person to a friend that Clay Edwards ever had.

Clay Edwards left for Vietnam as a young man and came home an old one. A major portion of Clay's sanity was lost over there in Vietnam and he never got it back. Maybe, he didn't have it in the first place. Like everybody else around Darby, Clay went to work in the woods felling trees for a local logging operation when he got back. Clay's mom, Mary, passed away shortly after he got home. As for Clay's father, nobody had seen or even heard of Ronnie Edwards in a long, long time. Not since that night.

Clay's father was a hard-working alcoholic who, when he wasn't fighting in the bar, was practicing on Clay and his mother. One night, things were especially bad after he got home from the Antler Bar. After slapping Clay's mother around, he turned his attention to Clay. Clay had stepped in, trying to protect his mom but he was just a fourteen-year-old kid, and Ronnie Edwards was the type of man that tough men avoided. Maybe it was the fact that Clay stepped in this time to try to protect her or maybe Ronnie was just a little more tuned than usual. After slapping Clay to the floor, Ronnie ripped Clay's pants off him.

"Think you're a man? You little fuck! I'll show you a man! I've bitched slapped you, and

now I'm going to show how a bitch gets treated!"

Ronnie tossed Clay's jeans across the room and grabbed Clay's kicking legs by the ankles and flipped him over effortlessly. That's when he heard the sound, the only sound on the planet that could cut through his rage. Mary had ratcheted a shell into the chamber of the Winchester Model 12 shotgun that was leaning by the front door. Ronnie froze.

"Be careful, woman, or I'll stick that gun up your ass."

Mary's eyes were cold. There was absolutely no fear in them.

"Leave! Leave now and don't you ever come back! If you do, so help me with God as my witness, I'll kill you!"

Ronnie, for the first time in his life, felt a strange sensation and realized it was fear.

"Woman, you're going to fall asleep or not be watching, and when you turn around, I'm going to be standing there."

"After you leave, or die, you bastard, we're going over to my father's house, and I'm going to tell him what you tried to do to that boy tonight. Then in the morning, I'm going down to Sam's diner and I'm telling every logging crew in the place. By 9 a.m., I won't have to kill you. You'll already be dead, you son of a bitch!"

He knew she was right. Back then, what went on between a man and his wife, unfortunately, was overlooked. People made excuses for the bruises and black eyes. However, what Ronnie had done would not be tolerated and he knew it. He'd catch a bullet and everybody would swear it happened while he was cleaning his own gun. Everybody, including the sheriff out of Hamilton.

Clay and his mother never spoke of that night again. Maybe they should have, but they never did. Clay withdrew into himself. He had never been what you'd call social, and he became even less so after that night. When he turned seventeen, Clay entered the Marine Corp. Mary cried a little when she signed the papers, and she cried a lot after he got on the bus to the Induction Center in Butte, Montana. The screaming and threats of the drill instructors in boot camp didn't faze Clay. He had grown up with a man who actually acted on his threats. After graduating as a rifleman with an expert marksman badge, Clay got the eagle, globe, and anchor pinned on his chest, and he was shipped off to join a Marine combat platoon serving in the Republic of Vietnam.

A year later, he was back in the States, or the world, as everyone coming back from Vietnam called it. Discharged from the Marines, Clay headed home to Darby. A little more than a year later, he was sitting at the end, on the corner of the Antler Bar with his back to the wall when he watched the fall of Saigon on the TV. He'd seen the men in his unit die and bleed, and for what? Once a Marine, always a Marine.

A short time after the fall of Saigon, Clay's mother passed away. When they buried Mary Edwards, everyone in town attended her service. It spoke to the type of woman she was and how people thought of her. At the reception after the service, Clay noticed a young woman working in the church kitchen washing dishes from the potluck. He couldn't take his eyes off her. She was so pretty that it hurt his eyes just to look at her. She looked up and saw him staring at her. She dried her hands off and walked towards him. Clay desperately wanted to turn his head to look away but he couldn't, no matter how much he willed himself to do so. It wouldn't be the last time self-will would desert him.

"Hello! My name's Becky Sorenson. I'm terribly sorry for your loss."

It turned out that Becky Sorenson was a student at the University of Montana in Missoula. She was in Darby that weekend staying with a friend she knew from childhood who also attended the university. Both girls belonged to the same denomination, and it was just the natural thing for her to help with the church that weekend.

Clay couldn't speak; he didn't know what to say to her and yet, he wanted to blurt out his entire life story to this woman he just met. Somehow, he managed a weak thank you. She let go of his hand. He hadn't even fully realized that she was holding on to it.

"I should get back to the kitchen. I just wanted to…" she stopped mid-sentence.

They stood looking into each other's eyes. Becky felt as if Clay could see into her very soul. It was as if they were the only people in the room or for that matter, the only people on the planet.

"I should go back and help in the kitchen," she muttered.

Clay just nodded. She turned to leave, and as he watched her walk away, he could feel himself suck air back into his lungs. It was as if she stopped his breathing.

Becky found an excuse to stay in Darby that summer with the Wilson family. Her and Kathy Wilson had been friends since they were young girls going to summer camp together. Clay inherited his mother's place, a modest log home on a piece of ground that was so pretty it looked like a postcard. Clay had known the Wilson family all his life. That wasn't surprising, given that Darby was your typical small town community in Montana where everybody knew everyone in town.

Clay spent his weekdays logging in the woods and his weekends coming up with an excuse to help Gary Wilson around his place. It was Gary who actually introduced Clay to Bob Watkins and his wife Fran. Fran had become fast friends with Becky, and wherever Becky was, Clay could be found close by. He hadn't spoken two dozen words to Becky since the funeral; he didn't need to. Clay Edwards said everything that he needed to say to Becky Sorenson with his eyes.

Bob and Fran did what they could to help bring these two together. Bob talked Clay into helping him do several odd jobs, and Fran always made sure Becky was on hand at lunch or at dinnertime. As quiet and reserved as Clay was, Becky was the exact opposite. Her personality just bubbled and she talked a mile a minute, which was okay because Clay could listen to her for hours. In the evenings when the four of them were together, Bob would catch Fran's eye and the two of them would slip away leaving Clay and Becky at a picnic table or walking along the riverbank alone.

Weeks went by and the summer began to come to an end. One evening, Clay was walking ahead of Bob on their way down to the river to do some fishing.

"What are you going to do about it?" asked Bob.

"About what?" Clay replied, looking over his shoulder with a puzzled look.

"About summer ending, is what."

Clay looked at Bob as if he were nuts or something. "Summer ends every year about this time, Bob, just what would you like me to do about it?"

"Well, Clay, you're absolutely right, and when that happens, school starts and when school starts, Becky's going back to Missoula."

Clay stopped walking. It was as if someone punched him in the stomach.

"Know what I think?"

"No, Bob, I don't," replied Clay.

"I think you better ask that girl to marry you before she goes back to school."

All the color drained from Clay's face.

"Marry me! Marry me? What the hell makes you think a girl like that would want to marry me?"

"Well, she sure isn't hanging around because you're a great orator," Bob said with a smile. He could tell by Clay's expression that his shock was turning into anger.

"Hey, Clay, I'm sorry if it appears like I'm teasing you or funnin' ya, because I'm not. I think that you are head over heels in love with Becky. In fact, it's so obvious that a blind man could see it. And, both Fran and I think that Becky feels the same way about you."

Clay Edwards had jumped off the skids of a Huey helicopter into the middle of a rice paddy while it was being swept with Viet Cong machine gun fire, and he was not even close to being as scared then as he was that day standing by a river that flowed through the back of his own property. He felt Becky's hand slip into his. He could feel her eyes. Clay swallowed hard and turned to look at her.

"I was thinking a man could build a new log house someday up on that hill over there. Maybe put it so the back deck looked down on the river. Most likely be cool in the evening, especially if a breeze was blowing across the river."

His legs felt weak, and he was afraid that they would desert him and he'd just fall to the ground in a clump. Becky's eyes began to tear, and for the first time in their relationship, she couldn't find her voice. Clay swallowed again, and when he spoke to her, there was no longer a crack in his voice or fear in his tone. It had been replaced with conviction and purpose.

"I'd like to build it for you, Becky. I'd like it to be our home. I can't offer you much like other men could, and I know deep down inside that I don't deserve someone like you. And, regardless of what you say, I'm going to love you for the rest of my life. That's just the way it is. Becky Sorenson, will you marry me?"

She knocked him over when she jumped into his arms. Clay could feel her tears on his neck and could tell that she was shaking her head yes.

It was a beautiful wedding held on the very spot where Clay had proposed to her. Bob Watkins stood as Clay's best man. Kathy Wilson stood as Becky's bridesmaid.

CHAPTER 3

Lesya Zhirova was born to poor Russian immigrants who brought her to the United States at the height of the cold war between the USSR and the USA. Her father, Boris, was an electrician in Moscow before the family moved to the US, but unfortunately, he never learned to speak fluent English, and so he would never practice his trade on US soil. He made just barely enough money for his family to survive on by doing odd jobs around the New York City neighborhood that they called home.

Boris was able to learn just enough English to get a driver's license, and he became a cab driver for a short time, but the man brought with him a great love for his country's finest treasure, Vodka, and he never quite understood why it should be illegal to drive and imbibe. It took only a few complaints from customers to the dispatch office and two DUIs in a matter of three weeks for Boris to be effectively retired from the taxicab business.

Lesya's mother was a chronic complainer who fussed over her daughter constantly, but somehow, even the manner of her fussing over Lesya always turned out to be all about her and her own troubles. In fact, there was never a single moment since the time that Lesya could first remember, that her mother said anything positive to anyone for any reason. If she did, there was always a twist.

"Lesya, I love you so much," she would often say, but would follow it with, "and you should be lucky to have someone that loves you because no one has ever loved me, not even your father."

If her father happened to overhear this statement, which he always did because she raised her voice so that he would be sure to hear it, he would curse quietly in Russian and sometimes leave the room. This always left an opening for another remark from her mother.

"Run away, you old drunk, I feel better when you are out of my sight," she would say with as much disgust as she could muster, followed by, "Lord knows, it's devastating for me to be in the presence of a man who reminds me all day long with his pathetic face that I ruined his life."

The negative comments and constant bantering between her parents was so common in their household, Lesya tuned it out and mindlessly ignored it as much as possible. Sometimes, she would fantasize about which parent she would trade in if a new parent salesman knocked on the door offering upgrades. However, she always came to the same conclusion that the decision was too difficult, and then would imagine that the salesman would just have to take both parents, even if that meant that there would be no parent at all.

Lesya avoided the conflict at home by turning her attention and every free moment to reading as many books as she could get her hands on. In her books, she found escape from her daily concerns, and the stories allowed her to propel herself into riveting adventures and bold new futures. She started reading American classics like Huckleberry Finn and Catcher in the Rye, but eventually ended up with a strong interest in science books. When she read the Hot Zone for the first time, Lesya became fascinated with viruses, especially the Ebola virus, and she checked out and read all of the books on the topic of virology at the local library.

She was fascinated that something so small that it could not be seen, even by a microscope, could wreak such havoc on human beings. She read about the virus hunters who performed epidemiological studies and solved viral mysteries, she read about how viruses spillover from one species to the next, and she read The Coming Plague with great interest. Her reading helped fuel her love of science, and she deliberately and methodically constructed a dream to become a virologist.

As Lesya moved from middle school to high school, her body began its transformation to womanhood and she began to be noticed by many of the boys in her school. Her portly preteen form had transformed, seemingly overnight, to a tall and shapely dark-haired beauty, even though her personality had not adapted to her new look. She was quiet and reserved, even a little embarrassed by her new body.

Lesya was asked out by a number of boys early in her high school years, and went on several first dates. Unfortunately, most of those dates ended after a couple of awkward hours with no noticeable chemistry between Lesya and her date. She found most boys her age to be too immature and too focused on cars and sports. Even worse, she found that the smart guys who managed to ask her out were even worse than the jocks because they were so focused on themselves and their future plans that it seemed that she was just another thing that they could add to their resumes to show some future university admittance board that they were well-rounded.

She eventually gave up on dating, deciding that she wanted to spend her time doing the things that she loved, which was studying science. For her, science was the only thing that made sense. It was the one thing in her life that she could count on for inspiration and comfort in a world that was otherwise drab, uninspired, and way too predictable.

Her high school biology teacher noticed Lesya's passion for science and identified several opportunities that she could participate in to further her education and foster her enthusiasm for the subject. In her junior year in high school, her biology instructor encouraged her to participate in a competition that was being held by the Society for the Future of Science, which held an annual competition open to all high school students in the

US interested in organizing, designing, and conducting an independent research project with the help of a mentor.

Lesya contacted a virology and epidemiology professor at Columbia University in New York City and asked him to be her mentor for a project that would study the epidemiology and pathogenesis of Lassa fever virus. The professor agreed to serve as a mentor and provide the information and materials that she would need to perform her research, but he left all of the details up to her.

Lesya spent every spare hour over the next six months setting up and conducting her research study, which was designed to gather as much information as she could about the Lassa fever virus, its spread, and its epidemiology, and then she generated a model of how this disease would spread in the future. When her project was completed, her model was able to infer the year the virus first spilled over into humans, determined a putative evolutionary rate, and predicted how and where the virus would spread over the next 50 years, accounting for such variables as deforestation, climate change, and human population growth in the endemic regions, etc.

To Lesya's surprise, she and her project were selected as one of the 40 finalists by the Society for the Future of Science, which meant that she was invited to participate in a weeklong trip to Washington DC, along with all of the other finalists, where she would spend her days with the other contestants exploring the city and showcasing their science projects to the public, to other scientists, and even the president. The week's festivities were to culminate in a gala black tie event where the Society would announce the top five projects and present an award check in the amount of $50,000 for the winner.

Lesya was both excited and terrified to be going to Washington DC, and decided to ask her father to escort her there instead of her mother. Of her two parents, she felt that he represented the lower risk of embarrassing her, even though he could barely speak English and would probably be drunk most of the time. However, that was less of a concern than her mother's constant flow of self-centered negativity.

The Society had spared no expense in the arrangements for the trip. Both Lesya and her father were flown to Washington, DC with first class seats, and there was a driver awaiting their arrival when they stepped out of the secure section of the airport. They were taken to the Hilton where they were checked into a nice room and given the itinerary for the week.

The first evening was set up as a mixer for parents and students, where students in one group and parents in the other were allowed to get to know each other. Lesya hated these types of situations. She was not a social person by nature, and she particularly felt threatened by people that she thought would be smarter than her. At the student mixer, she grabbed a soft drink and a small plate of snacks and sat down on a bench by the wall, trying with all her might to slip into the patterns on the wallpaper so as to go unnoticed for the evening. Unfortunately, her strategy did not work.

"My name is Victor," an uncertain voice announced, as she watched the tall, lanky body associated with the unusually squeaky voice move closer toward her. "What's your name? Where are you from?"

Lesya looked at the boy who was now holding his hand out in an attempt to shake her hand. Suddenly, the can of Sprite that he was grasping precariously along with a plate in his other hand, came toppling out, spraying her from head to toe as it made its drop to the floor with a thud.

"Oh my God," the boy exclaimed as Lesya let out a little scream. "I am such a klutz!"

Victor attempted to help clean the Sprite from the front of her dress with his napkin, but ended up nearly fondling her in the process.

"It's okay," she said meekly. "I wasn't having much fun here anyway. I'll go change."

"I am so sorry," he said.

Lesya turned away from him to head back to her room and Victor called after her.

"You never told me your name. Maybe you don't want to now!"

"My name is Lesya," she said as she walked through the crowd to get back to the hotel lobby.

Victor was smitten. The tall, dark-haired girl was gorgeous, and he had to get to know her. He vowed that he would make it up to her. He watched her walk through the crowd, and was even more attracted to her because of her meek and unassuming demeanor. Everything about her said that she was grateful to be experiencing this moment, even though it was obvious she did not feel worthy. It was an endearing quality and it stood out in this crowd.

Lesya liked Victor, even though she thought he looked a little goofy. He was too tall for his own comfort and his Adam's apple protruded noticeably from his neck, as if his neck had not completely filled in yet. His voice was too high for someone his age, and his face was covered in pimples. His blondish-red hair was already receding slightly above his prominent forehead. His eyes appeared to be sunk too far into his head, but that was probably because of his prominent forehead. He was not unattractive, but he looked just like you would expect a future academic type to look. Fortunately, his personality seemed to be breaking that mold.

As the week progressed, Victor sought out Lesya every moment that he could so that he could talk to her. He was not a great conversationalist, but he made up for that with his sense of humor. Although Lesya was quite shy, she had a hearty laugh and it warmed Victor's heart to hear it. By the end of the first three days, the two were inseparable.

On the fourth day, the group went on a tour of all of the monuments, and Victor and Lesya spent the entire day together. They discussed the history behind the monuments and the great city that they were visiting, and they shared their own perspectives on what it meant to be a citizen of this great nation. Victor was touched deeply by Lesya story of how her family had arrived in the US while she was just a baby. They were first generation immigrants who were forced out of Russia because of extreme poverty and social upheaval. Her strength amazed him.

When they got back to the hotel that evening, there was an hour before dinner, and everyone was heading back to their rooms to freshen up. Victor did not want his time with Lesya to come to an end, even though he knew that they would sit together for dinner. He didn't want to be away from her.

"I guess I'll see you at dinner," he said to her, as she turned down the hallway toward her room.

"Yes, see you at dinner."

"I want you to know something, Lesya," Victor said to her. "You are beautiful and smart and humble, and I love being with you. I am not usually good with girls, but I don't even care about all of that stuff when I am with you."

Lesya blushed as she looked him in the eye. She loved being with him, too, and it scared her. She wasn't sure what to say, so she tilted her head slightly and to her surprise and his, she kissed him gently on the lips.

"See you at dinner."

Victor could barely contain himself until dinner. The kiss dominated his thoughts, and his stomach flipped a somersault every time he thought of Lesya. He decided to take a cold shower and change clothes before going to the dining room.

Victor sat at the same table as Lesya and her father, as was the usual, but unfortunately, Victor's mother sat between him and her. Victor found that he could barely look at Lesya because he feared that his heart would jump right out of his chest. After what seemed like an excruciatingly long dinnertime, the parents were invited to the bar for a nightcap while the students were shown around the ballroom where the gala dinner would be in just two days. All 40 of the students had created a poster displaying their research project, which on the night of the gala they would present to scientists from around the country.

Victor stood beside Lesya during the overview, and tried to sneak in a couple of jokes, but Lesya remained focused on the instructions that were being given by the Society staffer. She was feeling a bit awkward toward Victor, and she wasn't sure if she should have kissed him. She was having doubts.

After the presentation was over the students were released for the evening to go off to bed. Victor and Lesya talked for a few minutes, mostly about the events that they would be doing the next day. Victor stood by awkwardly as the rest of the students disappeared, longing for another taste of her sweet lips. His stomach flipped with the thought.

"You can come by my room later tonight after your mother goes to bed if you want," Lesya said to break the silence.

Victor was stunned. He was hoping to spend more time with her, but he never expected this.

"Won't your father be there?"

"Are you kidding? They gave him a free drink. I won't see him again until tomorrow morning if he comes back at all."

When Victor knocked gently on the door, Lesya answered immediately. He wondered if she was standing on the other side of the door waiting to open the door at the first sound. She looked up and down the hallway, and when satisfied that no one would observe them, she pulled Victor inside the room.

Lesya was dressed in a silky white nightgown that covered her entire body from the base of her neck to her knees. Victor entered and sat down on one of the queen beds that Lesya motioned for him to sit on. She sat down beside him.

"I have really enjoyed every minute I have spent with you," she started. "I have never had a close friend, because I have been afraid that they would laugh at me and hurt me for being poor and having strange parents. You are the first person that I have ever met who sees me as me, not as an extension of them."

"You are beautiful to me," Victor said, "inside and out. I can't imagine living my life without you and yet I have known you for less than a week. I don't want this trip to come to an end."

"You are so sweet," Lesya said as she caressed his left cheek with her right hand and kissed him again, a little harder and lingering a little longer this time.

Victor put his hand on her back and rubbed it gently up and down her silky nightgown, noticing that he could feel no bra strap underneath in the process. Without saying a word, Lesya gently pushed him onto the bed and removed his shoes and then his socks. She tickled the bottom of his right foot playfully, but he barely noticed because he was so self-conscious about other things that were happening to his body.

When Lesya removed his shirt, he reciprocated by trying to untie the bows on the front of her nightgown. Lesya laughed out loud as he fumbled with the knots, and eventually she had to show him that they were decorations that did not really untie anything. She slowly pulled her nightgown over her head, revealing her naked body to him. Victor felt embarrassed to see her naked, but quickly let that go as Lesya removed his pants first and then his briefs. Victor released his embarrassment by looking at her naked body, which was beautifully shaped and perfectly formed. She reached over him and turned off the light that was on the nightstand between the two beds, and then she slid her naked body on top of him, gently connecting her body to his.

Victor had imagined a million times what this experience would be like, and in the moment, he realized how inadequate his imagination had been. Never had he felt closer to anyone, never had he felt so right with the world, never had he felt so much love for another human being.

When she was finished, Lesya rested her head on Victor's chest. He could feel her naked breasts pushing with a little more pressure against his chest with each breath, and the warm air coming from her mouth tickled the few chest hairs that he had been able to grow. Victor lay there with her on top of him, soaking up every moment, until he felt a stream of warmth trickling across his chest and running down his side. He realized that Lesya was crying.

"Are you alright?" Victor asked.

"It just isn't right," she said.

"I'm sorry, did I do something wrong?"

"No, it's not you. It just isn't right."

"Maybe we should have waited," Victor stated, feeling ashamed that he had made her cry.

"No, you are perfect, it was perfect, but it just isn't right for me, Victor. It just didn't feel right."

Victor tried to console her and tried to understand what she meant, but Lesya just kept repeating the cryptic message over and over. She eventually told him that he should leave, and she hugged him tight and kissed him on the cheek as he made his exit.

Victor was confused, but Lesya was even more confused. She had been having sexual thoughts about other girls for a couple of years, but ignored them, thinking that it was just part of going through puberty. She would occasionally catch herself looking at another woman and would quickly look away and justify it, telling herself that the girl she was observing was wearing a nice skirt or a lovely blouse.

Her experience with Victor was sweet and beautiful and she was glad that she had it, but it confirmed for her that she was meant to be with another woman. She felt terrible that she would have to tell Victor this because she really did love him, and she really wanted to keep the close relationship that had grown between them.

When she told Victor that she thought she was gay, Victor was both shocked and relieved. Shocked because he did not see that coming in a million years, and relieved because he had been torturing himself since that evening because he felt that he must have done something wrong to cause such a reaction from her. Although his male ego took a beating, because sex with him helped her realize that she liked her own gender better, Victor could not, would not let go of the close relationship that had developed between them.

The next time that Lesya cried was when Victor's project was selected for the Society's grand prize of $50,000. She was genuinely happy for him. Her project received second honorable mention and came with a cash prize of $30,000. For the first time in her life, Lesya knew that her dream was about to begin. The prize money would be enough to pay for college.

Victor and Lesya remained friends through college and then graduate school. Whenever the other encountered any difficult times, they contacted each other and often spent hours on the phone just hanging out. Lesya told Victor of her exploits with other women, and Victor listened compassionately, hoping, always hoping that she might realize that she was just going through a phase and that she really was meant to be with him.

He waited patiently in secret agony, savoring every moment that they hung out together. However, Lesya eventually settled down with a partner, Alania, and called Victor less and less frequently. Victor moved on by pouring himself into his career, and he never really looked back. In addition to his work as an academician, he founded a non-profit organization that focused on saving the planet. He occasionally went on a date, but really never hit it off with anyone after Lesya.

Lesya completed graduate school with a doctorate degree in microbiology with a research project that focused on filovirus pathogenesis. She eventually gave in to her father's urgings, and agreed to take a position as a postdoctoral scholar in Moscow working with a Russian virologist who studied the Ebola virus. To her surprise, she loved Russia and she did very well there. At the end of her three-year appointment as a postdoctoral fellow, Lesya accepted a staff scientist position at the Virology Institute in Moscow.

CHAPTER 4

Life in Washington, DC had never normalized for David Gilbert, despite the fact that he had lived in the city for 15 years. He had spent most of his earlier years in a small rural farming town in Iowa, where he served as a priest at the local Catholic church. However, it was clear to him after only a few years as a priest that he could not continue to be Father Gilbert for his whole life. Despite the fact that he knew that he could not lead a faith he had a hard time believing himself, he was swayed by the bishop of the local diocese to stay for much longer than he had intended. He managed to remain a man of the cloth for 17 years before he could no longer force himself to go through the motions.

When he walked away from the church, he suddenly found himself in a harsh and cold world with few friends and only one family member, his "old maid" Aunt Gertie, who lived in the DC neighborhood of Columbia Heights. He had contacted her and made arrangements to stay with her for a while until he could figure out his next move. At the time, he was 43 years of age, had no employable skills, no real savings, and nowhere to turn. Despite all of the problems that leaving the pulpit brought him, it didn't really matter because at least he was free. He no longer had to speak a truth that he did not believe in.

In DC, his situation at his aunt's house transitioned quickly from her helping him to him being her caretaker. Gertie was an old woman when he arrived, but now she was in her early 90s and still doing well enough to be around for several more years. However, she was nearly blind and more than half deaf, and got a little confused at times. David assumed the role as her caretaker, and made the best of his life in the capital.

The most disturbing aspect to David of living in this city was the indifference of the people toward one another. In Iowa, whenever he walked down the street, he always made eye contact with anyone that he encountered along the way and they always exchanged pleasantries. In addition, there was always a certain level of patience and politeness that guided people's behavior in the Midwest. In DC, there was no such courtesy. He learned quickly that most people do not look you in the eye or exchange greetings on the streets of this city, and if they did, they wanted something, usually a handout.

Moreover, the overt rudeness or perhaps complete indifference of people in the DC area was a shock to David. He was nearly overwhelmed the first time he went to a grocery store and had to contend with people moving in all directions around him and in his personal space, reaching in front of him or over him to get items without so much as a look of acknowledgement. He never got used to the fact that most people in the city appeared to operate from a place where they did not really see the other people around them. He hated that feeling, he hated that this was the status quo in this city, and he vowed that he would not let himself be conditioned to behave in this way.

The most surprising aspect of moving to DC was his Aunt Gertrude. David and his family had visited his father's sister from time to time while he was growing up, and she visited them every other year, however, he never really knew her as an adult. The only real memory he had of visiting with her as an adult was at his father's funeral, which he officiated, and he had so little time to spend with her at that time that he was unable to connect with her. To his pleasant surprise, he found Aunt Gertie to be one of the brightest minds that he ever encountered in his life, and he absolutely loved having deep and meaningful conversations with her.

To say that David was confused when he arrived at Aunt Gertie's house was too simple of a description. He was raised Catholic and his family was very proud when he decided that he would study to become a priest. However, to his consternation, he found that the more he learned about his religion, the less spiritual it seemed to him. There was a strong hunger inside him to be open to the mysteries of the universe, and what he was taught at seminary seemed to artificially set limitations to experiencing the mystery. He wanted to be open without limits to fully experience life, and in his experience, the church doctrine was established to define, outline, decree, construct, and limit spirituality to one narrow and hollow worldview.

In retrospect, he realized that he did not agree with these doctrines by his second year in seminary, but he could not tell if he was truly in disagreement with the doctrines or just insecure with his own ability to present them, so he ignored that inner doubt. Within three years of being a priest, he knew that he did not fully believe or accept the doctrines that he was teaching and he felt like a fraud because his parishioners seemed to worship him as much as the doctrines he taught. He reassured himself at the time by telling himself that it was a good life, that he was doing good in the world, and that the Catholic doctrine helped others live a good life. In addition, when he spoke to his bishop about his misgivings, the bishop reinforced those tenets by telling him that humans are flawed and that following a doctrine can help everyone be better people.

He hung on to these ideals for several years, but eventually he could no longer allow his own cognitive dissonance to drown out the still small voice in his own soul that demanded a deeper and more meaningful experience. And so, his spiritual journey took a major turn in his mid-40s, and he would never have guessed that his 76-year-old aunt would be his next spiritual teacher. In fact, when he first moved in with the woman, he was cautious because he assumed that she held the same staunch Catholic beliefs that his father had. To his surprise, he learned that she had a similar spiritual curiosity as his own.

"I learned long ago that God is too large to fit into one religion," she told him, "therefore, I do not allow myself and my thinking to be confined to one point of view. Let me read you this statement that Einstein once wrote: *'A human being is a part of the whole called by us Universe, a part limited in time and space. He experiences himself, his thoughts, and feelings, as something separated from the rest, a kind of optical delusion of his consciousness. This delusion is a kind of prison for us, restricting us to our personal desires and to affection for a few persons nearest to us. Our task must be to free ourselves from this prison by widening our circle of compassion to embrace all living creatures and the whole of nature in its beauty'*."

David had never heard the statement that Einstein had written in a letter of condolence to a father who had just lost a young son to a poliovirus infection.

"For me, religions are limited in time and space," she continued. "I believe that they are all good, and serve a good and useful purpose, except I do not agree with or accept that you must believe in one fully in order to reap some reward in the afterlife. I don't know if there is an afterlife, and I will not live this life worrying about the next. Unfortunately, religions too often become prisons that we must escape from so that we can experience more of the mysteries of the universe, and more compassion toward those around us."

David knew that he had arrived at the starting point of his next spiritual journey, and he was ready to see where it might take him. He began to read some of the books that his aunt recommended and he started to do some of the things that she did. He quickly learned that she had lots of interests. For example, she made it a practice to meditate daily and she belonged to a sangha that met three times a week to meditate and to discuss topics related to compassion and love. David started to attend this group with her and was surprised at how much it increased his compassion.

In addition, Aunt Gertie was a naturalist who loved to be out in nature. She took him on several hikes around the Washington, DC area, and he was surprised to find that there were so many natural respites so close to the madness of the city. On one of these hikes, they took the Northwest Branch trail along that branch of the Anacostia river through the Rachel Carson greenway. The trail was an easy hike that meandered along the river with lots of wildlife to be seen in all directions.

"I attended a lecture that she gave once," Aunt Gertie said while on the hike.

"Rachel Carson?" David asked, only thinking to say that name at the last minute.

"Yes, she was a very interesting lady. Did you know that she was one of the first activists to protest the use of DDT in insecticides?"

"I did not know that."

"She pretty much raised public awareness on that issue singlehandedly. The DDT caused malformation of bird eggs, making the shell layer so thin and fragile that they would be crushed by the mother when she sat upon them to incubate them. This was a particular problem for eagle eggs."

"Wow, that is fascinating," David replied. "Where did she present?"

"Oh, it was several years ago at the Smithsonian institute. They frequently had lectures from scientists and activists of the day. Still do from time to time."

Aunt Gertie was also a movie fanatic. She loved the movies and she insisted that David take her as often as they could. Usually every weekend. David was not accustomed to going to the movies because there was only one movie theater in the small Iowa town that he lived in for so many years, and it only played two movies at a time. It was not much of a draw, and he found little reason to go there by himself.

"I love stories," Aunt Gertie had told him. "Stories are the real souls of human beings. We connect to one another through our stories."

David wasn't quite sure what she meant by that, but she spoke with such confidence that he did not feel comfortable asking her to clarify. Instead, he played along.

"What do you want your stories to say about you?" he asked her.

"Ahhh, you have hit the nail on the head," she said. "I think about that often. When people tell the stories of Gertrude Gilbert, I want them to laugh and cry, I want them to remember warmth, compassion, love, and humor. If, when I die, there are three or four stories of me that provide those qualities, then I will have lived a marvelous life. And, maybe those stories will outlive me."

David had never thought of personal stories as having so much meaning, but in the manner that she described them, he realized that she made a good point.

"Have you ever wondered what the story of humankind will be?" she asked. "You know, from the perspective of the evolutionary scale. Humans in their earliest form have only been around for 3.5 million years or so on a planet that is 3.5 billion years old in a universe that is 13.5 billion years old. We often think that we have made so much progress as a species in the last 200 years, but in the context of the evolutionary scale, 200 years is nothing. We could last another 5 million years and then go extinct and in the context of evolutionary time, we would have meant nothing... been only a dull blip on an infinite canvas."

"I have certainly never thought of it in those terms," he said.

"And in the context of one human lifetime," she continued, "just imagine... we may be the only conscious beings to ever experience the profound beauty of this universe. In an evolutionary sense, we are the eyes and the ears and the hearts of the universe. We have evolved from the very molecules of the cosmos to stand before her in the awe of her beauty. We are the universe looking out at the universe admiring the universe."

"Sort of makes mortgage payments and taxes and all of our daily worries seem so insignificant," David said after a few moments of reflection.

"The odds of us getting to experience life are so infinitesimally small, that every birth is a miracle. So, my nephew, in the sacred words of the poet Mary Oliver, 'Tell me, what is it you plan to do with your one wild and precious life?'"

CHAPTER 5

The Genesis Project was the brainchild of Victor Kraus. The main purpose of the project was to advocate for balance and sustainability on the planet by developing and promoting policies that would benefit all of the earth's inhabitants. The project had five strategic missions: 1) sustainable use of resources, 2) human population control, 3) land management to curtail encroachment of human activities into pristine wildlife reserves, 4) global pollution control, and 5) protection of endangered species.

Victor was a tireless advocate for the project, and while he spent much of his time as a professor at Columbia University studying wildlife infectious disease ecology, he dedicated all of his free time to the project. When the Genesis Project first started, he was hopelessly optimistic that science and reason would have an impact on the behaviors of rational human beings. However, he quickly became frustrated when he realized that most politicians could only see as far as the end of their terms, and most rational human beings only cared deeply about their own lives and assets.

While the Genesis Project failed at gaining much traction in the public eye, the project was successful in pulling together a handful of dedicated and zealous scientists who were committed to the cause of saving the earth. The small group of 15 scientists met quarterly in person and weekly online to discuss the current issues and to develop strategic plans for exacting the change that they felt was necessary to save the planet.

"The Ebola virus outbreak in West Africa is directly related to human encroachment," Victor said to the group assembled for a quarterly Genesis Project meeting.

"The Chinese bought all of the mineral and mining rights in that area 20 years ago, and then spent billions building the infrastructure necessary to transport their resources to the coast so they could be shipped back to mainland China. The very infrastructure that they built was used by the populations in that region, which allowed the virus to spread at heretofore unprecedented rates."

Victor paused for a moment and looked around the room at his colleagues. He had been contemplating how to approach them with a plan for more drastic action, and he was hoping that this presentation would be the catalyst for his radical idea.

"There have been over 28,000 human cases of Ebola virus disease in less than a year, and at last count, there were more than 11,000 deaths and that number could continue upward as more of the cases die. The impact on human life in this region has paled in comparison to the number of gorillas and chimpanzees that have been lost to this virus. The real story here is not the virus itself, but humans encroaching into areas that they do not belong and providing transmission routes that destroy other species."

The mood in the room was grim, but the other scientists listened intently to what he was saying. Victor continued with as much passion as he could muster. However, in reality, he had moved beyond passion and was now operating from pure outrage.

"In 2003, the SARS outbreak was traced back to the Chinese wet markets where it was determined that human merchants in those markets basically established artificial ecologies that allowed that virus to spillover from bats to other animals and humans. As a result, the Chinese government killed 6 million civets, and who knows how many bats have been culled out of fear that they will transmit the disease."

"The bird flu has resulted in the culling of millions of chickens by the Chinese, and that disease is also traced to human behavior. Chinese chicken farmers living in their barns to protect the flock from thieves and scavengers and corrupt government officials likely contracted the first cases of that influenza virus. Do you see the pattern here?"

"Human beings are encroaching on new territories, engaging in unsanitary practices, bringing together species that do not ever come in contact with one another in nature, and the results are catastrophic. In response, they react in fear and destroy animals by the millions, because instead of seeing the reality that they caused the problem, they blame the animals and kill them off."

Victor took a moment to examine the faces in the room. He was hoping for full buy-in, and it was obvious that his audience was indeed on the same page with him. He decided it was time to deliver his new solution.

"Let me ask you this, esteemed colleagues, do you think there is any reason to believe that this is going to get better as the population on this planet doubles in the next 20 years? Right now, over half of the landmass of this planet is dedicated to raising food for humans or to feed the animals that they will slaughter for food. What do you expect that number to be when the human population doubles in size in the next 20 years?"

"Right now, the earth is in the midst of its sixth mass extinction, and we are currently losing plants and animals at a higher rate than at any time since the extinction of the dinosaurs. In the next three decades, 30-50% of the species on this planet will be extinct. What's even more frightening, over 95 percent of species that are currently threatened with extinction are at risk as a direct result of human activities. What will these numbers look like when the human population triples or quadruples in 30-years-time? These are the questions that have been haunting me, and I, for one cannot stand by any longer and allow one species to mindlessly destroy all of the other species and this planet. It is time for drastic action."

Victor finished his presentation, leaving the obvious question of what to do about this problem lingering in the air as he sat down at the table with his colleagues. He gently wiped a little sweat from his balding head and dried the brim of his forehead. He then filled a glass with water from a pitcher that was sitting on the conference table, and took a sip. He was surprised at how easy the words had come to him for this talk. While he always gave a riveting talk, this time he was filled with a new calm. The forcefulness that had driven so many of his previous talks was still there, but this time, instead of showing itself as belligerence, it manifested as resolute peace. He was at peace with his new plan, and he hoped that his colleagues would be too.

"I think you are preaching to the choir in this room," said Dr. Jane Raber, an economist who specialized in Agriculture and Applied Economics. "What did you have in mind?"

"The first mass human extinction," Victor replied in a steady voice devoid of emotion.

A murmur arose from the group as they contemplated what he meant by that statement. While Victor had little trouble convincing the rest of the scientists of the Genesis Project that drastic measures were needed to stop the human population explosion that had already pushed the Earth to its limits and threatened to topple it completely in the next half century, his specific plan was not met with the type of support that he would have liked.

However, Victor expected that some members of the Genesis Project would need convincing. His years working in science had taught him that it was fundamentally impossible for those trained to think critically to agree upon anything without weighing the evidence carefully and fully debating all sides of the issue. He had come prepared for the debate.

"We are out of time, and there is no other way to stop the unrelenting population explosion, short of intervening in a drastic way," Victor stated. "Look, we have been beating the climate change drum for 25 years, and it is just barely acknowledged by the general public and little more than a nuisance to be addressed during campaign speeches for most politicians.

"This will never be taken seriously by most human beings. The human mind evolved to deal with immediate and pending dangers it is not good at preparing for the future. By the time the alarm bells go off in most human minds, the planet will be beyond the point of no return. We must act now."

"But what you are proposing, Victor, is too radical," stated Dr. Van Cliffton, a well-known epidemiologist who specialized in organizing field investigations as a professor at Emory University.

"What will it take, Van?" Victor asked. "Jonas Salk said it best: *'If all the insects were to disappear from the earth, within 50 years all life on earth would end. If all human beings disappeared from the earth, within 50 years all forms of life would flourish.'* The longer we wait, the more species that will disappear. Soon, it will be too late. There will be nothing to do to save the planet, because there will be nothing left to flourish."

"But your plan is unnatural. It's unethical," Dr. Clifton stated. "You cannot take it upon yourself to wipe out civilization as we know it."

"Victor, I agree with Van, this is not a decision that can be made by one person or even by one group," Dr. Roger Friedman spoke up. "I am with you on the call to action. Hell, I've spent my 35-year career dedicated to environmental studies and the impact of climate change on animal habitats. Something has to be done, but you are reaching too far with this approach."

"My distinguished colleagues," Victor began, "you speak of ethics and of no one being qualified to make such a decision, but let me ask you this. If not us, then who? If not now, then when? Surely you have noticed that our own Congress can't pass any bill of any substance without years of debates, negotiations, concessions, and modifications. They are notorious for either solving the wrong problem or not understanding the full scope of any problem they attempt to address. By the time a bill is passed, the original intent is so watered down and the bill is so full of pork that it hardly represents a useful policy. We have spent years trying to influence environmental policy on the hill. What impact have we made? We have one senator who believes in the cause enough to join our group. What else do we have?"

"We cannot be so shortsighted as to think that we know the solution to this problem and so foolish as to believe that the 15 of us in this room can solve it," said Dr. Kevin Keene, a U.S. Senator from Vermont, who was a former medical researcher at Duke University.

"Taking no action is akin to signing the death warrant for the planet," Victor continued. "Take no action, and die with history. Stand up, take a bold action, and save the planet. You then become the only history that ever mattered. You speak of ethics, but what ethics are being followed on the planet today? Is it moral to consume unconsciously while the rest of the planet wilts? Is it moral and ethical to buy your 55th pair of shoes at the cost of the rainforest? To watch TV in your $500,000 house filled with items extracted from the earth and built from the great forests that are disappearing from this planet? To consume animals at will, to dominate animals for your eating pleasure, to desecrate wildlife areas so that you can grow more of your own food?

"My friends, it is time for new ethics. Ethics founded upon sustainability and balance. An ethics that accounts for the needs of the entire planet instead of the one barbaric species that evolved to the highest level of dominance. We are the ones to do this because we are the ones that know what's at stake. And, we are not destroying mankind, we are reducing it to a sustainable level."

A silence fell over the conference room as the members of The Genesis Project contemplated the debate and weighed their conflicting emotions. Victor was worried that the group might not go along with his idea, and it occurred to him that even a single holdout would likely be enough to stop his plan. For if one person did not like the plan and refused to go along, that represented a potential breach that could ruin everything. Fortunately, he had planned for every possibility.

"Okay, for the sake of full disclosure, tell us the details of your plan," said a solemn-looking Dr. Ron Glick, an emeritus professor of medicine at the University of Colorado.

"Yes, we need to know that plan; however, I suggest that you keep the details of the plan to a minimum in case we ultimately do not support it. We need to be able to maintain plausible deniability," Dr. Anna Gold said. She was the only attorney among them, and as a scientist and an expert in law, she knew that what he was about to say could be considered collusion at the best and premeditated crimes against humanity at worse.

"The goal is to reduce the human population by a minimum of 80%," Victor started. "To do this, we have devised a very specific plan. The agent that we will use to do this is a chimeric measles and Ebola virus. The chimera has been developed and tested, and it is very effective so far. The chimera was specifically engineered to get past the transmission limitations of the Ebola virus so that it can be spread while the infected person is still free of symptoms and via the aerosol route. This will increase its infectivity by at least 15-fold."

"Where did this virus come from?" asked Dr. Cliffton.

"In collaboration with a Russian scientist," Victor stated. "We can have her describe it to us in detail at the next meeting if you wish."

"Let's wait until we decide if this is something that the Genesis Project can support," Dr. Gold interjected. "Please continue, Victor."

"The plan is multidimensional, with the goal of making it appear that a natural Ebola virus outbreak spreads quickly across the world and becomes an out of control pandemic. First, we hit a major city in China with the natural Makona variant of Ebola virus in early May. We designed this stage of the attack to look like a natural Ebola virus outbreak that was imported from West Africa. This will get the attention of the world, and all of the major countries will mobilize their epidemiology teams and medical personnel to help in China. We fully expect this outbreak to get out of hand quickly, and we expect China to cover it up, which will only make matters worse for them but better for our plan."

"A couple of weeks later, we introduce the Ebola virus Zaire strain in other major Chinese cities, which will throw the public health officials off, and cause widespread panic as everyone realizes that the virus is out of control and no one even knows what they are dealing with. After the Chinese outbreak is in full swing, around the first of June, we will systematically release the chimeric virus that we have named the Typhon virus after the 'father of all monsters' in Greek mythology."

"At first, we will release Typhon virus at every major airport hub and in every major city in the world. This will require some coordination, and we will need an army of volunteers to help disseminate the Typhon virus. We will distribute the virus at these hubs for ten consecutive days."

"Are all of the virus preparations ready to deploy? How will this all be paid for?" asked a slightly mortified Dr. Raber.

"The preps can be ready within days of our decision. As for funds, we have about 10 million dollars in our political action committee account, and I have been diverting all of my grant dollars to this cause. So have many of you."

"Okay, carry on, Dr. Kraus," Dr. Clifton said. "Tell us more about the Typhon virus."

"The Typhon virus is engineered in such a way as to allow the Ebola virus to acquire two novels functions. First, it can be transmitted like the measles virus, through aerosols generated by sneezing. Second, it can be transmitted for two or three days before the infected person shows severe symptoms. Typhon virus combines the infectivity of the measles virus with the lethality of the Ebola virus. We estimate that the Typhon virus will have a mortality rate of roughly 80%. Moreover, all of the models that I have run predict that we will get about 86% coverage of the human population. That means that an additional 10-12% of the population will need to be disposed of to reach our goal. That may require dissemination into more specific regions, and I have designed a plan for roving dissemination teams to be mobilized if necessary. However, I doubt that we will need to use these teams because I expect that human panic may actually take care of the surplus without our help."

"How do we know who will survive?" asked Dr. Raber.

"We don't. In fact, I believe the only ethical way to do this is to subject ourselves and our families to the same chances for infection as the rest of the world. I plan to help disseminate the virus, and I will do nothing to protect myself. We let the virus select the new human population of the earth."

"This plan leaves too much up to chance," Dr. Clifton said, "I mean, let's say the thing works as expected and reduces the human population of the earth to about one billion. How long will that take? What will become of the governments around the world? There is likely to be anarchy everywhere, and perhaps war. That could have a greater impact on the planet than humans over time. And what about those who survive? What if the virus wipes out all of the intelligent people and leaves pockets of uneducated backwoods folks who will repopulate the planet? Then we are just delaying the problem, but it will return a few generations later."

"The truth is that we cannot predict what the world will look like when this is done, except for the key goal. The population will be reduced by roughly 80%. And honestly, if that is all that we accomplish, then that will be worth it. It is my hope, though, that those who survive will consider this as a wake-up call and an opportunity to change. As for your question about how long this will take, the goal is to infect 100,000 people worldwide with Typhon virus. The virus has a basic reproductive rate of 16-20, meaning that on average, everyone who becomes infected will infect 16-20 other people. If we assume the lower number in the range, we would expect this to take a total of six generations of infection or a total of 18 weeks to infect all of the humans on the planet with a multiplicity of infection of greater than one."

"So basically, you would see six waves of death with each wave being exponentially greater than the last. A concentric circle of global death," Dr. Gold stated, shaking her head.

"The only way that I could agree to this plan would be if we can protect specific people from infection to ensure that the new world is equipped with a few leading scientific thinkers to help with the rebuilding process. I think that the members of the Genesis Project and their families should be protected so that we can make our intentions clear to the world," Dr. Raber stated, as many of the others in the group nodded in agreement.

"That is possible," Victor stated. "There is a vaccine that protects against the Typhon virus. It is not approved by any regulatory body; hell, no one even knows it exists. However, if we save ourselves and our families, then we will have to decide who else to save. Then it gets complicated," Victor stated. "But we can do that if that is what it takes to reach consensus."

"Isn't there an Ebola virus vaccine in development? And what about the measles virus vaccine? How do you know that these two vaccines will not protect against the Typhon virus?" asked Dr. Keene.

"Those are excellent questions, Kevin, but we are already one step ahead of you. The viral proteins on the surface of the Typhon virus have been engineered so that they are novel. No pre-existing immunity will protect against this virus because no immune system will ever have seen anything like it."

"There is one other concession that must be guaranteed, if you want me to go along with this plan," stated Dr. Gold. "The Genesis Project must play a pivotal role in the rebuilding of the earth after the event. In order to do this, we have to remain squeaky clean. I am willing to authorize the attack, but only if you can guarantee that it will never be traced back to you or to us."

"That's the beauty of this plan," Victor said, smiling. "It is designed to come out of nowhere, and the only clues will lead the public health authorities on a wild goose chase. By the time they figure anything out, there will be nothing and no one left to investigate. You have my word that no one will ever know where this attack came from and that the Genesis Project will be a prominent contributor to the rebirth of a sustainable planet. I am excited because this plan will allow us to fulfill the mission that we set for our group years ago!"

After a few more questions and a little more discussion, the group reached consensus. They agreed that they would release the Typhon virus as Victor outlined and that each member of the group and their families would be vaccinated ahead of time. In addition, it was decided that each member would make a list of people that they thought would be important for building a new world as potential candidates for vaccination.

"As you alluded to in your plan, it is going to take an army of volunteers to disseminate the virus. Where are we going to get that army?" asked Dr. Raber.

Victor smiled. "The enemy of our enemy is our friend," he said.

CHAPTER 6

The conversation in the center of the Antler Bar had changed from the Middle East to something less contentious. Now the debate was over which pickup was the overall best truck for your average Joe. Carl was now fully engaged as he considered this to be his area of expertise. The three men were just as loud and opinionated about this topic as they were about the Middle East or any other topic. Given enough beer, these three would argue about how sticky a fly strip needed to be.

"Tell ya what," Phil said. "Let's ask Bob and Ethan what they think."

"Well, no offense to Bob...I mean, Bob you're pretty smart and all, but you're smart in a, like...you know, a schooling-type smart. Know what I mean?" Carl asked.

"Jesus Christ, Carl! You telling Bob that he ain't smart enough to have an opinion on who makes the best truck?"

"I didn't say that, Burt, dammit and you know that. I'm just saying."

"What are you saying, Carl? Come on and say it!"

"Hell, he drives a Toyota, for Christ's sake, with a four-cylinder 22R in it. I mean that

Ain't a real truck! No offense, Bob."

"None taken, Carl."

"Ethan, what about your two bits on this?" Phil asked.

"That ain't really going to work either," Carl said

"Come on, Carl! Now Ethan can't have an opinion?" Burt was beginning to enjoy ribbing Carl.

"God dammit, Burt! Yeah, he can, but Ethan's mounted in a 94 Ford F350 one-ton and it's got a 7.3-liter diesel engine. It's just apples and oranges to compare it to gas rigs."

"Haven't been able to get any decent apples for baking lately."

Everyone, including Vicki behind the bar, stared at Phil with a *What the hell?* look on their faces.

Ethan took a sip of his beer and said, "Well, boys."

Vicki cleared her throat.

"Sorry! And, lady! I'll tell ya."

Right then Carl said, "Hey, shut up, Ethan!"

Ethan continued his thought.

Carl shouted, loud enough for everyone to hear, "SHUT UP!"

They all stopped, surprised.

"Listen," Carl said, as he pointed at the TV.

The crawler said, Fox News Alert.

"Vicki, turn it up would you?"

"The president is about to speak to the nation. This is an unscheduled address and will be broadcast on all networks and cable channels," announced the pretty blonde reporter.

Her co-anchor pointed out that it was not unusual or unprecedented for this administration to, essentially, seize the American airwaves, which according to this reporter was not surprising considering this president's prior executive actions. He was interrupted by the pretty blonde reporter.

"Ladies and Gentlemen, the President of the Unites States."

The president walked to the podium holding a rolled-up paper in his hands. He seemed to be nervously twisting the paper with both hands. His eyes were cast down, his head tilted, looking at the floor in front of his feet. He put the papers on the podium and grasped the sides of it, as if to steady himself. He lifted his head and looked into the camera.

Bob and Ethan looked at each other. Both had seen numerous presidential addresses. They all tried to look serious or presidential, whatever the hell that meant. But this guy, well, he looked scared.

"My fellow Americans, I come to you today, not only as your president, but also as a father, a husband, and a member of the human race. What I'm about to report to you, will come not only as a shock, but frankly, will cause people to be fearful and panic. I implore you to remain as calm as possible. Our nation, and our species, perhaps, and I emphasize perhaps, faces a threat not seen in modern history. On the recommendation of the Secretary of Health and Human Services and the Assistant Secretary for Preparedness Response, experts at the Centers for Disease Control and Prevention, Civilian Health Authorities, USAMRIID, and the Joint Chiefs of Staff, I have asked that emergency powers, along with the powers granted by the Constitution, be granted temporarily to the Office of the President. With overwhelming majorities of both Houses of Congress and the leadership of both parties, this request has been voted on and granted. Therefore, after consulting, and with the consent of all of the Justices of the Supreme Court, I am declaring a state of emergency. I have placed American Armed forces at their highest state of readiness. America's nuclear force status has been moved to DEFCON Four. I have federalized all National Guard troops. All military and National Guard personnel are ordered to report to the closest military installation immediately.

"The reason for taking these unprecedented steps is to safeguard this nation and its citizens from what has been determined to be a bioterrorist attack upon our soil. There are, in numerous locations across this nation and around the world, confirmed cases of Ebola virus disease. It has been scientifically determined that there are multiple strains of this virus circulating, and there is evidence that these viruses have been intentionally released upon thousands of innocent people worldwide. As we learned during the Ebola virus outbreak in West Africa in 2014 and 2015, this virus is highly contagious and it carries with it a high mortality rate.

"Due to these circumstances, I am implementing martial law across the nation and closing our northern and southern borders. I am ordering the closing of all schools and businesses. Federal troops will be moving into cities and towns to back up and assist civilian law enforcement. Curfews will be implemented and lethal force is authorized to prevent looting. On my orders, all commercial and civilian air traffic is grounded. Those planes currently in the air have been ordered to the nearest landing strips. Any aircraft deviating from these orders will be escorted by military aircraft and forced to land. If they do not comply, they will be shot down.

"Simply put, ladies and gentlemen, I implore you to go home and stay in your homes. I am working with Emergency Management services to ensure that power and water will remain on at all times. Food and other necessities will be distributed door to door by local emergency responders and military personnel will be delivering these items in bulk to neighborhood drop points. If, at any time, any person is feeling sick or showing symptoms of the virus, they will be transported immediately to a secure medical facility. Directions for how to report symptoms will be distributed to you within the next few days. The Emergency Broadcast System (EBS) will be available on all local channels providing important information 24 hours a day. If this virus proves to already be in the general population, our best hope for containing it is to isolate those who have it and, to limit the exposure of sick people to others. That is why it is so important for everyone to remain in their homes. Citizens stranded at airports will be taken to holding facilities along with any foreign nationals. All financial institutions will be closed. All wages and prices have been frozen by national mandate. Individuals will not be charged for electricity, water, food or other goods during this crisis. Working with the Secretary of the Treasury and the Chairman of the Federal Reserve, I can assure you that plans arc in place to protect the future economic status of the Unites States of America.

"The next twenty-one days are critical in determining the outcome of this crisis and the future of our nation and our world. I'm sure that all forms of communication have, by this time, already been overwhelmed. I am suspending all cell communications until such time as an emergency rationing system can be implemented. I will do the same with internet Wi-Fi services if it is determined to be a hindrance to the public health efforts that are being employed to protect our people. Any hoarding of goods will be dealt with harshly.

"We must remember that we are all in this together. No one, and I repeat, no one is immune from these executive orders. I can assure you that these orders will be rescinded as soon as it is deemed safe. I have also taken steps to ensure the continuity of our government and our constitutional form of government. America is not a just a place on the world map. It is a belief that all men and women are created equal; that each of us has the right to pursue life, liberty, and justice; that we hold to religious freedom, choosing to worship as each individual sees fit. We, the people of the United States of America, believe in freedom. These beliefs shall not perish for any reason. They will endure and so shall we. I ask you to say a prayer to whatever higher power you believe in, for our nation and for our world. May God bless you and may God Bless America."

"Holy shit, holy shit!" Carl turned and looked at Bob.

In fact, everyone was looking at Bob.

"Bob?" Burt asked.

"Well, I guess that we should do what the man said. But we, ah... I doubt that anyone in Darby has been exposed to this virus. We need to gather people at the church before we all hole up in our homes. Everybody around here is pretty self-sufficient. But we should gather up supplies from downtown here and distribute them where needed. Then we'll split up." Bob looked from face to face to make sure that everyone was on the same page.

"Burt, you, Phil, and Carl can kinda take charge of that if you would."

"But the president said we're under martial law, I mean, *fuck me!*" stated Carl in a high voice.

"Carl, you're right, he did say that, but I doubt the Army is going to show up anytime soon. And the chances of us getting supplies, well, it might not happen for a while," Bob replied. "So, I really think it's alright to do what I suggested, okay? We have got to get ahead of the panic that is sure to come from this speech."

"Ya, I guess it makes sense. I mean shit, man, right now, none of this makes sense; but okay."

The other two nodded.

Vicki spoke up at that point. "Here, boys." She had poured everyone a shot and put a bottle of what they were drinking by the shot glass.

"What the hell, bottoms up," Bob said.

After the drink, Bob looked at Ethan and motioned him to the door.

"Hey, where you guys going?" Burt asked with a note of fear in his voice.

"I'm heading to my lab in Hamilton and Ethan's going to walk me to my truck. So calm down, Burt, and do what I asked, okay?"

Then Bob and Ethan walked out of the Antler Bar. Ethan wondered if it would be for the last time.

CHAPTER 7

Whatever David decided to do with the rest of his one wild and precious life, he knew that it would have to be in service to others. That is one thing that he got out of being a Catholic priest for all of those years: he loved being of service and he loved helping people. He also knew that he would not confine himself to any particular set of rules, but instead he would let his heart be his guide. And so, he opened himself and his life to finding those that he could be of service to.

David and Aunt Gertie were regulars at the sangha where they meditated at least twice a week, and David found this community of friends to be intelligent, friendly, compassionate, and dedicated to helping others. He loved the sense of connection that he got by going there and he thrived in the community. At first, he started by just attending, and then he took a service position with the group helping to set up and take down the room before and after the meditation and discussion sessions. Soon, he was leading an occasional meditation and discussion, and then taking classes to become better versed at leading group meditations.

The sangha did not have any specific doctrines or dogmas that were required to be followed or any particular beliefs that members had to follow. Instead, there were five mindfulness trainings that encouraged training compassionately in five areas, including Reverence for Life, True Happiness, True Love, Loving Speech and Deep Listening, and Nourishment and Healing. The particular mindfulness trainings that were studied by his sangha came from the Vietnamese Buddhist monk and teacher, Thich Nhat Hahn, who David had read extensively and came to consider one of his spiritual teachers.

Aunt Gertie was also intimately involved with the group and enjoyed participating in the discussions and the occasional weekend retreats that the group sponsored. She and David attended several of these retreats over the years, and came to cherish their time in the silence together. David also spent a lot of his time reading and listening to podcasts that he downloaded to his cell phone. One of his favorites was a show that played on NPR called On Being, hosted by Krista Tippett.

While listening to one episode of On Being entitled The Wisdom of Tenderness, David became inspired by the work of Jean Vanier, a philosopher and Catholic social innovator who was a teacher of the wisdom of tenderness. Vanier founded the L'Arche movement, which centered around people with mental disabilities, and his teachings brought together the most paradoxical religious teachings to life: that there is power in humility, strength in weakness, and light in the darkness of human existence.

David followed Vanier's experience and developed a group of like-minded individuals dedicated to fierce compassion. The goal of his group was to compassionately help those in need, regardless of what their needs happened to be. His group reached out to social service organizations throughout the DC metropolitan area, and offered direct help to those in need. He decided that the group would focus on doing the actual work of helping others and stay away from the administrative stuff, such as raising money and maintaining an official office.

The group called itself the Compassionate Neighbors Organization, and they signed up for all kinds of opportunities to help others. They visited the sick, helped feed and clothe the homeless, visited the elderly, painted and repaired the homes of those with low incomes, tended to those who were sick, helped homeless veterans, listened to grieving families, and provided any other service that was asked of them without charge. The group quickly became very busy, and many of its members dedicated nearly all of their free time to the cause.

David was fortunate in that his Aunt Gertie fully supported him and this cause, which allowed him to dedicate all of his time to the work. Aunt Gertie helped as often as she could, as well, but her declining health made it difficult for her to spend too much time out on the streets. Therefore, she mostly volunteered to sit compassionately with those in need and offer deep listening.

"So often, we don't need someone to tell us what to do or to even think of our problems as something that needs to be solved," she often said. "We just need someone who can listen deeply and compassionately as we speak our truths in a safe and non-judgmental environment. We have to be able to be vulnerable with each other and to be a safe set of ears for our friends who suffer."

Even at 91 years of age, Aunt Gertie participated in the work of the group as an active listener. Her favorite activity was to go to the hospital or the local hospice and just listen to the stories of those who so desperately needed to be heard. Sometimes, she would listen for several hours without a word in reply, except perhaps an occasional acknowledgement that she was still paying attention. Not only was this useful to the person talking, but it filled Gertrude with deep gratitude, because she loved the stories.

When Aunt Gertie's health took a turn for the worse, David spent much of his time attending to his ailing aunt. Her body had been in slow but steady decline the entire time that David lived with her, but her mind remained as sharp as ever. However, as the pain of her arthritis became constant, and her breaths became labored as the result of congestive heart failure, her warm and tender spirit gave way to a weariness that was apparent on her face and palpable in her voice. Her stories of great spiritual adventures shifted to stories of how her life fit into the greater picture.

David was troubled by her suffering, but there was little he could do but sit with her, listen to her stories, and wait. In many ways, it seemed as if he was helping her process her life in the context of the whole, and while he wanted her to be free of suffering, he felt a resistance arise in him when it occurred to him that he was helping her die.

"I do not want you to die," he said to her one afternoon as she lay in her bed by the window, watching the birds.

"See that bird, the gray one with the black cap?"

"Yeah, I see it," David said, looking in the direction that her head was turned.

"That's the gray catbird. They make the most interesting 'mew' sound... that's where the 'cat' name comes from."

David did not allow the distraction to derail his previous thoughts.

"Beautiful," he said.

There was a long silence, and David thought that maybe his aunt had fallen asleep.

"I don't really believe in death, I believe in recycling," the old woman finally stated after several minutes of contemplation. "The universe does not waste anything, and it will not waste me. I am going back to stardust, David. The form of me that you know will become the molecules of life everywhere. We are but a small part of a great biological engine, but we had our moments in the sun as this assemblage of molecules with consciousness, and soon it will be time to transition on to the next. I am ready, and it is nearly time."

David was silent.

"Take me with you wherever you go, feel my love warming your heart always, know that I am smiling with great pride and admiration every time you touch a soul, and make a beautiful story that is worthy of being told for all generations to come," Aunt Gertie said as she reached out, grabbed his hand, and gave it a squeeze.

"I will take you with me everywhere; you are my greatest teacher and I love you so much," he said as the tears started to flow.

"Now, would you go get me a cup of hot tea?"

David went to the kitchen and prepared the tea, but when he returned, he discovered that Aunt Gertie had already begun her next journey.

Over the next several days, David was consumed with funeral arrangements and taking care of all of the loose ends associated with his Aunt Gertrude's passing. He arranged for her funeral service and was present with her attorney when her will was read. Aunt Gertie left her house and all of her savings to David. With the gifts that his aunt left him,

David would be able to live out the rest of his life doing the work of his organization. He was immensely grateful.

The first night that David returned to the sangha after Aunt Gertie died, they had a memorial service for her where everyone shared fond memories and stories of her. It was a wonderful evening filled with love and compassion, and David felt the love and support of his newfound family. At the end of the dharma discussion, one of the members of the group, who had recently traveled to France to attend a retreat at Plum Village, alerted the group that there was a new virus circulating and killing people in Asia. He described the loving-kindness meditation that the monks and sisters at Plum Village had performed for those who were suffering from the illness caused by the virus. The group decided that they would close their evening meeting by doing the same metta meditation for those suffering from the illness.

The next day, David turned on the news on the TV to see if he could learn more about the virus outbreak in Asia, and he was surprised to find that there were several cases in China and Korea, that there were different strains of virus apparently circulating, and it was popping up in other major cities around the world. David breathed in deeply. He knew that it was coming to Washington, DC, and he suspected that if it was hitting other metropolitan areas, that it was probably already present.

Within three days, David's intuition proved to be correct. Washington, DC announced that there were a handful of cases in the area, some being treated at the National Institutes of Health hospital in Bethesda, Maryland where they had a biosafety level four containment facility for treating people with highly contagious pathogens with high mortality rates. However, this unit only housed four patients and it was already at capacity. So, other patients were being treated at different hospitals in the area following the revised guidelines for working with dangerous pathogens issued by the CDC during the 2014-15 Ebola virus outbreak in West Africa.

Within days, however, the situation in the Washington, DC metropolitan area deteriorated rapidly as dozens of new cases were reported and hundreds of suspected cases were isolated. It did not take long for emergency government quarantine policies to clash with those who felt they were being held captive, and as panic escalated, irrationality ruled the city. In some cases, those in quarantine refused to be held and no one was able or willing to enforce the new policy that required all suspected cases to be isolated for 14 days. Many of those who left isolation in violation of the new law, were in fact infected, and they took the virus out into the city with them.

As more cases were announced, news reports of total devastation in Asia circulated, and rumors of a deliberate terrorist attack circulated, most citizens in the capital focused on doing whatever they could to keep themselves safe during the looming outbreak. Others used the opportunity to take whatever they wanted, which led to widespread looting. Between those running to the store to buy as many supplies as they could and those inclined to take whatever they wanted, the resources in the city disappeared quickly. Much of the damage had already been done by the time the president declared martial law.

There were reports of violence as store owners had gunfights with would-be looters, and in many cases, even though the police were called, there were too few of them to respond to every issue. As the unrest continued, less and less officers felt compelled to do their jobs and many turned their attention to saving their own families.

Government officials made public service announcements on every medium possible, asking citizens to remain calm and to return to their homes to await instruction, but the announcements were widely ignored because there was a strong sense that the government was too far behind on an appropriate response to this disaster and therefore, they had no clue how to deal with the situation.

The Compassionate Neighbors Organization spent all of their time trying to relieve the stress and fear of people on the street. They offered hugs, food, water, and compassionate listening to anyone who requested help. However, the situation on the street was such that most people were so consumed with taking care of them and theirs, that they barely noticed David and his group or anyone else for that matter. This was driven in part by the fear that everyone on the streets could be infected with the virus and therefore contagious.

David and several other members of the Compassionate Neighbors Organization watched the emergency presidential address with much concern.

"Wow," a friend named Paul said. "I never thought it would actually come to this during my lifetime. I'm feeling really afraid."

Several other friends stated the same sentiment and many of them discussed what they would be doing to protect those that they loved. David remained silent. He knew that the natural response to such a catastrophe was self-preservation. He felt the urge himself, but he could not, no would not give in to it.

"Friends, now is the time that we have spent years practicing for. We must stand up and be a force of good in the world. We have to be the example. The world is running rampant with fear and greed; we must demonstrate love and compassion. Terror can only be defeated with love and tolerance."

David decided that he had to do the compassionate thing, regardless of the danger it would bring to him and his organization. He had to be a force for change, so he opened up his home to anyone who was on the streets who needed a place of refuge during this uncertain time. In a matter of days, he had a house full of terrified new friends to love.

CHAPTER 8

Outside the bar, Bob turned to Ethan. "Follow me to my place," he said and then he simply got in his truck and started it. A smile crossed his face. *"Screw Carl, I like my truck even if it's a four-cylinder Toyota."*

When Bob turned off the main road, he checked his rearview mirror, and sure enough, Ethan was right behind him. Bob lived pretty well off the beaten path. By the time they got to Bob's house, both men had a familiar glow that they picked up at the bar. They pulled into the yard and parked in front of a nice log home with a well-groomed yard.

A beautiful German shepherd jumped to its feet when they pulled up, and when Bob got out of his truck, the dog leaped from the deck and headed toward him at a dead run.

"Come, Cowboy, come on," Bob said slapping his knees. The dog went straight to him and flopped right onto his back like a big puppy. Bob bent down and scratched the dog's stomach.

When he was done, the shepherd jumped up and headed toward Ethan. Ethan dropped to one knee.

"Hey there, boy. How's Cowboy doing?" Ethan asked in a playful voice while scratching the dog's ears.

Cowboy, a five-year-old German shepherd, had come to Bob by way of the Ravalli County Sheriff's Department. The sheriff had put in a request to the US Drug Enforcement Agency (DEA) for a canine to help with the growing methamphetamine problem in the county. It was thought that a drug-sniffing nose would help tremendously.

The shepherd was delivered along with a trainer who was supposed to help get the dog acquainted with its new partner. When the trainer introduced the dog, everyone assumed the name Cowboy had to do with the fact that the dog was being shipped to live in Montana. They would find out later that this wasn't the case.

The trainer ended up leaving before he completed the training because of a family emergency. The DEA promised another dog trainer who turned out to be a no-show. The sheriff teamed Cowboy up with Monty Weston, who was one of his deputies. Monty assured the sheriff that not only had he been around dogs all his life, but he had in fact trained several bird dogs in his day. Monty was one of those guys who had pretty much done everything in his lifetime and was a self-reported authority on all of it.

Unfortunately, Cowboy and Monty were like gas and water. The dog had a mind of its own, and sadly, Monty decided that the best way to deal with the dog was by beating the stubbornness out of the animal. When

Cowboy tried to take a chunk out of Monty's arm, the sheriff was forced to act.

Bob happened to be in the sheriff's office the day it happened. Monty stormed in, arm bandaged, demanding that he be allowed to put the animal down.

"Well, first off Monty, you're not going to do anything unless I say so," stated Sheriff Jim Maxwell. "Rumor has it you've been beating that animal."

"Bullshit, Sheriff, that fucking dog don't listen. What do you want me to do? Have an intelligent conversation with it and use reasoning to get him to obey my orders?"

It occurred to Bob that it would be impossible for Monty to have an intelligent conversation with anything, but he opted to keep his thoughts to himself.

"Tell ya what, buddy, you best remember who you're talking to and whose office you're standing in. Am I clear?" the sheriff paused. "I'm sorry, Monty, I didn't hear you."

"Ya, you're clear."

"Good. Where's the dog now?"

"It's in the back of my fuc…" he caught himself. "It's in the back of my squad car. I can't get it out."

"Leave it there, I'll take care of it. What'd the doctor say about your arm?"

"He told me to take it easy. It's pretty bruised but he released me for light duty. Here's the paperwork." Monty handed the sheriff a note from the doctor.

"Well, go find something to do; like I said, I'll take care of the dog."

"Sheriff, I want that dog put down."

"Monty, you hard of hearing? I said get the hell outta here."

Monty stormed out much the same way he'd stormed in. The sheriff looked at Bob.

"Shit, I'm going to have to put that dog down."

"Come on, Jim, you're not serious are you?"

"Ya, Bob, I am. I mean Monty is Monty and all but the dog bit him. I've got to do something with it."

"The fact that Monty is Monty, can't you just send it back?"

"I'm beginning to think they sent it here to get rid of it in the first place."

"Alright, what if I take it?"

"I don't think I can let you do that, Bob."

"You're the sheriff. I always thought that the sheriff could do whatever he wanted to."

Jim picked up his unlit cigar and put it in his mouth and smiled. "I wish you'd tell my wife that. Hell, if I don't put the dog down, that idiot will file a complaint and a work comp claim."

"I'll make a deal with you. If I can get the dog out of your cop car and into my truck, I get to keep it."

"Bob, what if that animal bites someone else, like a kid or something? Your ass and mine are hanging out there a mile. And what do I tell Monty, huh?"

"Put Monty in charge of some bullshit deal and that will more than make him happy. I'm willing to take my chances on the dog. Come on, what do you say?" Bob pleaded.

The sheriff smiled again. "I wouldn't mind knowing where that fishing hole is that you keep finding those big Cutthroats in?"

"That's pretty dirty, Jim."

"It would save the taxpayers money. I could pull that tail off you. Deal or not?" He put the cigar back into his mouth.

"Deal. Can't believe you'd stoop that low."

"I get the fishing hole either way, even if you can't get the dog out of the car and into your truck."

Bob nodded and the two men got up and headed out to the parking lot. Bob pulled his Toyota around by the patrol car. He got out with a brown paper bag in his hand and opened the passenger door of the truck.

The sheriff opened the back door of the patrol car. Cowboy was laying on the back seat looking at them. When they approached, the dog stood up and snarled at them.

"Okay, Bob, unless you've got a good-looking female German shepherd in that sack, I'm curious to see how you're going to do this."

Bob looked back at him and smiled. He opened the sack and took out a sandwich that was wrapped in wax paper. He showed it to Cowboy then took a bite out of it and made sounds like it was the best thing he'd ever tasted. The dog's ears perked up and it leaned forward. Bob walked backward to his truck pretending to eat more of the sandwich as he went, and he continued to make sounds to stimulate the dog's appetite. He put the sandwich on the seat of the Toyota, clapped his hands together, and gently called to the dog.

Cowboy jumped out of the patrol car and ran over and jumped into Bob's truck. Bob shut the door and looked at the sheriff who was standing there with his cigar drooping downward in his mouth.

"I'll be damned," he said, taking the cigar out of his mouth.

"Fran's meatloaf," Bob said.

"I'll be damned," the sheriff repeated. "What are you going to do if he's still hungry after he's done with the sandwich?"

"Guess I'll give him the chips and pickle," Bob said, just before driving off.

"When you two are done playing with that mutt, get your butts in here," Fran yelled from the front porch.

The two men looked up and then head to the house.

"Thought you might have been home a little earlier. What with everything going on, Bob."

"Well, Fran, I'll tell ya."

"Ya, I bet you will," she turned and walked in the house.

Bob quickened his step and gave her a good-natured slap on her rear end.

"Did we drink our lunches, gentlemen? Of all days, you had to do this today?"

"I'm thinking that of all days, this day would be a bad day to be completely sober. And, I believe you should join us in a drink, my dear. Am I right, Ethan, or am I right?"

Normally, Ethan would stay out of a Fran and Bob conversation like this. But, every now and then, he would interject if it felt safe.

"I couldn't concur more, Bob," replied Ethan.

"Jesus. I'll make you two something to eat. But, if you're pouring, I'll take a Crown and Diet Pepsi. Heavy on the Crown; apparently, I've got some catching up to do."

Fran went to the kitchen and started making turkey sandwiches. Bob went to work on passing out drinks.

"Ethan, Turkey 101 on the rocks. Fran, Crown and diet and a bit of Glenlivet for myself. Well, it feels as though someone should say something."

"How about this, Bob? How about you tell me what you think is going on and what you know is going on," said Ethan. "Because, it sure the hell is more than what you were willing to share at the bar."

Fran turned around with a plate in her hand.

"What'd you tell 'em at the bar?" She set the plate down in front of Ethan. "Here, eat this and I won't take no for an answer."

"Hadn't thought of saying no," Ethan said, as he took a big bite of the sandwich.

She placed Bob's plate in front of him. Bob took a drink and looked at his plate.

"I'm afraid this whole deal could get really bad," Bob said.

"Like, how bad is bad? Like...?"

"Like, society changing! If it is what I think it could be, things won't be the same from here on out."

"Okay, so you're still not telling me anything."

46

"Ethan, I'm not telling you because I don't know for sure. In fact, I don't think anyone really does. Fran and I, though, do need to discuss something with you. Or, rather, ask you for some favors," he continued on before Ethan had a chance to answer.

"We're going to ask you to keep Cowboy for us. Fran and I are leaving for Hamilton. We'll be staying at the lab. They've called us in for lockdown. Unfortunately, they won't allow us to bring Cowboy. We'd like you to stay here if you would. You've got your fifth wheel at your mom and dad's place and you could even pull it here if you'd like. But, it would just make more sense if you stayed at our house. I guess I should say it would be best if you'd just stay in the house. We've got enough food set aside to last you for probably close to a year if not a little longer."

Ethan shifted uneasily in his chair. Everybody took a couple of pulls on their drinks.

"I guess I could do that," Ethan replied somewhat nervously. "So, it could last?"

"Like I said, I don't know. But, I think that the fact that I got called in… or more like ordered to basically move to the lab facility, coupled with the fact that all civilian labs have been placed under military authority, doesn't bode well. You heard what the president said. We have essentially become a military state, and he just hit a few of the highlights. There's a lot more happening behind the scenes."

"Looks like we could use a refill," Fran said.

Bob continued, "I'll show you how to run the ham radio in the basement. You'll be able to pick up ham operators from all over the world. In fact, I have a dozen or so operators I'm in fairly regular contact with. It will be the best way we have of keeping track of the situation worldwide. We've got one at the lab, too. I'll give you the call sign so that we can stay in contact with the outside world. We'll also want to stay in touch from time to time. It's setup to run on AC or DC current."

"When you say 'stay in touch from time to time,' it sounds like you're wanting me to pass you information as much as the other way around."

Fran handed everybody a freshly filled glass.

"I'm about half shit-faced," Bob said, as he took a drink. "I better show you the radio and some other stuff you'll find handy. Follow me."

Ethan stood up and kind of rocked a little. "Shit, I think I am shit-faced," he said with a goofy smile.

"Great, the world is coming to an end as we know it and you two are going into survival mode in the bag. I'm going to pack a few more things," Fran said as she left the room.

Once downstairs, after showing Ethan the storage room with dry goods, Bob took him into what he referred to as his man cave. It was a room about the size of a small bedroom. The ham radio was on a desk with a map of the world hanging on the wall next to it. There were pins in various locations throughout the world on the map. A reloading bench was on the opposite wall and Bob's gun safes were at the end of the room. Other various items were scattered around. Bob opened one of the safes.

"If you need to leave, make room in your pack for these. This is a solar-powered charger. You can use it to charge this handheld GPS, this headlamp, and this flashlight. I'm also going to give you a satellite phone."

"So, did the government issue this stuff or what?" Ethan asked.

Bob grinned. "Oh hell no. Got it at Cabela's. The house has solar panels on the roof and I've got a couple of mobile solar panels that you can use to charge some batteries. You can't run the whole house on the batteries, but it will keep the radio going, run the water pump, the refrigerator, and a few lights. I'll show you how all of that works in a minute. Any of my firearms you can have to use. But, you already knew that."

Bob then reached up and took down a small box from the top shelf of the gun safe. He turned and looked Ethan in the eye.

"We never had kids. Wanted to but Fran found out she..." Bob paused, lost in thought for a moment.

"After the miscarriages..." his voice trailed off again. "Anyway, it was a boy."

"Jeez, Bob, I never knew."

"How would you? It was a long time ago. I bought this when I found out she was pregnant. I've never told her about it. I was going to give it to my son. I'd like you to have it, Ethan. Been meaning to give it to you for a while." He handed the box to Ethan.

Ethan looked at the item in the box. The word 'Case' was printed on the green box in red letters. He opened it and saw a bone-handled Case knife. It had a fork on one side and a spoon on the other. The knife blade was in the middle.

"It's called a hobo knife," Bob said. "Here, let me show you."

Ethan handed him the knife.

"Here, watch." Bob flipped the spoon out and then with his thumb he pushed upward on the bone handle and the spoon and handle separated from the rest of the knife. He then did the same thing with the fork side. After laying them on his desk, he opened the blade. Thus, the knife became three separate items.

"Hoboes used to carry them. These things are handier than a stiff dick on a wedding night," he said, as he reassembled the Case and handed it back to Ethan.

Bob put his arms around the young man and hugged him. It took Ethan a moment, but then he hugged Bob back. Ethan couldn't remember the last time a man hugged him.

"I'm scared and I'm not sure why," Ethan whispered.

"Me, too," Bob whispered back. Except, he knew why he was afraid and he had good reason.

After Bob was done bringing Ethan up to speed on everything that he would need to know to run the house, everyone found themselves back in the kitchen.

"I'll need to head back to my place and grab a few things. I won't be gone long, if that's okay," Ethan said.

"Absolutely. Take Cowboy with you, okay? He's yours to look after." Bob was starting to choke up. "We won't be here when you get back. I'm not saying goodbye, don't believe in it."

Fran put her arms around Ethan.

"We love you," she said as she squeezed him tight.

"Me, too," Ethan said, his voice cracking.

"You've always been loved, Ethan, not just by us. But your..."

"I know," he said before she could finish.

They walked him to his truck. Ethan opened the passenger door.

"Come on, boy," he said. Cowboy looked at him and then looked toward Bob.

Bob bent down and hugged the dog. "Go on, boy."

Cowboy jumped in the truck. Ethan got in after the dog, fired it up, and put the truck in reverse without looking back as he drove off. There were tears rolling down his cheeks.

Bob put his arm around Fran.

"Didn't see this coming," he said, but as he said it, deep down inside he acknowledged that because of his chosen profession he knew it had always been a possibility. Or if the harsh truth were known, just a matter of time.

"Come on, old man," Fran said taking his hand.

He looked at her. "I'm glad you're here, I wouldn't have wanted anyone else to share my life with," he said.

"Same here, it's been a ride, Bob, and you know what? It's not even close to being over."

CHAPTER 9

"Lesya, it's Victor. How are you?" Victor asked into his cell phone.

"Victor, it's so nice to hear your voice. Are you doing well? How was your meeting?"

"The meeting went fine. I am doing well. I am scared, but I am doing well."

"Why would you be afraid? This is something that you have wanted to do for as long as I have known you. It is in your blood; you should be proud."

"I am proud, Lesya, but the damndest thing has started to happen. Everywhere I go, I see people just being themselves, being kind to one another, helping each other, even helping animals. I have witnessed so many beautiful things in the past few days, it makes me question my plan."

"What do you mean?"

"For example, I took an Uber ride to the hotel the other day and the driver had an incredible story. He came to the US from Trinidad 25 years ago. He was a cop there and was shot three times in one year before his wife brought him to the US and burned his passport. He had to start over in the US, which he did right away. He has his own business, raised his four kids and put them through college, and now is just making a little extra money so that he can spend his last years traveling with his wife. I am not sure I can pull the trigger on killing him and thousands just like him."

"What will he be like in ten years when there is no food and the planet is failing? It's easy to look around in this moment and see that everything appears just fine, but as you've told me a thousand times, that's all part of the justification that we use to maintain the status quo."

"You are right, of course, just a moment of weakness, I guess. I am feeling like a horrible person for coming up with such a plan."

"Of course, that is natural. But what you are about to do, what we are about to do, is change the world, not destroy it. We are saviors not monsters."

"That's what I love about you, Lesya, you get me," he said. "You are the only person on this planet who has ever gotten me."

"Victor, I love you, and I always will. Is the plan a go?"

"Yes, Lesya, it's a go. Prepare the vaccine and grow up a bunch of the virus preps. We are going to need plenty. Do you have the natural isolate stocks ready to disseminate?"

"They will be ready for delivery in two days. Are you ready? Are we doing this thing?"

"Yes. I'll be in touch with the final details. Goodbye, Lesya."

"Goodbye, Victor."

Victor put down his cell phone and sat for a moment in his chair. It would soon be happening. A lifetime of hard work was about to culminate into a real world solution. When his conscience gave him trouble, Victor reminded himself of the purpose. He had constructed a mental image of what the world would be like with a population of 10 billion greedy humans consuming everything in sight and demanding more. This fabricated image fueled his cognitive dissonance, which allowed him to sleep at night feeling that he was justified in his actions and that he was a kind, generous, and decent human being. And of course, it always helped when Lesya offered her support.

Over the course of the next couple of weeks, dissemination of the natural Ebola virus isolates in China went as planned. The dissemination team used two Ebola virus variants, Zaire and Makona. The plan was to first hit the port where ships carrying products harvested from West Africa would arrive in mainland China, delivering massive quantities of the Ebola virus Makona variant. The goal of using this isolate was to mislead the whole world into believing that the virus was imported from West Africa. From there, they would hit every major city in China with the Ebola virus Zaire variant because it had a higher mortality rate and any drugs or vaccines that might be used against the Makona variant would be less effective against the Zaire variant. It would take weeks for the public health teams to realize that they were dealing with a different variant. By that time, the Typhon virus would be released upon the world.

As for dispersing the natural Ebola virus preparations, the plan was to spray the virus into large crowds with the goal being to coat the skin and mucous membranes of as many people as possible. They knew that these viruses were not spread by the aerosol route, so they expected it to be more difficult to infect people, and they knew it would spread much less efficiently than the Typhon virus.

Victor and Lesya had come up with very creative ways to introduce the virus to various crowds in China. In several places, they made it appear that malfunctioning sprinkler heads in very busy subway stations accidentally sprayed water on hundreds of passengers, but these fake sprinklers were spewing out virus. They used water mist stations originally designed to cool people down by spraying them with mist, to infect hundreds more who sought comfort from the heat only to be covered from head to toe with virus. Their most devious dissemination route was to drop 50 Yuan bills that were soaked in virus into large crowds, which created a frenzy of people and bills all wallowing around in a desperate attempt to get a few dollars along with their inevitable death sentence.

Once the virus had been disseminated in China, it became a waiting game. Most people infected with Ebola virus would go through an incubation period of 8-12 days, during which time the virus would be replicating inside them, but they would not have symptoms or be able to transmit the virus. Once symptoms arrived, it would usually only take a few days before they would be too sick to move around and would require hospitalization. They would be contagious at around the time that severe symptoms came on, but would generally be immobilized, making it difficult to infect others. Death would occur for most within 6-8 days of symptom onset.

Victor knew that it would be at least two weeks before the first cases started receiving any attention in China, and it would be at least three weeks before the first deaths would occur. Moreover, it would likely be weeks before China announced anything of the outbreak to the rest of the world. China did not have a good public health track record. During the SARS outbreak, they tried to hide the developing epidemic out of fear that it would stop tourism. Unfortunately, the plan backfired and China's subterfuge undermined tourist confidence in the government, leading to severe economic losses north of 30 billion dollars for the region.

Victor had calculated every step of his plan. He wanted it to appear that the Ebola virus outbreak started in China and grew out of control. In order to make it appear that this was the case, he knew that the Genesis Project would have to disseminate the Typhon virus a few weeks after they disseminated the natural Ebola virus preparations.

The Typhon virus had similar characteristics as the Ebola virus in that it would require an incubation period of about 12 days; however, there was one key difference. From day 12 to day 14 or 15, the person infected with this virus would have only mild cold-like symptoms and would be highly contagious. Most of these people would likely be up and about, sneezing Typhon virus into the air wherever they went. And because the virus had been engineered to also be transmitted via aerosols, on average, each person would likely infect 15 to 20 other people. Roughly 80% of the people infected would die within 16 to 18 days of infection.

In addition to serially infecting different populations across the earth, Victor's plan was devious in other ways. First, if all went as planned, no one would be aware that this was an introduced attack until weeks had gone by. By that time, it would be nearly impossible to track down where it came from or who was responsible. Second, the sheer number of infections occurring simultaneously would prevent the Centers for Disease Control and Prevention, the World Health Organization, or altruistic groups like Medecins de Frontieres from doing contact tracing. With so many infections, it would be impossible to trace anything, and that would make it difficult to stop.

By the time the first reports of an Ebola virus outbreak leaked out of China, Victor and the Genesis Project had dissemination teams delivering Typhon virus in all major cities throughout the world and at all major airport hubs. Victor sat in front of his television, watching the nearly constant loop of what CNN was calling Ebola-China, A Deadly New Frontier. They showed the same footage of the index case being isolated in a Chinese hospital with nurses and doctors in large bio-containment suites tending to him. As Victor predicted, they had made the connection and were reporting that the virus came from West Africa. The Chinese government reported that there was no evidence of a viral outbreak and insisted that they did not have an Ebola virus outbreak in China, that this was a case imported from West Africa. The problem was the man had never been to West Africa.

The repetitive loop of information on the TV was interrupted by a knock on the door. Victor was startled. No one ever knocked on his door, particularly if he wasn't expecting it. He looked through the peephole and then quickly opened the door.

"Lesya, what are you doing here? Oh my God, you look like shit."

"Victor, oh my God, I am so glad to see you."

Lesya entered and embraced Victor, holding him tight. Her eyes were red, she had obviously been crying. Her mascara had run down the side of her cheeks.

"You came all the way from Russia?"

"She's dead, Victor."

"Who is dead? Lesya, who is dead?"

"I had to kill her, Victor. I told her about our plan and she was going to go public. I can't believe she was going to go public."

"Who did you kill?"

"Alania. She would have told the world of our plan."

Victor held her close to him. Her body shook as she wept.

"I tried to get her to take the vaccine and she refused. I had no other choice, Victor. She was crazy. She would not listen to reason. She said that I was the monster. She just couldn't grasp the higher purpose. I did the right thing, didn't I?"

"Of course," Victor said aloud, as a sense of panic came over him. Lesya had just killed her partner of several years for the cause. He wasn't sure if that was the right thing to do, it seemed kind of messed up, even to him, but he damn sure wasn't going to tell her that.

"You did the hard but necessary thing," he said, looking her directly in the eyes.

Lesya looked deeply back into his eyes, and reconnected with the feelings she had for him when she was younger. She wrapped his head in her arms as she kissed him passionately. Years of pent-up sexual frustration exploded to the surface of Victor's consciousness. He ripped her clothes off, sending strips of fabric and several buttons flying to the floor and then removed her undergarments.

Lesya surrendered to Victor's sudden show of dominance. Although it caught her by surprise at first, it excited her. She let go of all of her worries and troubles, and let him do with her as he wanted. It felt good to be with someone who knew what they wanted, and who was willing and able to go get it. Victor took her passionately on the coffee table as CNN was reporting more breaking news out of China. Lesya screamed with pleasure as the announcer declared that five new cases of Ebola virus were suspected in the great city of Beijing.

CHAPTER 10

Robert Watkins was a fourth generation Montanan, who was as in love with Montana as anyone to ever live in the state. Maybe this love was bred into him by the previous generations of the Watkins family, or maybe it was just that Montana made him feel free. Whatever it was, Bob could not get Montana out of his mind, and he liked it that way.

Bob spent most of his time outdoors when in Montana, and was an avid hunter, an excellent fly fisherman, and everyone in the county knew the man could shoot. He had hit a few legendary shots from time to time that kept his reputation intact. For example, he once dropped an elk from about 400 yards out, with a single shot that landed perfectly in the animal's heart.

When Bob went away to graduate school in Texas, it was quite a shock to his system. He had gotten his bachelor's degree at Montana State University in Bozeman, where he studied Microbiology and Immunology, but wanted to go on to get a doctorate degree so that he could do research and teach. While he had his heart set on doing his graduate studies in Montana, all of his advisors recommended that he go out of state to get his advanced degree. They told him that it was important to show that he could excel in a variety of different academic environments.

He eventually decided to accept an offer from the University of Texas Medical Branch (UTMB) in Galveston, Texas because it had an excellent virology program and one of the only biosafety level four (BSL 4) laboratories in the United States. Bob knew that if he ever planned to come back to Montana and find a job as a scientist or researcher, he would have to have a broad enough training to qualify him for all of the microbiology/virology jobs that could eventually come open, because he knew that there would be very few of those opportunities in the state.

Training at UTMB gave him a leg up on the competition because the school provided training in a number of areas that would make him a highly competitive candidate for working at the Rocky Mountain Laboratories in Hamilton. Bob's graduate studies focused on the vector-borne Dengue virus, and he studied the immune response in primary infection with one serotype of the virus and the complications associated with a minority of cases that all seemed to be secondary infections with a different serotype that caused an exacerbated clinical syndrome called Dengue Hemorrhagic Fever or Dengue Shock Syndrome.

After graduate school, Bob did a postdoc at the US Army Medical Research Institute for Infectious Diseases (USAMRIID) in Frederick,

Maryland where he continued to study vector-borne viruses, but there he also expanded into Ebola virus research and became recognized as an up and coming virus hunter. In the mid to late 1970's, Bob served as a scientist on the expedition led by Dr. Carl Johnson from the CDC's Special Pathogens branch to search for the animal reservoir of the newly identified Ebola virus. He would make several trips and spend many months in Africa in search of the elusive Ebola virus reservoir, but unfortunately, the reservoir was never identified. Years later, some scientists claimed that bats were the reservoir, but the evidence did not convince Bob.

After his stint at USAMRIID, Bob applied for a staff position at the Rocky Mountain Laboratories (RML) in Hamilton, Montana in the Laboratory of Vector-Borne Viruses. He eventually rose to the level of chief of that section and worked closely with other sections at the lab to study a variety of viral diseases focusing on emerging and re-emerging viruses like Ebola virus, MERS coronavirus, and Dengue virus. He was among the first scientists at RML to use viral genotyping and computational biology to study the molecular epidemiology of the Ebola virus outbreaks in humans.

Bob had spent years at the bench actually doing hands-on research, but those years had passed pretty rapidly as he rose up the ranks at RML. As he approached retirement, he spent most of his time attending conferences, giving talks, meeting with collaborators, mentoring postdoctoral scholars, and writing research papers. The scientific life had taken its toll over the years, and Bob was tired. He was ready for retirement, and as his enthusiasm for it increased, he found himself out in the Montana countryside more and more.

He was exhausted by the amount of work he put into helping control the West African Ebola virus outbreak of 2014-2015. He worked around the clock with a team from RML in Guinea, where they set up a lab that performed diagnostics for one of the largest Ebola Treatment Units in the area. He had spent six-week stints at the lab at three different times during the outbreak. He was glad to see the outbreak wane, and he was relieved to step foot on Montana soil again. He thought that he would be retired by the time the next outbreak popped up. Unfortunately, that was not to be the case.

The Ebola virus outbreak in China was strange. There was more to the story than China was telling, he was sure of it. First, it appeared to start with hundreds of cases occurring simultaneously. That did not happen during the largest Ebola virus outbreak on record, which was traced back to a single index case, and so Bob was sure that this was not simply imported cases coming from the previous outbreak. Sure there were likely to still be a few cases floating around in Guinea, but a single case or two making its way into China would not explode like it had. There were at least 200 cases reported on the news, which Bob knew was just the tip of the iceberg, even as China was still denying that there was an outbreak.

Not only that, but new cases had started to come in and rumor had it that these were different variants of the same species of Ebola virus. The first outbreak in China was caused by the Makona variant of Ebola virus, but there was evidence that there were other cases caused by the Ebola virus Zaire variant. Similar but different. Both deadly, but the Zaire variant was probably a little more lethal. This observation was weird because there were never two virus variants associated with a single outbreak. This was strange, and Bob knew that there something unnatural going on. Moreover, Bob was well connected in the scientific community and he knew that there was much more going on than any government was reporting publicly. He had been getting lots of emails from around the world. This whole thing smacked of a bioterror attack.

When he was ordered to return to RML indefinitely, he knew that his hunch was right. The order came from the White House through the secretary of the Department of Health and Human Services. All RML essential employees were ordered to return to the laboratory indefinitely. Each lab chief was given the authorization to order three FTEs to their labs in order to complete their teams, and Bob was fortunate in that he could order his wife Fran to go with him. In addition to being among the best wives in the world, Fran just happened to be one of the best research technicians he had ever worked with.

Bob had first met Fran when he took his first position at RML, and while he found her quite attractive, she was not easy to talk to in those days. Bob later found out that Fran was very talkative, but she became very quiet around guys that she found attractive. The two spent the first several weeks playing hide and seek, Bob hoping for chance encounters, and Fran afraid that she would bump into him and have to say something.

From a distance, Bob liked everything he saw of Fran. She had the look of someone who spent a lot of time in the great outdoors, and she drove an old car with racks on the roof that she used to carry her skis. She wasn't the kind to wear makeup or care about her appearance to the point of vanity; she was practical and organic. Bob loved that about her.

While Bob had grown up in the Flathead Valley of Montana, north of Hamilton by several hours, Fran was a local girl who grew up in Corvallis and went to the University of Montana in Missoula where she graduated with a bachelor's degree in Microbiology. She never really had any intention of going further in her education; she was content with a BS degree. She had seen the lifestyle of the academic types, and she was not about to leave Montana or live in Montana and be a slave to grant writing and managing lab crises.

Instead, when a research technician position opened at RML, Fran applied and was happy to put in her hours at the lab bench, with little worry or concern about funding or management. That suited her just fine. She would much rather spend all of her free time under the beautiful Montana sky. In fact, she did not have a lot of friends at the lab because she did her job and did it well, but left at 5:00 p.m. every day to do her own thing.

She knew that most of the academic types who took positions at the lab came from distant places much different than Montana, and she knew that most would be gone within a few years. It was the typical trend that Montana residents witnessed all the time. The beauty of the state attracted new residents who did not have what it took to survive there. Not only that, but most of the academic types were so self-absorbed and self-important that she could barely stand to be around them. Bob was different.

Bob had arrived at RML as a native of the state, and he took the job there because he loved two things: Montana and science, and in that order. It would only be a matter of weeks before he loved a third thing that would knock Montana to number two on his list of loves: Fran. Fran could tell that Bob was different and that he loved Montana, and she really liked him. However, she found it hard to believe that a doctor would want anything to do with her.

Bob finally grew tired of trying to accidentally on purpose bump into Fran, so he finally took it upon himself to sway circumstances in his favor. He came in on a Friday morning, a little later than Fran and parked his pickup truck right behind her car. Then, he sat back and waited for Fran to track him down. Sure enough, around 5:15 p.m., Fran found him in the lab and asked him about his truck.

"Excuse me, Dr. Watkins," she said timidly as she approached him, "your truck is blocking me in and I need to leave."

"Please call me Bob. And yes, I know my truck is blocking you in. I will only move it if you agree to have a drink with me."

Fran couldn't decide if she should be flattered or angry.

"Come on, what do you say?" he begged playfully.

"I don't fraternize with academic types," she retorted without letting on that she was kidding.

"Thank God," he said without missing a beat, "there is nothing more exhausting than an academic!"

Bob's ploy worked. Fran agreed to have a drink with him, and then a dinner date. Soon the two were spending weekends hiking, and fishing, or hunting and skiing.

When Bob became chief of his own lab, he hired Fran as his research technician. In most fields, this type of nepotism would be frowned upon, but in science, it was commonplace, and no one raised an eyebrow. Fran was the type of scientist that every researcher dreamed of. She knew what she was doing, she knew how to do it well, she was creative, resourceful, intelligent, independent, and extremely competent. In addition, she worked well with others, provided they were not pretentious or arrogant. She pretty much ran the lab behind the scenes, especially when Bob was travelling, which he had to do a lot of in the past few years. So, when Bob was given the orders to select three FTEs, Fran would have been his first choice, even if she wasn't his wife.

When Bob and his small crew ended up at RML, they were surprised to find that a few samples had arrived from China, three samples from South Korea, and a handful of samples from a more recent outbreak that was occurring in Jakarta, Indonesia. The samples were serum samples collected from patients who had died and the samples were processed in Trizol, a reagent that kills all viruses but preserves the nucleic acids. Bob's team processed these samples for sequencing, with the goal of identifying the pathogens that were in the samples by determining their DNA code. Bob's lab specialized in a new technology called Next Generation Sequencing, which allowed for sequencing all of the DNA in the sample.

His team had processed the samples and sequenced them. The processing included a step for reverse-transcribing any RNA in the samples to complementary DNA so that these nucleotides could be sequenced by the DNA sequencing machines that he had in the lab. Bob liked to do the bioinformatics analysis himself, so he began the process by using human genome sequences to filter out all of the sequence reads that matched human sequences from each of the samples, leaving only sequences that were nonhuman to analyze. He then built larger sequences from the small reads, known as contigs, and then used consensus sequences for each contig to query databases of known sequences to see if the DNA in the human samples matched anything that was known.

The samples from China were mixed. Some of the patients were clearly infected with the Ebola virus Makona variant, while others were infected with Ebola virus Zaire. That was odd. Never before had he seen any Ebola virus outbreak with multiple virus variants present. The samples from South Korea were all Ebola virus Makona variant, and they were identical to the sequences from China. It was pretty clear that the South Korean outbreak virus came from China.

However, the most puzzling sequences came from the Jakarta patients. These sequences looked like the Ebola virus Zaire variant, but there were measles virus genes mixed in with the Ebola virus genome sequence. This was just not right, and Bob knew it. It was odd, because both viruses were from the same order, Mononegavirales, but it didn't seem possible that they could be recombined into one genome. Bob wondered if it was possible that some weird recombination event occurred in a patient infected with Ebola virus and measles virus at the same time. It seemed more likely to him that this was a sequencing error.

As Bob stood up from his desk to head to the lab to discuss this sequencing anomaly with his lab crew, his telephone rang.

"Hello? Yes, this is Bob Watkins," he said into the receiver.

"Lesya Zhirova? Of course, I remember you. How are you, Lesya? Well, I am not currently sitting, but I can take a seat. What's going on?"

CHAPTER 11

Ethan backed up to the fifth wheel camper beside an old shed that was several feet from the house and shut the truck off. He just sat there for a minute trying to wrap his mind around everything that was going on. It was finally Cowboy's bark that brought him out of his thoughts.

"Ya, I guess we better get our shit together," he said aloud, as he patted the dog on the head.

They headed to the shed behind the RV. Inside it, Ethan kept most of the gear he had accumulated. Right inside the door, he reached for and grabbed his "bug-out" bag. It was a Badlands Summit pack that already contained most of what he would need if he ever had to head out in a hurry. The first thing he did was find his mess kit and add the Case Hobo knife that Bob had given him to it.

Once inside the fifth wheel, Ethan laid out all of the other items he would take with him on the living room floor. He placed his Tika 30-06 rifle with a three to nine powered Leupold gold ring scope in the middle of the pile. To say he could hit what he was aiming at with that rifle was an understatement. Next to it, was the rifle he would take with him if he had to leave Bob's place. It was a semi-automatic Marlin stainless steel .22 rifle with a synthetic stock.

After countless debates at the Antler Bar, no one could shake Ethan's belief that the little Marlin was the best all round survival rifle. Many of the "experts" at the bar argued that you needed heavy-duty firepower for survival, but Ethan reasoned that if a person was ever in a situation that required a lot of firepower to get out of, chances were he'd already be screwed. Besides, if it ever came to that, Ethan was at his best tactically in close encounters. As he tried to explain to all the other "experts" in the bar, the .22 was the best all-around rifle for a number of reasons.

First of all, it was the perfect rifle to shoot down small varmint animals without destroying their value as food, and he had proven on several occasions that a single well-placed shot would kill a deer. Second, a person could fire several rounds quickly, which would stop the advance of any combatant, particularly those without military training. Finally, what Ethan considered to be the best reason for carrying the Marlin as the primary survival weapon was the fact that a person could carry over five hundred rounds of ammunition in a Crown Royal bag. In addition, Ethan knew he would be able to find .22 shells all over the state of Montana and probably the US. Everyone that he knew of had a .22 and the shells were cheap, so most had several rounds in stock at their homes.

Ethan carried about one hundred .22 rounds in his small mickey Crown bag. He came by the bag honestly after helping Fran drink the Crown. He placed the rounds next to the Marlin and his Bowtech Assassin compound bow that was set up to carry three grim reaper broad tipped arrows. He carried an additional six on his pack. He added two Springfield 1911A1 45 ACP pistols with five clips each to the pile. One of the pistols was in a combat leg holster so it was accessible when he had the pack on, and the other was the first thing he would touch when his hand went inside the pack. His K-Bar knife was on his gun belt along with a canteen and clip holders. The last two items he grabbed were his Filson Wool cape coat and his Camo Gore Tex rain jacket that he would wear over the Filson if necessary. Last but not least, he threw his Caterpillar baseball hat into the pile.

When he was done piling up his necessities, he loaded everything into his truck. He couldn't help but look across the field at the log home that stood empty. He could feel the emptiness radiating from the house. Ethan adjusted his Caterpillar baseball hat that he had placed on his head while loading the truck and then reached in the cab window and took his truck keys out of the ignition.

"Come on, Cowboy," he said as he started walking toward the house.

He stepped into the dark and musty smelling house and stood just inside the door. It was as if there was an invisible barrier that wouldn't allow him to enter any further. He slowly turned his head to look toward the kitchen table. Instantly, he was fourteen years old again coming home from school. Ethan could remember thinking it was odd that his father's pickup would be parked in the driveway at that time of day. He expected to see his mother in the kitchen as always making him a snack to tide him over until dinner. But on that day, both of his parents were sitting at the table.

His mother, Becky, had a cup of tea in front of her. His father, Clay, a cup of coffee. He remembered vividly that his mother looked up and made eye contact with him, but his father's eyes were cast down at his cup. It was as if he was studying it for some reason.

"Ethan, honey, come sit down by me." Becky had motioned him to a chair across from her.

Ethan put his book bag down and sat. Something wasn't right, and that scared him a little. His mother held both her hands out, allowing her arms to rest on the table.

"Give me your hands."

He placed his hands inside his mother's. Ethan stole a glance over at his father. Clay had not moved, he just sat there staring at the cup and clenching and unclenching his fists.

"We have something we need to talk to you about, okay?"

Ethan nodded.

"I'm sick, honey," she said. "You know how I've been so tired lately and how my back hurts all the time? Last week when I was gone for two days, I was seeing doctors in Missoula. They did some tests, Ethan," she looked at Clay.

Clay couldn't speak. He wanted to; in fact, he knew that he should help her tell Ethan about his mother's illness. That was something that he felt they should do together, but he couldn't speak. Becky continued. She squeezed Ethan's hands tighter.

"I have cancer, and I have it real bad."

His father sucked air into his lungs and stiffened even more.

"I'm not going to get better, baby. You're so precious, you're the most precious thing I've ever had," she told him as she rubbed one of his hands with both of hers. "I'm going to need you to help your dad. You'll do that for me, won't you, baby? He'll need you."

Ethan nodded again and then turned to look at his father. The tears were rolling down Clay's cheeks and literally dripping off his chin. He was crying without making a sound. Ethan had never seen his father cry before. For that matter, no one had ever seen Clay Edwards cry before.

Ethan desperately wanted to jump into both of their arms at the same time. He wanted to be comforted by both of them, and he wanted to comfort his dad. The moment was too emotional. Clay stood up, and without looking at either of them, he walked out the door.

"Come, let me hold you, okay?" his mother said.

They held each other for a long time, until they both ran out of tears. She had told him she was dying of cancer, but he knew that he would be losing both parents. She was the one physically dying, but Ethan knew that his father would never recover from this loss.

It didn't take long for the cancer to consume Becky. At first, she was able to stay at home. But with each passing day, she moved a little slower, did a little less, and complained of more and more pain. Finally, the day came when she couldn't get out of bed. Then one day, an ambulance came and took her to Saint Patrick's Hospital in Missoula. After that, it was just a matter of days or weeks they were told.

Ethan spent every moment that he could with her, and so did his father. However, Clay never said much. He only talked when he needed to or to answer Ethan's questions about this or that. Ethan never questioned his father about the condition his mother was in. What was there to question? She was going to die. Nor did he ask about the future. What would they do? What would it be like? He had these questions, but never asked them. Perhaps, he never asked because he knew that his father had no answers to any of them.

Becky, on the other hand, told Ethan how special he was and she talked freely about how much joy he had brought to her. She said it so often that he almost believed it himself. On one visit, Ethan left the room to go get coffee for him and his father, and he returned to find his father bent down over his mother. He could see his shoulders shaking and knew that she was gone.

Bob and Fran Watkins took care of most of the details for the funeral. They buried her on the hill overlooking the river on the spot where Clay had told her that he would build their home. After the graveside service on the hill, everyone in attendance was invited down to the house for the reception. Ethan was walking through the field holding Fran's hand when he turned to see his father standing alone by the grave.

Clay was remembering the first time that he saw her in the basement of the church. He thought of his own mother. He thought about asking God why, but quickly decided that would do little good. The sadness and powerlessness he felt in the moment made him think of the night that his had father left. He hadn't thought about that night in years. In fact, he hadn't had any reason to remember that night since he found Becky.

"Fuck God," he said as he turned and walked down the hill.

Clay stood by the door nodding to people as they left. Bob and Fran were the last ones to go. Bob leaned close to him as if to hug him, but Clay leaned away from it, so Bob stopped and put his hand on Clay's arm. He gave it a quick squeeze and then let it go. Clay did not resist when Fran reached up and touched his cheek. As soon as Bob and Fran left, Clay went to a kitchen cabinet and took out a bottle of Wild Turkey.

"Don't know why they bother making the eighty-six proof stuff," he said as he took the cork out of the bottle and poured some into a water glass. He took a long pull from the glass. When he was finished with the drink, he looked at Ethan.

"Want to know something about you and me, Ethan? We're cursed. That's right, we got some kind of Edwards curse. My old man, that rotten prick, had it. I got it, and so do you. Cursed. What do you think about that, boy?"

Ethan didn't know how to respond. What do you say when you're fourteen years old and on the day you bury your mother your father tells you that? Ethan didn't say anything, he just walked away. Clay never put the cork back in the bottle that night, nor would he ever again.

Clay and Ethan got by as best they could, but Clay became a daily drinker who was always drunk. In fact, it was unusual to find him not drunk or well on his way to getting there. He had to quit working in the woods because his drinking made him too unsteady with a chainsaw. His new plan was to make homemade furniture in the garage and sell it to, as he put it, *"those dope smoking hippies in Missoula."* Hardly any furniture ever got made.

It was mostly Bob and Fran who looked out for them. Ethan went to school, and given the circumstances, he did alright. Bob hired Ethan to do yard work in the summer, which just happened to include a whole lot of fishing. In the wintertime, Ethan would shovel snow with Bob and help Fran do projects. Fran always had a project of some kind going on for which Bob and Ethan would always give her a good-natured hard time. Bob and Fran always sent him home with food for two, and Fran would just happen to include a lunch for school.

Ethan had always had parts of both his mother's and father's personalities in him. After his mother's passing, he withdrew, but as time went by, you could see more and more of Becky coming back out in him. Maybe Clay saw her in him, too, and it was just too painful for him to be around it or maybe it was just the booze. Whatever the cause, father and son grew further and further apart.

On his seventeenth birthday, Ethan came home and told his drunken father that he was joining the Marine Corps and would need his signature to do it. Clay signed the papers and drove Ethan to the induction center in Butte, even though Ethan had told him that he didn't need to drive him. Clay told him that he wanted to, even though he was half in the bag when they left for the three-and-a-half-hour journey.

Clay was pretty much sober by the time they got there. He did have a few beers on the drive, however, primarily to keep the shakes away. Clay walked with Ethan to the door of the Induction Center and stopped Ethan from entering as he was holding the door open. Clay put his hand on Ethan's shoulder.

"I'm... I should have done better. I was. I'm..." he turned and walked away.

Ethan watched him get in his truck and then turned and went inside the building.

Months passed and Clay continued to drink himself blind, but Bob would not forsake his friend. Bob paid the taxes on the place and kept the power on. Bob was sure that Clay was in an alcoholic daze and didn't know what he was doing. He was hopeful that he would eventually let go of the grief, put down the booze, and get on with his life. He knew Clay well enough to know that he was strong enough to pull himself through.

Then one day when Bob showed up in his pickup truck to check on Clay, as he got out of the truck, he saw Clay standing on the porch. It took him a second to notice that Clay was cleaned up. He had on a nice shirt and a clean pair of jeans. He also had what looked like a piece of pipe in his hand.

"Hey, buddy, thought I'd stop by and see how you are…" He stopped, they both knew how he was doing.

"Little busy right now, Bob. Why don't you swing back by tomorrow if you would? In fact, I could use your help up on the hill. How does early morning sound?" Clay asked.

"That will work. Maybe, we can wet a line together afterward," Bob replied.

"Ya, maybe."

Bob turned to go.

"Thanks for watching out for my boy," Clay said.

Bob was in his truck driving down the driveway when he looked into his rearview mirror and saw Clay toss the pipe that was in his hand out into the yard. He couldn't quite make out what Clay was throwing away.

The next morning, Fran handed Bob the sandwiches she had made for him and Clay, and he put them in the cooler.

"Not sure what time I'll get home. "If I can, I'll try to talk him into going fishing for a little bit," he said and then he kissed her cheek and headed out to Clay's house.

After knocking on the door and checking to see if Clay might be in the garage, Bob looked up toward the hill. He walked slowly up the hillside because the realization of what he would find up there grew with each passing step.

Bob found his friend laying on the grass with his Winchester shotgun not far from him. Its barrel had been sawed off just above the shell tube. Clay's body was lying on its back, the blood on his shirt had turned dark. Clay had cut the barrel off the gun and trimmed the stock so that he could hold it against his chest when he pulled the trigger. Bob took his jacket off and gently placed it over his friend's face.

Ethan was out in the field training with his recon unit when the Humvee pulled up. A lieutenant talked a moment with Ethan's staff sergeant.

"Edwards," the sergeant called.

Ethan jogged over to him.

"Yes, Staff Sergeant."

"You are heading back to base with the lieutenant."

"Yes, Staff Sergeant."

No one spoke during the ride back to base. When they arrived, Ethan was ordered to report to see the chaplain, and he was led into the chaplain's office by an aid. When he walked into the office, the chaplain and Bob Watkins stood up. Ethan looked first at Bob then the chaplain. He knew that seeing Bob meant there was bad news from home.

"Sit down, son," the chaplain said and motioned to a chair. He then told Ethan his father had died, and offered a few words of comfort. "I'll leave you two alone for a moment."

Bob and Ethan stood as the chaplain left the room.

"How?" Ethan asked.

"On the hill overlooking the river."

"Did he do it?" Ethan asked.

"Ethan, I…"

"Did he do it, Bob?" Ethan asked looking him in the eyes.

Bob nodded. "He's not in pain anymore."

"Ya, what about me?" Ethan thought.

The memories were overwhelming. Ethan backed out of the house and shut the door. He hadn't made it any further into the house this time than he had on any of his other attempts. He looked down at Cowboy who looked back up at him. It almost appeared that the dog was caught in the memories, too, for he never left Ethan's side the entire time they were in the house.

"Fuck, what a shitty fucking day!" Ethan said. "Come on, boy, let's get out of here."

CHAPTER 12

Jin-Ho Yeo hated his job. The stress ate at him every single day, even on his supposed days off and especially on holidays. He was surprised to learn, when he first started his teaching position 11 years earlier, that the pressure from the South Korean government and the high school administration was not nearly as constant as the pressure he felt from his students themselves.

Mr. Yeo taught advanced mathematics and economic theory to third-year high school students at a South Korean high school where the students were competing for a limited number of freshman positions in South Korea's most prestigious universities, the Seoul National, Korea, and Yonsei Universities, known collectively as the SKY universities.

Mr. Yeo was very familiar with a saying pervasive in South Korean culture that expressed the country's expectation for education: *If you sleep three hours a night, you may get into a top SKY university; If you sleep four hours a night, you may get into another university; if you sleep five or more hours a night, especially in your last year of high school, forget about getting into any university.*

Sadly, many of the students who failed to get into the best universities, took their own lives. Suicides among this age group were higher than ever, and seemed to rise in frequency every year. Mr. Yeo had lost 31 former students to suicide in the 11 years that he taught at the school. He hated how competitive education had become in the country, and he put a lot of pressure on himself to help these kids learn as much as possible. In fact, he often went above and beyond the call of duty to ensure that his students would have a competitive edge when applying to universities.

This year, he had made arrangements to take 50 of his third-year students to China in early May to study at the Peking University in Beijing, China. He had spent weeks making the necessary arrangements with the South Korean government, with the Chinese government, and with the parents of the kids. Unexpectedly, the most resistance that he received was from the kids themselves, as they were afraid that the trip would prevent them from studying enough. Mr. Yeo had to bring 5 tutors that each tutored multiple subjects along on the trip to ease the fears of this students.

The Peking University had been very hospitable, putting together a challenging and exciting curriculum that would provide a unique academic experience for Mr. Yeo's students. They spent 10 hours a day for two straight weeks attending the trainings that focused upon mathematical modeling of biological systems, computational biology, and bioinformatics. The students loved the experience, even though many of them spent several additional hours after the trainings were completed for the day studying with the tutors who also made the trip.

Mr. Yeo was very pleased with how the whole trip had gone. Everything was seamless. The travel plans had proceeded without any hitches, the housing in dorm rooms on campus was perfect, and the trainings were exceptional. Mr. Yeo was pleased with the overall experience, especially, because the trip did not start out so great. After flying into Beijing, the group had to catch the subway to campus, and while standing on the platform waiting for the train, a sprinkler had malfunctioned and sprayed all 56 members of the group, including students, tutors, and Mr. Yeo himself. Although not ideal, Mr. Yeo believed that it was good to get the bad luck out of the way on the first day, and it had been smooth sailing ever since.

The day before the group was to head back to South Korea, two students were getting sick with cold-like symptoms. On the day that the group boarded the airplane for their journey, 17 students, 2 of the tutors and Mr. Yeo were all experiencing similar cold-like symptoms. The two students who were sick the day before had developed severe diarrhea by the next morning, and had to make several trips to the lavatory during the flight.

The first day back in South Korea, 42 of the students and all of the adults were experiencing symptoms of some type of infection. Several of the students were severely sick, but because they feared that staying home would cause them to lose ground on their studies, all 50 students were at school that day and the next. On the third day back, all of the students attended school, but one student collapsed in the cafeteria during lunch, several were sent to the school's infirmary, and Mr. Yeo was taken out in an ambulance.

On the fourth day back, news hit South Korea that China had an Ebola virus outbreak, and the 50 students that were recently in China were sent home on quarantine and told to wait for further instructions. Several of the students were sent to hospitals over the next few days, and by the end of the first week back, all 56 of those who had travelled to China were hospitalized, and several had died, including Mr. Yeo and three of the tutors. A total of six students had no symptoms but were hospitalized for observation, and while most of these later developed mild symptoms of Ebola virus disease, they all survived. The other 44 students did not fare so well, as 41 of these students died and the three that survived full-blown

Ebola virus disease had severe neurologic damage. The six adults who made the trip did not fare so well. All of them succumbed to the disease.

The mortality rate among this group was much higher than the rate observed during the outbreak in West Africa, which led South Korean public health officials to conclude that this was either a modified Ebola virus or this group of South Korean citizens had been exposed to very high concentrations of the virus. Both of these scenarios pointed to a single possibility: this was a direct bioterror attack by China.

CHAPTER 13

"Members of the Genesis Project, we have a problem," Victor said tentatively, looking around the table at each member who was assembled for the emergency meeting of the group.

In the days since the dissemination began, the group was nervous, and Victor had spent many hours on the telephone with each member calming nerves and sharpening their resolves. There was a lot of second guessing going on, and a lot of remorse as dead bodies started to accumulate in China and other parts of Asia. The members of the Genesis Project knew that the worst was yet to come, and although they had agreed in principle with the idea of reducing the human population, in practice it was horrific.

Many members were frightened that they would be found out, and the group had made Victor promise that this would be an anonymous attack, that no one would ever be able to trace it back to them, and that when it was all over they would be called upon to help rebuild the new world. Victor had made these promises, and he had reassured them that the plan was flawless. He had told them that no one would ever know who perpetrated this act upon mankind.

So far, a couple weeks into the completion of the dissemination plan, no one had a clue that this was a deliberate attack upon humans. The dissemination teams had delivered their product perfectly. Of course, much of the dissemination technicalities had been worked out ahead of time by Victor and colleagues that he recruited. He had spent months working with a bioengineering colleague to develop dissemination sprayers that would spread 250 milliliters of fluid, containing more than 250 million Ebola or Typhon viruses in droplets or aerosols that were the perfect size for transmission.

Several devices were designed and engineered to look like ordinary objects found in public places. One device was a virus disseminator designed to look like a fire sprinkler commonly found in public buildings. It simply required attachment to the ceiling after the timer had been set. At the appropriate time, the sprinkler would spray all of its contents on whoever happened to be standing within a 25-30-foot radius.

Another dissemination device was designed to look like a smoke alarm and this device was set to spray the same quantity of virus as soon as it detected movement. Hundreds of these devices had been set in hallways, pedestrian tunnels, and jet bridges where large numbers of people walked by. In jet bridges, the movement of the bridge when adjusting it to an airplane would trigger the dissemination of virus, leaving a vapor that contained 250 million viruses trapped in the jet bridge as planes were loaded or unloaded.

In all cases, the dissemination devices had been carefully installed without notice, and were removed without arousing suspicion the next day. Victor was very pleased to report to the Genesis Project members that thousands of dissemination events had been successfully deployed, and no one had any idea of what was about to hit.

At the last group meeting of the Genesis Project, he proudly reported that the world was 18 weeks away from complete and total rebirth. He remembered the silence in the room when he made that statement, and he remembered it because his laughter echoed off the walls of the chamber. It wasn't that he enjoyed killing people, that was just part of the bigger purpose. No, Victor was giddy. He was beginning to feel like his life was about reach the level of *dream come true*.

Then all hell broke loose.

"The dissemination teams that we worked with to improve the conditions on this planet are about to go public," Victor stated. "But, don't worry, they will not be alive for long, we just have to ride out this first wave of negative publicity."

"What the hell are you talking about?" yelled a very angry Dr. Gold.

"Let me explain. There was no way to disseminate the world's greatest solution without calling upon people who had the most to benefit from destroying civilization. Who else would be crazy enough to kill billions of people in 18 weeks? Therefore, through some connections, I was able to meet with and recruit the leadership of the Supreme Jihadists, the world's largest terrorist organization. I had several meetings with them and convinced them that it was their God's will for them to usher in the new world."

"Dear God, you turned the Typhon virus over to terrorists? Those animals have no regard for human life. They will kill indiscriminately!" Dr. Clifton shouted.

"Like I said, let me explain," Victor continued. "This group has terror cells in every major city in the world, and they are not afraid to donate thousands of martyrs who think that they will get 17 virgins each when they die and go to heaven. So, fuck them. Let them die and do something useful in the process."

"This makes no sense," Dr. Raber stated. "Why would they agree to kill just to kill? They usually have an agenda and they want the world to know that it was them. That is how terrorism works. Without a responsible party, no one knows who to fear."

"Promises were made," Victor said, almost as if it were a joke. "I approached the leadership of the organization and I told them that I had the world's most lethal virus, that I was planning for a new world, and I wanted to make sure that they were part of it. In fact, I promised them that in return for their services, I would vaccinate all of their leadership and provide 500 additional vaccines for them to use on anyone that they wished. In addition, I promised them that they would be the only Muslim organization to be recognized by the new world government, and I promised them that they would be among the most powerful sects in the new world."

"Those are promises that you cannot deliver, Victor," Dr. Clifton stated firmly. "You have no idea how the new world government will form, and you cannot make any promises regarding any positions of power."

"Of course not," Victor continued, "but they didn't know that. They bought it hook, line, and sinker. The only wrinkle in the plan was the day that I went to give the top leadership the 'vaccine,' they insisted that I also take the injection from the same vial. Poor bastards had no idea that I was injecting them with Typhon virus. They also had no idea that I had already been vaccinated, so I gladly injected myself from the same vial, knowing that I was already protected."

"Jesus Christ, Victor, you double-crossed them," Dr. Gold said, shaking her head.

"Of course I did. Do you think for one minute that I want some fundamentalist Muslim group in my new world? Fuck them. They can perpetuate the worst calamity of all time on humankind and then die in the dirt with the rest of them. Look, we have the opportunity here to select who will live and who will die. Let's not mess it up because we suddenly have morals along the way.

"Besides," Victor went on, "by the time they figured out that they had been infected, which would take 10-12 days, all of the dissemination work was done. They finished their work just in time to go home and infect their families and then die. The problem is, one of the older members of the terrorist leadership got sick and died of Typhoid virus after only eight days, so the others figured it out. Somehow, they know that their whole organization is about to be wiped out and they are threatening to go public and tell the world that the Genesis Project did this."

Victor did not tell them that the Supreme Jihadists were unaware of the Genesis Project until they threatened to go public and implicate Victor. It was Victor's attempt to defer blame to the organization that led to them finding out that the Genesis Project was involved.

"Oh, for Christ's sake," Dr. Gold started, "that is exactly the type of scenario that I was afraid of. Why didn't you tell us of this plan?"

"Are you kidding me? Are you actually serious? You of all people should know exactly why I left out the details of all of my plans. You were so worried that I might implicate all of you, that you wanted… what was it you called it? Deniable plausibility? Well, fuck you all. You have been nothing more than puppets, all of you. I needed you for one reason and one reason only… You are my counsel of doom that came up with the idea to destroy humankind and who ordered my participation. If I go down, I will show the whole world, or at least what is left of it, hundreds of hours of secret video that I taped of each of you discussing the events that led up to the first massive human extinction. If you think for one minute that I will take the fall for this group, you are dead wrong. I will spin this so fast against you all that you will still be dizzy when the mobs come to hunt you down and kill you in the streets."

"I do not believe in heaven or hell or good versus evil," Dr. Clifton stated, coldly. "However, the unadulterated human greed and lust for power that flows through you is the most grotesque display of human nature gone awry that this world has ever witnessed. You have taken high ideals and good science and turned them into self-serving power. You disgust me, Victor."

"Save it for the cameras, Van. They will be here soon enough. By the time this whole thing is unsorted, you will all be dead, and I will be building a new world from a position of power. I'm going underground, you are all on your own."

The chamber erupted in outrage as Victor stormed out. While Dr. Gold tried to calm the committee, the room was soon overcome by panic as the new reality settled upon the Genesis Project members. The world was soon going to know them all by name, and history, if one anyone were lucky enough to survive and courageous enough to write it down, would have several new names to add to the list evil masterminds and mass murderers.

CHAPTER 14

"Jesus Christ, Bob!" Ethan said into the satellite phone. "It's everywhere. I haven't talked too much on the ham radio, but I've been listening and Jesus, I can't... I don't... I mean, it's everywhere. They're saying people are dying like flies. The whole damn world is falling apart."

"It's not good, I'll give you that," Bob replied.

"Not good? Not good? Shit, Bob, that's like saying... I'm not even sure what it's like saying. I mean, these people are saying the dead are piling up in the streets. And, anybody that can move is leaving the cities. Some countries are even shooting healthy people who are trying to leave so it doesn't spread. It's like... Hell, I don't know what it's like."

"Ethan? Ethan, listen to me."

"WHAT? What are you going to tell me, it will be alright? What?"

"SO, WHAT THE HELL DO YOU WANT ME TO TELL YOU? GODDAMIT, STOP ACTING LIKE A SCARED BOY SCOUT. YOU ARE A MARINE, START ACTING LIKE ONE. You want me to say it? That this is the Apocalypse? Because, guess what, buddy? That's exactly what this might be."

The phones went silent.

"I'm sorry," Bob said. "I'm..." he paused. "I'm sorry."

"Shit, man, I'm just scared. I mean, it's like I haven't really seen or spoken face-to-face with another person in a while. It's... I just keep thinking, 'what if, like, I'm the last guy?' You know? I know how stupid is that."

"It's not stupid at all. Believe me, nobody, and I mean nobody, is wired to deal with something like this. It's going to sound stupid, but you'll know what I mean when I ask it, okay?"

"Alright."

"How are things out there?" Bob asked.

"Well, you're right about how it sounds, but I get what you're asking. All in all, not too bad. We found a way to communicate without getting close to each other. Carl apparently had a stack of old CB radios at his place. He left them outside folk's homes with antennas and coax and instructions on how to hook them up. He told people to take the batteries out of their cars to hook them up to. So far, the power has stayed on."

"We've been told that actually in certain areas the power grid may be one of the last things to fail. All the dams are automated so, short of the lines going down, it, hopefully, will last for a while. The CB idea is good," Bob said.

"Ya, who would of thought Carl would be the new ma bell?"

Both men let out a weak laugh.

"How's Cowboy?"

"Cowboy's fine, in fact, better than fine. Fran?" Ethan asked.

"She's good. Kinda on my ass about the hours I'm working, but that's nothing new."

The phones went quiet.

"I've been hunting and hanging the meat in trees in the front yards of some folks," Ethan said to break the silence. "I hung some meat at the Wilson house and it's been hanging for three days. I've been checking on it. You think…?" he stopped talking mid thought.

"Gary was traveling out of town, wasn't he?" Bob asked.

"He showed back up. I'm not sure when or how because the government shut everything down, but I saw him in the yard one day when I was checking up on things," Ethan replied.

"Ethan, can you remember exactly when you saw him?"

"Well, I don't know for sure, but maybe a little over a week ago. I mean, I've kinda lost track of days, you know what I mean? No real point in keeping track of them."

"Stay away from the house," Bob said, his voice harsher than he intended.

"I thought maybe I should…"

"NO, THEY'RE GONE. Sorry, but if they've got the virus there's nothing you could do for them, nothing. The only result may be that you end up being infected, too. So, please don't, alright?"

There was no response from Ethan.

"Ethan?"

"I promise, Bob, I promise."

"Thank you, and start keeping track of the days again, especially if you see someone and then you don't. Understand what I mean?"

"Yes, you're asking me so that you can determine how long it's taking to kill our friends, right?"

Bob ignored Ethan's statement, but he was right.

"Ethan, I want to include another person in our call, okay?"

"Ya, sure who is it?" Ethan asked.

"Mr. Edwards, this is Lieutenant General Tyler Short."

"You with Bob? Bob, is this guy in Hamilton with you?"

"Mr. Edwards, I'm with Homeland command and where I'm at is not your concern."

"Ya, well guess what, General? Maybe I think it is."

"You listen to me, Edwards, the president has called all past military personnel under the age of 65 back into active service by executive action. So, you're once again a corporal in the United State Marine Corp. And as Dr. Watkins said earlier, now's the time to start acting like it."

Ethan chuckled. "Are you fucking serious, man? FUCK YOU, BUDDY! Bob, who is this clown? I mean, give me a fucking break."

They could hear Bob sigh.

"Gentlemen, this conversation isn't going to get us anywhere. Ethan, he's under a mountain in Colorado. Or at least I'm pretty sure he is. And, you're in my basement in Darby. So, the two of you need to start over because, guess what, boys? We all need each other or we don't have any hope of any of this working, OKAY?" Bob ended.

Ethan cleared his throat. "Of what working?" he asked.

"General, would you like to tell my friend what we are thinking?"

"Alright, Edwards. It's like Watkins said, I'm located at Cheyenne Mountain in Colorado. We got off to a bad start. I'd like to rectify that."

"It would go a long way if I could get some straight answers," Ethan replied.

"I'll do the best I can."

"What's that mean?" Ethan asked with a tone to his voice.

"It means he'll do the best he can, alright, Ethan?" Bob stated.

"Hey, I just don't get it. I mean all the secrecy. Who is left to keep secrets from? If what's coming over the radio is true, the majority of us are dead or going to be soon. So, what's the point?"

"I'll tell you one of them right now," General Short responded. "We've still got a bunch of guys sitting in hardened silos with their fingers on nuclear buttons to put it simply. Not to mention the ones in submarines. I mean one... ONE trident nuclear submarine has enough power..." he paused a moment and then continued. "Also, there are surface ships with nuclear-armed tomahawks. Getting the picture? So, having said that, it's a pretty good bet that there are several other countries with pretty much the same scenario. Right now, the world is teetering on the brink of complete destruction."

"Okay, what you said makes sense. But, like who the hell am I going to tell?"

"It's not who you might tell, Edwards, it's who might be listening," the general said. "Okay, here's the reader's digest version. Once again, there are other nations with the same intelligence assets that we have. Granted, maybe not to the same extent. But, let's say for example they hear that the virus originated in the good old US of A; think maybe some Russian might get tipped over or just feel compelled to punish us for allowing that to happen and take out a few American cities? I mean, it's like you said, what's the big deal most everybody's dead, right! Or it gets out that the bad guy is from the Middle East and two guys up in your country outside, say Conrad, Montana, decide to turn a couple of keys and send some missiles over the horizon. Thinking they must be aimed at the right people, right? When in fact they don't have a clue who they just launched on. There's a lot of these things out there, son, and pray to God that we can keep a handle on them. We have no way of knowing what kind of command structure remains inside other countries' militaries. To tell you the truth, I hope ours is operational. I think it is for the most part. But, if somebody, and it's not going to matter who, lets a nuke off... Well, then the few of us left are going to wish we died from the virus. Because, as bad as it is with the virus, if it goes nuclear, it will get worse not just for our species but for the whole planet."

Ethan was silent. "Guess I owe you an apology, General. Sometimes I have a tendency to think small picture. So, it's as bad as what I think?"

"Actually, it's probably worse than you think, Corporal," the general said, using Ethan's Marine Corp rank for the first time. When Ethan didn't respond or raise objection, the general continued.

"It's a pile of shit, son, and everybody's in it up to their eyebrows. But, maybe we've got a sliver of hope and we are doing everything we can to prevent a nuclear holocaust. We do have something that we would like to talk to you about."

"Yes, sir, I'm all ears," Ethan said immediately.

"Good. Like I said, we've still got some assets left. One of the most important ones is the ability to monitor world communications. If you think that we shut everything down after that Snowden NSA bullshit, well then you just don't know your good old Uncle Sam as well as you think. So, I'll just get to the point," the general said.

"We've got lots of intelligence from operatives on the ground that tell us that whoever made this bioweapon also made a vaccine. Unfortunately, most of the operatives are silent now. My intelligence sources tell me that the vaccine never made it out of Russia, and that it is now being concealed by the Russian government. However, Dr. Watkins tells me that he received a phone call out of nowhere informing him that the vaccine is not only in the United States, but in the possession of a man who may be heading to Glacier Park, which I'm informed is around 200 to 250 miles from you depending on your route. You with me so far?"

"Yes, sir," replied Ethan, "just not sure how I'm fitting in."

"You will. Watkins says you're a smart guy."

"You should maybe consider the source, General," Ethan said jokingly.

"I know the source and that's the only reason I'm talking to you. I'll continue," the general said without any humor.

"Yes, sir, please do."

"The communication indicates that...," he paused. "You sure, Bob?"

"Absolutely certain, General, as if he were my own son," Bob solemnly replied.

"Alright then. Edwards, the man who we think may be responsible for all this might be holed up somewhere in Glacier Park. He is the founder of a group of people called the Genesis Project, and some members of this group have been arrested for this atrocity."

"General, sorry, sir, but aren't you afraid that, well, sir, like you said, somebody might be listening?" Ethan asked.

"When I said that other nations had the same capabilities that we do, that was the truth for the most part. We're just a whole lot, and I mean a whole lot, better. I'm sure our satellite link is secure. Back to Genesis. The leader of this group, for lack of a better term, is an asshole called Victor Kraus. Unfortunately, we have no intel on this Victor Kraus. The last we knew, he was still in Maryland. So, the official position of the U.S. Army is that Victor Kraus is in Maryland and no vaccine exists in the U.S. Watkins, why don't you take it from here?"

"Alright, General," Bob sighed before he began. "Ethan, we need you to find Victor for us. Like the general said, we have no idea if he is in the park, and what we lack is...,"

"Boots on the ground," Ethan finished Bob's statement.

"That's right, Ethan, we need boots on the ground as you put it and they are your boots."

"I can do that," Ethan said. "If that fucker is in the state of Montana or for that matter still on the planet, I'll find him, I fucking guarantee it. And, I'll snuff his flame," Ethan said angrily.

"And that is exactly what we don't want you to do," Bob said.

"You lost me."

"We think he's got a vaccine and he may have hidden it."

"Holy shit."

"So, as you can see, he doesn't do us any good if he's dead. We need to get him or his computer or whatever will tell us what we need to know. We need to find those vaccines; the fate of the human race may depend on it."

"Corporal, if in fact Dr. Watkins is right about this, and this guy has a vaccine, and we can acquire it and announce to the world that we have it and will distribute it; well, not only does it probably save the human race, but hopefully, it will also give pause to a nuclear disaster."

"So, you willing to go find this guy?" Bob asked.

"One thing needs to be clearly understood, Edwards," the general said solemnly, "this mission does not exist. You are on your own until you identify Kraus. Once we have intel that he is indeed in the park, we can allocate resources to extract him. Until then, you are unofficial and pretty much on your own."

"When do I leave?" Ethan inquired.

CHAPTER 15

Lesya heard Victor storm in through the front door of his apartment, and she realized that she did not have much time.

"Bob, the virus was engineered to be the most lethal virus on the planet. There is a vaccine, but there are only a few thousand lots. I don't have time to go into details here, but the mastermind behind the attacks is a man named Victor Kraus. He is dead set on wiping out the human population, and this is an intentional attack. If something happens to me, Bob, find Victor. He will likely go into hiding out west. I've got to go, he's coming," Lesya whispered into her cell phone before she quickly terminated the call and dropped the phone into her pocket.

"Where are the vaccines?" Bob asked as the phone line went dead.

"Who were you talking to?" Victor asked, as he charged into the apartment and started gathering items that were precious to him.

"Just an old colleague who was asking questions about the outbreaks. Nothing interesting, I get dozens of these calls a day."

"We have to get out of here, they are coming."

"Who?"

"The media, law enforcement, the government, whoever is left to fight against the virus."

"Victor, there is panic everywhere, are you sure that anyone would be concerned with looking for you?"

"The Supreme Jihadists are making an announcement to the world. Lesya, soon the whole fucking world, or whoever is left, is going to know that the Genesis Project distributed the virus, and that you made it. We are going to be hunted down and killed. Our legacy, all that we fought for will die if we do not handle this correctly. We have to get out of the city and get out now."

"Victor, this was a mistake. We should never have released this virus on the world. In theory, it made sense. From a global perspective, it made sense, but people are dying all around us. I do not want to live in the world, no, I cannot live in a world where I was responsible for the deaths of millions."

"I am not leaving you behind, Lesya, I love you. I need you. You are my partner."

"No, Victor, I was your puppet. You played me beautifully, and I mindlessly followed you to the end, but I cannot follow you any longer.

Alania was right, I am a monster. You are a monster. We cannot go through with it, Victor, we must do whatever we can to help the people that we have infected."

"We are not doing that, Lesya, the plan goes on."

"No, Victor, I cannot continue."

"Lesya, for Christ's sake, you killed your partner for this cause. Are you now going to let that act of murder be for nothing?"

"That's what I am saying here, Victor. This is not me. This is not us. This is not right; I cannot go through with it. Alania's murder made me realize how insane I had become."

Lesya cried freely now, defeated. "It wasn't until I was standing over Alania's dead body that I woke up. I strangled her for you, Victor… for a cause that you carefully constructed in me with a series of moral compromises, hundreds of carefully designed compromises that led me deep down the rabbit hole. I didn't even know how far I had gone until Alania was lying dead before me."

Victor walked to the kitchen counter and grabbed a Güde Damascus Santoku knife and then walked over to where Lesya was standing. He slowly reached behind her and grabbed an apple from a fruit bowl, placed it on the chopping block counter, and violently chopped the apple in half, sending the two halves flying onto the floor.

"You and I are one," he said, holding the knife up for effect. "There is only one way for us to split up, and I am afraid that does not bode well for either of us."

"Victor, you were a good man. You have always had the world's best intentions in your heart. You are a wonderful speaker, and convincing debater. You are passionate about this planet and its life forms, but you are blind to what you have done. What we have done. It's over. My conscience will not let me continue."

Victor looked at Lesya. She was firm in her resolve. He knew that she meant what she said and that it was too late to convince her that she was overreacting. She was suffering from a moral dilemma and it would be the ruin of her and of his plan. He could not bring her into the new world, for she would always be there to remind him of who he was, of who he had become.

"I have loved you since the first day I saw you," he said.

Lesya looked him in the eyes, but instead of seeing love reflected back at him, Victor saw that she pitied him. In her eyes, he saw what he really had become to her, a pathetic, small, shallow, feeble intellectual lulling himself to sleep with various forms of cognitive dissonance. The reflection pierced him, hurt him, infuriated him.

"Be well, Victor," she said. She knew what was coming.

After a long and awkward silent stare into Lesya's eyes, Victor turned to leave the kitchen. And then, with one sudden and fluid movement, he glided the exquisitely sharp knife blade smoothly against Lesya's throat, slicing her carotid artery and jugular vein. Her body fell to the floor with a loud clump. Victor let out a primordial scream and tears flowed freely down his face. He bent over her still body, moved her hair gently from her face, and kissed her ever so tenderly on the lips.

"You always were a prick tease," he said to her lifeless form. "When I fell in love with you, you became a lesbian. It only makes sense that when I am ready to fulfill my destiny and reduce the impact of human life on the planet, that you would help develop the plan but then refuse to see it through."

Victor left Lesya's body on the kitchen floor and continued to gather the items that he would need for his journey. Fortunately, he had planned for such a contingency; in fact, he had planned for every contingency that he could think of. He knew that something like this could happen, and so he had developed an escape route that included caches of gasoline and supplies at various hiding spots across the US. He loaded his Range Rover with the supplies that included food, clothing, medical supplies, his master plan for the new world, and all of the vaccines that Lesya had brought from Russia. In total, he had vials to vaccinate about 3100 people. Lesya had brought enough vaccine for 3500 people, and the Genesis Project had used enough to vaccinate 400 people that they had hand selected.

Victor wasn't quite sure how to proceed with the situation with the terrorists. He knew that they would go public and he guessed that they would put a price on his head. That was the least of his worries. He figured that all he had to do to avoid them was stay away from them for a couple of weeks and the virus would do the rest. However, if they went public and the news was to get out and ruin his reputation, then that could impact his ability to implement his plan in the new world.

Victor needed time. He needed time to think about how to move forward and he needed time to see how everything settled. Maybe no one of consequence would know or care if he was involved with the outbreak. Regardless, he was sure that with a little time and a lot of studying of details, he would be able to spin the whole thing in such a way that he would convince whoever was listening that he was not involved. He just needed a safe place to go until the dust settled.

When Victor spent time with his father studying prairie dogs in the Dakotas during summer breaks when he was a kid, they always took a trip to Glacier National Park for some hiking before returning to Frostburg for the school year. Victor and his father frequently stayed at Many Glaciers Lodge during these trips, and often hiked the Gunsight Pass Trail to Sperry Chalet. It was this park that first introduced Victor to the most magnificent splendors of the natural world and the potential impact that climate change was having on the disappearing glaciers.

Glacier National Park had always been Victor's oasis, and he knew that if things did not go as planned that he would need to escape to the park for some time to think and reflect, to rebuild and reformulate. Victor's escape route was designed to provide everything that he would need to get from his apartment in New York City to his hideout in Glacier National Park. So, as soon as his Range Rover was loaded, Victor set a course for due west.

CHAPTER 16

Much like Victor predicted, the Typhon virus outbreaks swept across the earth in systematic circles of death. The Ebola virus outbreaks that were initially started in China ended up causing less than 500 hundred cases for each variant, resulting in a total of 764 deaths. The reason for the relatively small numbers of cases and deaths was because these viruses caused such severe morbidity that by the time the infected person was contagious, they were too sick to move around, and therefore, they were not able to efficiently spread the infection.

These outbreaks died out relatively quickly due to the public health measures that were employed to stop them. It seemed that the public health world did learn a thing or two during the Ebola outbreak in West Africa. China did everything that it could to prevent the news of these outbreaks from spreading around the world, but social media made this impossible. Reports of the outbreaks were on Twitter and Facebook as soon as they were known, and US news channels were reporting them in real time.

The outbreak in South Korea was also limited by the severity of the disease, and other than the students and teachers who were directly exposed, there were only a handful of additional infections and deaths associated with that outbreak. Public health measures, including contact tracing, helped contain the outbreak. The political ramifications of that outbreak far outweighed the damage caused by the disease.

China had refused to admit that it had Ebola virus, but it was widely known that several Chinese citizens were infected with it. When the 50 South Korean students came back from China and became sick, it appeared to the South Korean government that China had initiated an attack, and they alerted the US and other allies. Word on the streets of South Korea was that North Korea was working with China to perpetuate the attack on South Korea in an attempt to pull the US into a conflict in which China would have a strategic advantage.

In response, the North Korean government felt that South Korea and the US were planning an overthrow of the government, and so the regime readied its missile launch capabilities, aiming long-range missiles with nuclear warheads toward the United States and short-range nuclear missiles toward South Korea. As intel poured in on the military actions around the world, the US responded by preparing its military for imminent action by raising the Defense Condition to DEFCON 2, for only the second time in US history, the first being during the Cuban Missile Crisis. Russia and China also responded by alerting their militaries and readying their nuclear weapons for discharge, and on all continents, the major military powers began to build their alliances and prepare their allies for war.

Tensions were high for several days, but then the rising number of cases of Ebola-like illness around the globe helped South Korean and US governments to realize that if there was a bioterrorist attack, it most certainly was not limited to South Korea. In fact, the numbers of bodies that were being reported worldwide was staggering. Large cities the world over were being decimated by the virus, and it seemed to be rapidly spreading in all directions. The first official tally claimed that more than 1,000 lives were lost in 27 countries, including over 100 cases in the US. The second official tally, which came ten days later reported 17,683 deaths in 81 countries, with more than 2,800 deaths in the US. The third report stated that there were more than two million deaths, with dead bodies in every country that was reporting on the disease. All of these reports contained the same caveat: These were the known cases, many additional cases were likely, and these were not included in these counts.

In the US, there were more than 200,000 reported cases, and it was clear that the worse was yet to come. Public health measures were implemented in an attempt to control the virus, but as new cases sprang up, and health care facilities became overwhelmed, experts at the Department of Health and Human Services concluded that the damage had been done. Now, it was a waiting game and the focus had to shift from identifying the source to controlling the pandemic. Martial law was implemented to prevent large groups from gathering, as such gatherings were fertile grounds for infecting others. In addition, large quarantine camps were established at military bases and at some large postal facilities.

Just after the first wave of death was reported, the Supreme Jihadists claimed responsibility for the attacks; however, they later changed their story saying that they were hired by a group called the Genesis Project to do the attacks. They provided a list of members of the Genesis Project, and they named Dr. Victor Kraus as the mastermind behind the attacks. Furthermore, they claimed that Dr. Lesya Zhirova had engineered a mutant Ebola virus that contained genes from the measles virus. However, a conflicting news report came out a day later refuting that Victor Kraus and the Genesis Project were involved in any way in the attacks. Instead, they reported that Dr. Zhirova was working for the Russians who had hired the jihadists to destroy human lives and disrupt the economic stability of the whole world. It was reported that the Russians had intentions of taking over individual nations and establishing a world government.

With all the conflicting reports in the news, no one knew who was to blame. Several members of the Genesis Project were detained for questioning and jailed for conspiring to commit terrorist acts. At least five members of the Genesis Project were beaten to death in the streets within hours of their pictures being shown on the national news. An all-points bulletin was issued for Victor, who was wanted for questioning in connection with the terrorist attacks and for the murder of Lesya Zhirova, whose body was found at his New York apartment. Official documents from the Russian government authorizing the attacks were also found in Zhirova's briefcase at the scene of the murder, and this information, which was later determined to be counterfeit, was leaked to CNN news.

Many of the Supreme Jihadists had been hunted down and arrested, although many of their members had already been lost to the disease. The leadership of the group wanted to clear their name, and so they divulged all of the information that they could to the authorities. They explained how the devices were set up and activated to disseminate the virus, how the different sites were infiltrated, and how the virus was transported to them.

The Department of Homeland Security determined that Victor Kraus was indeed the mastermind and they set up a nationwide manhunt looking for him. Their best guess was that he would return to his family home in Frostburg, MD; however, when they arrived at the home, there was no sign of Victor. In fact, the home was boarded up, and looked like no one had entered it in many years. Even so, the house appeared to be fully furnished and completely set up for living. After that lead, the trail headed west to the Dakota's where Victor and his father had spent many summers together.

CHAPTER 17

Ethan unconsciously shook his head. *"So, I'm on my way to Glacier National Park to find a guy I've never met named Victor who may or may not be there, and if so, may or may not have a vaccine for a virus that he may or may not have created that has changed society as we know it. And to top it off, what's left of humanity could depend on me finding this asshole. It's a good thing nobody out there knows that their existence rides on a guy with a C-average in high school and a slight drinking problem... In fact, a shot would taste pretty good right about now,"* he thought.

He geared down into second and made the switchback turn and then continued to climb on the old logging road. His Ford diesel took a little coaxing to get going from sitting so long, but a little starting fluid worked wonders. There was one main road running in and out of Darby, Montana and that was Highway 93. The highway travelled north from Darby going through Hamilton then Missoula. From Missoula, Highway 93 continued north around Flathead Lake, the largest freshwater lake west of the Mississippi River, and then into the Flathead Valley and on to Glacier National Park. This would have been, by far, the best route to the park. Unfortunately, it would also be the most populated route.

Both General Short and Bob had warned him about staying away from the more populated areas. Not only would there be the potential for infection, but widespread panic had hit, and there was no telling what he might encounter on the road. In addition, time was of the essence. According to the intel that the general had, they had one chance of finding Victor, so they decided that it would be better to be safe than sorry. Ethan decided that the safest route was to take back roads into the Bitterroot National Forest crossing over into Idaho.

After hunting and logging in this territory his whole life, Ethan knew the area like it was his own backyard, which in reality it was. His plan was to take logging and forest service roads until he hooked up with Highway 12 at Lolo Pass. He would then drop back down on the Montana side of the Bitterroot range and pop out around Superior, Montana. Then, he would head north toward the Flathead. He figured that his fuel should hold out if everything went as planned; however, even though he knew the area, getting turned around and lost would still be a distinct possibility. Or as he liked to refer to it, there would be plenty of opportunities for joining the Fukarwe tribe as in, "where the fuck are we." He hoped that the GPS unit that Watkins had given him would help, but his own experience with such devices left him uninspired.

Ethan left at daylight so he wouldn't need to use his headlights. Even though he was travelling on logging roads, he would be winding his way up and down the faces of various hillsides and headlights in the dark meant that he could be spotted. It was amazing at what distance a headlight or spotlight could be seen, as more than one poacher had found out the hard way.

It was dusk when Ethan hit asphalt, which he knew was Highway 12. Ethan grinned as he got out to pee and let Cowboy stretch his legs. He was pretty proud of himself. He'd only stopped twice to check the GPS and that was just for reference. After driving another twenty minutes or so, he pulled off the highway and drove into the trees a short distance. He knew he was close to the Lolo Pass Visitor Center at the top of Lolo Pass, which was pretty much on the Idaho-Montana border.

After grabbing his Marlin, he headed off to find the center, as it would be a good place to spend the night. He just wanted to make sure nobody else had the same idea. Ethan stopped in the tree line behind the center and looked through his Vortex Viper binoculars.

"Looks okay to me, what do you think, huh?" he asked as he reached over and gave Cowboy a scratch behind the ear.

Ethan returned to his truck where he had parked it and grabbed his pack and then returned to the visitor's center. It didn't take him long to break in. After making sure that the place was in fact empty, he did a little exploring.

"Jackpot," he said with a huge smile on his face and a three-quarter-full can of Folgers coffee in his hands. "It's been awhile since I had a cup of Joe. If we happen on a bottle of Turkey, maybe I'll change my view on the whole God thing. What about you, boy?"

Ethan worked on getting something ready to eat for him and Cowboy. The smell of coffee boiling in an open pan on his little propane camp stove caught his nose. Ethan took the coffee off the stove and poured some into his canteen cup.

"How about some Denti Moore stew?" he asked Cowboy. "Just like mom used ta make."

The statement made him pause. He wished he hadn't said it. He opened the can lid, leaving it partially attached, and placed the stew on the burner.

"Be just a minute, boy," he said as he took a sip from the canteen cup.

"SHIT," Ethan said rather loudly. It had been awhile since he'd drank hot coffee from a metal canteen cup, which required a bit of an art form to avoid burning your lips on the hot metal.

"Guess it's going to take awhile to get back into the swing of things."

That comment made him think about the shape he was in and he looked over at Cowboy as he carefully stirred the stew. He kind of liked having the dog around to talk to.

"Okay, so I ain't in the shape I was when I was humping sand in the desert. I'm older, slower, and got aches and pains. This is depressing. Damn it, Cowboy, I wish we had a drink. Ah hell, it will all come back to me, wait and see, we're going to do alright. Looks like dinner is ready."

He looked around, found a magazine, and poured about half the stew on it and spread it out so that it would cool faster and then placed it down on the floor for Cowboy. He then dug in his mess bag and pulled out the Hobo knife.

"I won't let you down, Bob," he said as he looked at the knife. "Won't let ya down."

Ethan awoke around first light and went into the restroom. The water and toilet still worked, so he gave himself a monkey bath in the sink and did, as he referred to as, his morning reading. Ethan had found an old people magazine in one of the desks. He thumbed through it as he sat on the toilet.

"*Jesus*," he thought as he read about Hollywood stars and their problems. "*Man, I can't believe this shit. What's worse, I can't believe that other people, every day people, are interested in this crap.*"

He closed the magazine in disgust, wondering if the whole virus thing was payback for losing sight of the really important things.

"*After all, how important is the halftime act at the Super Bowl or any of that kinda crap?*" he wondered. "*But, regardless of how vain humans had become, what made this Victor guy think he could play God? I'm not even sure there is a God. Maybe that is why it bothers me so much that this asshole has attempted to step into that role.*"

Ethan looked up and saw Cowboy standing in the doorway. "What? Who knows when I'll be around indoor plumbing again? Get outta here, I can't finish with you standing there watching me! Damn it, get."

Ethan planned on abandoning his truck that day after getting several more miles down off the pass. Little did he know, however, that one of mother nature's rodents had a different idea for his truck. Ethan did one more sweep of the visitor's center and he found a box of Lipton tea he had overlooked during his excitement of finding the coffee. He hoisted his pack, grabbed his rifle, and headed back to his truck.

Ethan paused as he approached the truck, and observed it from his hiding place in the woods.

"*See, old habits do come back,*" he thought to himself.

When he was sure no one else was around, he walked up to the truck and placed his pack in the bed.

"Come on, Cowboy, let's go," he said, holding the door.

The dog jumped into the cab and Ethan followed. He placed the key in the ignition and turned it on, expecting to see the "Wait to Start" light reminding him of the mandatory 15-second pause required for the glow plugs to heat up in the diesel engine. Unfortunately, no messages lit up on the dashboard.

"What the hell?" Ethan said aloud as he turned the key again. "Nothing! Jesus Christ, what's next?" he said, getting out of the truck and popping the hood.

What he saw after looking for a moment was that a pack rat had chewed through the wiring harness of the program control module. The truck wasn't going anywhere.

"WELL FUCK ME RUNNING," he shouted as he kicked the driver's door shut. "You stupid bastard, why didn't you open the hood last night? God dammit, I can't believe it."

Cowboy barked at his outburst.

"Fuck off, Cowboy," Ethan said as he slammed the hood.

Anybody who grew up camping in the woods knew that pack rats loved to crawl into engine compartments as they cooled in the night. Moreover, wiring to a pack rat was like crack cocaine to an addict, and the little creatures just loved enclosed spaces. One way to prevent this was to open the hood at night to prevent these rodents from holing up in the engine compartment.

"Shit," Ethan said as he hoisted his pack. "Guess we're walking a lot sooner than I thought, huh, buddy?"

Cowboy gave him a *"fuck me? well, fuck you!"* look. Ethan picked up on the look.

"Get over it," he said to the dog. "Come on, you know I didn't mean it."

He started to walk away and then stopped and turned around. Cowboy hadn't moved.

"It's up to you, but I'm going to need help getting this done, so come on," he said, slapping his leg. Still, the dog didn't move.

Ethan turned and started to walk again. He'd only taken a few step when he looked down and saw Cowboy alongside him.

"Thanks, buddy," he said.

CHAPTER 18

Victor stood on the shores of Lake McDonald in Glacier National Park. It was about 6:00 a.m. in the morning and the lake surface was perfectly still and crystal clear. The snow-capped mountains surrounding the lake reflected in a mirror image on the smooth surface of the lake. A cool breeze blew gently across Victor's face as he took in the spectacular sight. It was the first day of summer in the rest of the US, but Glacier Park had its own seasons, and it would not feel like summer there for at least a couple more weeks.

"In the presence of nature, a wild delight runs through the man, in spite of real sorrows. Nature says, -- he is my creature, and maugre all his impertinent griefs, he shall be glad with me," Victor said aloud, quoting an essay on Nature by Emerson that Victor's father was fond of reading to him.

Victor felt at home in nature, away from the mad world of men, and he especially felt at home in Glacier National Park now that the whole world was falling apart. Just as he had planned, and right on schedule. He thought about the line from Emerson's essay, wondering if Nature would claim him as one of her creatures and be glad with him. He felt that Nature would be pleased with him, and he felt good about where the earth was headed.

Victor had always felt out of place in large cities, and he was particularly disgusted by the largest cities that he had visited or lived in. When he first moved to New York City, he was shocked by the horrific display of humanity everywhere around him. Congested traffic, swarms of people, miles of concrete and asphalt were bad enough, but he was even more horrified by the amount of consumption and the mountains of pollution and waste that the population created. The Hudson River was a cesspool of waste; the manhole covers in most city streets spewed stench in the form of smelly steam that rose from them like twisted clouds.

Victor attended a conference in Hong Kong early in his career and was mortified by what he saw. The city was so large and so compact that there was no visible bare ground anywhere. The city prided itself on the fact that it was the largest, most densely populated city in the world. It claimed to be the world's tallest residential city because so many residents lived in high-rise buildings. At the time of his visit, more people in Hong

Kong lived above the 14th floor than in the entire city of Chicago, totaling more than 3 million people.

By the start of the 21st century, over half the population of earth lived in cities, and nearly two million square miles of the earth's surface had been paved over to develop these urban centers. To Victor, the excessive consumption of resources and the complete lack of awareness regarding their impact on the environment made him hate mankind. Humans were blind to what they were and therefore, they could not, would not stop it. He was convinced that humans would not stop until the entire surface of the earth looked like New York City or Hong Kong. It disgusted him at the time, and that disgust grew stronger every day. He imagined how these cities would look now and in the next 20 years, and a smile streamed across his face.

After standing on the shore watching the reflection for several minutes, Victor returned to his Range Rover and continued his journey toward Many Lakes Lodge. A magnetic sign on the side of his vehicle read National Park Service, Emergency Services. Victor had covered all of his bases long before he headed west. He knew that there was a strong chance that he would have to hide out in Glacier Park during the cleansing period, and he had made the necessary plans. He had several magnetic signs and phony credentials made that would allow him access to places that would be closed off.

Glacier Park had been ordered closed due to the pandemic, but Victor gained access by providing credentials of a veterinarian with the National Park Service Emergency Services. He explained to the ranger on duty that he was sent to monitor the animal populations in the park to make sure that the new super virus did not infect them. He told them that he would need access to a cabin or a room and that he would not need any additional support. Victor knew that any attempts to verify his credentials would likely go unanswered, and in fact, found that the ranger offered no resistance at all.

The ranger was just happy to have another professional to talk to. He explained that his job had been mostly reduced to a security guard preventing people from seeking refuge in the park. He recounted several stories of people arriving at the locked gates, begging for entry so that they could camp out in the park until the pandemic passed. The ranger had been surprised at the numbers of people who showed up, and was at first amused, but he had become a little less patient as it became clear that everyone that showed up at the gate represented a potential opportunity for his own infection.

The ranger gave Victor a key to access Many Glacier Lodge, and issued him a Delorme inReach SE 2-Way Satellite Communicator with a rechargeable lithium battery so that the park service could keep track of his whereabouts when he was in the field. The phone would also allow Victor to reach them in the event of an emergency. After signing a few forms, Victor was set. He was safely inside his favorite place on planet Earth. It felt good, especially since his journey to the park had become increasingly risky as he travelled.

As Victor drove across the country from New York to Montana, he had a magnetic sign that read Centers for Disease Control and Prevention on the side of his Range Rover. As he cruised along back roads and secondary highways, it was as if he was driving deeper and deeper into a hurricane of panic. People along the route in New York were scared, tentative, and acted more than just a little worried. By the time, he reached the Midwest, stores were empty, gas stations were out of fuel, and traffic jams clogged up all of the major roadways as people tried to escape population centers. By the time he reached the Dakotas, civilization had collapsed. Most stores and homes were boarded up or burned down, there were no services available, and Victor worried about highway bandits. In fact, he was leery of any car he saw on the road, but fortunately, they were few and far between on the back roads that he traversed.

Victor walked onto the large and deserted deck of Many Lakes Lodge, carrying a few of his supplies. He had driven as fast as he could across the US, stopping only at his cache sites that were strategically placed about 300 miles apart and he was now ready to settle in and get some rest. It was a little unsettling to be the only person at the lodge, but Victor loved solitude. And, it felt secure because along with him being the only one at the lodge, for all intents and purposes, he essentially had the National Park Services protecting him. Essentially, he had 1,583 square miles of pristine wilderness all to himself.

Inside the room, Victor turned on the television. The local access to cable TV had been lost, and the only thing that Victor could find was a channel of streaming information that was coming in on the EBS. The announcement reiterated the requirements of martial law that had been implemented and was being enforced in the area. A curfew had been established from sun down to sun up and public gatherings were prohibited. Foods and medications were being delivered to and distributed by local grocery stores, based on a rationing system that was described.

The EBS also provided some very brief updates about the situation. It reported that more than 14 million people in the world had died as a result of the virus, including over 5 million in the US. Instructions were provided for how to care for an infected love one, warning people to not take their sick relatives to healthcare facilities. In addition, instructions were also provided for how to dispose of dead bodies. Coroners and local morgues had been even more overwhelmed than local health care centers.

The next morning, Victor got up at daybreak and hiked up to Grinnell Glacier on the Grinnell Glacier Trail. The hike was a strenuous 7.6 miles, climbing over 1,800 feet to an altitude of 6,515 feet with spectacular views of the Grinnell Lake and the Grinnell Glacier. Victor had hiked this trail many times with his father, and it was one of his favorites. They had always seen bighorn sheep and occasionally grizzly bears from a distance when hiking this trail. But even more profound for Victor was standing on the glacier itself. It had retreated significantly since the time he first stood on it with his father over 40 years earlier.

"Hopefully, we can reverse this process," Victor said aloud while standing on Grinnell Glacier. "I have done my part to save you. Soon, climate change will begin to reverse as less and less humans consume less and less resources."

Victor remembered his father in this moment. He remembered him standing on this very glacier and crying tears of sadness as he explained how humans were impacting the planet to a young Victor. His father's tears always surprised Victor because he always cried at the strangest times. When bad things happened to family members, he stood by stoically with little emotion. But, when an animal was hurt or killed, or human error led to a catastrophe like an oil spill, or if more evidence on the impact of climate change on the earth was reported, his father would cry.

Victor loved his father; in fact, he idolized him. He never felt closer to another human being on the planet, and he measured all of his relationships based on that one. When Victor's father died, Victor was devastated, and he never really dealt with the grief. Instead, he continued to speak to his father as if he were now a voice in his own mind. Victor wondered what his father would think of his plan. He couldn't help but imagine that his father would be deeply pleased and he sensed that it would bring a warm smile to his face. Those smiles were even more rare than were his tears.

Victor planned to hike the Gunsight Pass Trail to Sperry Chalet the next day, so he returned from the Grinnell Glacier Trail early in the afternoon. Victor had intended to use Sperry Chalet as his hideout if security at Many Lakes Lodge became compromised in any way. He brought enough provisions to create a cache of supplies there, and he had done enough research to know that the chalet had enough food to make it through a winter if necessary. He would establish the chalet as his final backup plan, his last resort.

CHAPTER 19

The first wave of the Typhon virus attack was spread over ten days, because the dissemination schedule designed by Victor and the Supreme Jihadists called for releasing the virus on thousands of people at public transportation hubs around the world for ten consecutive days, starting around the first of June. In this manner, Victor estimated that at least 10,000 people per day would become infected. The first signs of disease would be 10-12 days later, and all of those who were infected would be contagious 2-3 days before they became overtly sick.

In this manner, the expansion of the Typhon virus was designed to be both linear and exponential. Linear in that approximately 10,000 people per day for ten consecutive days would be infected. Exponential in that each of those 10,000 people would infect 16-20 additional people, expanding each wave by at least 16-fold. By Victor's estimates, if everything went as planned, for each 10,000 people originally infected with Typhon virus, it would take only six waves of infection: wave one would infect 10,000; wave two would infect 160,000; wave three would infect 2,560,000; wave four would infect 40,960,000; wave five would infect 655,360,000; and wave six would infect more than 10 billion or potentially everyone on the planet.

However, Victor knew that dissemination would not be that smooth. In order for this to work, every infected person would have to infect 16 others and those that were infected would have to penetrate into the most remote places on earth to ensure that all were infected. This simply was not possible. However, Victor knew that he could at least improve upon the odds by adding the linear step at the time of the original dissemination, ensuring that thousands of different people over several different days would become infected and carry the virus into different areas. Given that more than half of the earth's population lived in urban areas, Victor expected the largest cities to be hit the hardest and to be the first to recognize that an epidemic had arrived.

In fact, as Victor predicted, this was exactly what happened. Major cities around the globe were hit hard by the virus, which caused widespread panic, looting, and massive migrations from the cities as citizens tried to flee from the disease only to be taken by starvation or worse, by bands of thieves that formed to prey upon those who had anything of value. Local militaries were dispatched to control the crowds and attempt to stop the crime, but these efforts were of little value and many troops defected as doom settled in on a region.

Air travel and mass transport were halted almost immediately after the first major outbreaks became known, but that was about three weeks into the attacks, so by that time, nearly 20 million people worldwide were potentially infected and in place to infect others. There were no diagnostics available to determine who was infected and no one knew that those who still appeared healthy could be infectious. This was new, and most experts still assumed that the sick would not be contagious until after they had become debilitated by the symptoms. Nearly all emergency public health policies that were enacted, were based on the old paradigm, and this proved to be dead wrong.

By the time martial law was established in most places around the world, around three weeks into the attack, more than a million people were infected, and chaos had become the norm. Government officials in many countries had gone underground to protect their leaders, leaving the governing on the ground to emergency military personnel. They maintained martial law in most major cities, but it was impossible to control the panicked crowds who looted and destroyed buildings, stores, and factories in an attempt to gather whatever resources they needed. There was a strong sense in every major city in the world that their governments had deserted them. They did not take this passively.

Small groups of citizens formed in many cities for the purpose of survival. It was widely accepted that no help was coming, for there was nothing to provide. Therefore, these groups became focused on gathering the resources that they needed to survive and to protect their own. This led in many cases to gang rivalry and hostility as these groups competed for the limited resources that were available. In addition, given that it was impossible to tell who might be infected, in some cases, an infected person would be allowed into a group only to infect other members. Thus, a powerful group could easily be wiped out in the manner of a few days.

Some groups recruited suicide infectors who would become infected and then join a rival group only to wipe them out 10-12 days later. Other groups built confined communities that they protected by force. Military bases and other assets were frequent targets of attack as groups attempted to acquire weapons and ammunition for their own use, and to take over structures that could be protected.

On the international scale, tensions among world governments were at an all-time high. Russia was convinced that the attacks were backed by the US to reduce the exploding population in China, and that the US had fabricated the story about Lesya Zhirova to incite public hatred of Russia. The Russians were convinced that the US intended to destroy both Russia and China in the process. China, Russia, and North Korea solidified their alliance against the US. However, when the major governments went underground, communications between them became less frequent. Diplomatic channels between Russia, China, and North Korea on the one side, and the US, Japan, and the European Union on the other were crippled in the process.

North Korea became impatient with the lack of communications and took matters into their own hands, firing nuclear missiles first at South Korea and then at Japan. In addition, North Korea fired several nuclear missiles into space from a southerly route, a maneuver that they had practiced several times, because they had calculated that it would have devastating consequences for the US electrical grid. America responded by deploying several nuclear warheads aimed at targets in North Korea. The US Seventh Fleet provided defense by using their missile defense system to shoot down the missiles aimed at Japan and were able to intercept and destroy several of the missiles headed for outer space, missing only one missile that was headed in that direction.

Fortunately, diplomatic communications between the US, China, and Russia were reestablished in time to avert complete nuclear proliferation, because through those communications it became established that North Korea was acting alone and without the consent or approval of Russia or China. The three major superpowers were able to reach a short-term diplomatic agreement, whereby all three tentatively agreed to back down and remain on high military alert.

The US breathed a sigh of relief that nuclear proliferation had been averted, at least for the moment. However, they were not in the clear and much damage had been done. Both Koreas were devastated by the attacks, and the nuclear warheads that were intercepted in the air on the way to Japan had exploded, sending massive quantities of nuclear material into the ocean waters near Japan. There would be devastating consequences as a result, and these would have an impact the world over.

And then suddenly and without warning, the lights went out in the US. As it turned out, North Korea's mission to knock out the electrical grid of the US by detonating a nuclear missile at precisely the correct location in space to generate an electromagnetic pulse (EMP) that would cause the grid to implode worked as planned. The single nuclear missile detonation that occurred in space after the US missile defense system missed it, ended up knocking out the US electrical grid and with it much of the North American Aerospace Defense Command's (NORAD) ability to defend the US from future nuclear attacks.

CHAPTER 20

In the days following the presidential declaration of martial law, life in the DC area spiraled out of control. Despite pleas from public officials to remain calm and cooperative, enough cheaters ignored these warnings and went into the streets to get whatever resources they could to help themselves survive the coming plague, and this caused a ripple effect. The actions of a few cheaters led to the feeling that there would be nothing left for those who followed the suggestions of the public health officials, and it soon became apparent that despite their best efforts, the officials could not control the people or the resources available. This led to complete anarchy.

David and the Compassionate Neighbors operated the house on Girard Street, offering medical services, food, water, and support to anyone who was in need. However, they saw firsthand how a few frightened and careless citizens created the chaos that was overtaking the city, and in fact, not everyone who showed up at their front door was there for help. Some would drop by to see what the group had so that they could steal it, while others were only interested in any medications that the group was distributing. It did not matter what their motive was, David and his group helped everyone feel welcome.

"You have to love your fellow brothers and sisters more than you love your things," he was fond of reminding everyone.

However, this open door policy led to thefts of their supplies, and some of the other members of the Compassionate Neighbors began to monitor the situation without David's knowledge. All they really tried to do was make sure that there was enough for everyone who came by, especially since there appeared to be no end in sight for the number of people seeking help, but their supplies were low.

"We are running out of supplies, and we need to get more," one of the members brought up to David one afternoon.

After several moments of thought, David replied with a couple of questions. "Does anyone know where we can get supplies? Are there food banks that are open? Grocery stores? Hospitals? Any other ideas?"

No one knew for sure what was available and so they sent groups of friends out to see what they could find. After a couple of groups left, David sat down and turned on the television to see if there was any information available on the news. What he saw shocked him.

From the looks of it, the world had gone to hell. The CNN reporter was standing in front of the White House, which was less than five miles from David's front door, reporting on the current state of the U.S. government.

"At this hour," the reporter stated, "the president is urging everyone to stay calm. There have been a number of cases of this illness among prominent members of both houses of Congress, and the president and his family and the vice president have been taken to separate but secure locations. The president's cabinet, at least those who have been cleared of illness, have also been sent to safe locations until this outbreak is under control. At this time, the president is signing emergency executive orders that will implement the Continuity of Government plan that will allow the government to operate in emergency mode from these remote locations until such time as this virus is under control.

"The most recent report from the World Health Organization is that more than 121 countries have reported cases of the viruses that is being called the Typhon virus. Communications have been lost with several of these countries; however, the president stated emphatically, that many of the NATO countries are still in contact with one another and emergency protocols have been implicated to protect this alliance."

"Earlier today, we heard from the Assistant Secretary for Preparedness and Response from the Department of Health and Human Resources who gave some very important details about this virus and how to prevent contracting it. First, she stated that the virus was indeed an engineered biological entity, which means that this event is considered a bioterrorist attack. No one has stepped forward to officially claim responsibility for this attack, although there is plenty of circumstantial evidence floating around that suggests that the virus was created by the Russian government, supported and funded by a U.S.-based group called the Genesis Project, and distributed by a Muslim extremist group known as the Supreme Jihadists. The man who founded the Genesis Project, whose picture is now on your screen, is wanted for questioning, although he denied any knowledge of the virus before going into hiding.

"The assistant secretary also cautioned everyone to stay home and await further instructions, warning that those who are out and about in the community are at greater risk of being exposed to the virus. The National Guard has been deployed in the district and in several states to supply food, water, and medicine to those in need. Safe zones and houses are being established and plans will be announced very soon."

"The director of the Center for the Disease Control and Prevention announced that the Typhon virus has been detected in nearly all 50 states, and those who have recently travelled by airplane are at a greater risk of having been exposed to the virus. It is recommended that those who have potentially been exposed put themselves in voluntary quarantine, staying away from other members of their family for at least two weeks to ensure that they are not infected and to prevent infection of others."

"Wow, that was gruesome," David said aloud as he turned off the television.

Within an hour, two groups of friends who were sent out to look for resources returned with grim news. They reported that the streets were filled with people running around grabbing things, pushing shopping carts full of supplies everywhere. The roadways were plugged up with way too many cars trying to navigate the city streets. Grocery stores were full of people, and in some cases, the crowds had rushed the doors and refused to pay for the goods that they were taking. There was panic and pandemonium everywhere they went. The National Guard was everywhere, but they were unable to gain control of the situation.

They did manage to make it to one of the homeless shelters and talked with the people in charge there. The shelter agreed to provide several cases of bottled water, a few cases of canned goods, and some out-of-date potato chips and other snack items. However, they were running low on fresh items like meat and vegetables. They were hoping to get a shipment from some of their regular sources, but no shipments had arrived in the past three days, so they were not sure if anything else would be arriving.

The shelter said that their numbers had dwindled a little, and they thought that some of their clients may have moved out of the area or been killed by the virus. No one knew for sure what was happening or what would happen in the future, but it was clear that whatever provisions arrive on a regular basis in the past could no longer be counted on.

David nodded solemnly as he listened to the two groups describe what they had seen out there. He updated them with the information that he heard from the news.

"Was there any update on the nuclear tensions between China, Russia, and us?" one of the friends asked. "I heard on the radio the other day that the virus was made in Russia, sent to the US for distribution in China. China was really angry and was threatening war with Russia and the United States. Then there was an outbreak in South Korea, which caused North Korea to panic. Last I heard, it sounded like a nuclear threat was very real."

"No, there was no mention of that. Let's turn the TV back on to see if they have gotten to world events yet. They were pretty much discussing domestic issues when I looked last."

David turned on the television, and it appeared that the same news crew was now discussing international events. There was a picture of the mushroom cloud over Hiroshima behind the news anchor's head. Unfortunately, before the anchor could say a single word, the TV went blank.

"That's odd," David said. "It looks like the power just went out."

CHAPTER 21

When the power went out in Glacier Park, Pappie Anders didn't even notice it at Sperry Chalet. It was the middle of the day, and other than a little news about the outbreak and all the deaths worldwide, Pappie was content doing his job and enjoying the beautiful surroundings that he was fortunate enough to get to live in. At 76 years of age, Pappie had seen better days, but never happier ones, for he was completely at home in the solitude of this mountain chalet that he was charged with maintaining.

Pappie had lost his wife of 47 years, Jean, just two summers ago, and since her passing, he pretty much spent his time in nature. It was the place that he felt closest to her and to whatever God there might be. He was never much of a churchgoer, and he didn't have a lot of patience for religious doctrines or dogmas; they all seemed to run a little hollow to him. But, he could not deny a strong sense of a powerful creative force that was ever present in nature, pushing through the struggle of life with glorious and spectacular abandon. His eyes were attuned and his heart was open to such experiences and he saw them all around him.

Pappie had always loved Glacier Park, and in particular Sperry Chalet. The first time he and Jean hiked the Gunsight Pass Trail to Sperry Chalet, they weren't sure that they would ever make it out of there alive. They started at Siyeh Pass Trailhead at 8:00 in the morning and they had plans to meet a friend for dinner at Lake McDonald Lodge after a nearly 27-mile hike. However, the hike proved to be much more strenuous than they thought it would be and they encountered all forms of weather, including snow in July during that hike. Instead of completing the hike by dinnertime as they had planned, they only made it to Sperry Chalet.

They were out of water, and all of their snacks had been consumed. Fortunately, the chalet allowed the two stray hikers to come in, have dinner, and replenish their water supply. After dinner, the couple continued their hike and finally made it to Lake McDonald Lodge around midnight. The last several miles in the pitch dark were terrifying and Pappie was so tired he kept falling asleep between steps only to be jolted awake when his foot hit the ground. They never forgot the hospitality they experienced at the chalet, and in fact, it became an annual trip for them up until the time that Jean got sick.

After Jean died, Pappie did not know what he would do. He had worked at several jobs in his life, and was well beyond the seven average career changes that most people experience during their lives. For his final job, he put in 17 years driving and delivering for Pepsi Cola, which he retired from about ten years earlier. It was a decent job with a decent retirement, and with the steady income, he was able to help get his kids through college and settled in their own adult lives. The only thing that Pappie was ever really good at was loving Jean, and quite honestly, he was lost without her.

About a month after Jean died, Pappie noticed an ad in the help wanted section of the Daily Interlake, the local newspaper that he had delivered to his home in Columbia Falls, Montana. The ad was for a caretaker for Sperry Chalet during the offseason months of October through April each year. Pappie was sure that he would not get the position, and he certainly did not need the small stipend that came with it. However, a part of him felt as if Jean was saying that he should go to the chalet and meet her there. He applied and to his surprise was hired to be the caretaker.

Pappie was surprised to get the call from Glacier Park in mid-June of this year asking him to assume his caretaking duties as soon as possible. He was informed that the park was shutting down and locking all entrances until further notice due to the pandemic. He was advised that he would be on duty as soon as he could get to the chalet and until further notice. Pappie did not hesitate; he headed to the chalet later that day after informing all of his children where he would be. He couldn't think of a better place to be holed up than in the middle of nowhere in the greatest piece of real estate in the world.

Pappie's routine at the chalet was, well, rather routine. Each day, he went through a checklist of items to ensure that the chalet was properly maintained, and then he went on various hikes in the area. He watched birds, studied flowers as they bloomed, waded in cool streams and waterfalls, observed bighorn sheep for hours, and occasionally watched a bear or wolf from afar. Pappie always carried his backpack with him that contained all of the essentials that he would need to survive in the woods if he were to lose his bearings and get lost. On his right hip, he carried a fresh canister of pepper spray to ward off bears and on the left hip, his trusty Glock 9 mm pistol.

Each day after lunch, he would touch base with command and let them know that things were going okay, and order any supplies that he might need for the coming month. The park service delivered provisions once a month, by horse in summer months and by snowmobile during the winter. The chalet had all of the modern conveniences except for one: there was no cell phone or television reception at all. Pappie could occasionally pick up a radio station out of Canada on a solar radio that he brought with him, but that was inconsistent at best. He got most of his news from checking in with the rangers each day and with a stack of out-of-date newspapers delivered each month.

As was the usual, Pappie was up at first light and after a light breakfast, he did his routine maintenance items and was on the trail hiking by 9:00 a.m. He liked to get an early start so that he could get back in time for a late lunch around 1:00 p.m. Then, he would do a little reading and relaxing in the afternoon until dinner time, and after dinner, he would be off to bed. It wasn't the most exciting schedule, but it suited him well.

The looming pandemic in the outer world was always on his mind, especially since his kids and grandkids were out there. However, they all lived in small Montana towns that had not yet had any reported cases of the virus, so, he felt pretty good about their chances of avoiding the pandemic. He got daily updates from command, and there were always messages from his kids letting him know that everyone was safe. The rangers that he talked to at headquarters had become increasingly concerned about potential intruders into the park, and they warned him to be vigilant about not letting anyone near the chalet. He was to alert command if he saw anyone.

It felt a little strange to Pappie to have this assignment while the whole world was going to hell. He almost felt that he was the last person on earth, and he couldn't imagine what he would do if he saw someone else. Particularly, given the concern about spreading the virus, and his orders to protect the chalet. It was strange indeed.

When Pappie returned from his morning hike, it was around 12:30 p.m. and the June sun was as high above the chalet as it would be for the day. He first noticed that there was a problem when he tried to make contact with the rangers at headquarters. His solar two-way radio was fully charged and seemed to relay his message, but there was no response. The chalet was completely off the grid, so it never had electricity in the first place, thus, Pappie was right at home with the current situation and had no idea that most of the U.S. was without power.

Victor left Many Lakes Lodge as soon as the power went off. He knew that something big was going down, and he also knew that he needed to be in a more secluded spot to ride this out. He was aware of the nuclear attacks because the EBS had provided information on how to prepare for nuclear fallout, how to treat loved ones who might be exposed, and how to be safe in the event of a direct nuclear attack. He was dying to know who was involved, but he had no access to information and he dared not attempt to contact anyone.

The scenario unfolding was not exactly what Victor had planned, the whole world destroying itself with nuclear weapons, but he took solace in the fact that humans would mostly kill themselves and the rest of the life on this planet would come back. Evolution would see to that. Humans were the aberrant life forms that were out of control and beyond the reach of evolution, but that was already changing. Soon, the canvas would be wiped clean and evolution could tinker away.

Victor decided that he would move into Sperry Chalet and hunker down there for several months while he waited this thing out. He attempted to communicate with park headquarters, but as he suspected, there was no reply. The battery-operated devices were likely still able to communicate, but the radio at dispatch had been rendered useless without power. Victor wasn't sure what would cause a large-scale power outage, but if the grid went down, then he knew that chaos would soon override all attempts to manage the pandemic. He really hoped that this was the case.

Victor drove his Range Rover to the Sperry Trailhead and parked in the lot adjacent to the trailhead. He then loaded as many supplies as he could carry into his pack, locked his vehicle, and headed up the trail toward Sperry Chalet. He left his vehicle in the parking lot because he planned to make a few trips to get all of his supplies to the chalet. Once he had transported everything, he would move his vehicle so that it would not be so obvious that someone had taken that trail and might be at the chalet.

The six-mile hike into the chalet was strenuous and exhausting, particularly with a heavy backpack on. At the five-mile mark, Victor could see the chalet and he perched himself on the side of the hill with his field glasses in place so that he could study the area surrounding the chalet. Given the emergency closure of the park, Victor wasn't sure if they would revert to their offseason protocols. When he spotted Pappie, Victor's heart raced. He watched him closely and for several minutes trying to determine if the old man was there alone or if there might be others at the chalet, too. This was a problem.

"Good afternoon," Victor shouted from the trail as he approached the chalet.

Pappie was outside watering a few plants around the front of the dining hall, and was startled by the stranger's voice.

"Hello there," Pappie called back. "No one is supposed to be in the park right now, it's closed and so is the chalet."

"Yes, I am aware of that," Victor said. "I'm Jim Wilson, a wildlife veterinarian with the National Park Emergency Services. I'm checking in on the park's wildlife. This virus is typically limited in what it can infect, but we want to keep a close eye on the animals, especially bears and wolves that are already in perilously small populations."

"Oh, yes, headquarters mentioned that you were going to be in here poking around, I'm glad to know you, Dr. Wilson. My name is William Anders, but most folks just call me Pappie."

"Oh, please, call me Jim."

Pappie extended his hand and shook Victor's with a firm handshake. Afterwards, Victor turned toward his backpack which he had dropped on the trail heading up to the chalet. When his back was turned momentarily, Pappie instinctively checked to make sure that his pistol was on his side. Pappie had not let on, but he recognized Victor. His picture had been all over the newspaper in the last shipment that he had received a few days earlier.

"Do you mind if I stay here for two nights while I check on the animals in the area?" Victor asked.

Pappie did not want to scare him off, and he did not want to let him go. Even though he figured his bosses at headquarters would not want him to allow a guest to stay, he felt that it would be his best chance of capturing the bastard who was in the process of destroying humankind. He just wasn't sure about how to go about it, so he made a plan to alert headquarters as soon as he could.

"Yeah, they said you might drop by for a night or two. That will be no problem. I see you brought your own supplies."

"Yeah, and I have several more in the car at the trailhead. I am going to head back down there in the morning to get another load," Victor stated. "So, why do they call you Pappie?"

"Well, it's a long story, but the short version is pretty straight forward. We were so poor when I was a boy, I had to wear hand-me-downs that my own father wore when he was a boy. All my friends thought I dressed like their grandpas and so they teased me and called me Pappie. I guess it just stuck."

Victor looked at him incredulously, not sure if the man was telling the truth.

"That's a funny story," he said dryly. "Pappie, can you take me to a good location in the morning for observing bears?"

"Well, as you know, the bears are very skittish. You'll be lucky to see one, but I can take you to a great spot up on Comeau Pass where I sometimes spot a grizzly from a distance. We will have to leave around first light, though, so that we can be in position by the time the animals start moving."

"That sounds great," Victor said.

Pappie set Victor up with a room in the hotel section of the chalet and he invited him to share dinner with him in the mess hall. Pappie prepared a couple of cans of chili con carne and served it with a little grated cheese, a few diced onions, and corn chips. Victor had volunteered to cook dinner using his own supplies, but they agreed that he could cook the next night.

After dinner, they retired to their individual sleeping rooms for the night. Pappie burned all of the newspapers that had Victor's picture in them in the fireplace just in case Victor saw them and realized that Pappie might know his identity. It was a perfect night for a little fire anyway, for the early summer chill could be felt throughout the mountain chalet.

Pappie attempted to get a message out to headquarters alerting them that Victor was at the chalet and that he was the person that the whole world was looking for in connection with the pandemic, but there was still no reply. He tried several times that evening and again first thing in the morning.

Just before first light, Pappie was up in the mess hall fixing breakfast and getting the coffee ready. Victor came in a few minutes after Pappie got there, and greeted him warmly.

"The coffee sure smells good," Victor said. "Nothing better than the smell of freshly brewed coffee on the cool mountain air."

"That's a fact," Pappie said. "So, how long have you been a vet, Jim?"

The question caught Victor by surprise. "I guess it's been about 23 years," he lied.

"What is the strangest case you have ever had to deal with?"

Victor thought for a moment. "Ahhh, that would have to be the time that a doe and two fawns were run over by a hay cutting machine. It was a mess, and I was surprised the farmer hauled all three of the animals to my clinic. Unfortunately, the mother died, but I was able to save the two fawns. They recovered and were eventually donated to a zoo."

"I'll bet that took some doing," Pappie said. "We better grab our food and hit the trail so that we can be in position when the sun starts to rise over the mountains."

The two men placed small packs on their backs and headed up the trail away from the chalet. Pappie made sure that everything was locked before he left, and he checked his bear spray and pistol as he headed up the trail. Victor followed close behind, and walked as silently as he could. The trail took them 2000 feet up in elevation and was about 3.5 miles long. When they reached the peak, Victor was ready for a break, and he was surprised at how well Pappie handled the strenuous hike.

Pappie found a good spot to sit upon that allowed for a perfect view in several directions and pulled out his field glasses to look for signs of animals. He finally settled his focus on a meadow about 500 yards away. He was about to turn toward Victor and offer the glasses when he felt something cool against his neck and then felt warm blood pour over his shirt and onto his lap. He had lost control of his body and felt himself fall backwards as the world became dark. The last words he heard were from Victor.

"Six billion and one. No offense, old man, I just couldn't have you meddling in my affairs."

CHAPTER 22

Three days of hiking put Ethan and Cowboy on the valley floor. Taking a break just inside the tree line, Ethan noticed a calmness and absolute silence. He had, of course, been in the woods many times in his life and would often pause to listen and hear only the wind in the trees. The trees would creak and groan as if alive, and it eventually occurred to Ethan that they were. Sometimes while at work, he would stop everything after falling a tree. Just shut his chainsaw off and listen. When he did this long enough, he could hear voices in the breeze. It was even more eerie on still hot days in August, when it sounded as if the trees spoke to each other.

Ethan Edwards could be described as a lot of things but being an environmentalist wasn't one of them. Bob had told him they were conservationists because they believed in the wise use of the environment and its resources. Bob said that God gave man dominion over the earth and that it was man's job to manage the planet. And, depending on how much Glenlivet Bob had consumed would determine just how shitty of a job man was doing with managing those resources. However, Bob always concluded that in the grand scope of things, man was still a young species and perhaps would grow up as time passed to be good stewards. That, or Mother Earth would brush humanity off like an old woman brushing lint from her shoulders.

The biggest thing that bothered Bob about environmentalists was that they were conceited in thinking they could or should control the balance of resources and lives on the planet. Bob liked to say that human beings would be around just as long as God wanted them to be. Not one minute more and not one minute less. Ethan didn't know about all of that God business, but he was keenly aware of what he considered to be the planet's gifts.

Ethan enjoyed the feeling of wonder and excitement he felt when a Cutthroat Trout broke the surface of the river and took his fly. The way he felt when he put his hand on the deer or elk he had just taken, pausing a moment to give thanks. He had seen country so beautiful that it took his breath away. So, who was he giving thanks to? God? Ethan avoided the question or at least he thought he had avoided it. He didn't like the God question, but it always seemed to pop up.

"We better keep going, got at least a few hours of daylight left. Probably should find a secluded place to hole up for the night," Ethan said to the dog.

As he began to proceed across the valley, he thought he heard music in the distance. *"Surely there wouldn't be music out here,"* he thought. He just couldn't believe that someone would be out in this remote wilderness area, but sure as hell he could hear singing. He knew he was approaching the Clark Fork River and thought that perhaps the river was playing tricks on his ears. He looked down at Cowboy who looked as if he agreed with Ethan.

"Well, hell, let's check it out, boy."

Ethan dropped his pack in a stand of trees, and with his Marlin rifle in hand, he carefully worked his way through the woods. The music grew louder. He crouched on the rise and looked down on a man cleaning a nice bunch of Cutthroat Trout on the river's edge. What looked like a CD player was on the bank playing a Robert Earl Keen song.

"I saw him sing at the Top Hat in Missoula one time," Ethan said.

The man froze. "Well then, you obviously appreciate good music, my friend. May I turn around so I can have the pleasure of seeing with whom I'm conversing?"

"You should do it slowly and it would be best if you keep your hands out in front of you," Ethan replied.

"Of course." The man stood as he turned.

"Now, carefully take your left hand and remove the pistol from its holster."

"I'd rather not do that. Lots of unsavory folks about nowadays. Present company excluded, of course. But where are my manners? Miles Gilmore at your service and obvious disadvantage."

Cowboy growled.

"I see your canine friend doesn't approve of me."

"He don't approve of a whole lot. Mr. Gilmore?"

"Yes, sir?"

"Slowly take your left hand and remove what appears to be a Springfield XD from its holster. Place it on the ground and take two steps away from it. The topic isn't open to further debate," Ethan said as he slowly moved his Marlin so that Gilmore was looking down the barrel.

Cowboy growled again as if to add emphasis.

"I can see that. Even though you have a rifle, although not a very big one, pointed at me." "Although big enough. It ain't about the size, it's what you can do with it."

Gilmore smiled. "So, I've heard. I'll remove my pistol now."

He slowly took the pistol out and put it on the ground and stepped back two steps.

"There, feel better, Mister...? I didn't catch your name."

"I didn't give it."

"Don't you find it…?" Gilmore paused. "I want to say *odd*, but on further reflection, I suppose it's not. I'll call it *human*. Don't you find it human that with all that has happened our first inclination as humans is to assume a defensive position with each other?"

"Christ, this guy sounds like Watkins," Ethan thought.

"Edwards. Ethan Edwards."

"Ah, Mr. Edwards. And your rather unfriendly canine companion?"

"That's Cowboy," Ethan replied.

"Of course it is. Well, now what, Mr. Edwards?"

"Not sure, actually."

"Perhaps, we could start with you pointing your BB gun at something else."

"A fellow shouldn't make fun of another man's gun, especially when he doesn't have one."

"I can't tell whether you are aware of the penis references you continue to make when you're talking about your weapon or if it is just your manner of speech. Either way, we are at a point in the conversation where you, my good man, seeing as how you have the gun, get to decide what takes place next."

"Shit, this guy is worse than Bob when it comes to the philosophical bullshit," Ethan thought.

"I need to get north across the river. If you could direct me to the nearest bridge, I'd appreciate it."

"Well, Mr. Edwards, I…"

"Ethan. Just call me Ethan."

Gilmore looked at Ethan's face for a moment.

"Very well then, Ethan, there's a bridge about four miles upstream from here. Although, I wouldn't recommend traversing the river in that fashion," he continued. "I'm fairly certain that it is being held by, what shall we call them, Highwaymen, as in days of old, if you are aware of the term."

Ethan couldn't tell if Gilmore was speaking down to him in a condescending fashion or if that was just the man's way of talking. Regardless, this guy was beginning to piss him off and he wasn't exactly sure why.

Cowboy bared his teeth.

"I believe that your dog truly does not care for me." Gilmore smiled as he said it.

"Like I said, he's not overly social."

"You did mention that, in a fashion. I'll tell you what, Ethan. Why don't you and Mr. Cowboy follow me back to my humble abode where we can dine?" Gilmore looked down at the Cutthroat Trout lying on the grass.

"Then, after dark, I will float you across the river in my drift boat. Then, you can be on your way."

Ethan cradled the Marlin in his arm. "That sounds like a pretty good offer."

"Then, may I gather my things and by that I mean all my things?" Gilmore asked.

"I don't see why not and thanks for the offer, Mr. Gilmore."

"Don't mention it. I'm sure I'm going to enjoy your company and perhaps even your friend will warm up to me."

The hike to Gilmore's home was an easy one that began as they angled away from the river slightly. It must have been about three miles when Ethan saw a home and a couple of outbuildings at the foot of a hill. Gilmore stopped and turned around to face him.

"Be it ever so humble."

"Looks like a nice place," Ethan said, meaning it.

"Yes, actually, it has served its purpose quite well. Ethan Edwards, I've been wondering where I've heard that name before and it has finally come to me. Are you not aware of it?" he asked.

"Guess not," Ethan replied.

"Hmm, it was John Wayne's name in the film the *Searchers*. Most consider it his best performance. What is it that you search for, young Ethan?"

Ethan was taken back by the question. It was as if Gilmore somehow knew more than he should.

"What makes you think I'm searching for anything?" Ethan asked.

"We all search for something, son. It's why we are here." He paused. "Although, very few of us ever fulfill our quest. Shall we?" He turned around and continued in to the house.

Ethan shook his head behind him and thought, *"This is one strange dude."*

The inside of Gilmore's house was plain but comfortable. Ethan placed his pack by the door along with the Marlin. He left the .45 pistol in its holster on his hip, as did Gilmore with his pistol.

"Make yourself at home," Gilmore said as he motioned toward a chair at the kitchen table.

"I'll put some water on to boil. Although, I don't have anything but some of my own herbs for a homemade tea."

"Hey, I've got some coffee I can contribute to the cause," Ethan said as he went to get it out of his pack. He noticed what he thought was a disappointed look on Gilmore's face. But it was there for just a moment.

"You don't say. See, I knew this was going to be a mutually pleasant evening. I'll warm up some stew I made yesterday, if that is alright with you. Waste not want not, as the saying goes. I'll even add a bit of herb to it seeing as how we'll be missing out on my tea."

Gilmore continued to talk as he prepared their food.

"As I was saying earlier, it is a shame that when the structure of society fails evil seems to flourish. A person can't help but wonder if the belief that there is good in all of us is erroneous. Perhaps it's just the opposite, that evil is the base of man's makeup, and therefore, it triumphs in the end. Perhaps, we only tell ourselves otherwise so that we can avoid the consequence of an unpalatable truth. What say you, Ethan?"

"Guess I think there's good and bad. Always has been. I think some people overthink it. Good people will always try to do what's right first off. Bad people will always look for what's in it for them or how something is going to affect them. I believe good people aren't as scared as bad people and that we all have the same thing in all of us for the most part."

"Interesting, a bit of bad in the best of us and a bit of good in the worse. Simply put, but I like it. But, what about evil, Mr. Edwards?" Gilmour asked, as he placed a bowl of stew in front of Ethan and one on the floor for Cowboy.

"*Bon appétit*. Enjoy, I myself am not hungry at the moment but please while it's warm," he turned and went back to the sink.

Ethan blew on a spoonful of stew. Cowboy went to his bowl, and as he stuck his nose down to it, he bared his teeth and growled a deep menacing growl. Gilmore started to spin around at the sink with his right hand attempting to pull his pistol from its holster. Ethan's hand went to his leg with lightning quick speed. He pulled the .45 from its holster and had it above the table all in one fluid motion. His first shot caught Gilmore center mass in his chest, the second just below his throat. The 230-grain full metal jacket bullets did what they were designed to do with devastating effect. Gilmore was dead before he hit the floor.

The noise from the gunshots left Ethan's ears ringing. He moved his jaw around to clear his ears, knowing that the ringing would eventually pass from previous experience. He reached down and retrieved Gilmore's pistol, keeping his own pointed at him even though there was no doubt he was dead. Ethan looked at the man. His eyes had glazed over and were devoid of life. After a quick search of the kitchen, he found a pill bottle with a crushed up white powder in it. He turned and looked at his bowl of stew and then at Cowboy's.

"Thanks, buddy. Guess all that police dog training came back to ya. Told you it would come back to us."

Thinking in that vain, Ethan kept his .45 pistol ready to shoot as he searched the rest of the house. There were three bedrooms up on the main floor. All of them appeared to be lived in. When he opened the basement door, he was met with the strong smell of bleach. However, there was another odor there that the bleach was attempting to cover up. Cowboy growled again.

"Ya, I hear ya," Ethan said as he slowly started down the stairs, his pistol up and ready.

At the bottom of the stairs, he found a light switch and flipped it on. A battery-powered light came on, illuminating the space. Off in the far corner of the room, Ethan saw a pile of heaped-up clothing. Most of the pile was made up of men's clothing, but there were women's clothes there too. A chill went through him. Next to the pile of clothing was a table with an assortment of watches, wallets, rings, and eye glasses. Ethan turned and noticed that across the room there was a door with a hasp and a padlock on it. Cowboy stood in front of the door, staring at it ready to spring forward. Ethan crossed the room.

On the wall next to the door hung a key on a nail and it was obviously for the padlock. With the .45 pointed at the door, he heard the lock click as he turned the key. It sounded like a gun being cocked and made him flinch. As he swung the door open, a horrific smell rolled out of the room. Ethan recognized the smell. It was the smell of stale blood. He then noticed a light switch on that side of the door. When he turned it on, the room became brightly lit. The room appeared to be some kind of a torture chamber. There was a soiled bed with chains lying on it and handcuffs hanging from the ceiling. On a table near the bed was an assortment of knives and various hand tools covered in dried blood.

What he saw made him vomit and he ran out of the house to do so. He stood on the front porch sucking clean air into his lungs and blowing his nose trying to get the smell out of his nostrils. He knew from past experience that every time he thought of this place that smell would come back. It reminded him of the smell of the prison cells in an Iraqi compound they had liberated. Memories of those cells always brought back that terrible stench. Ethan turned and looked at the house.

"This sick bastard wasn't acting alone, Cowboy. He's got helpers," Ethan said to the dog as he recalled Gilmore's comment about Highwaymen on the bridge.

He recalled that all of the bedrooms in the house appeared to be slept in, and it occurred to him that this might be where the so-called Highwaymen stayed. The day was fading and dark was quickly approaching.

"Let's hangout and see who shows up, boy."

About forty minutes passed and Ethan heard them coming before he saw them. Three men, all armed with automatic or semi-automatic weapons, were headed toward the house. The men carried their weapons in a relaxed fashion, walking abreast of each other as they approached. When they got in the yard, one of them yelled.

"MILES, you old pervert, where you at?"

"Maybe he's got somebody in the basement?"

"Fucker better not start without us. Like he did with that little blonde number. She was fun while she lasted."

"Doesn't appear to me like it matters a whole lot to you, Henry; I think you actually enjoy the boys more than the girls nowadays."

The three men were at the bottom of the porch steps. The one named Henry turned his head to comment to one of the others. The man next to Henry suddenly stopped talking as his stare fixed on Henry's chest. Henry's eyes looked down as both men noticed the razor sharp arrow protruding from his chest. Before they could say anything, the man who had been speaking reached for his throat where he clutched the shaft of a second arrow. The third man spun around blindly firing his weapon until it was empty. As the panicked man struggled to reload his gun, Ethan stepped from his hiding place, aimed the Marlin, and shot the man in the knee. He dropped his automatic weapon and crumpled to the dirt. As he rolled around, Ethan gave him a hard kick in his back knocking the wind out of him. The man gasped for air.

"Shut up, fucker," Ethan said as he pushed the rifle barrel in the man's ear. The man quit moving.

Ethan stood over him.

"Your pal, Miles, and I were having a conversation about good and evil. He asked me something about what a guy does about evil. I didn't have an opportunity to answer him, so I guess you'll do. YOU LISTENING?" he asked as he pushed the barrel harder against the man's ear.

"YEAH, YEAH."

"Good," Ethan replied.

"Evil... you kill it," he said as he pulled the trigger four or five times.

CHAPTER 23

It was a little eerie for Bob and his lab crew to have to work under military surveillance. It wasn't exactly surveillance in the typical sense, but the place was completely locked down, and military personnel were in every room. Bob couldn't seem to even scratch his ass without some private making a note of it. However, it came in handy when the power went out because with all the troops and fortifications, the US government had also shipped all of the latest supplies for field units, including large generators and solar-powered devices, such as two-way radios.

The general had been assigned by the president to command the RML complex, and he and his battalion had fortified the complex so that it could be rigorously defended from all sides. Their mission was to protect the lab complex at all costs, and to procure a vaccine or drug for the Typhon virus. The RML was in a remote location and had all of the most modern scientific equipment that would be necessary for working with this deadly pathogen.

To escape the law and order of the military presence, Bob and Fran found a secret spot on the roof of one of the lab buildings where they set up a couple of plastic chairs and spent a couple of hours there each night, enjoying a nightcap while Bob puffed on a cigar. He had received a gift of a box of Cuban cigars from a dignitary from Sierra Leone while he was there fighting Ebola virus, and although he had never really smoked cigars, he found that he really liked the refuge a nice cigar gave him from his stressful routine.

"Too bad that guy didn't give you more cigars," Fran said. "Looks like your box is just about empty."

"Yeah, I'm here to tell ya, a nice cigar is like one of your drinks… it will knock your socks off!"

Fran smiled. She loved this man, and she loved every moment that she got to spend with him. The current situation was so uncertain, she found herself worrying about their future for the first time in many years. Sure, she worried about him when he was off in West Africa fighting Ebola virus, but Bob knew that virus and so did she, so she felt a bit of comfort knowing that he was so competent with that virus. The Typhon virus was a whole new deal.

"Well, here you go, a nice drink to go with your nice cigar," she said, handing him a drink.

"The perfect trifecta! A fine cigar, a fine drink, and with the world's finest woman. And to top it off, I get to enjoy all of this under the beautiful star-filled Montana sky."

The starry nights in Montana were always beautiful, but they were even more spectacular with the city lights of Hamilton knocked out by the power outage. Everywhere they looked they saw brilliant stars.

"You are going to go, aren't you?" Fran asked after a few minutes of quiet awe.

"I'm afraid I'm going to have to. I told you about the call from Lesya Zhirova. She mentioned that the madman Victor Kraus has a vaccine. We have to get our hands on that vaccine if we want to make any impact on this pandemic."

"Bob, honey, that is a job for a younger man. Let Ethan handle it."

"I'm afraid he is in over his head, Fran. We are asking a lot of him, and he is not as stable as I let on. Besides, he will not know what the vaccine might look like or how to handle it to make sure that it is handled properly for transport back here."

"We don't even know if this vaccine works, or how it was made, or even if it was tested in humans or approved by any regulatory body."

"We don't have a choice, it's all we got."

The truth of the matter was simple. The only lead that Bob had on the vaccine was that Lesya said there was one. He knew Lesya, but not well, and he certainly was not up to speed on the science that she had been doing. Most of her work was done in secret in Russia and mostly published in Russian science journals. He had attempted to do a literature search on her work, but there were only a few publications available in English. Nothing was mentioned about the newly engineered virus or any vaccine work.

To complicate matters even more, a member of the Genesis Project told the press that there was a vaccine for the Typhon virus, and since that leak in the national news, every major research center in the US was at risk of being attacked by desperate people trying to find a cure that would save their loved ones. As panic blazed across the population, the word on the street was that the US elite had a vaccine, but they were only giving it to the rich and the well connected. This fueled public outrage, which resulted in large and dangerous mobs that marched on clinics, hospitals, university laboratories, and the like. In most instances, the mobs marched without opposition as police and military forces were much more worried about the possibility of catching the virus than of the violence the mob might cause. In many cases, these groups destroyed those facilities, and left the buildings ablaze.

RML was an asset that the US government committed to preserve and protect, and Bob's lab was charged with figuring out how to slow down the Typhon virus. Based on Bob's conversation with Lesya, he knew that there were a couple thousand vaccines available somewhere in the Midwest with Victor Kraus, and he knew that he needed to get his hands on them to figure out what components were used to make the vaccine.

Bob had spent years working with the Ebola virus, and he knew what difficulties this virus presented to those who would develop therapeutics to counter it. First of all, it was an RNA virus, which meant that it evolved quickly. Therefore, any vaccine or drug would likely only be effective for a short period of time before the virus adapted and became resistant. He had seen this happen with several drugs that were developed against Ebola virus but had failed to really ever be effective enough to try in humans.

Another feature that made the Ebola virus difficult to block was the fact that the virus shielded its viral glycoprotein in carbohydrates that hid the receptor-binding domain until the virus was inside the endosome. This meant that the immune system would never see it, and therefore, would not be able to prevent the virus from attaching to the receptor and infecting the cell. In fact, antibodies raised against the glycoprotein with the carbohydrates attached also did not neutralize the virus well enough to prevent infection. These were a couple of reasons that helped explain why vaccines against Ebola virus were so difficult to develop.

Bob was fully aware of these issues and had developed some workarounds for the Ebola virus, but he did not have any idea how the immune system handled this new virus, and he needed to either do a whole lot of basic virology and immunology to learn about how this virus worked or he needed to get his hands on one of those vaccines so that he could examine the components it contained and then replicate them.

During the West African Ebola virus outbreak, several investigational drug products were used under compassionate use protocols authorized by the FDA, and in fact, some of these had been tried without much success against the Typhon virus. There were other developmental products being tested and some people in other labs at RML were attempting to figure out if any antiviral drugs approved for the treatment of other viruses worked against Typhon virus. This seemed like a long and tedious road to Bob, because in reality, it took several years and millions of dollars to develop most drugs, and that was after a virus had been pretty well studied. This was a new virus that was killing so fast that by the time a new drug was developed, there would be no one left to give it to.

Bob needed that vaccine, as it was his best shot at figuring out how to reproduce a therapeutic that could be used to protect the uninfected immediately. The need was even more urgent because all of the latest reports that Bob received indicated that the Typhon virus was even more virulent than Ebola virus, and its mortality rate was greater than 90%.

In addition, those that survived the infection did not fare well. Although those recuperating from the infection had only had a few weeks at most to recover, most had developed encephalitis or meningitis and experienced severe effects on nervous function, including reduced motor neuron control and muscular atrophy. Moreover, the virus seemed to accumulate and persist long-term in immunoprivileged sites, like the eyes, the cerebrospinal fluid, and the semen, and many people who survived infection were blind. Recovery from Typhon virus was almost a fate worse than death.

"General, I believe I need to go with Ethan to get that vaccine," Bob said to an impatient-looking General Short during one of his visits to RML.

"I'm afraid that's not possible," the general replied. "You are a top priority and I need you right here working. In the eyes of the US government, you are a high priority asset."

"The fastest way to a vaccine is if I can get my hands on the one that they already have. If I can figure out how they made it, I can replicate that and we could have a vaccine in a matter of weeks. If I have to do this from scratch, it's going to be years. We don't even know how this new virus replicates, what cells it infects, what receptor it uses, or anything really. You need to let me go to Glacier Park with Ethan."

"First of all, we don't even know if Kraus is in the park. Second, I thought you said that we could count on the corporal," the General snorted.

"He is as trustworthy as they come, he just doesn't have a clue about what he's looking for. This mission is critical. That vaccine may mean the difference between the survival of mankind or complete annihilation. I would rather be on the ground looking for the vaccine; that is a better use of my time. My lab crew can do all of the preliminary work on the virus while I am gone, so we won't be a minute behind schedule either way."

"What do you imagine it's like out there, Doctor? Do you think you arc just going to waltz out there and get in your pickup truck with your hunting rifle and drive on up to Glacier Park? There are a thousand desperate sonsabitches within 20 miles of here with nothing to lose. They will shoot your ass just for the gas in your truck. Who knows what you'll find near Missoula. I can't spare the men or the vehicle to get you there."

"I have a way to get there, General. It won't cost you a single man or truck."

"This is a conversation for another day, Doctor. If Kraus is indeed in Glacier Park, then we might, and I do mean *might,* discuss this further. Until then, I would suggest that you focus on what you can do right now."

Bob nodded. The general was right, but Bob had an eerie feeling that he would eventually come face-to-face with the mastermind who unleashed hell on the world.

CHAPTER 24

Victor stood on the mountaintop, soaking in the spectacular views. After a few minutes of breathing in the cool mountain air with his eyes closed, he removed his pack, took out his journal, and scribbled down the following lines:

I am but a small part of a vast and beautiful world,
The eyes of the universe, the ears of the timeless orbs,
I stand here humbled by endless skies,
by the snow-capped peaks that whisper my name for eternity.

In the morning, when the sun awakens on the new world
I will be the humble and courageous servant,
I will stand in awe as the ambassador of change,
I will bow to a new and beautiful evolutionary reform
That will usher in a new millennium.

Balance will be restored,
Life will be renewed,
Nature will win,
Mankind will be reduced to its righteous place
At the bottom of the pyramid
Where they will struggle to survive.

Victor read the poem aloud, and then closed the journal and placed it back in his pack. He then removed a tarp that was strapped to the bottom of the pack and unrolled it. Just as he expected, Pappie's body had been largely devoured in the night by wolves or bears or other carnivores. His body was disassembled with large portions missing. Most importantly, his neck was completely devoured, and there was no sign of the precise cut that had taken his life.

Victor took out his digital camera and photographed the horrific scene from every possible angle. When he was finished documenting the scene with photos, he placed latex gloves on his hands and then gathered up the various pieces of Pappie's body and placed them on the tarp. When he was finished, he pulled the four corners of the tarp together and tied it up as a sack that he could drag on the trail behind him. He then pulled Pappie's remains back to Sperry Chalet and buried him in a shallow grave that he dug the day before. He documented the grave with photos and covered it with large rocks. He placed all of Pappie's belongings, including his gun, in a box inside the chalet.

When he was finished burying the old man, Victor completed the process of covering his tracks by recording his story in his journal. Victor knew that he needed to cover his tracks and spin his story. His image had taken a hit on the national media, and if anyone survived that knew of him, he would have a lot of questions to answer. He had a little time to develop his story, and he was sure that when the time came, he could convince everyone that he was not to blame, that in fact he had tried to stop it.

In the journal, he described how he arrived at the chalet the day before and found no one there, so he broke in and stayed the night. The next morning, he hiked various trails until he came upon Pappie's remains up on Comeau Pass. He described how traumatized he was to see a dead body, and despite the horrific challenge that it presented, he felt that it was the humane thing to do to drag the remains to the chalet grounds and bury them so that no other animals would devour his remains.

He described finding the can of pepper spray half discharged, when in fact, he had discharged it himself just before heading down the trail. He described how he tried to contact headquarters, which in fact he did send several messages on the satellite phone, but received no response. When he was satisfied that he had documented a perfect cover up, he put his journal away, put on his large empty backpack, and headed back down the Sperry Trail to his Range Rover.

Victor made a few trips from the chalet to his vehicle and back, carrying as much as he could, over the next two days. When he loaded his last supplies into his backpack, he hid it off the trail and then drove his Range Rover a couple of miles down the road and parked it in the Lake McDonald Lodge parking lot and disconnected the battery. He then returned to the trail, put on his pack, and hiked back to the chalet. With the last of his supplies safely in the chalet, Victor was set. With what he brought in and what was already at the chalet, he would have everything he needed for several months. With winter only a couple of months away, he would soon be snowed into the mountain chalet, and safe from whatever was happening in the world until spring.

Now it was time to formulate his plan for revising his public image, write his version of history, and further develop his plan for the new world. He started by writing his version of the events leading up to the release of Typhon virus. The story that he would use to sway public opinion in his favor and save his reputation. Fortunately, portions of this story were true, which would lend credibility to the whole. In addition, most of those who knew the truth were already dead, and with a little luck, Victor hoped that the rest would be dead by the time he needed to repair his image.

The heart of his story was his relationship with Lesya. He started by detailing how they met when they were in high school and how she had become obsessed with him. For years, he wrote, she tried to convince him to love her and when he refused, she became a lesbian. Then, as her career developed, she confided in him that her father worked for the military intelligence branch of the Russian Spetsnaz, and he had been assigned to raise her in the US and train her as a virologist that would return to Russia to lead the Virology Institute in Moscow where she would be in charge of the bioengineering of human viruses.

When the Russian government ordered her to engineer a virus to wipe out humankind, she contacted Victor and played him perfectly. She tried to convince him to get on board with reducing the population, and while he refused, he agreed to meet with her when she came to New York to discuss the plan further. During that visit, Victor agreed to take the vaccine because she insisted, but he was convinced that he had talked her out of destroying civilization. Instead, he invited her to be part of the Genesis Project where she could help inform public policy that would change humanity.

Then, he wrote, Lesya double-crossed him in an attempt to force him into collaborating with her. She went to the members of the Genesis Project and told them that he had approached her and convinced her to engineer a virus that would wipe out humans. She told them that it was his idea, and she convinced them that they should back the project. Once she gained the backing of the Genesis Project, she tried to use that to convince Victor that he should lead the effort. However, he refused and threw her out of his office. It was then that she and the Genesis Project proceeded without him. He also explained that she and the Genesis Project used a vaccine to bribe various people and turn them against him. Their mission was to spin it so that he was the evil one so that he would take the fall if it was ever learned that the attacks were planned and implemented by the group.

After the attacks began, his story continued, she told the Supreme Jihadists, who were paid by the Russian government, to blame Victor for the attacks and she provided a script for them to read. She also worked with the Genesis Project to blame him and wrote scripts for all of them to follow when speaking to the media or the authorities. Victor concluded his story with Lesya showing up at his apartment where she attempted to call the authorities to turn him in for a crime that he had no part in. When he tried to throw her out of his apartment, she grabbed a knife, and in the struggle that ensued, he managed to stab her in the throat. He had fled because he was afraid for his life, and the uncertainty of what she told the press made him fear that he would be arrested or killed.

When Victor was finished writing his story of how the Typhon virus attacks came about, he reread it and polished it. He then made a list of loose ends that might need cleaning up. He heard that several members of the Genesis Project were killed, but some of the others had been arrested and these members would have to be dealt with in one manner or another. Another item on the list that was important was the fact that there were vaccines. He wanted to make sure that they believed that he had no idea where the vaccines were. Victor knew that the vaccines would likely be the only ace he had up his sleeve, and he would need them when he handpicked the leaders of the new world. Another item to be addressed was Lesya's lab in Russia. He would have to make sure that there was no evidence in that lab that connected him with the attacks.

With the story written and ready to send out into the world, Victor knew that he would have to get out before it and make sure that the loose ends were tied up. That is, if the virus had not already done so for him. However, he was pleased with the story and he felt that his plan was solid. He was sure that he could spin this and have whoever was listening believing his version with very little work.

More important to Victor was his plan for the new world. He had been working on this plan his whole adult life, and now it was time to write it out and start fine-tuning it. There were three primary elements to the plan: resource sustainability, balanced consumption, and controlled human population growth. No longer would man have dominion over the planet. They had lost that privilege, and Victor was going to do all that he could to prevent them from ever having the chance again.

CHAPTER 25

Ethan woke up to the sound of rain hitting the tin roof of the construction trailer that he'd spent the last three days living in. He lay there in his makeshift bed for a while just listening to the steady stream of rain dancing melodically across the roof. It felt like the earth was trying to cleanse itself of the virus and the chaos that was ushered in with the pandemic. It could use a good cleansing he thought.

After several moments of slipping in and out of sleep, Ethan stirred and rolled off the bed he made out of a door and two saw horses. He needed to pee and his back was starting to cramp up from sleeping on this hard bed. He stumbled to the door of the trailer, opened it, and relieved himself, noting that he needed to do so as quickly as possible to avoid getting too wet. He looked down at Cowboy.

"Hey, get tough and go do your business," Ethan said to Cowboy, as the dog looked at him and then headed out into the rain.

Ethan was thrilled when he stumbled upon the construction site a few days earlier, not only because he had been traveling in the downpour and was soaking wet, but also because he was cold, hungry, and completely worn out. He hiked at a brisk pace for several days in an attempt to get the events at Gilmore's place out of his sight and out of his mind. He needed a few days to regain his strength. Cowboy, on the other hand, appeared to enjoy the increased pace.

Ethan stumbled upon this shelter quite by accident. He had been working his way north in the open spaces, looking for a shelter, and he first noticed the construction site from the crest of a hill he'd climbed hoping to find something that would get him and Cowboy out of the weather. From the crest, he could barely make out the shapes of several structures below him in the misty fog, and it looked like there could be a couple of small buildings scattered across the field below, so he and the dog headed down the hill toward them.

As he approached the site, he was able to see more clearly and the buildings turned into pieces of construction equipment. There were large D9 caterpillars and enormous excavators with their arms and buckets extended away from their bodies. He also noticed a couple of John Deere 844 front-end loaders close by. Ethan stood there for a moment and looked at the equipment through the rain. He couldn't help but think that the machinery looked like steel dinosaurs from an age gone by. He then realized that in all likelihood, that is exactly what they represented.

After sloshing through the mud for a few minutes, he noticed the trailer a few yards away from all of the equipment. It wasn't a small trailer, but more like a large portable construction office designed to be pulled by a large truck. He walked up the steps leading to a main door and discovered that it had a padlock on it.

Ethan removed his large pack from his back and took out what he referred to as his master key, which in fact was a sturdy old pair of bolt cutters. After cutting the lock, he retrieved a flashlight from the pack and entered the trailer. The beam from his light was dim, and he realized that not only did he need to see the sun again, but so did the solar backpack charger that he used to keep what little equipment he had powered up. A quick survey of the trailer revealed what he expected to find in a construction trailer. There was a desk with papers piled on top, a few file cabinets, and a telephone on the desk. He couldn't resist the urge to check for a dial tone, and was not surprised to find the line was dead.

Ethan felt a smile grow across his face when he spotted a small wood stove in the corner of the office. The stove was vented through the roof with a chimney system that was designed to be dismantled when the trailer was ready to be moved. He quickly located several large bundles of grade stakes at the back of the trailer and used them and some stick matches by the stove to get a fire going. He then built his makeshift bed and spent the next three days sleeping and hoping that the rain would subside.

After three days, it was time to move on. Not only did he need to find supplies, but the walls of his newfound home were starting to close in on him. In addition, the abandoned construction site was a little too eerie. He could imagine that before the pandemic, this place was abuzz with activity and several men worked long hours on the machines that now stood stoically in the yard, slowly returning to the earth they once moved and molded.

Ethan suddenly realized that he had quit peeing and was just standing there in the rain holding his dick. He let out an embarrassed laugh and called out for Cowboy. It wasn't like anyone was watching, but none-the-less, he felt a little self-conscious. It was then he noticed that that rain had started to stop, and he could see the sunlight breaking over the mountains. Returning inside, he made himself some tea, if you could call it that. His last tea bag had been used so many times that he put it in the cup more for psychological effect than for any flavor he might get out of it. Next, he took out a can of chili he had scavenged from his last stop.

Ethan didn't want to spend a lot of time thinking about his last stop. After gathering the supplies he could carry in his pack, he emptied Gilmore's house of food products and put all of it in one of the small out buildings. Ethan figured someone who needed it might stumble upon it. He then dragged the dead bodies from the yard into the house, along with

Gilmore, placing them in the living room. Next, Ethan gathered bedding and anything else that was flammable and spread it around the walls in the living room and lit it all on fire. He didn't care who saw the smoke or flames, he just wanted this place and its memories erased. He stopped once and looked back as black smoke poured from the windows.

Ethan opened the chili and placed it on the stove to heat. Fortunately, he hadn't found it necessary to break into his emergency rations, and wasn't about to until he had no other options. He looked at his watch and noticed that it was near the designated time to contact Bob. Ethan grabbed the satellite phone and popped the battery in it. He'd last spoken with Watkins right after what he described as "the incident at Gilmore's." Ethan had told Bob everything that happened. Not much else was said, because quite frankly, there wasn't much to discuss.

On this call, Watkins told him that the international scene was deteriorating. When Ethan asked what that meant, Bob simply reported that there was even more fear that someone might let the nuclear genie out of the bottle. As he described it, one of the threats was an EMP that could occur after a nuclear detonation.

Ethan was aware of the potential for an EMP and the damage it could do to electronics, but most of his information came by the way of speculation that was discussed at the Antler Bar more than once. However, Ethan was aware that the Humvees and other military vehicles had old-style ignition systems so they would be able to run after an EMP. But, as an added precaution, he and Watkins had come up with a schedule when they would attempt to reach each other. When not in use, they agreed that they would take the batteries out of the satellite phones. Watkins told Ethan that he had questioned General Short about potential communication problems. The general's answer was true to the general's general approach to his job.

"All those billions of dollars for defense over all those decades didn't buy five thousand dollar hammers. When people say we've got shit that nobody knows about, well, guess what? We've got shit that nobody knows about."

So, both Ethan and Watkins assumed that General Short would keep their lines of communication open.

Ethan would not have been able to find the words to describe what he was feeling when Bob informed him of North Korea's nuclear launch and America's retaliation. There was no sure way to tell, but it was highly likely that the Korean peninsula had become uninhabitable. The American civilian power and communication grid was basically knocked out. And, it wasn't like any repairmen were working on restoring it. Apparently, General Short had been telling the truth. Military communications had taken a hit, but according to Short, they were coming back online.

The American command structure was in contact with its Trident Ballistic Submarine forces and was working feverishly on re-establishing communication with its ground forces around the world. Bob told Ethan that Short had informed him that the US military was still a formidable force both domestically and internationally. How much of what the general was saying was bullshit or just wishful thinking, Bob couldn't tell.

"How are you holding up, Ethan?" Bob asked.

"Better than most of the rest of the planet," he replied.

Ethan told Bob that he was fairly sure that he was calling him from the Flathead Valley, and if all went as he had planned, he'd begin moving through it the following day.

"So, there's one other thing we need to figure out," Bob said when Ethan was done talking.

"I'm listening," Ethan said.

"Well, we need to have someone in place who will be able to question Victor or identify the vaccines once you find him."

"Hell, Bob, why don't we just have Scotty beam him to me. I mean shit, I'm not even sure I can find the son of a bitch. Then once I do, I have to figure out how to get some lab geek up there?"

"Ethan…" was all Bob got out before Ethan started again. Bob knew from past experience that it was best to let him rant for a bit.

"So, this ain't a clean petri dish test tube environment. Is this going to be some Rambo military scientist or what? Just who is the dumb BASTARD I'm supposed to magically get here?"

"You done?" Bob asked.

"For the moment," Ethan replied.

"Okay, so I was thinking that Burt Long has a plane, right? And—"

"Whoa, whoa, how the hell does Burt… Wait a minute, Bob, just who are you guys going to try and get up here?"

The phone was silent.

"Bob?"

"Alright, no rants, got it?" Bob started. "And dammit, I mean it."

After a short pause, Bob in a dry voice simply said, "I'm the lab geek that has to get to you."

"Okay… Um, and this ain't a rant. But, Bob, you ain't exactly in… I mean, I don't want to piss you off or hurt your feelings but hey, buddy…"

"I ain't no spring chicken. Is that what you're doing a piss poor job of saying?"

"Ya, that pretty much covers it," Ethan said.

"Tell ya what, slick, you just worry about finding Victor and let me worry about me. Because the fact is, I'm the only guy here with the knowledge and experience necessary to recognize what needs to be recognized. And that's just the way it is."

"Alright, alright. But, don't tell me I'm the only person who isn't gung-ho about the idea. I can only imagine what Fran has to say about this."

"Me too, I've kind off broached the subject, but I haven't told her yet. Now, do you want to hear my plan or what?"

"Lay it on me, buddy."

CHAPTER 26

When the power from the generator was finally connected and the rangers at Glacier National Park headquarters were able to check messages they received from Pappie at Sperry Chalet, they were surprised to learn he had a visitor at the mountain outpost. Moreover, attempts to contact him continued to go unanswered, even though the radios they used were unaffected by the EMP. The officer in charge knew that something was up, although, he found it hard to believe that *the* Victor Kraus that the whole world was talking about, at least those who were alive and on the news, might be at the chalet.

He looked again at the text message he received from Pappie a few days earlier just to be certain, and sure enough, it read: *Send several officers to Sperry Chalet. Dr. Victor Kraus just showed up here. He has no idea that I know his identity. Plan to arrive at exactly 9:00 a.m. on whatever day you can get a team up here. I will be prepared at this time each morning.*

The district manager sent out an announcement over the radio to call all of the rangers together. There were only five rangers who were still on duty, including the district manager, as most of the others had left their posts to attend to family members or had disappeared without any notice whatsoever.

"This is District Manager Lorrents from Glacier National Park headquarters," his announcement began. "I'm calling all rangers back to the main office. We have an emergency. Dr. Victor Kraus may be in the park at Sperry Chalet. We need to go in and get him if possible."

"Isn't that the guy that unleashed this virus on the world and who is supposedly hoarding all of the vaccines?" one of the rangers asked.

"Affirmative, meet at headquarters ASAP. We are going into the chalet as a team in the morning. We need to bring this guy out."

The district manager attempted to call for backup, but for all intents and purposes, he lost contact with the outside world. The phone lines were dead, his cell phone was dead, and Wi-Fi on the only laptop computer that was not destroyed by the EMP was dead. The only thing that worked was the radio he and the other rangers were using, and he had no idea how large of a range that would be. Regardless if he could get backup or not, District Manager Lorrents was not about to leave one of his elderly caretakers in the presence of a mass murderer. He had to act and he planned to use everything at his disposal to take the man out of there alive.

"Dumb ass amateurs," Victor thought to himself as he heard the message broadcast on Pappie's radio. *"What can you expect from federal government employees..."* Not only did the message alert Victor to the plan, but it gave him time to prepare for the posse.

Victor went into survival mode. The first thing he did was bury the two cases of vaccines for the Typhon virus in two different locations far away from the chalet. First, he located a landmark that was distinct in each of the two areas and then dug a hole four feet deep and placed a small crate that was sealed and weatherproofed into each hole. This was no small task as the soil was extremely rocky, and it took him a couple of hours to dig each hole using a pick and shovel he carried from the chalet.

Once the holes were dug and all but two of the vaccines were safely in place, he buried the crates carefully and covered the fresh dig marks with leaves and twigs to ensure that they were hidden from sight. Then, he carried the tools back to the chalet and prepared for his showdown with the park rangers. He decided to keep four vaccines with him at all times to use as a bargaining chip if a situation arose that might require a negotiation.

Victor was not the athletic type, although he was certainly the outdoorsy type. He could handle himself in nature; he was just not built for or coordinated enough for hand-to-hand combat. However, what he lacked in agility he made up for with intelligence. Back inside the chalet, he took out his collection of Ninjutsu throwing knives and checked them for sharpness. He owned a beautiful set that he purchased while attending a conference in Japan, and he spent hundreds of hours practicing his craft with these very knives after he got them. All six knives were razor sharp.

Next, he took Pappie's Glock 9 mm out of the box of possessions and checked to see if it was loaded. The clip was full. Victor had fired a handgun exactly two times in his life, and he knew that he could not count on his shooting skills to win a gunfight against four or five armed men. But, he reasoned, at close range, a gun could come in handy.

Then, he mapped out his strategy. He figured there were three ways that the rangers would try to get him. First, they would come in with guns a blazing and try to take him by force. Second, they would play dumb and try to catch him without incident, and third, they would try to sneak up on him and catch him by surprise. Therefore, he developed counterattack plans for all three of these scenarios.

In all three cases, his counterattack hinged on getting the rangers into the smallest and darkest room in the sleeping cabin, so he placed a couple of knives in that room in strategic locations, and then initiated a plan that could sway the odds in his favor. He sent a text on Pappie's radio with the following message: *I can't use this radio because I told Victor that I lost contact with the outside world. He sleeps in Room 6 of the sleeping lodge.*

If you want to catch him off guard, show up here at 6 a.m. and you should be able to get him without incident. Pappie.

Entering the sleeping lodge from the main entrance, Room 1 was the largest room and it was to the immediate left, while Rooms 2-6 were to the right down the hallway. Room 6 was at the end of the long dark hallway. The room had one rustic queen-sized bed and only a small window. Victor would wait for the posse in Room 1, and when they entered, he would hit them from behind while they were in the hallway. He figured that they would send in a couple of rangers and a couple more would likely stand guard outside the bunkhouse, so he had to figure out how to get those rangers who were on the outside, too. For that, he figured that if he took out the rangers on the inside quietly, those on guard duty would soon come in to see what happened, and when they did, he would be ready.

District Manager Lorrents got Victor's message, thinking that it was from Pappie, and he devised his plan to go in and get Victor while he was asleep in Room 6 of the sleeping lodge the next morning around 6:00 a.m. He and the four rangers in his charge went over the plan in great detail. They would start at the trailhead at 5:00 a.m., hike into the chalet, and three men would go inside the sleeping lodge to get him. One man would stand guard at the front door and a second ranger was assigned the back window of Room 6.

Victor was ready when they arrived, and waiting in Room 1. When the three rangers entered the sleeping lodge, two of them quietly walked down the hall, while one stayed back by the main door. Victor disposed of the three men easily. First, he sliced the first man's throat cleanly, catching him by surprise from behind. The man slumped to the floor and Victor caught him as he fell to prevent a sound. The second man was killed by a well-placed knife that Victor threw from behind. The knife caught the man in the back of the neck just below his skull. However, when the knife pierced his neck, he let out a small groan that alerted the third ranger, District Manager Lorrents, who turned to face Victor with his handgun drawn. Victor caught him in the right eye with a long sharp knife that penetrated deep into his brain, killing him instantly, but not before his gun went off sending a single bullet into one of the logs of the sleeping lodge.

"Shit," Victor muttered.

The gunshot alerted the other two rangers, and Victor tried to stabilize the quickly deteriorating situation.

"We got him," Victor yelled out. "Get in here and help us."

The ranger at the front of the lodge went running into the front door, and at the precise moment he noticed the dead bodies of the other rangers, he yelled out a warning.

"They're all dead," he yelled, just before Victor caught him from behind with a knife that ended his life.

The last remaining ranger took cover behind the lodge, and in a state of panic hid there, trying to figure out what to do next. Victor wasn't sure how many men had come for him, but from the message he listened to, he was expecting five. So, he assumed that there was another man out there waiting for him.

"This doesn't have to end badly," Victor called out to the man. "I do not want to kill you."

There was no response. Victor carefully looked out each window of the sleeping lodge to see if he could see the fifth ranger. He did not see any signs of him. He positioned himself at one of the windows were he could see the trail leading away from the chalet, in case the man tried to escape, and he decided he would lay low, waiting for him to make the next move.

The ranger sat behind a small clump of Alpine fir trees. As far as he knew, all four of his friends were dead and Victor was in the sleeping lodge waiting for him. He had a radio, but he knew that no one was out there to hear his pleas for help. He heard Victor's message, but how could he trust someone who just killed four rangers?

"I don't get paid for this shit," he thought to himself, as his mind raced.

After several minutes of silence, the ranger decided he needed to get out of there and go back to headquarters to see if he could get a hold of someone, anyone who could help him. From his hiding spot, he hiked up the hill, staying hidden as best he could and then got on the Sperry Trail just above the chalet. Victor saw the man just before he disappeared on the trail heading away from him. He gathered his knives and went after him.

The man was hiking at a pretty good pace, but Victor caught up with him quickly about 500 yards down the trail. From a vantage point about 30 feet above the man, Victor launched one of his knives that caught the man in the back of his right shoulder, disabling his arm on the same side of his body as his handgun was strapped. The man let out a sharp groan as he attempted to unholster his gun with his left hand. By the time he got his gun out, Victor was upon him. With a second knife, he pierced the left shoulder of the man, leaving him without the use of either arm. The man fell backwards onto the rocky ground, with blood pouring out of each wound.

"Oh, Jesus," the man said.

"This didn't have to go this way," Victor said.

"Sure, I could have surrendered to you up there and you could have killed me without any fight," he replied.

"Who else knows your here?" Victor asked.

"We alerted the Federal Marshal Service," the man lied. "They will be coming for you, mother fucker."

"Look, I am not a bad man," Victor replied defensively. "You don't even know me."

"I know everything about you I need to know. You kill people from behind and without warning. You are the very evil the Bible warns about. I never believed in Satan as a person until I met you."

Victor laughed.

"Have you ever believed in a cause greater than yourself, you fucking idiot? Have you ever made sacrifices for something worthwhile in this world?" Victor asked in the condescending voice that he had mastered.

"When I die by your hand in the next few minutes, I will die with a clean conscience," the man said. "I have lived my life in service to others. I do not have to answer to you for anything, Satan."

"And I suppose you turned the water off while brushing your teeth so that you could save the planet, you fucking moron. Let's get on with this."

Victor removed a large knife and violently thrust it into the man's forehead, twisting it vigorously as the man gurgled his last breath.

"Da da domp domp domp, another one bites the dust," Victor sang as the man died.

Once again, Victor found himself in cleanup mode, but he was tired of digging holes to bury the dead. So, instead of burying them, he returned to the chalet, gathered the four dead bodies from the sleeping lodge, removed their guns and the contents of their pockets, dragged the bodies a few hundred feet from the chalet, poured kerosene on them, and burned them. Then he took the keys, his knives, a handgun, and a container of kerosene and hiked down the trail.

He did the same with the body of the fifth ranger, and then continued down the trail to the trailhead. Once there, he used the keys he had gotten from the district manager's pockets to start the truck they used to come get him. He drove to park headquarters, searched it for any information that they might have on him, and then set the building on fire. When he was confident that the building and all of its contents would burn to the ground, he drove back to Lake McDonald, parked the truck in the parking lot, and then hiked back to the chalet.

CHAPTER 27

The day before the events at Sperry Chalet about 275 miles due south from West Glacier, Montana, Lamar Young sat at his ham radio listening for more news that he could report to his clan. As an elder in his Mormon community in Salmon, Idaho, Lamar was charged with protecting his people and his church's message. He was not too surprised to find that there were hardly any recognizable sounds on his radio after the power went out. Regardless, he spent a couple of hours each day trying to find a signal.

The clan that Lamar was in charge of was comprised of 56 men, women, and children. There were 23 men, including himself, 16 women including his wife, Shelly, and the rest were kids. Five of those kids were his own, and they were all under the age of 10. Lamar and his family were part of the Salmon Idaho Stake and the Salmon Ward of the church, and they had made several friends over their years of attendance there.

Because of the tenets of the church, which required congregants to stockpile supplies in the event of an emergency, many Mormon stakes and wards had everything they needed to survive the pandemic, provided they could maintain a cool head and not allow outsiders in. Lamar led his ward to a Latter Day Saints retreat center on a small lake just outside Salmon. They brought all of the supplies they would need for several months, and the men brought enough weapons to adequately protect the compound. They were prepared to fight for their lives if it came down to that.

Lamar could hardly believe his ears when he finally heard a very faint message broadcast from his radio.

"Did they just say that Victor Kraus is in Glacier Park?" he said out loud to the radio while fine-tuning the knobs a little.

He then listened intently to the faint message that followed. It confirmed what he heard the first time and mentioned that Victor might have vaccines against the virus that was causing the pandemic.

Lamar's heart raced. The man who single-handedly set out to destroy the world was a five-hour drive away from him and he likely had the only vaccine in the world. With that vaccine, Lamar could save his people. The stories had been pouring in. All over the mid- and northwest, hundreds of Mormons had been lost to this pandemic. In Salt Lake City, the main Mormon temple had been destroyed by vandals and thieves seeking anything of value. If he could get that vaccine and deliver it to his people, he might very well become the next modern day saint.

Lamar used his radio to contact elders from two other Mormon communities close by and told them of what he heard. Within an hour, he had assembled a small group of six men, well trained with guns, who were committed to making the trip to Glacier Park to find those vaccines. Lamar's clan had an old propane-powered king cab pickup truck that could easily make the trip, so they planned to get together and head for Glacier Park the next morning.

Lamar Young was a good man, a great husband, and an even better father. It pained him to leave his family behind during such uncertain times, but he truly felt that the message that he received over the radio was as much from God as it was from whoever had transmitted it. The night before his trip, he called his family together for prayers and goodbyes.

"I wanted to have a family meeting so that I can explain a few things that you need to be aware of and so that we can send out some prayers together as a family," he said as he looked into the eyes of each of his children and his wife.

"I have to go on a trip in the morning, and I wanted to let you know that I will be gone for a few days," he started. "I am going with several of our friends, many of whom are the dads of your friends. We are going to drive to Glacier Park to see about getting some medications that will help the world."

"Will you be in danger, Daddy?" his oldest, a son named Luke, asked.

"The world is an uncertain place right now, son, I honestly have no idea what we might encounter," he replied.

"Are you taking guns?" the young man asked.

"We are, but remember what I taught you about guns? A gun should be considered a very useful tool and never a weapon. We are going out into the world as Christians, and we will not rely on the power of a gun over that of our Lord."

"Why is there medicine in Glacier Park, Daddy?" his seven-year-old daughter Elizabeth asked.

"Well, the man who created the virus that is killing people has a vaccine and he is in Glacier Park. We are going to go find him and see if he will give us the medicine."

"Is he the devil, Daddy?" Elizabeth asked.

"No, honey, he is a man who made a bad decision. We do not know him or what motivated his actions, therefore, we cannot judge him. He has not been introduced to the one true church, so he has not had the blessings that we have. We must forgive him and let God be the judge. Our job is to love each other, period. Without question."

"Let's say a prayer that Daddy will return safe to us and he will be blessed on a journey that will only bring good things to the world," his wife Shelly said.

The family bowed their heads and prayed for several minutes. When the prayer was over, Lamar hugged and kissed each child and put them to bed in different beds in the one large room that they shared. When the kids were all tucked in, they sang *Jesus Loves Me* together as a family.

When the kids were safely tucked into bed, Lamar embraced his wife.

"Be careful out there, it's dangerous," she said. "We have heard all about the horrible things that people are doing to each other out there."

"These are indeed scary times, my love. But, I truly believe that this is a mission ordained by God. Why else would I be the one to hear that message?"

"We can do a lot of good in the world if you can bring that vaccine back here. I believe that God has blessed you and that you will be safe. I know to doubt that is to doubt God's plan, so I know that you will come back to me and I know that this trip will be a success."

"That's right, Shelly, I believe that, too. Shall we do our reading?"

It was a tradition in the Young household, no matter where that household happened to be, that Shelly and Lamar would read together from the Bible and the Book of Mormon every night for an hour after the kids were in bed. They read with the kids every night, too, but their time studying together was often the highlight of the day for them. And so, like every other night of their marriage, the couple read and prayed together before going to bed.

Bright and early the next morning, Lamar was up loading the pickup truck for the journey to Glacier Park. The plan was that he and two of his men would pick up another man from a neighboring Mormon community and two more from a second community a few miles north of town. Lamar and his two men loaded everything that they would need, said their goodbyes to family and friends, and then climbed into the old pickup truck and headed off. It was barely daylight and most of the kids were still in bed. However, Lamar could see his son Luke in the rearview mirror waving at the truck as it drove away.

After Lamar had picked up the remaining men, they stopped at a roadside pullout, and Lamar asked everyone to get out of the truck.

"Gentlemen, I want to start this trip off right. First and foremost, we are brothers. We are driving off on a dangerous journey, and I want you to know that my top priority is to get us all home safe and sound. Vaccine or not. Second, I believe that this mission is ordained by God. Just think of all of the people in this world who are desperate to have the information that we have and of all the places that Victor Kraus could have gone. But we have the information and we know where he is. We have been called, and this is a sacred journey."

"Amen, Brother Lamar, I believe that fully," Tom Fredericks said.

"Third, the world is an uncertain place right now, and we have all heard horrible stories of what has been happening around the world. I have no idea what we will encounter on this journey, but I do know this… We are Mormons, and we will be conducting ourselves as Christ would at all times."

The other men agreed to this and signified their agreement by saying 'Amen.'

"And finally, no sacred journey can officially start without a prayer. Bishop Peterson, can you please lead us in a prayer for this journey?"

Bishop Peterson was a beloved man in the Mormon community of Salmon, Idaho, and although he was a little older than the other men, he was the first one that Lamar invited on the trip. Bishop Peterson had such a strong sense of peace and such a resolute faith that his very presence was enough to inspire others to persevere when things were tough. That kind of strength was difficult to find, and was by far, more important than physical strength in Lamar's mind.

When the Bishop was finished praying, Lamar hugged each man and told them that he loved them. They all expressed the same sentiment to one another, and then loaded up the truck and headed north toward Montana.

They debated about which route to take, but finally decided that it made the most sense to take major highways, because they would likely still be in pretty good shape, and they were concerned that back roads might lead to ambushes or take them through communities that were protecting themselves from outsiders. They knew that there had to be many small communities out there, particularly in the west, that would not be afraid to defend their turf by force. So, they headed north on US Highway 93, on a route that would take them right through the Bitterroot Valley and through Missoula and then on up to Polson. At Polson, they would take Highway 35 around Flathead Lake, and then cut over to Highway 2 into Glacier National Park.

If all went as planned, they expected to be in Hamilton in an hour and a half, to Missoula an hour after that, to Polson within four hours, and to West Glacier around noon. Unfortunately, their first delay happened within 20 miles of Salmon. They had just driven past the Walker Lane exit on US Highway 93 N and were about to cross the bridge over the Salmon River when Lamar noticed smoke coming from the north end of the bridge. He slowed the truck to see if they could get a closer look at what was happening, and then came to a complete stop a few hundred yards before the bridge.

It appeared that a large pile of logs had been set ablaze right on the bridge, and it was sufficient to block both lanes. There were no other vehicles in any direction on the highway or the surrounding area, no signs of any humans in the area, and no houses or buildings in site. Lamar took out his binoculars and studied the burning logs. They were charred, but without a lot of damage by the fire, indicating that the fire had been lit relatively recently.

"I'd say we are right in the middle of a trap," Lamar finally said. "I am betting if we had driven on the bridge, something would prevent us from ever leaving it. I think it's time to go back to the last exit and find an alternative route."

"That may be what they are planning for," the bishop said. "It is the closest exit to this place and the real trap could be right there waiting for us."

"Good point," Lamar said. "Maybe we should go back a few exits and reroute. Regardless of what we decide to do, we need to get moving, we are sitting ducks out here."

The group got back in the pickup and turned it around, heading southbound on the northbound side of US 93 North. As they started to pull away, Lamar noticed several men with weapons running up the bank from under the bridge and standing in the highway watching them disappear.

"I'm betting they lit the logs about 30 seconds too soon, Praise the Lord," the bishop said. "It's all about seconds and inches, ten more seconds and a few more inches and we could have been had. Thank you, God."

They travelled southbound for a couple of miles and then took a ramp off the highway and pulled out their map. Unfortunately, there were not a lot of options for heading north, so they decided that they might have to come up with a different strategy. They mapped out a route using secondary roads and a few fields to get passed the bridge that had been blocked, but the new route required that they cross an older bridge by a fishing access on the Salmon River. They were very cautious as they approached that bridge, and they took their time studying it before making the crossing.

Once across the river, they continued on secondary roads until they were a few miles north of where they had encountered the problem on US 93 N, and where they could get back on the highway when they were ready. On the side trip on the secondary roads, they encountered a few homesteads, all of which had been burned to the ground, and Lamar stopped at them all to see if there was anyone there who needed help. No one was anywhere around these homes, so Lamar had his men gather up charred-looking material, including burned tarps and tar paper, burned plywood, anything that looked burned and that could be draped over the truck to hide it.

His new plan was to completely cover the truck with burned materials so that it looked like a vehicle that had already been destroyed by fire and then drive it slowly at dusk and at night without any lights on. If they saw lights or any activity on the highway, he would pull the truck off the road, turn it off, and they would hide in the truck behind the burned materials until they were safe.

When the men were finished camouflaging the truck, it looked more like a large burned pile of debris than it did a vehicle. Lamar was pleased with the effort, and they decided to spend the remainder of the daylight hours in the safety of a side road that hid their truck under the cover of the trees.

CHAPTER 28

Ethan had been to the Flathead Valley before but wasn't overly familiar with it. Given the current state of the world, his plan was to skirt along the eastern edge of the city of Kalispell moving northward to the small blue collar town of Columbia Falls and into what is referred to as the North Fork, because the north fork of the Flathead River flows through it. Ethan had fished the North Fork River, which acts as a border to Glacier National Park, but that had been years earlier. He felt at a distinct disadvantage trying to navigate this territory so many years later. He decided to take it one step at a time.

By mid-afternoon, Ethan had managed to get to the northern end of Kalispell. He tried to determine what was happening in the scenic valley town, but everything seemed quiet. Too quiet. He continued following the Flathead River north. It was a warm and sunny day, the kind of day that made you happy to live in Montana, Ethan thought, and that hadn't changed. In fact, living in Montana meant more to him now than ever before.

"Let's take a short pause for a good cause, what do you say, boy?" Ethan asked Cowboy as he dropped his backpack.

After hiding his backpack, Ethan assembled the collapsible Ugly Stick fishing pole he took from his pack, put a red Mepps spinner on the end of his line, and headed to the river.

"Maybe we can catch us a nice Cutthroat for lunch," he said to Cowboy as he cast the Mepps lure out into the river. Cowboy looked up at him, gave an excited bark, and headed off with him.

On his second cast, a Cutthroat Trout hit the spinner hard. Ethan gave the pole a good jerk to set the hook, and then the fight was on. Ethan was using an Ugly Stick ultra-light pole built for backpacking with six-pound test line on his Daiwa reel. He could tell instantly that even with the lightweight set up he was using that he'd hooked a hell of a nice fish. He tightened down the drag on the Diawa as much as he dared to. The last thing he wanted was this monster snapping the line. The large trout headed down river with the current, stripping line off Ethan's reel. He had to step out into the river and follow the Cutthroat downstream, because he knew that if he could stay with it, the fish would eventually tire and he and Cowboy would have a nice lunch.

The Cutthroat started to wear out, and Ethan continued reeling in line to bring the fish closer to the shore. His whole focus was on landing the large fish. He rounded a gradual bend in the river and that is when they saw each other.

A woman was standing in the river with the water just above her waistline. He was in it up to his knees. She immediately dropped down in the water up to her chin. Ethan was startled by the sight of the naked woman and he jerked a little too hard on the pole, snapping the line and throwing himself off balance. He struggled to keep his feet under him as he backed up. Finally, he caught his footing and his balance. He stood there with his pole in his hand, the broken fishing line dangling from the end of it.

"Howdy," he finally said, with a touch of annoyance in his voice.

The woman just stared at him.

"I was fishing and had this fish on and I..." he stammered, trying to explain himself.

"Do you mind? It's a nice day, but this isn't exactly warm bath water," she interjected.

"Oh, ya, sorry," he said, as he turned his back to her.

Ethan could hear her moving in the water and then heard her on the shore. He continued to try and explain himself.

"So, this trout hit my hook and I mean, hell, it was a monster, so I was following it and I mean it wasn't like, I was looking... I mean, I didn't see anything. Really, I..."

"You can turn around now," she said with no amusement in her voice.

Ethan turned around. The woman before him was tall and had on a flannel shirt that was too big for her. Her legs were still bare, her wet hair hitting her shoulders. She was absolutely beautiful. He stopped talking.

"Put your hands up and slowly walk to the shore," she said to a dazed-looking Ethan.

"What?"

"You deaf? Put your hands up and walk to the shore."

It was only then that he noticed she was holding what appeared to be a .357 magnum pistol with both hands, and it was pointed directly at him. Ethan slowly raised his hands and moved toward the shore angling his way toward her at the same time. It occurred to him as he did so that he should stay away from rivers from now on. Once on shore, he looked at her. *Jesus, she was beautiful!*

"Okay, now what?" he asked.

"Keep your hands up."

"They are up," he said, about half mad.

"What are you doing here?" she asked.

Ethan displayed an exasperated look on his face.

"Like I was saying, I was fishing," he said as he looked at the pole in his left hand. He held it up for emphasis.

The woman's face registered a "well that was a stupid question" look.

"Is that there pistol a double-action or single-action?" Ethan asked.

She looked confused.

"Because if it's a single action, you need to pull the trigger back in order for it to fire," he said as he moved slightly toward her. There was now about seven feet between them.

"It's the kind that shoots bullets," she responded.

"So, what's your name?" he asked.

"I'm asking the questions," she said with as much authority as she could deliver in her voice.

"And, so far, some really good ones," he said sarcastically, as he moved a little closer.

"Stop moving toward me or I'm going to shoot you."

"Well, that would most likely piss my partner right off," Ethan said.

"I'm not falling for that."

"Don't tell me, tell Cowboy," he said, and then he turned toward the dog. "Cowboy, where are you, boy?"

Cowboy responded with a bark, and the woman looked in Cowboy's direction to investigate. Ethan took two quick steps and dropped his fishing pole as he moved out of the line of fire. At the same time, he reached out and grabbed her left wrist pulling her toward him. The gun went off.

Ethan slid his hand to the pistol and twisted it from her grasp and tossed it up the bank into the grass. Placing his right leg behind her, he pushed her over it and followed her to the ground, pinning her down with his chest across hers. She struggled to fight back and tried to hit him with her free hand. It took him a couple of tries, but he eventually caught her other wrist and held both of her hands to the ground. She was pissed. He could feel her breathing through his chest.

"GET OFF ME!"

"Calm down."

"GET OFF ME," she repeated even louder.

"I will as soon as you calm down. I'm not going to hurt you."

"YOU'RE DAMN RIGHT YOU'RE NOT."

"Look, lady, calm down. For Christ's sake. I'm really not going to hurt you."

He could feel her breathing start to slow.

"What's your name?" he asked.

He got no response.

"I'm Ethan Edwards."

After a moment, she said, "Samantha. My name is Samantha."

"Okay, Samantha, I'm going to let you up now, alright?"

She nodded.

"But, when I do, you need to remain calm. Otherwise, we'll end up in the same position and have to start all over again. Agreed?" he asked.

She nodded again.

"I'd feel a lot better if you said something, Samantha." Ethan was using her name as often as he could, hoping it would help keep her calm.

"I agree," she said.

Ethan let go of both of her hands and slowly pushed himself off her and stood up. She propped herself up on her elbows for a second then rolled to one side and stood.

"Damn, she is something to look at," Ethan said to himself.

Ethan turned and went up the bank to where he had tossed her pistol. With his body blocking her view, he flipped the cylinder opens and popped the shells out of the pistol. As he turned around, he slid his hand into his pocket and got rid of the bullets.

"So, here's the deal, Samantha. I'm just passing through. I don't want any problems," he said as he walked toward her. When he was close enough, he held the pistol out to her. She looked down at the gun.

"Take it," Ethan said. "It's yours, and by the way, it's a double-action Colt Python in case the subject ever comes up again."

She hesitated and then took the gun from him. She didn't point it at him, which Ethan took as a good sign.

"Alright then. Well, I lost my lunch when I lost that fish, so I better…" He didn't finish his statement.

"SAM, SAM," they heard someone yell "SAM, YOU ALRIGHT, SAM?

Ethan looked at her.

"You better answer."

She looked right into Ethan's eyes for a second.

"OVER HERE," she called out. "I'M OVER HERE!"

Ethan and Samantha stood looking at each other. A couple of minutes went by and a lanky man came out of the trees. He held a Ruger mini 14 in his hands, and he pointed it at Ethan when he saw the strange man close to Samantha.

"Sam, are you okay?" he asked.

"I'm alright, Mike," she replied.

He looked at Ethan, and Ethan knew that if she had said any different, things would have gone bad very quickly.

"I'm really alright, really. This is Ethan Edwards. Ethan Edwards, this is my friend, Mike."

"Nice to meet you, Mike," Ethan said.

"Ya, we'll see," was Mike's response.

"Mike, put your rifle down. He's alright," Samantha said as she gave Ethan a bit of a smile.

Mike lowered his rifle.

"There's a ranger patrol around, I spotted them earlier. That's why I was coming to find you."

"What's a ranger patrol?" Ethan asked.

"I'll explain later," Samantha said as she pulled her jeans on. "We better get out of here before they find us."

"Too late," Mike said as he pointed up river with his rifle.

Four men mounted on horses were riding toward them at full speed.

"What do we do?" Ethan asked as his hand dropped to the forty-five on his leg.

"Not that," Samantha replied. "Let me do the talking, okay?"

It only took a few moments and the men were on them. They stopped a few feet from the small group. All of them carried AR15 assault rifles at the ready. The man in the center spoke first.

"Heard a gunshot, Sam, was that you?"

"Actually, Dale, it was. Kinda stupid how it happened. I was checking it and thought for some stupid reason that I was setting the hammer on an empty cylinder and obviously it wasn't and the damn thing went off. Scared the shit out of me," she said with a slight chuckle.

"Bet it did. Surprised that you'd do something like that, Sam. If I remember right, one of the first things you told my wife when she went to your pistol course was to never do that."

Ethan shot Sam a quick look.

"So, she knows how to handle a gun," he noted mentally.

Dale then shifted in his saddle.

"Who's your new friend, Mike?"

Sam spoke up.

"That's Ethan Edwards," she said. "He heard the gunshot also; that's how we were introduced."

"Is that right? Well, you know the rules about strangers in the county. You'll have to come with us, Edwards."

"Just where am I going?" Ethan asked.

"Any strangers have to report to the commissioner," Dale said, "and I'm going to need that forty-five from you also."

Ethan looked directly at him.

"That's not going to happen, buddy," Ethan replied.

Dale's horse moved under him.

"Whoa, dammit. Look, mister, there's four of us and one of you. How do you think this is going to turn out?"

"Not real well for me," Ethan said, "but I'm betting not real well for at least two of you either. And, you're going to be one of the two, that much I'll guarantee."

The men looked at each other. Before something stupid happened, Samantha piped up.

"Jesus Christ, you guys stop measuring dicks. Dale, I'll take Ethan's gun and I'll deliver him to the dump as soon as we can hike there, alright?"

"Don't think I can allow that, Sam," Dale said, his voice grim.

"Well then, you're going to have to shoot Mike and me, too," she replied. "Isn't that right, Mike?"

"I guess it is now," Mike said.

Dale thought about it. Ethan knew he was going to agree because the odds had changed, and if this guy was going to make a move, he would have and should have done it by now.

"Alright, you've got three hours. After that, I'm coming looking for you and there won't be any talking," Dale said, sounding tough in an attempt to save face in front of his men.

"You have my word," Sam said. "And, thanks, Dale."

They turned their horses and rode off.

"Who's this commissioner and did he mean dump as in a garbage dump?"

"Come on, gather your shit," Mike said. "We better get going, we'll explain on the way."

CHAPTER 29

As the outbreak consumed the Washington, DC metropolitan area, anarchy became the rule of the day. Martial law seemed to have little impact on the number of shootings and violent street scuffles that grew into larger and larger battles. From the beginning, martial law was overwhelmed by panicked crowds that took matters into their own hands. Angry mobs of infected people charged on hospitals and government buildings in an attempt to get help, but many of them were shot by National Guard troops that had been mobilized in an attempt to quiet the unrest. However, the violence only led to more panic, and more and more citizens rose up as it became clear that no help was on its way and the cavalry would not be coming to rescue them.

In nearly every corridor of the city, mobs overtook the forces that were sent in to govern them. The troops retreated behind secure walls and waited until the madness calmed down. It was only a matter of time before the virus calmed things down for them, and then they could return to clean up the city and tend to the survivors.

David walked down 14th Street in Columbia Heights and could not believe his eyes. Businesses were burned, papers and clutter filled the streets, and destroyed vehicles were everywhere he looked. He could hear screams and acts of violence occurring in all directions. Even more alarming, dead bodies were strewn everywhere. Some of the dead were obviously killed by acts of violence, but even more appeared to have died of the virus. Dried blood was caked around the noses and mouths of those that he believed died as a result of the infection.

The Giant grocery store was destroyed; the front glass windows were broken out, and the inside of the stored was completely empty. Shelves were knocked over, food wrappers were thrown about, and the checkout lanes were burned. He noticed a few desperate people inside the store looking for anything that the looters may have left behind. One old man was eating from a bag of Purina puppy chow.

Across the street, the Sticky Fingers vegan bakery was all but destroyed. The glass storefront was also broken and the place had been burned. He could see that there were a few food items left in a dark and busted-up cooler in the front of that store. He looked closer and realized that the items were vegan chicken salad sandwiches and a seitan crab cake. He could not help but notice the irony that a man would rather eat dog food than vegan food.

Many of the apartment buildings that surrounded the lovely 14th street square had been attacked, and many of the apartments had broken windows and items strewn across their balconies. Some had dead bodies stacked on them. As David looked around, he noticed a young boy sitting on one of the balconies and he called out to him.

"Hello," he said to the boy.

The boy did not respond, and in fact, when David looked at him again, the boy tried to hide behind a plastic outdoor chair that was on the balcony.

"You do not have to be afraid," David said, "I will never hurt you. What is your name?"

The boy remained in hiding behind the chair.

David thought for a minute and finally decided he would go into the building and attempt to get to the boy. The inside of the apartment complex was extremely dark, but since the electricity went out, David got into the habit of carrying a small flashlight with him wherever he went. He clicked it on and made his way through the ruins of the lobby. Looters had destroyed the place, and he could barely make it through all of the debris. Fortunately, the building was made of brick, otherwise, the fire that had been set to burn all of the beautiful oak woodwork in the lobby might have destroyed the whole building.

David eventually found a staircase and began climbing up the stairs. Before going into the building, he counted the floors and determined that the boy was on the sixth floor. So, he climbed the stairs until he reached the sixth floor and then went into the hallway. A strong scent of gasoline overtook his nostrils as he walked down a very charred hallway toward the apartment that he thought the boy might be in. Unfortunately, he could not tell for sure which one it was. So, when he was close, he began to knock on doors.

When he got to apartment 614, he thought he must be close, so he knocked on the door. There was no reply. He knocked again, louder. Still nothing. After a third knock, he tried the door only to find that it was locked. Next, he knocked on the door of apartment 616.

"Get the fuck out of here, I will shoot you," an angry voice replied.

"I'm not here for any other purpose than to help a small boy," David replied.

"Yes, of course," the voice said snidely. "And I am not here for any other purpose than to blow your ass away."

David thought about offering the voice on the other side of the door some compassion, but realized that he was in a dangerous situation and at a distinct disadvantage. So, he left. At apartment 618, he knocked on the door and received no answer and after the third knock, he tried the door and found it unlocked. He slowly entered the apartment shouting out 'hello' as he entered each room.

The apartment was a mess; it looked like somebody had broken in and was looking for something. Clothes and household items were scattered all over the floors. David searched the apartment and found no one there. Then, he went out onto the balcony to see if he could see the small boy. From his vantage point, he could see that the boy was, in fact, on the balcony of apartment 614, the first door that he knocked on.

"I am not here to hurt you," he yelled to the boy. "My name is David, and I just want to know if you need anything."

The boy was startled when he first heard the voice and he shifted behind the chair again in an attempt to hide from David.

"What's your name?"

The boy remained still.

"Do you have anyone to take care of you?"

No reply.

"Can I come in and check on you?"

The boy did not respond and did not move.

"I'll tell you what, I will go knock on your front door, and if you would like me to help you, all you have to do is answer the door, okay?"

David returned to the front door of apartment 614 and knocked. He waited for several minutes and then knocked again. After knocking three more times, David realized that the boy was probably alone and that he was probably not going to answer the door. He contemplated his next move, wondering if he should break down the door or if he should leave the boy alone, but he could not bring himself to leave.

David returned to the balcony of apartment 618 to check on the boy, who was still in the same position as the last time he looked. He reached into his cargo pants and removed a crunchy peanut butter Clif Bar and held it up for the boy to see.

"I have food, and I would be happy to give it to you if you let me in," he said. "I'm going to go back to your front door and knock again, okay?"

David returned to the front door of the boy's apartment and knocked again. This time, he heard the sounds of the locks turning, and after a few minutes, the front door opened slightly and a little hand came out reaching for the Clif Bar. David placed the Cliff Bar in his palm, and the kid snatched it and slammed the door shut and locked it again.

"I am not going to hurt you," David said to the closed door. "I will sit out here and wait until you feel comfortable talking to me. If you open the door, I will talk to you and will not come in unless you want me to."

David sat at the door for a couple of hours and recited nursery rhymes, sang songs, recited poems, and told stories. He hoped that the sound of his voice would reassure the young boy and that he would eventually feel comfortable enough to open the door and let him in. However, he did not know if the boy was still at the door or if he had gone back to the balcony to hide.

"It's going to get dark soon, and I know that it has to be scary in there when it's dark outside," David said. "I can take you home with me. We have lots of food and lots of other people who will help take care of you. You will be safe with us."

There was still no reply and no signs of movement on the other side of the door.

"I know this is scary, and I don't want to make you more frightened," David said, "so, I am going to leave now and I will come back tomorrow to check on you, okay?"

As David started to leave, he heard the locks turning on the door, and so he got down on his knees so that he would be at eye level to the boy. The door opened and the little boy stuck his head out to see if David was still there.

"Hello, I am David, what is your name?"

The boy was terrified.

"Can I come in?" David asked.

The boy shook his head to let him know that it would be okay to come in.

The inside of the apartment was dark and smelled of death. David flipped on his flashlight and shined it around the living room. The place was nicely decorated and was in good shape.

"Where are your parents?" David asked.

The little boy grabbed David's free hand and held it as he led him to the master bedroom. Inside the dark bedroom, David shone the light to reveal a horrific scene. The bodies of a man and woman were motionless on the queen-sized bed. Both bodies had begun to decompose, and they both had signs of Typhon virus. The woman's eyes were closed but caked with dried blood. Her entire body was coated with decaying vomit and blood. The man was lying on his stomach with dried blood gluing his face to the bed sheets.

"I am so sorry," David said to the boy. "Are these your parents?"

The boy shook his head. Large tears were flowing down his cheeks. David reached down and hugged the boy.

"Is there anybody else in here?"

The boy shook his head no.

"How long have you been in here alone?"

The boy did not respond.

"Can you tell me your name?"

The boy did not respond.

"How old are you?"

The boy held up five fingers.

"You are the bravest five-year-old boy I have ever met," David said. "Let's get some clothes for you and we can get out of here. I will take you to my house where you will be safe, okay?"

The boy shook his head in agreement.

David spent the next several minutes gathering clothes from the boy's dresser and putting them into a backpack that he found in the boy's room. When he was finished, he looked through the pantry to see if there was any food they could take. He found only a few canned food items, including a can of tomato sauce, two cans of kidney beans, and a small can of tomato paste. The boy had eaten all of the other food, and several wrappers were scattered around the kitchen floor.

Just before he was ready to leave, David stepped out on the balcony. It was already dusk and getting darker by the minute. Six stories below, David noticed lots of activity on the streets. Groups of thugs were roaming the streets looking for anything of value and clashing with anyone that they encountered. David knew that if he took the boy out of there at dark, they would probably encounter one or more of these groups on the walk to his house. He decided to wait until morning.

"I think it is too dangerous to leave right now," he told the boy. "I think we should stay in here tonight and then leave first thing in the morning. Are you okay with having a sleepover?"

The boy shook his head up and down.

In addition to the noise on the streets, David could hear the sounds of activity in the hallway of the building, indicating that some of those groups had likely found their way inside the apartment building. Fortunately, the front door was sturdy and made of metal, so he hoped that it would be strong enough to withstand any attempts to break in. To be safe, David stacked several heavy pieces of furniture behind the door in an attempt to fortify it in case someone tried to break down the door.

He then made a bed for himself on the floor of the little boy's room. He noticed that the boy had a nameplate on his desk that said 'Aiden.'

"Your name is Aiden, isn't it?" David asked the boy.

The boy shook his head up and down.

"Okay, Aiden, I am going to sleep right here on the floor beside you and then when we wake up, we are going to go to my house, okay?"

David put the boy in his bed and tucked him in and then lay on the couch cushions that he had used to create a bed for himself on the floor. They had been in bed only for an hour or less when sounds from the hallway woke David. It sounded like several voices were right out the front door. He heard the doorknob jiggle as someone tried to gain entry.

Then, there were loud thuds on the door, thuds that sounded like a large hammer or axe banging on the outside. After several minutes of pounding, David heard the sounds of voices screaming and then heard a loud blast that had to be a gunshot. The first shot was followed in rapid succession with a second shot, which was followed by the sound of screams and running in the hallway. David wasn't sure what to make of those sounds, but it sounded like the guy next door, who threatened to kill him earlier, may have shot one or more of the thugs trying to break down the door.

There was silence after the second gunshot, and David was grateful that the man had scared away whoever was trying to get inside the apartment. He looked up at the bed next to him, but it appeared that the boy was still asleep, although David found it hard to believe that he would be able to sleep with all of the noise coming from the hallway.

"I think it's okay now," he said quietly.

David lay there for several minutes and was about to fall asleep when he felt Aiden's small body lay down beside him on the floor. The boy was shaking violently, and David could feel his warm tears on his arm. He reached over and pulled the boy toward him and held him tight as he wept.

"It's going to be okay, Aiden," he whispered. "We are going to be just fine."

CHAPTER 30

Victor saw the smoke to the north of Sperry Chalet while hiking to the top of Gunsight Mountain. He could not see flames, but he knew that it was probably a forest fire caused by a dry lightning storm. Those types of fires occurred frequently in wild lands in the West, and now that there were no resources or people to fight them, they would burn freely. Victor felt a tinge of guilt for wiping out the human race that would have likely fought this fire because he did not want nature to run rampant and burn his beautiful park.

Victor returned to the chalet, ate some dinner, and then decided that he would hike toward the fire in the morning to get a better idea of how big it was and to see if he could determine its trajectory. If it burned down the chalet, he knew that he would be screwed. Not only that, but he knew that the vaccines that he had buried would not likely withstand the heat from a forest fire. He had to do a reconnaissance run to determine his next steps.

At first light, Victor was on the move, headed north toward the smoke. He decided that he would head toward the Granite Park Chalet, which was about 25 miles north. He mapped out his route carefully, as he wanted to make sure that there were safe places along the way to seek shelter and to protect himself from the fire if conditions grew out of control. His plan was to take the Gunsight Pass Trail to the Loop Trail and then take that trail to the Going-to-the-Sun Road. He would then walk for about five miles along that road until he reached the Highline Trail, which he would take to the Granite Park Trail, which would take him directly to the other chalet.

Victor figured that it would take him approximately 12 hours of hiking with his backpack to cover the nearly 24 miles, so he packed supplies and provisions for several days. He also packed his knives, and one of the pistols that he had taken from the rangers who came in to get him. Victor wasn't quite sure what to expect along the way, but he was hoping to grab a few more supplies from the other chalet, so he brought an empty canvas bag just in case he might need it.

Victor made good time on his journey, and when he reached a highpoint on the top of the Going-to-the-Sun Road, he was able to put eyes on the fire. Through his binoculars, it looked like the forest fire was close to Swiftcurrent Mountain just north of Granite Park Chalet. However, the smoke from the fire made it difficult to see for sure. He continued on his journey and was just about to the junction of the Highline Trail and the Granite Park Trail when he heard voices. Victor stepped off the trail and found a safe place to hide, and then removed his knives from his pack and placed them strategically on his body so that he could access them quickly.

The voices grew louder as they moved toward him, and within a few minutes, he could see what appeared to be a family of four moving down the trail. Two kids led the way, a boy and a girl, both of whom appeared to be 10 to 12 years of age. They were followed by a middle-aged couple, the man was tall with a full beard, and appeared to be in his early 40s and the woman had sun-bleached hair and the kind of deep golden tan found upon those who spend their summers hiking in the mountains. Both the man and woman carried large backpacks that were filled to capacity.

"Stay close," the man yelled ahead to the kids. "Don't leave my sight."

"Uhhh, you are so slow," replied the boy with a playful tone to his voice.

"I'm packing more than just me," the man replied. "Should I just throw your stuff off?"

"Whatever," exclaimed the girl.

Victor stayed in his hiding place as the foursome approached, trying to decide what to do. They would soon be near him, so he knew that if he was going to dispose of them, he would have to do so quickly. As he got a better look at the adults, he noticed that they were both carrying holstered pistols on their hips.

"Whoa, you had me scared there for a minute," Victor said as he stepped onto the trail from his hiding place. "I haven't seen many humans these last few weeks, so I was a bit surprised when I heard voices up ahead."

The man stopped in his tracks and reached for the pistol on his side. After looking at Victor, he relaxed a bit, but the woman took her pistol out of the holster and had it in her hand.

"Who are you and what do you want?" the woman asked.

"Well, I could ask you the same thing," Victor started, "but one thing's for sure... I don't want anything from you."

"What are you doing here?" the man asked.

"Well, I've been caretaking at Sperry Chalet, and I saw the smoke from that fire. I thought I better get a good look at it to determine if it would be a threat to me."

"I thought Pappie was the caretaker over there," the man responded.

"Oh yeah, Pappie is the main caretaker, but he got called back to town. Seems that one of his grandkids came down with the virus... he was very distraught. I'm his replacement."

"I'm so sorry to hear about that. How terrible," the man replied.

"My name is Jim Wilson, I'm a wildlife veterinarian for the emergency park services," he said, reverting to his former alias as he offered his hand to the man.

The man shook his hand and then Victor reached out to shake the woman's hand. She returned her pistol to its holster and then shook Victor's hand. The two children had stopped and were standing there observing the conversation.

"And now tell me your names," Victor said playfully, despite the fact that he found it completely annoying that he had to ask.

"This is my family," the man said. "My wife Jane, my daughter Rebecca..."

"Becca," the daughter corrected.

"Yeah, she goes by Becca, and this is my son Benjamin, or Ben as he likes to be called. I'm George Bailey."

Victor shook the hands of Becca and Ben and then turned back toward the parents.

"What are you all doing in the park?" Victor asked.

"Well, until this morning, we were living in the Granite Park Chalet, taking care of the place. However, that fire you are seeing is getting pretty darn close to that chalet, so we decided to head over to Sperry Chalet to see if we could hang out there until help arrives."

Victor looked at the couple taking careful notice that their demeanors had changed when they realized that he was in charge of Sperry Chalet. He also knew that he had too many suspicious things laying around in the chalet, so he knew that he would have to be very careful if he decided to allow them to stay there.

"So, can we stay at the chalet with you for a few days?" Jane asked.

"Of course," Victor said, "you can stay as long as you need."

"Oh, thank you," George replied. "We are grateful."

"Have you had any contact with headquarters?" Victor asked.

"Nothing. We have been up at Granite Park for several weeks and have heard nothing. My uncle is the caretaker there," Jane said, "but he insisted that he would stay and go down with the ship. He wants to do whatever he can to save the chalet, he loves that place."

"I can understand that," Victor said, "I feel the same way about Sperry Chalet. Well, let's head back, it's a good ways away. Can I help carry anything?"

The man shook his head. "Not right now," he said, "maybe after our next break. Are you okay, Jane?"

Jane nodded and the five of them headed down the trail leading back to Sperry Chalet. They hiked back down the trail and then onto the Going-to-the-Sun Road, and decided to stop for lunch at one of the pullouts along the road.

"Seems eerie that there are no visitors here this time of year," George said. "I have no idea what will become of places like this when our government resurfaces, but hopefully they will be preserved." "Oh they will be, mark my words," Victor said forcefully.

"You know something that we don't?" Jane asked.

Victor thought a moment before speaking. He was aware that he was probably letting the cat out of the bag, but quite frankly, he didn't care. He knew that he could eliminate these people if he so chose, and it was time that he started to assert himself.

"The whole planet will be treated like a park when the new administration comes into power. Human greed and sloth have ruled for too many years, and it is time for a paradigm shift."

"Well, I can certainly get on board with that, but you are speaking as if you are in the know. How do you know this?" George asked.

"I have friends in high places," Victor replied smugly.

There was an awkward pause until the kids started fighting over the trail mix.

"I get the last handful, Ben! Dad, tell Ben to give me the last handful..."

"No, you took a larger handful than me last time, so I should get the rest."

"Guys, you need share," Jane interjected.

"Ben, let her have the rest," George replied.

"You always go with her side, you are so unfair," Ben said, looking at George.

With the fight resolved, the three adults packed up their backpacks and led the way down the road toward Sperry Chalet. As they progressed, the last few miles of hiking were tough on the kids who had been hiking since early that morning, and they were tired. It was well beyond dinner time by the time they reached the chalet, and Victor was sick and tired of the incessant bickering that went on between the two kids. He could not believe that the parents would just let them continue fighting and arguing all day long. It was all that he could do to not intervene, and the anxiety it provoked in him reinforced his desires to destroy mankind.

Once at the chalet, Victor would not let the family into the main lodge because all of his papers and personal items were spread around in there and he did not want them to see anything. So, he directed them to the sleeping quarters where he planned to assign them each a bed. The hallway was dark when they entered the main door, so George turned on a solar lantern to lead the way.

"Jesus, is that a blood stain on the carpet?" George asked when he noticed a dark stain on the hallway carpet that led to the rooms.

"Grizzly bear blood," Victor said without missing a beat. "A sow got into the cabin a few weeks back and we had to put her down."

"Oh my God, that must have been scary as hell," George said.

Victor just nodded and kept walking down the hall.

"Did you keep any teeth or claws?" Ben asked.

Victor was still seething mad about the nonstop fighting that he had to endure, and so he ignored the boy.

"Well, did you, mister? Did you keep any claws or teeth?"

"Shut your mouth, you little…" Victor blurted out, but managed to stop himself.

George and Jane looked at each other and George was about to say something when Victor went barging by.

"I'll meet you in the kitchen in 30 minutes to help prepare dinner," he said as he walked passed the couple and exited the sleeping quarters abruptly.

"What an odd man," Jane said.

"And by odd, do you mean *asshole*? I'm about to punch this asshole in his mouth," George replied.

"Mommy, I'm scared. That man is mean and there was a bear in here. Are we going to be safe here?"

Jane bent down to look her daughter in the eyes. "Of course we are, Becca, Daddy and I will be here to watch over you." She hugged the girl.

"Okay, everyone, pick a bed," George said.

After the family selected their beds and unpacked a few supplies, they gathered up some of their food and headed toward the dining hall. When they arrived, they found a completely different Victor. Victor knew that he was about to lose his cool and he stepped away, cooled off, and regained his composure. He decided that it might be best if he kept these people around for a while since he was bored out of his mind and the winter would likely be long and lonely without some company.

Victor greeted the family warmly and apologized profusely for his earlier attitude. He explained that he was exhausted from all of the hiking he did that day, and he blamed his sour mood on that. To make up for it, Victor prepared a large pot of oatmeal with brown sugar, dehydrated apples, raisins, walnuts, and fresh huckleberries that he had picked a few days earlier.

The family sat down at the table and dug into their food. He had made a large enough pot of the oatmeal that everyone could eat as much as they wanted and it was really good. They wasted no time finishing their bowls and having seconds.

"These huckleberries are delicious," Jane said. "Did you pick them around here?"

"Yes, there is a very nice patch of them along a hillside just about a mile from here. I like to pick them every day or so."

"Well, they sure do make this oatmeal come to life," George said. He was feeling a little relieved that Victor had apologized, and he certainly could relate to his exhaustion.

"I really must apologize for what I said earlier about the whole earth being a park," Victor stated. "I don't really have friends in high places, I just have high hopes. I really hope that we humans who survive will take notice of what our species had done before, and make some adjustments to help our planet and ourselves."

"I couldn't agree more," George said.

"The earth is so wonderful and there are so many beautiful creatures, but somehow we lost sight of that."

"I heard a rumor before we left town and headed up to the chalet that this might have been a deliberate attack," Jane said. "It scares the hell out of me that one group would try to wipe out the human race. We lived in scary times before the pandemic; I hope that will change after."

"I certainly agree," Victor stated. "I hold great hope for our future. I hope we can build a new world your kids will be able to enjoy and share with their kids."

The next couple of days, Victor played it cool and served as the exceptional host. After the first night, he cleaned up all of his personal items so he could invite the family into the main lodge. He did not want to incite any suspicion because he developed a plan that required this family trust him completely.

The first evening in the lodge, the family played Monopoly with Victor, taking advantage of a cache of games available to guests of the chalet. During the days, Victor showed the kids how to do some basic gardening and he took them all to a large huckleberry patch where they picked a bunch of fresh huckleberries.

In the evenings, after the kids were in bed, Victor visited with Jane and George and they shared many wonderful conversations. Victor assumed the background of his alias as a wildlife veterinarian so that he could tell false childhood stories to build trust. He was afraid the news may have provided details of his own life that might be remembered by his guests if a fact jogged their memory, so he avoided getting too close to the truth.

George and Jane were completely won over by the man. They were skeptical at first, and even a little cautious, but as the days wore on, and Victor played his part perfectly, they felt a genuine friendship developing. Not only that, but as it turned out, Victor was really good with the kids. As a child, Victor was so isolated and so "trapped in his own head" he had taught himself all kinds of cool things, and he taught the kids many of these things he learned on his own.

He taught them about several bug species that were around the chalet, he introduced them to all of the local plants that could be eaten, and he showed them plants that were poisonous. He taught them magic tricks he had learned as a boy, and he even taught them some rudimentary knife skills, being careful not to reveal too much of his own knowledge. The kids grew to love spending time with him, and he seemed to genuinely like hanging out with the kids, except when they were fighting.

"So, tell me about your uncle," Victor said to Jane at dinner one night. He was concerned that the man could show up at the chalet unannounced and Victor did not like surprises.

"He's kind of a gruff old man," Jane said with a chuckle.

"And stubborn as hell," George added.

"What motivated him to look after the other chalet?"

"Boredom I think," Jane answered, "he retired a few years ago, but just could not stand sitting still at home. He volunteered to look after the chalet, although, truth be told, he would have probably been fired this year if the pandemic didn't happen. His bedside manner is not so good, and he had a few confrontations with folks last year that led to disciplinary action."

"Oh, that's funny, guests can be a pain in the buttocks, no doubt."

"He certainly thought so," Jane said.

"He beat some guy up for wanting to stay at the chalet after it was closed," Ben added.

"Okay, Ben, that's not your story to tell," Jane said, playfully.

"Maybe we should go get him and bring him here where it is safe," Victor offered.

"No chance he would come," Jane said. "We begged him to come with us, but he said that he was too old and too comfortable to let a fire drive him away. He said, and I quote, 'I am not afraid to die, and I would just as soon die of a forest fire than fall prey to some jackass' diabolical plan."

Victor laughed. "Sounds like my kind of guy."

"He's a real piece of work," George replied.

George was experienced at trapping and wanted to set a few snares around to see if he could capture any small animals they could eat, and he brought the idea up to Victor that evening after the kids had gone to bed.

"I think that is a really good idea," Victor said. "We really need to conserve as much of our food as possible, and supplementing it with some meat is a great idea."

"I've seen a lot of rabbits running around, and I think I could catch a few. If you don't mind watching the kids in the morning, Jane and I will go set several snares around the area at first light."

"That sounds great, you two should do that, and if you're up for it, you could hit the huckleberries when you are done. There should be several more berries ripe by tomorrow."

Early the next morning, George and Jane went out to set the traps with the plan to pick some huckleberries afterwards. They were delighted to have a few hours to spend together without the kids underfoot, and they made quick work of packing up their supplies and hitting the trail.

Victor was up and watched them go. He too was excited, because he had a plan of his own. He had the realization while he was hanging out with the kids that he missed out on fatherhood, and he felt that these two kids could be exactly what he needed to complete him and his mission. He decided after only a few days with this family that he would kill the parents and raise this kids himself. In his mind, it was the perfect solution to his most disturbing problem; the fact he might not be able to overcome the bad press and rise to the position of leadership he planned for in a new administration. The kids would be Plan B. He would train them to carry out his mission if he couldn't get the job done, and he needed to start their training as soon as possible.

"What a beautiful morning," Jane said as they started down the trail.

"That is a fact, baby, I love this park in the late summer and fall. The cool mountain air and the beautiful light before the sun rises above the mountains is just incredible."

"When's the last time we had a break from the kids?" Jane asked.

"Well, that would have been several months ago. Remember, we hired a sitter and went to the show to see the movie *Wild*. Maybe, I remember it because the sitter cost me more than dinner and the movie."

"That makes sense," Jane laughed. "I'm betting that was our last movie for a long time."

George nodded, and then stopped, took a few steps off the hiking trail and reached in his pack. He found the perfect spot to set a snare next to an Alpine Fir in a shady area that was surrounded by rocks. After the snare was set, the couple moved along the trail and set several additional traps leading up to the huckleberry patch.

The huckleberries grew on the side of a steep hill that required careful footing to reach. The hiking trail was carved into the mountainside below the huckleberries and provided a staging area for picking. However, the trail was narrow in that area and on the other side of the trail was a sheer drop off that went for several hundred feet. There was a large rock that protruded from the trail over the drop-off that a person could stand on to take in a spectacular view of the valley and the river below.

When Jane and George arrived at the huckleberry patch, Jane took off her pack and set it on the trail while George stepped onto the rock to take in the view. He did it every time he came up here, despite Jane's warnings that he could fall off.

"This is truly one of the most spectacular sites I have ever seen," he said as he looked out over the panoramic view. "Truly spectacular."

Jane listened mindlessly as she focused on getting her huckleberry picking supplies from her pack, but when she heard the strange thumping sound, she turned in George's direction just in time to hear him scream as he fell off the rock to his certain death. Jane freaked out.

She jumped up and ran to the edge of the rock, releasing a haunting scream that echoed throughout the valley below.

"GEORGE," she screamed, as she dropped to her knees and crawled to the edge of the rock to see what had become of her husband. She wailed as she peered over the edge and saw a tiny speck of color several feet below.

"Oh my God, oh my God," she muttered. "He fell off the cliff. I told him he was going to fall off that cliff. Oh, my God."

In a panic, Jane ran back to her pack, threw it over her shoulder, and started running down the trail. She had only made it a few feet when she ran right into Victor.

"Oh my God, Jim, thank God you are here," she blurted out. "George fell off the cliff, we got to go get him. We got to go down there."

Victor consoled the distraught woman and then walked to the edge of the rock and looked down. He removed his binoculars and studied the colorful spot on a pile of rocks several hundred feet below.

"I am afraid he did not survive," Victor said as he put down his binoculars and looked back at her.

Her body gave way as she let out a scream and collapsed onto the trail.

"Oh my God, what will I tell the kids?" she cried.

Victor returned to the trail where Jane was weeping, helped her to her feet, and hugged her shaking body. She wept uncontrollably as he tried to console her, but he could not find the words to comfort her. This situation posed a dilemma for Victor. When he threw the rock that hit George in the back of the head and knocked him off the ledge, he assumed she would have seen it and his next move would have been to push her off the ledge, too. However, it appeared she did not see how it happened.

His plan all along was to kill both parents and raise those kids on his own. Now he contemplated the possibility of letting her live with the goal of eventually winning her over and having her as his new wife. A ready-made family.

"Are you sure he is dead?" Jane said between wails.

"I'm sure."

"I've got to see for myself. Give me your binoculars."

Jane took Victor's binoculars and returned to the edge of the rock, this time standing up. She looked down at the spot where George's body lay and cried out in agony when she saw his twisted form on the rocks below.

"This is so complicated," Victor said aloud, from beside her. "Let me see those binoculars."

Jane handed them to him and looked at him with a puzzled look.

"It would be a shame to lose a good pair of field glasses," he said as he pushed her over the ledge.

CHAPTER 31

"Where's the rest of your stuff?" Mike asked Ethan.

Ethan paused for a few seconds before he answered. It was obvious he didn't show up with just a fishing pole, a pistol, and a dog. Ethan called out for Cowboy. After a few minutes, the dog came running.

"I was wondering where your dog went," Samantha said.

"He's got a mind of his own and kinda comes and goes pretty much as he wants. But, he's got a knack for showing up when it counts. He's saved my butt a few times here recently. I should warn you, though, he's not overly friendly."

Samantha crouched down and held out her hand to the dog.

"Hey, Cowboy, come and introduce yourself," Samantha said in an inviting voice.

Cowboy gave Ethan a short look and then went over to the woman. Sam patted his head first then scratched behind his ears a bit and gave him a good back scratching. She finished by giving Cowboy a big hug and telling the dog that she was happy to meet him.

"He seems pretty friendly to me," she said as she got up and started walking up river.

"Come say hi to me, too," Mike said as he bent down to Cowboy and gestured the dog over.

Cowboy gave Ethan a look, looked at Mike for a moment, and then walked past both of them and headed up river, walking next to Samantha.

"So, explain this whole dump commissioner deal to me," Ethan said as they hiked along the riverbank, retracing his steps.

"Alright, we'll go first," Sam said over her shoulder. "When this whole virus thing broke out and they shut down all travel and basically implemented the whole martial law thing, nobody was infected up here. Unfortunately, some tourists on their way to Glacier Park came down with the virus. The sick ones were transferred to Kalispell Regional Hospital, and the rest were detained at the airport. Everything seemed like it was under control. Then, one of the airport TSA agents snuck off.

"At pretty much the same time, more of the people quarantined at the airport started showing symptoms. The county commissioners tried to secure the place with law enforcement, but from what I've heard, not a lot of guys showed up. And, who can blame them? They were being asked to stop people from leaving an area infected with a deadly virus. Could you imagine if you were a part-time posse member or a sheriff deputy and you didn't have a hazmat suit? How close would you be willing to get? Anyway, long story short the virus got out.

"That led to all out panic. There was a run on all the stores. Anything that could remotely help a person survive got snapped up. And being Montana and all, everybody was packing a gun. People started shooting each other over bottled water. It was pretty much total anarchy." She stopped and turned around and looked at Ethan.

"It's fear... everybody just... well, it's pure fear," she said.

"And then the Commissioner, Anthony Harms, rides in," Mike said from behind Ethan as they started walking again.

"Commissioner Harms, it seems, rounded up some stout-hearted members of the county's swat team, a few deputies, some ex-military types that he deputized, and the sheriff. They went rolling into the parking lot of Wal-Mart in an armored truck, a couple of Humvees that the sheriff picked up after the wars in the Middle East, and a few four-wheel drive pick-ups. They pulled up right in front of the store and everybody jumped out of their rigs and formed a couple of lines. One line faced the parking lot the other faced the store. Oh ya, forgot to mention, every one of them was dressed in black. Not sure how they managed that but anyway..."

"The commissioner and the sheriff got out of one of the Humvees and stood between the two lines. Harms got on a bullhorn, and he started saying 'attention, attention' to all of the civilians that were there gathered around. Bear in mind, the panic was over a virus that was transmitted from one person to another and he was calling everybody closer together... go figure."

"So, what were you doing there?" Ethan asked.

"Hey, it was free shit at Wal-Mart. You want to hear the rest or what?" Mike asked with more than a little tone in his voice.

"Sorry, sorry. Ya, definitely, can't wait. Head toward that clump of trees," Ethan said pointing the way, "that is where my pack is."

"Okay, so like I was saying," Mike continued, "Commissioner Harms, the sheriff, and their guys were there with this crowd around them and pretty much everybody had a gun. Harms got on the bullhorn and told everybody that basically all of the looting and anarchy bullshit was over starting right now because he was restoring order. So, the crowd started kinda shuffling a little bit. Then the commissioner told everybody that they could keep their guns but that until further notice, everybody needed to disperse and stay at their homes until they were notified by his office."

"Someone yelled 'FUCK YOU, HARMS, I DIDN'T EVEN VOTE FOR YOUR SORRY ASS.' Harms stepped through the line with the sheriff behind him and without the bullhorn shouted out for the guy who yelled that to step forward, if he had any balls. So, this big fucker started working his way through the crowd. When he stepped out of the crowd and I could see that he was packing what looked like an AK-47, might have been an SKS, anyway, doesn't really matter... across his chest. He told Harms that he was the guy who shouted. Harms told him that he didn't give a rat's ass who he voted for, if he didn't move his ass, he was going to get arrested. The guy kinda chuckled, looked around, and then yelled 'Fuck You, Harms, and the horse you rode in on' and then kinda turned to the crowd and laughed."

"Without another word, Harms pulled a 1911 .45 pistol from his holster, and as the guy turned back to face the Commissioner, Harms shot the bastard right between the eyes, sending a mist of blood and brains all over the crowd. Everybody just kinda stood there shocked for a minute and then the sheriff stepped forward and said, and this is no bullshit, he said, 'You can't do that, Commissioner, you just can't do that.' At which point, Harms shot him at point-blank range in the temple, spraying his brains over the parking lot. Harms then spoke into the bullhorn and told the crowd that he wasn't fucking around anymore."

"The commissioner turned around and said, 'Dale, you're the new sheriff,' then he walked in front of the rest of his guys and told them something that we couldn't hear. The next thing you know, all of his guys formed one line facing the crowd. Harms was on the bullhorn again and said 'ready,' and when he did, all of his guys lifted their weapons in a firing position. He then turned to the crowd."

"'You people go home and stay there. Further instructions will be posted or conveyed to you. Tell anyone and everyone you see that order has been restored and any kind of unauthorized action will be dealt with swiftly and harshly. Do it now.' So, people went home, and from that point on, he basically installed himself as a dictator."

"Sounds to me like a pretty ballsy move he pulled off in that Wal-Mart parking lot," Ethan said.

"More like he doesn't give a shit if he lives or dies," Mike responded.

"He lost everyone. His wife, two sons, two grandsons, everyone," Sam said.

"Everybody has lost somebody," Mike said.

Ethan thought for a moment. He hadn't really lost anyone. He'd lost his people a long time ago. In fact, he kind of gained a purpose of sorts. They arrived at his backpack.

"That's a nice bow," Mike said when he saw Ethan's Bowtech on his pack. "In fact, judging by just what you've got on the outside of this pack, I can tell you paid attention in Boy Scouts."

"Never was one," Ethan replied.

"Ya, didn't really think so. But, I'd say from what little I've seen of you, you've learned something from somebody."

Ethan looked at him for a moment then at Samantha.

"Look, I'm assuming that when we get to this dump place, whatever that means, someone is going to search through my stuff. There are a few things that they can't find."

Mike and Sam shot each other a glance.

When Ethan turned back from digging in his pack, he had the satellite phone and the solar-power system in his hands.

"Nice phone. So, I'm assuming you call someone or someone calls you with that thing because you ain't packing it around for the fun of it. So, remember when I said we'll go first? Well, guess what buddy, it's your turn," Sam said, her voice taking on a serious tone.

"And I will. Look, I'll explain everything, I promise. But, it's not a five minute or as we're walking along type of a conversation. I'm hoping that you guys will take care of this stuff and my bow and I've got a couple of other pistols that I'd just as soon nobody else knew about. Not only that, if you've got these things then you know that I'll show up to get them back," Ethan explained

"Who says we want you to?" Mike asked.

"A couple of reasons. One, I can tell you both want to know the deal on the phone. And two, somebody pulled a big pistol on me today and because of that I lost my dinner. So, the way I see it, I've got dinner coming," he said looking at Sam.

"Yeah, well guess what, James Bond? I'm pretty sure if we hit redial on that fancy phone, someone will answer by the second ring. And as far as dinner goes, you haven't gotten out of the dump yet," Sam replied.

After walking for a little over an hour, they crested a hill and as the dump came in sight they saw four horsemen riding toward them.

"Looks like we've got an escort," Ethan said.

"Yup, just remember what I told you. Let them look through your stuff and answer Harms' questions and he'll probably let you go. You've got an ace in the hole. But, he can be a real prick if he wants to," Mike said.

"So, what's my ace?" Ethan asked.

"Don't go there, I'll kick your ass, Mike. It's not that funny anymore," Samantha said.

"Hell, Sammy, you know it's true and you know you use it," he turned to Ethan. "Seems Commissioner Harms is partial to Miz Samantha."

"No shit?" Ethan said.

"No shit," Mike replied.

"Fuck both of you," Sam said as she turned and walked away.

CHAPTER 32

At the first sign of dusk, Lamar fired up the camouflaged pickup truck and he and his crew headed north on Highway 93 with the headlights turned off. They were able to cruise along at a pretty good speed for a while, but soon the darkness required that they slow down so that Lamar could keep the vehicle on the road. The highway was eerily quiet with no signs of cars on the road and no signs of life along the way.

The truck had been camouflaged so that there were gaps that allowed the driver to see through the windshield and for someone to keep watch from the bed. The window between the cab and the bed was open and one man sat in the bed, keeping an eye out for lights. The other men looked through various gaps in the debris to monitor for signs of life to the sides of the vehicle.

After about 40 miles, Tom called out from the rear post that headlights were approaching from behind. Lamar pulled the truck over to the side of the highway off the shoulder and onto the grass and turned the vehicle off and placed the keys in his pocket. They waited there for only a few minutes when a car flew by at a high rate of speed with about six motorcycles following close behind.

It was difficult to see what was happening because of the poor visibility, but it appeared that the vehicle was being chased down by the motorcycles. Lamar and his crew sat quietly in the darkness of the truck. Lamar's heart was pounding so fast he was sure the others could hear it. After several minutes, Lamar opened the door and got out of the truck, about the same time a gunshot echoed from a distance up ahead. Lamar walked up to the highway and looked in both directions. There was nothing but darkness to the south, but what looked to be about a mile to the north, Lamar could see several headlights surrounding the vehicle in the road and could barely make out the sound of yelling. Lamar pulled out his binoculars and described the scene to the others who had joined him up on the highway, leaving the truck doors open and the vehicle unattended.

"They got them surrounded," Lamar said. "I think they shot a tire out. It looks like they are about to smash the windows of the minivan with metal pipes."

"Those people need help," the bishop said. "we have to go help them."

"I wouldn't do that if I was you," a strange voice said from behind them.

Lamar looked back to see who was speaking, and his heart fell when he saw that a strange man was sitting in their pickup truck with a semiautomatic SKS military rifle on his lap.

"This is quite the camo job you got here. Fact is, I wouldn't have even noticed this mobile pile of crap if you hadn't parked the damn thing right in front of my view."

The man was scruffy looking. He wore an old white T-shirt that was brown with filth and barely covered his large belly. His head looked like that of a lion, with dark curly hair darting madly in all directions on his head and a full dark beard rounding out his face.

"For future reference, you made this really easy for me. You should never leave your vehicle unguarded."

"Who are you and what do you want?"

"The name is Chuck... my friends call me what-the-fuck Chuck. I'm kinda nimble for a fat guy," the man said. "Thing is; I already have what I want. Question is, how is this going to play out?"

"We can't let you take our truck," Bishop Peterson said. "We will be happy to share our provisions with you, but we are on an important mission and we need that truck."

Chuck laughed.

"What is it that you need?" Lamar asked.

"Thing is; these are uncertain times. A man never knows what he is going to need, so I will just take it all. From my vantage point, it doesn't appear that you have much negotiating power."

Lamar looked at Chuck and then at his men. He thought about charging the man, but he knew that would end badly. Chuck wasn't exactly the kind of man who would buckle under pressure.

"The way I see it, is that we have about 10 minutes before those motorcycles come back by here and see you. They will not be as charitable as I am. So, here is how this is going to work. You are going to give me the keys to this pile of mobile shit and I am going to drive off. Then, you guys should hide until the motorcycles go by. They are mostly thugs, so chances are, they shot out one tire and killed the people in that minivan that went by and will leave it up there on the road. Probably a little gas in the tank and a spare tire. Should get you a few miles down the road."

"Can you at least leave us with some of our food and a rifle for hunting?" Lamar asked.

Chuck laughed again.

"Do I look like a dumbass? Okay, so I probably do. Look, you seem to misunderstand the situation. This is now my property. This is how the end of the world works, gentlemen. I am not a bad guy; I am just out here making an honest living."

"I'll give you the keys, you give me one rifle," Lamar said. "And one box of ammo. That way you won't have to shoot me, which will likely cause problems with those motorcyclists up the road."

Chuck thought about it for a minute. He certainly appreciated easy transactions.

"Okay, here is what I'll do. I will give you one rifle right now for the keys. Then I will turn this thing around and drive about 2 miles and drop a box of ammo on the shoulder of the road. You can walk back and get it after the motorcycles come back by."

Lamar was surprised that the man agreed to such a deal.

"Okay," Lamar said. "Hand me the 30-06 and I will hand you the keys."

The man reached behind him without taking his eyes off of Lamar and his men, and grabbed the first rifle that he felt. He checked the chamber for bullets, and when he was sure that it was empty, he got out of the truck and placed it about 20 feet behind the truck.

"And now the keys?"

Lamar threw him the keys.

"Pleasure doing business with you boys," he said. "Oh, and in case you get any ideas about coming to look for me, my place is situated such that I will shoot you dead long before you even know you are in my neighborhood. So, don't ruin your day any more than it has already been ruined."

Chuck fired up the truck, flipped a U-turn on the highway, and headed south on the northbound side of US 93.

"Did that just happen?" Tom asked. "Did what-the-fuck Chuck just steal our truck?"

Lamar laughed, and looked at the bishop. He wasn't sure if he would find that statement to be funny, but the Bishop laughed out loud.

"These are bizarre times, indeed," he said.

"Okay, guys, here is what we need to do," Lamar said. "Let's split up with you three going back to get the bullets and us three will go ahead to see if we can help those people. Those of us going ahead will take the rifle, because actually having it may be enough to prevent trouble. If the vehicle is operational, we will come back for you. If not, we will start walking back toward you until we meet on the road."

There were three additional gunshots in rapid succession in the distance.

"We need to get going, brothers. Keep an eye out for the motorcycles; we do not want to be spotted."

Lamar, Bishop Peterson, and another man headed north toward the car that was apparently being robbed as the other three men headed back to find the box of ammo. A short time after they started walking, the motorcycle headlights began heading back their way. Lamar and his guys hid in the tree line as they passed. He noticed one of the motorcycles pulled a large trailer that was full of items that probably belonged to the owners of the vehicle ahead. The other three Mormon men who were headed south to look for the ammo hid in a drainage culvert until all of the motorcycles had passed.

Lamar and his group reached the vehicle after about 20 minutes of careful walking and turned on their flashlights. The scene was bloody. The motorcyclists had indeed shot out one of the tires, which apparently caused the driver to lose control. There were dark skid marks and the vehicle had come to a stop pointing east toward the ditch. The driver's side window was busted out with glass and blood everywhere, and there were three dead bodies lying in the ditch, including an adult male, an adult female, and what looked to be a teenage boy. They had all been shot in the back of the head.

"Oh, this is just horrible," Bishop Peterson said. "Let us offer a prayer before we do anything else."

The bishop knelt on the ground by the three bodies and offered a heartfelt prayer, requesting compassion for the souls of the three murder victims, for mercy for the murderers, and for understanding and strength for the three of them who had to bear witness to such evil.

"We must give these three a proper burial," the Bishop said. "Let's check the van for a shovel."

Lamar searched the van, but found that it was empty. The van had only a driver seat and one passenger seat in the front. All of the other seats appeared to have been removed. He checked the ignition switch and found the keys dangling from it.

"The keys are here; I'm going to try to fire it up."

The minivan started.

"Looks like there's about a half a tank of gas, we just need to change that tire."

"I used to have one of these Chryslers," the Bishop said. "Everything is hidden down in the stowaway compartments. I'll check for a spare tire, and maybe with a little luck, there will also be a shovel."

The bishop stuck his finger in the ring latch that opened the first compartment and folded the trap door upward. He saw the flash before he heard the gun go off, and then he felt the bullet hit him in the chest. He took a few steps backwards as the gunshot echoed in his brain.

"Bishop!" Lamar yelled, running toward him.

The other man dove onto the shooter in an attempt to prevent another shot from going off, and managed to wrestle the small handgun from the assailant's hand. By the time Lamar got there, the bishop was laying on the ground with bright red blood oozing from his chest, and the other man had the shooter in a choke hold. The shooter was a girl of about 11 years of age. Tears were pouring from her eyes, and she was screaming and kicking, trying to get away.

"Lamar," the bishop said, his voice obviously labored. "Bring the girl to me."

Lamar was not sure what the hell had just happened, and he had no idea what the bishop was planning to do now. He brought the girl over to the bishop, who reached up and grabbed her hand.

"Honey, I am so sorry I scared you," he said. "I did not know you were down there. I am so sorry. Can you forgive me?"

The girl cried loudly.

"What is your name, honey?" The bishop was losing strength quickly and his voice announced that fact clearly.

"Sarah."

"Sarah, you listen to me. I know you just heard your family get murdered, and you are afraid. I want you to know something. These men I am with are good men, they are not going to hurt you, okay?"

Sarah nodded.

"Lamar, you have got to take care of this child. This is not an act of evil, this is an act of self-defense. You must forgive her completely and you must forgive me. I was not thinking. I should have known better. I would have had my own small kids hide down there."

"Bishop, you are going to—"

"Lamar, I am fading fast. You have to promise me that she will be taken care of. Promise me."

"Of course, Bishop. I promise."

"Sarah, I am so sorry I scared you. You are not a bad person. This was not a bad thing. You did the right thing. You tried to protect yourself. You are not to blame, understand? I will forgive you for shooting me if you forgive me for putting you in a position to have to choose to shoot someone in order to save your life. Can you forgive me?"

Sarah nodded.

"That's a good girl. These are good men; they will protect you."

The bishop grabbed the girl's hand and squeezed it gently, and then reached for Lamar's hand. For a brief moment, it felt like the bishop might be reaching out for a little strength from Lamar, which was the exact opposite of how their relationship had always gone. However, he did not need much strength to make the transition; the bishop died before Lamar finished the thought.

CHAPTER 33

As they approached the dump, Ethan saw firsthand what Sam and Mike had been telling him. The whole area looked like an archeological dig except that there were also men on horseback carrying shotguns. It quickly went from an archeological dig to a surreal prison camp. He could see tents and makeshift structures dotting the landscape. The place had a chain-link fence topped with barbed wire that surrounded the perimeter. Ethan figured the fence was probably there from before, but he was fairly certain that the sandbagged gun fortifications on each side of the road were recent additions.

As they arrived at the gate, the guy named Dale rode a little bit ahead of them and motioned for them to take a road on their left leading up a hill and past the main entrance to the dump. The heavy-looking gates were made of rod iron. Close to the gate, there was a Caterpillar excavator that Ethan was sure was in place to block the gates if it was deemed necessary.

"Looks like we're heading up to the big house," Mike whispered.

Sheriff Dale spurred his horse and rode ahead of them. After about ten minutes of hiking, a large log home came into view. There were several out buildings around the yard. The railing on the large front deck had firewood stacked behind the entire length of it. Two men, armed with riot shotguns, stood on the deck. Ethan thought to himself that the firewood gave excellent protection and provided a good firing position for anyone defending the porch. A man dressed in black camo walked out of the thick front doors; he had obviously already been inside to alert the commissioner of the arriving party.

"Going to need you to drop your pack, and I'm going to pat you down. It ain't open to negotiation," the sheriff stated.

"I can understand that," Ethan said. There was no reason to force anything at this point. Besides, he obviously was not in a position to force anything.

After Dale had patted Ethan down. He turned to Samantha.

"Where's his .45?" he asked. "Because he sure as hell has got more on him than this 22 Marlin."

"I've got his pistol, Dale," Samantha replied. "Remember? That was part of the deal that he turn it over to me."

"I'm going to need it," Dale said.

"I don't think that will be necessary, Dale," a voice from behind him said. "If Sam has the weapon secured, I'm satisfied with that."

"Besides, which one of us would volunteer to try and take it from her." He gave a slight laugh. "So, Mike, how's the black market treating you?"

"Didn't know we had us a black market, and in all honesty, I'm kinda hurt that you'd think I'd have anything to do with something like that, Commissioner," Mike replied.

"Well hell, the last thing we want to do is hurt your feelings, Mike." He then turned his eyes upon Ethan.

"So, this is our wayward traveler, Ethan Edwards. I'm Commissioner Anthony Harms," he said with a slight smile that held no humor in it.

"Just passing through, not looking to get in anyone's way," Ethan stated.

"I'm sure that's the truth, Mr. Edwards, but what with recent events and the fact that certain segments of our society have reverted to more barbaric ways... well, how would you say it? Makes us seem less hospitable to tourists than in the past. I'm sure you can understand our caution toward strangers. It's unfortunate, don't you think, that in the heat of the moment, some people propelled by fear seek what they consider to be safety in, how shall I say it? by forming groups of thugs.

"Some of them are just plain bad people or perhaps that badness is evil, if you will. It seems that evil is often just below the surface waiting for a chance to show itself. Then again, there are those of us who are still preaching love and tolerance, thinking that if we just explain the situation, everyone will work towards the common good. That we can all get along. That all we really need is a group hug. We do this while everything around us is being raped and looted and destroyed. Then at some point, we cower and hide, shaking with fear, waiting for someone to come and get us." The commissioner had turned his gaze from Ethan to Samantha during his time on his soap box.

He then refocused his gaze on Ethan.

"The question, Mr. Edwards, is which group do you represent?" he asked.

"Oddly, I was about to ask you the same question," Ethan replied.

Harms smiled.

"I'm in the other group. The group that stands its ground. That won't stand by and let chaos engulf what's left. My group believes that the only thing violent men understand is violence. But let's not discuss it standing on the porch, come into my office," he said with a wave of his hand.

Ethan headed up the stairs followed by Samantha and Mike. Harms noticed that all of them were heading into the house. He turned around and everybody stopped.

"Mike, as much as I enjoy your company, I feel that Mr. Edwards and I should have a private conversation."

He then turned to Sam. "And, I'm sure, Samantha, that he won't need legal representation."

"Well, Tony..." Harms winced as Samantha addressed him by his first name. "Ethan and I have a dinner date."

A genuine smile came across Ethan's face. It didn't go unnoticed by Harms.

"Can I assume that he'll be able to attend?" she asked.

"God knows I'd hate to interrupt your dinner plans, Samantha. I'm sure that as long as Mr. Edwards can assure us that his intentions are what he claims them to be, he can be on his way. Is that okay with you?"

He didn't wait for her to answer.

"Mike, should you happen to hear anything about a black market..."

Mike answered before he finished. "You'll be the first guy I tell, Commissioner. The first guy."

"I'm sure. Mr. Edwards after you."

Harms, from behind Ethan, told him to take the first door on the right. Ethan walked into a nice-sized office with nice leather furniture. The desk was on one wall, a bookcase on the other. There was a door to the left of the desk. Harms went around Ethan and sat down behind the desk.

"Take a seat," Harms said pointing to one of the high-backed chairs in front of the desk. "I kinda inherited this place from its previous owner. Ya gotta admit, the son of a bitch had good taste," Harms said as he opened a desk drawer.

"Virus victim?" Ethan asked.

"Actually, the poor bastard shot himself in the back yard. We found what I assume are family pictures of a pretty wife and two little girls and himself. We didn't find the woman or the little girls. Perhaps he couldn't live with not knowing. Who knows. But, if they show up they, will most certainly get their home back."

Ethan believed the man was being sincere and would honor his statement.

"So, Edwards, what do you think of Samantha?"

Ethan thought it was somewhat of an odd question.

"She certainly leaves an impression," he said.

"To say the least. She is one of my most favorite people on the planet. Before or after the virus. Actually, Mike, too." He stopped as if he knew he revealed too much.

The commissioner pulled out a bottle of J&B Scotch.

"It has to be five o'clock somewhere," he said as he poured three fingers into two glasses and slid one across the desk to Ethan.

"What should we drink to, Mr. Edwards?"

"How about the fact that regardless of what happens, a man can still enjoy a good drink," Ethan said with a slight grin.

"That I can drink to," Harms said. After taking a swallow, he cleared his throat a bit.

"So, what did your new friends tell you about me?" he asked. "And please don't insult me by saying that they didn't tell you anything."

"First off, I wouldn't insult you, Commissioner," he replied.

Ethan could tell that the fact he used Harms' official title was noticed by him.

"They told me you lost your entire family to the virus."

Harms took a larger pull on his drink.

"They also told me you don't approve of people shopping for free at Wal-Mart. That you can be a prick sometimes."

Harms let out a laugh.

"I suppose that there's truth in that statement. And what do you think?" he asked.

"I think you took control of a situation and that your move at Wal-Mart was pretty ballsy."

"I'm not quite sure if you're being sincere or trying to blow smoke up my ass," Harms replied. "And your story, Mr. Edwards?"

Ethan told Harms pretty much the truth about him being from Darby that he was a logger and that he was passing through the Flathead on his way to British Columbia. He told him that he had a cousin up there.

"I've heard that there is ground up there that a white man has yet to walk on," Ethan explained. "And if anyone could survive and was prepared to live in these uncertain times, it would be my cousin Bill."

Harms poured a couple more fingers of Scotch in their glasses and rubbed his nose.

"Rumor has it the bigger cities have all gone to hell and are in total chaos. I've had reports of gangs of bad people wandering from place to place killing, raping, taking what and who they want. That's not going to happen here... not while I'm still breathing. This community, what's left of it, is going to survive. I'm going to see to that and I'm going to do whatever I think is necessary to make that happen. How can I be sure that you aren't on some kind of a recon mission for a group like that?"

"Because you don't think that. I've got a feeling if you did, we wouldn't be talking over drinks," Ethan stated.

"No, I guess I don't. I could offer you a position here. I can always use another good man."

"Just what is here, Commissioner?" Ethan asked.

"Ah, you mean the dump. Well, I can explain a little bit to you. I think that we can agree that this country became a throwaway society. If it didn't work, why fix it? I mean, you'd spend three-quarters of the price of something new trying to get your used item fixed. And who the hell even knew how to fix anything anymore? When you took something back to the store, they just handed you a new one. Boots get a little old, buy new ones for forty bucks. Hell, when something new and shiny comes out we throw the old one away even if it still works. Or, they won't take your garbage bag of old clothing at the thrift store because there's no room. Take it to the dump. I'm not telling you anything that you don't already know. But one little virus changed all of that. There's nobody making shit anymore. Nobody is left to make it.

"So, where are those of us left going to shop? That's why we are excavating the local dump."

"What about the mounted armed guards?" Ethan asked.

"So, I've broken the dump up in parcels. You as a private individual can rent, from the county, up to three parcels and mine them. What's the rental fee is your next question, no doubt. It's half of what you recover. The county gets first pick of the items and then the renter gets a pick and back and forth it goes. Other parcels are mined by those people who have been arrested for breaking county ordinances. They are sentenced by one of our surviving JPs. Of course, the county gets all of the goods from the penal sites."

"Capitalism and justice all in one stop. Can't think of anything more American," Ethan said.

"Capitalism started when two cavemen sat around and traded rocks or sticks. And justice... without justice, you have anarchy and evil reigns," Harms replied.

"I heard something similar just recently." Ethan thought back to his conversation with Gilmore.

"We're also getting the methane gas that's produced from the garbage. I'm having it stored along with the other fossil fuels we were able to save. When the power went down, the stations had no way to get the fuel out of their tanks. The county had emergency generators. So did the equipment rental yards. When you've got all that, all you need is an electrician. Just so happens, we also have equipment from the local National Guard depots. Not a lot, but some. So, we have a very mobile force... in case of an emergency. That last statement sounds rather odd considering that our current situation could be considered an ongoing emergency."

"Or perhaps it simply proves how quickly humans adapt to their environment."

"I'm beginning to like you more and more, Edwards. When we secured the dump, we also came across a large amount of out-of-date prescription drugs. They get incinerated normally, but lucky for us, if you can call it that, the virus broke out right before the next scheduled burn. Old drugs are better than no drugs. I also ordered the library to be secured. Knowledge is power and that is a building full of knowledge."

Ethan was gaining a grudging respect for this guy. He didn't necessarily like him, but he realized that it would be a mistake to underestimate him. He was pretty sure that Harms knew what he was talking about. Ethan thought it was clever how the commissioner played his hand. For if he was, in fact, on a recon mission, Harms had pretty much let him know that he was prepared to fight and not only that, he had contingency plans in place and a way to move resources quickly. His message was clear: if you are here on a recon mission, perhaps you should look for an easier target.

About that time the door by his desk opened and a small boy walked in.

"She won't let me ride today," the boy said as he looked at Ethan.

"Come over here," Harms said.

The boy went to him and climbed on his lap. Ethan saw a change in Harms.

"Will, this is Mr. Edwards."

"Hello," the boy said to Ethan.

"Nice to meet you, Will," Ethan replied.

"Will, I've talked with you about not knocking and interrupting me when I'm in my office..."

"I know, but she won't let me ride today, and I thought..."

An attractive woman in her late forties or early fifties came into the room.

"I knew I'd find you here, you little shit," the woman said in a pretend voice that held no real anger.

"You're not going to give into him, are you?" she asked Harms.

"Mr. Edwards, this is Crystal," Harms said waving a hand toward the woman. "Crystal is, how should I put it? My first lady of sorts..."

"But not your first choice. Nice to meet you, Mr. Edwards," she replied.

Ethan saw Harms change again, this time his eyes went cold. Ethan also found it odd that Harms felt the need to explain any of it to him.

"So, what's your ruling, Tony? I'm sorry. I meant to say, 'Commissioner.'"

"Will, you need to listen to Crystal. No riding today and any whining about it and there will be no riding tomorrow. Now, if both of you could excuse us."

"Absolutely, I know how valuable your time is," Crystal said as she took Will's hand and led him from the room.

Harms turned back to Ethan with a somewhat embarrassed look on his face.

"Women..." Ethan said.

"Yes. Crystal and I have known each other for years. She found the boy wandering. She came to me with him and herself. We, let's say, have tried to comfort each other. It is what it is."

Harms drained his glass and added more Scotch to it.

"Thirty-three years," he said. "I was married to her for thirty-three years. Got to where we could finish each other's thoughts. There's a line in a country song that says *'I'm not me without you.'* I watched her die. I can't begin to... My wife was the best human being I've ever known. If a man was to sit down and write what he wanted in a wife, a mother, a friend... She was my soul mate."

The commissioner struggled for the right words.

"It took her fast. We both knew, but we tried to tell each other it was the regular flu or something. But, we both knew. After a short time, we also knew that I didn't have it. Everyone was under movement constrictions. Hell, I signed them. After she passed, I went to my oldest son's place. Yelled to him from the lawn, then from the porch. When I went in the house, I knew. You could smell death. Ya know what I mean? That smell?"

Harms could tell that Ethan knew exactly what he was talking about.

"I found them... my grandsons were in their beds... Little boys a few years younger than Will. My daughter-in-law and son in the living room," the commissioner continued, while taking another good-sized drink of Scotch.

"Know what my first thought was?"

Ethan just shook his head no.

"Who died first? I mean, did those two innocent little boys lay in their beds crying and suffering? Or did my son have to watch his sons die? Sometimes, I dream about that. I found my youngest boy the next day. Somehow, he'd managed to put on his Marine Corps blues. He was in his recliner. At first, when I looked through the window, I thought he was asleep. *'Oh thank God, he's just asleep,'* I thought. But then I knew."

He took another drink, his hand trembling slightly. He looked at Ethan. For a split second, Ethan saw his father. He understood Harms' actions in the Wal-Mart parking lot. It wasn't a ballsy move at all. It was an *'I don't give a damn if I live or die'* move. In fact, looking at the man, Ethan was pretty sure that Harms would have preferred the later. *'A man who doesn't care if he lives or dies is a dangerous man,'* Ethan thought.

Harms cleared his throat.

"I suppose almost all of us left can tell that same story, only a different version."

There was a knock on the door and Harms regained his composure before speaking.

"Enter," he said in a loud voice.

The sheriff walked in.

"Commissioner, we've gone through his stuff and these are the only weapons we found," he said as he put Ethan's Marlin, his K-Bar knife, and the Hobo knife Bob had given him on the commissioner's desk.

Harms leaned forward in his chair and picked up the hobo knife.

"I'll be go to hell... I haven't seen a Hobo knife in... By God, it's an older case, too."

"It was a gift from a very good friend of mine," Ethan said.

"I can tell from the tone of your voice it is very important to you. So, you should keep it closer to you, Mr. Edwards. Keep it in your pocket not in your pack." He handed the knife to Ethan who slid it into his pocket.

There was another knock on the door.

"Come," Harms said in a gruff voice.

One of the men from the porch entered.

"Sir, she's back. And she's got a big mean-looking dog with her," he said.

Everyone knew who he was referring to.

"Leave us, both of you. Tell her we'll be right out."

When the room was empty, Harms looked at Ethan.

"I hear what they whisper, what Crystal thinks... Samantha is special to me, but not in the way everyone assumes." He paused, making sure Ethan had heard his words and was listening. "It's her spirit, her independence... Actually, it doesn't matter. I'm not sure why I've even told you what I have."

Ethan thought he knew why, because he had to tell someone. It was almost as if it had somehow been a confession of sorts, an atonement for surviving.

"She likes you, Edwards," he said. "Otherwise, she wouldn't have come back to check on you. You're lucky. Be careful. Hurt her, and I'll kill you. It's not a threat, it's a promise," Harms said, and then drained what was left in his glass.

There was not a doubt in Ethan's mind that the commissioner was deadly serious about the promise.

"You've got one day to think over my offer. If the answer is 'no,' then you've got two days to be out of the Flathead."

"I understand," Ethan said.

"By leaving, I mean leaving alone. Just you and the dog, clear?"

Ethan didn't answer.

"Hmmm... Well, let's gather your things, we don't want to keep your dinner host waiting any longer. She's something special most of the time, but when she's pissed, watch out."

"Dale, take Mr. Edwards to his things and make sure he gets them. All of them. Then report back to me, alright?"

"Yes, sir."

"I'll find you or I won't; either way, I'll have my answer," Harms said looking at Ethan.

"Thanks for the drink, Commissioner," Ethan said as he followed the sheriff out of the room.

An hour or so later, there was a slight knock on the door and Dale entered.

"You wanted to see me, Commissioner?"

"Yes, have a seat, Dale. Would you like a drink?" Harms asked.

"No, thank you."

"Come now, don't make me drink alone," Harms said as he poured a swallow in Ethan's glass for the sheriff. And filled his half full.

"Tomorrow morning, send a couple of men out to Samantha's place. If Edwards isn't there, I want them to wait until he is. I want them to intimidate her. Make damn sure they understand not to lay a finger on that woman. If they overdo it, there will be hell to pay," Harms said.

"Ah, Commissioner, she doesn't, ah, intimidate too easily," replied Dale.

"It's not her I'm wanting to get a rise out of. I want to see how Edwards reacts. And I've got a feeling that when it comes to Miz Samantha, it won't take much to get him to react."

"How far do you want my guys to go with him? I mean, he looks pretty fit. But hell, he's packing a .22 rifle around during these times. I mean, granted, he has that .45 also, but I think the guy is more talk than show," Dale said.

"Tell your guys to give him a decent ass-kicking, but they're not to touch the woman."

Harms had a hunch that there was a lot more to Ethan Edwards than met the eye. And as far as the .22 went, a man could argue that it made sense. A skilled man with a .22 was more dangerous than an unskilled man with a bazooka. Harms was pretty sure that Ethan carried the small caliber rifle because although he was probably very good with it; his true talents were in close quarters.

"Do it early."

"Yes, sir," Dale said as he got up and left the room.

Harms took a large swallow, leaned back in his chair, and closed his eyes. After a few moments with his eyes closed, he muttered the words *'I miss you.'*

CHAPTER 34

It was a long night in the apartment on 14th Street in the Columbia Heights neighborhood of Washington, DC. There were no more sounds in the hallway for the rest of the night, but noises coming from the street made it difficult for David to sleep. However, it appeared that the boy did finally get to sleep. David lay there for another hour or so after he first woke up. When the sun came through the window, David got up and looked down onto 14th street. There was smoke, but it appeared to be quiet. He could not see any activity in any direction. He woke the boy up gently.

"Aiden, it's time to leave," he said.

The boy opened his eyes, and for a moment, it appeared that he did not remember that he had a visitor, but he soon recovered and sat up groggily. David helped him slip into some clothes and secured his little backpack that had Teenage Mutant Ninja Turtles on it.

"My house is just a couple of blocks from here," David explained. "We are going to walk there as quickly as we can. If we see anyone along the way, we are going to just keep walking, okay?" The boy nodded. Other than a few weeping sounds, the boy had not yet muttered a single word or made even a sound. David realized that he had to be terrified, and he was anxious to get the boy to safety. David stepped out into the hallway slowly and shined his light up and down the dark corridor. There were two dead bodies lying on the floor between this apartment and the one next door. David made a mental note on how he could get Aiden out of there without him seeing the bloody bodies. The hall was completely dark, which he decided he could use to his advantage. As he was about to go back in and get the boy, he heard the neighbor's door locks turn. He braced himself, unsure what to expect.

"Are you taking the boy out of here?" a man's voice asked from behind a crack in the door.

"Yes," David said. "I am taking him to a safe place."

"How do I know that you can be trusted?"

"My name is David Gilbert, I run an organization called the Compassionate Neighbors. I am taking him to our safe house."

"No shit," the man said, as he opened the door a little to show himself.

The man was in his mid-forties and was well-dressed. A scruffy beard was growing on his face. David guessed by his appearance that the man was probably an attorney or perhaps an executive.

"Your organization helped get my mother from the hospital to an eldercare center when she took a fall last year. That was a really nice thing you did for our family."

"I am glad to hear it," David said. "We live for opportunities to help others."

"Some old lady named Gertrude spent hours on the phone and would not give up until my mother was safely admitted. I had spent months fighting with those people..."

"That was my aunt," David said.

He remembered how tenacious Aunt Gertie could be when she was on a mission.

"She is a great lady, tell her I said thank you."

David thought about telling him that she had died, but decided against it. There was already too much bad news floating around.

"I'll tell her," David said. "Oh, and thank you for protecting us last night."

"In all honesty, I was only thinking of myself," the man said. "Are his parents gone?"

David nodded.

"Sorry to hear that. They were great neighbors, but sadly, I barely knew them. Seems as though I was too busy to be bothered with neighbors."

"Are you okay? Do you need anything?" David asked.

"I've got enough food to last me for a few weeks," the man said. "After that, I have a feeling there will either be help or nothing left to live for."

It was a solemn assessment, and David knew that there was truth in that statement.

"I'll check back with you in a few days. If you need something, just hang a red cloth from your balcony and I will come up."

The man nodded and closed his door. David stepped into the apartment and grabbed Aiden's hand.

"Okay, we are off. I am going to shine the flashlight in the direction that I want you to walk, okay?"

The boy nodded. David stepped back into the hallway with his back toward the dead bodies and shone the flashlight down the hall in the opposite direction. When Aiden was on his way out the doorway, David grabbed his hand and they made it down the hall to the staircase. Once inside the stairwell, David searched with the flashlight and when he was convinced that it was safe, he proceeded down the stairs with the boy.

In the lobby, David used the light to find a path and led the boy through the maze of debris and out into the early morning sunlight. The whole 14th Street square looked like a war zone. Without a word, David pulled on the boy's hand and they walked at a brisk pace. He headed north to the next block, turned down Kenyon street, and then made a right on 13th Street so that he could get off 14th Street that he knew would likely be much more dangerous. They then walked a few blocks to Girard Street to Aunt Gertie's row house that she had left to David. Fortunately, they did not see anyone along the way.

The organization had fortified the house to protect it from the roving gangs and looters, and since it was in the middle of the row, they only had to board up windows and doors on the front and back. David knocked loudly on the front door and shouted that it was David. The door opened, and several members of the organization came to welcome him and his new guest.

"Thank God you are okay. We were worried about you when you didn't come home yesterday," one of the Compassionate Neighbors said.

David explained the situation at the 14th street square and told them about the terrifying night they had in the apartment. The members in the house showered Aiden with hugs and welcomes, and David took him into the house and showed him around. He found a bed for him in the basement with some other children that the organization had taken in, and he brought him some food.

Over the next several days, Aiden adjusted to the new environment and the group scoured the neighborhood and brought new people in to help them. The house was filled to capacity, but they still searched for more. They could not rest if others were suffering, so their focus was on finding those in need of immediate help. They would deal with the long-term problems as they arose.

When Aiden first got sick, fear spread through the house like a wildfire. There were heated discussions about the possibility that he had the virus, and they debated what should be done with those who were sick. They had been fortunate to have made it this far into the epidemic without encountering the virus firsthand. It was finally agreed that the sick would be isolated on the top floor of the house in a little room that Aunt Gertie had set up as a meditation nook. David moved Aiden up there, hoping and believing that he just had a cold.

After the first two days, it became apparent that Aiden was infected with the Typhon virus, and the other people in the house refused to go near him. David reminded them of their mission to help others regardless of the personal sacrifices, but when push came to shove, it turned out that he was the only one who was willing to put his life on the line. He ended up taking several days' worth of supplies and plenty of water to the third floor and he set up an extra bed up there for himself. He stayed up there with the boy.

David was shocked when the boy spoke to him for the first time, and he was quite sure that he was probably feverish and delusional.

"Am I going to die like Mommy and Daddy?" he asked.

"I don't know, Aiden, but I plan to take could care of you," David replied.

The boy slipped back into a deep but restless sleep. For about six days, David sat by the boy's bedside and fed him broth, gave him water, sang to him, and told him that he was going to be just fine. On day seven, David started to feel a little under the weather himself, and so he went downstairs to inform the others.

"Hey, everyone," he yelled from behind the closed door that led to the third floor. "Can you hear me?"

Finally, a female Compassionate Neighbor answered him.

"I think I am coming down with this thing," he said.

"How is the boy?" the woman asked.

"He seems to be stable, maybe even improving a little. He had a little bleeding from his nose and mouth and a mild rash, but that was a couple of days ago. His fever is better today. We are going to need more supplies and perhaps someone to take care of me, because if I have this virus, I will probably be flat on my back for several days."

"Okay," the woman answered. "You go ahead and get comfortable; someone will be up in a few minutes with supplies."

David waited for what seemed like a couple of hours, and then he finally heard someone making their way up the stairs. It was the same woman he had spoken to earlier.

"Thank you for coming, Anne," David said.

"I'm afraid that I am the only one who was willing to do it. We are experiencing a little friction downstairs," she said.

"Is everything okay?"

"Most of them are leaving, going out to find a place that is free of the virus. I tried to tell them that there would be no escape from the Typhon virus, but fear has taken over."

David was saddened by this news.

"I'm sorry to hear that. What about you, Anne? Are you okay with being here?"

"I am."

"Thank you."

David had always had a fond regard for Sister Anne. She was one of several nuns who participated in the activities of the organization, and she was always sweet and kind. Even when he told her that he stepped away from the priesthood, Sister Anne always treated him with kindness and respect, and she always demonstrated the love of her faith in all of her actions.

Sister Anne nursed David and Aiden for several days. Aiden continued to improve and within a couple of days, he got a little of his strength back. He could get out of bed and walk around, but only for short periods of time. Sister Anne had brought several books up with her, and the two of them passed a lot of time reading together and caring for David. David's condition seemed to grow worse by the hour. He started with a severe headache and fever, followed by chills, diarrhea, rash, and vomiting. A few days later, he developed a case of hiccups that was still persisting several days later.

The bleeding started on the eighth day of David's illness, and it was so severe, that there was no question that he was going to die. Shortly after David took a turn for the worst, Sister Anne began to feel sick. Soon, Aiden was doing the best that he could to nurse them both, but Sister Anne refused to lay down until she could not physically stand any longer. At least three times, she performed Catholic last rites for David, but all three times, he awoke the next morning with a little more fight in him.

Finally, David slipped into a comatose state, and did not move. He stayed like that for several days, and Aiden frequently placed his head on David's belly to determine if he was still breathing. Sister Anne's condition also worsened and she could not get out of bed. Before she was completely incapacitated, she sent Aiden downstairs to get some help, but when he went down there, he could not find anyone.

She sent him back to get more food and water, but all that was left was a case of 12 Clif Bars, two large cartons of Cheese-Its, and a giant sized bag of Costco potato chips. Aiden made a couple of trips up with the food, and several more to carry the remaining water bottles up. The situation was dire.

When Sister Anne died, Aiden covered her body with a blanket like he watched David do with his parents. Then, he lay down beside David's warm body and held him tight. For several days, David laid there motionless, as the boy fed him water. He could not get him to take any food, and the boy ate as little of it as he could.

When David finally woke up, he asked first for water and then for something to eat. The boy handed him a water bottle, but when he did not take it, he placed it in his hand. He then fed him fish-shaped, cheese-flavored crackers.

"Thank you, Aidan," David said in a weak voice. "How is Sister Anne?"

The boy did not respond.

"Aiden, I know that you are afraid, but I really need your help. Can you help me?"

The boy nodded.

"I need you to speak to me, Aiden, okay? I can't see. I need you to be my eyes for me, okay?"

Aiden could tell that there was something wrong with David's eyes. They were red and puffy, not like normal eyes.

"How is Sister Anne?" he asked again.

"She died already," he said. "She died already."

CHAPTER 35

Lamar knelt over the bishop's body and gently closed his eyelids. Even though all of the vibrant life that was in his body was now gone, his face still carried the look of love and compassion that he wore on a daily basis. Now, it looked a little more peaceful.

Lamar choked back the tears as he offered a prayer for their fallen leader. The other man with them had been in the bishop's ward, and he was devastated by the sudden turn of events.

"I loved that man," he said. "He was like a father and a big brother all in one."

Lamar nodded, and embraced the man who shook violently as he wept in Lamar's arms. Sarah sat on the floor of the van with her legs hanging over the runner for the sliding side door. She felt terrible about shooting that man, and she was still filled with terror. She wasn't sure who she could trust, if anyone. She tried to avoid looking at her family in the ditch, but she could not get the final sounds of their lives out of her memory. Her father's scream for mercy and then attempts to fight off the bikers. Her mother's screams and warnings. Her brother's defiance of the bikers. She clearly heard him call one of them a 'fucking pig.'

After a few minutes of grieving, Lamar searched the hidden storage compartments of the van. There was no shovel in the van and the spare tire was one of those compact temporary spare tires that had a road life of about 50 miles. In the other storage areas, he found a few food supplies and a box of shells for the .25 special pistol that the girl had down there with her. In the bin that she had been hiding in, they also found a sleeping bag and a pillow.

"Let's get this tire changed and load these bodies. We've gotta get out of here as soon as we can," Lamar said.

The two men put the compact spare on the front driver's side tire that had been shot out and then turned the van around to make it easier to load the bodies. Lamar had Sarah sat in the front passenger seat while they loaded the bodies up and stacked them in the van. When they were finished, Lamar climbed into the driver's seat and the other man climbed in the back and placed his head in the middle space between Lamar and Sarah.

Lamar drove south on the north side of the freeway. He drove slowly with only the running lights on so he could see the other men. He spotted them moving just a few hundred yards from where they had been. Lamar pulled the van over and got out.

"I'm so glad you are okay," Tom said. "We heard a shot and had no idea what was going on. What happened?"

Lamar's expression said it all.

"We lost the bishop," he said. "It was tragic. A small girl was hidden in the van, and when he opened one of the compartments, she fired the gun. A .25 special. Hardly enough power to kill a gopher at short range, but it hit him right in the chest in just the wrong place."

Tom's face grew solemn.

"The bikers murdered the girl's family. Shot the tire out and cleared out all of their supplies. There is enough gas in the tank to get to Darby or back to Salmon. The donut spare tire is good for about 50 miles."

"What are we going to do?" Tom asked.

"Did he leave the ammo?" Lamar asked.

Tom shook his head.

"The guy was true to his word. He left one box of 30-30 ammo for a 30-06 rifle. I am not sure if that was intentional or just Chuck living up to his name."

The remaining guys gathered around, looking for direction. The news of the bishop's death had brought a pall of sadness on the group, and it seemed like their mission had come to a rapid and unsatisfying end.

"Well, we are about, what? 40 miles from home?" Lamar started.

There were nods of agreement.

"And we have four dead bodies that need to be buried properly and a little girl who needs a lot of love and kindness. I am thinking we need to go back and start again."

"One thing to consider," one of the men named Larry said, "is that I have a relative that lives in Sula, MT just about 20 miles north of here. I have not heard from him since this whole virus thing started, but if I were a betting man, I would bet that there is a good chance that he is just fine and will have lots of supplies that he would be willing to share."

Lamar paused and thought for a moment. The trip had been a lot tougher than he expected, and it was not likely to get any easier as they got closer to the larger population centers of Darby, Hamilton, Missoula, etc. They simply could not take the girl with them, and they had to deal with those bodies. The bishop, in particular, deserved to be buried by his own people.

"Okay, let's do this. Larry and I will keep heading north on foot. We will plan to get to his cousin's place in Sula in a couple of days. We can meet up there. Tom, you take the van, the girl, and the rest of the men back to our camp. Get a proper tire and spare, fill up the tank, resupply the van, and then meet us at Sula as soon as possible. Larry will tell you where to find us there."

"What about the girl?"

"Have my wife Shelly look after her," Lamar said. "And you guys take the pistol and the box of shells. We will take the rifle, since it is pretty much useless with the wrong bullets, but it could still provide a little protection if used properly."

"You guys are making this too easy," a familiar voice said from the tree line.

Lamar knew that voice, but did not remember from where until he saw that goofy smile on the face of what-the-fuck Chuck.

"You have got to be kidding me," Lamar said, as he noticed the SKS pointing at the group.

"I hate changing tires," Chuck said, "and you just never know what danger looms at the scene of a robbery. Now, throw me that handgun."

Tom looked to Lamar for guidance, but saw none coming.

"Did I stutter? Throw me the handgun and the box of bullets."

Tom threw the handgun at him hard, hoping that it would hit him in the head and knock him out or even better, go off and kill him. No such luck.

Chuck laughed.

"Getting tired of this, I see. Gentleman, you had better start thinking or you are gonna start stinking. The road is no place for the mindless or the stupid. Not anymore. Now, I will need you to take those bodies out of my van."

The other men looked at Lamar, and he nodded his head. He knew the drill. Chuck was not going to negotiate anymore.

"At least you could give us a box of 30-06 bullets to go with the rifle you let us keep at our first robbery," Lamar said.

Chuck laughed.

"I wish I could do that, but as I told you, the road is no place for the stupid or the mindless. Lay the 30-06 and the 30-30 shells on the ground there by the van. Now that they have served the intended purpose, I will be taking those back, too."

When the men pulled the final body from the van and closed the doors, Chuck motioned for them all to step away.

"Another 20 feet," he said.

When he was convinced that they were at a safe distance away, he pointed his weapon toward the ground, headed for the van, picked up the 30-06 and the bullets.

"Pleasure doing business with you guys again. Please let me know when you are back in the area and perhaps we could arrange another business deal."

"I hope you don't get the Ebola," a small voice said. It was Sarah talking.

Chuck laughed.

"I hope you don't, either," he replied.

"I mean, my mom and dad had it bad, that is why we were on the road. We were trying to get to Missoula to the hospital up there. The van is probably full of the virus. I hope you don't get it," she said with remarkable poise.

"Jesus Christ," Chuck exclaimed, stumbling over his own feet to get away from the van. "Get these bodies and this piece of shit out of here."

Chuck ran back into the darkness of the woods in the direction that he had come from. Lamar looked from Sarah to the other men. She had just uttered their death sentences. Lamar wondered why she had not mentioned that earlier.

"Sarah, I did not know that your family had Ebola," Lamar stated. He wasn't quite sure what to make of the situation, and if the girl's story was true, then he and Larry had also been exposed.

"I don't like to lie," Sarah said, "but my daddy once told me that sometimes it's okay if the lie will do more good than the truth. We didn't really have Ebola," she said. "I just said that to scare him."

Lamar knelt down and hugged the little girl. The other men gathered around, too, and patted her on the back.

"You did the right thing," Lamar said. "And that was about the bravest acting performance I have ever seen."

Sarah smiled.

"Okay, guys, if we have learned nothing else, we have to keep moving. At least then we will see our enemies coming! Let's get these bodies back in the van, and proceed with our plan. Larry and I will head north toward Sula and see you there in a couple of days. We will not wait for you, so if we have left when you get there, we will let Larry's cousin know where the next meeting location will be."

"Sounds good," said Tom. "We'll get up there as quickly as we can. I think we have all learned that the passive approach is not the right approach. I will not make that mistake again."

"Just remember that we are Mormons, and at the end of the day, when we lie our heads on our pillows, we have to be able to live with our actions. Godspeed, gentlemen."

When the van was loaded with the bodies, the little girl and the three men got in and headed south down the northbound lane for a couple of miles until there was a turnaround connector road to the southbound side of the highway. Tom got the van onto the southbound highway and cruised along as fast as he could with just the running lights on.

Larry and Lamar headed north walking along the highway. They planned to spend the night somewhere safe but close by and then begin hiking at first light. Their goal was to stay close to the highway but hidden in the tree line as best as they could. The two men walked passed the scene where they recovered the van. Recovered it for Chuck... Lamar couldn't believe that he fell for the whole thing. Chuck had played him perfectly. He vowed to be more diligent and more attentive in the future. The rules of this new world had changed; he could no longer rely on the goodness of human nature.

Tom kept the minivan moving along the highway at a high rate of speed and made it about 25 miles without any signs of life. As he approached the very small town of North Fork, he knew that he was about 20 miles from Salmon, and about 15 miles from where Lamar's group had set up camp. He was close, and he was anxious to get there, but he also knew that he could never be too careful. So, he kept cruising along. Their earlier experience at the bridge was ever present in his mind, and he planned to retrace the last few miles using the route they had worked out on the way out of town.

Tom was not about to lose this van or place his friends in any more danger than he had to. When they got close to the bridge, Tom maneuvered the van to the other side of the highway, took the exit just north of the bridge, and retraced their route across the old bridge and along the old dirt road. The night was dark, and although the moon had been out at times, clouds moved in and out across the skies, hiding and revealing the moon in turns. The running lights on the van were sufficient to see a few feet ahead, but did not project out far enough to illuminate the road with enough distance to allow the driver to react to any foreign object in the road.

In fact, Tom had only begun to hit the brakes when the van slammed into the deer that he had only seen at the last minute. Tom managed to get the vehicles stopped, but the deer slammed directly into the radiator and then flew up into the windshield, sending shards of safety glass flying inward. Steam poured out of the front of the van and filled the inside with the smell of hot antifreeze.

"Dammit," Tom cried, "can we not catch a break here? C'mon, God, how about a little help?"

Tom slammed his hands on the steering wheel and then looked around to see if everyone was okay. For the most part, the passengers were a little shook up, but there were no injuries. However, the damage to the van made it impossible for it to go any further.

"Another challenge," Tom said. "Let's roll this thing off the road a little ways and then hike to my camp. It is the closest one to us and is just a little over 10 miles from here."

Tom and his group reached his camp just as the darkness of the night was giving way to the breaking dawn. It took the group about four hours of walking to get there, as they took it slow and hid in the brush any time they heard something that might be a threat. They were exhausted, and it was good to be back in a safe place. Tom woke his wife, who was surprised to see him, and she helped get beds for the rest of the group.

Later that day, Tom awoke and organized a group of guys to go after the van and retrieve the bishop's body. News of the bishop's death spread quickly through the camp, and because he was so well respected, Tom had no trouble assembling a group. He soon had a pickup truck and four men ready to go.

"Okay, brothers," Tom began, "we are going to load up the truck and drive straight to the van. It is disabled, so we just need to grab the bodies in the van and bring them back so that we can give them a proper burial."

"Here's the deal," Tom continued. "I've asked you all to bring rifles, and we need to be prepared to use them at all times. The road is not safe, and we cannot trust anyone. If we encounter anybody on the trip, I am not going to stop the truck, understood?"

The group nodded.

"I hate to say it, but for the safety of the group, I would advise you to shoot first and ask questions later."

The men jumped into the truck, and Tom headed back down the road toward the spot where the van had hit the deer just a few hours earlier. As they approached the van in the hot afternoon sun, Tom realized for the first time that the van was gold in color. He had only seen the vehicle at night and the events occurred so rapidly that he didn't even register the color. He pulled the truck behind the van, lining the two vehicles up so that the bodies could be taken through the back door of the van and into the back of the truck with as little effort as possible.

"Two of you need to stand guard, one at the front of the truck and one at the back," Tom ordered. "Keep alert, someone may be expecting us to come back for the bodies."

Two men moved into guard positions as the other two joined Tom at the back of the van. Tom opened the van door and the smell of warm decay hit them like a wall as the door swung open. One of the men turned and threw up, while Tom and the other man covered their noses and mouths with their hands and turned away.

"Okay, gentlemen, let's make this quick," Tom said. "Grab an end and let's get him into the truck."

The guard at the front of the truck was the first to hear the sounds of the motorcycles, and he alerted the rest of the group just as they had loaded the last body into the truck.

"I hear motorcycles coming our way," the man said.

Tom's heart raced.

"Okay, get in the truck and get in position to shoot. I am going to head toward camp as fast as this truck will go, and when we encounter this group on the road, we need to shoot them on site. Understood?"

"How do we know they are bad guys?" one of the men asked.

"Remember what I said earlier? Shoot first."

Tom had the truck on the road doing about 50 miles per hour heading toward camp when he encountered the motorcycle gang heading toward him from the opposite direction. He could not tell who fired the first shot, but what unfolded next appeared to play out in slow motion. There were several loud bangs as the men in the truck shot at the bikers. There was the sound of gunfire hitting the truck, windows exploded, a tire went flat, a bullet hit the radiator sending steam across the windshield. Tom kept the truck moving on the road for as long as he could, but it had taken too many bullets from the motorcycle gang to make it very far.

One of the men dropped his rifle out the window and was shot in the head as he reflexively reached for it. Two of the men were shot while attempting to reload, and the fourth man cowered in fear on the floorboard of the truck. As far as Tom could tell, they had not successfully shot any of the biker gang members, and his attempts to hit one or more of them had also failed.

Tom pulled out his handgun as the truck rolled to a stop in the middle of the road. They had only made it a couple of miles down the road, and so were too far away from camp for anyone there to know what was going on. He turned to the man on the floor.

"These men are going to kill us," he said. "It is time to for an exit strategy."

The man on the floor whimpered.

"I believe that God has a plan for us, and for this world. These men are pure evil, they prey on the weak and unprotected. I am not going down without a fight," Tom said. "I am going to lie down on the seat like I am dead and when they open the door of this truck, and I am going to shoot as many of them as I can."

About a dozen motorcycles surrounded the shot-up truck, and several men turned off their bikes and walked toward the disabled vehicle.

"Maroney, get your ass up there and clear the truck," the leader said.

A young looking biker eagerly ran toward the truck, and peered into the window.

"They are all dead," he said as he opened the passenger side door. "I'll gather up all the weapons."

The kid opened the cab door, and when he rolled Tom's body over to retrieve his weapon, Tom shot him in the forehead, sending his body backwards out of the cab. Tom quickly followed, firing his weapon several times toward the men standing around outside the truck. Tom was able to wound three additional men before several men returned fire and ended Tom's life.

"That's why you always send your biggest dumbass to check on who is still alive after a shootout. Okay, boys, get everything of value out of here and get back to the hunt," the leader said.

One of the men returned to the truck and was searching for more weapons when he found the man lying on the floor in tears.

"Hands up, motherfucker," he yelled.

The man held his hands up in a manner to show that he was surrendering. Several other bikers ran over to the cab to see what was going on.

"Well, I'll be a son-of-a-bitch," one of the bikers said. "Mark Williams, is that you?"

The man did not answer.

"Don't you remember me from high school? I'm Tom Haines. We took algebra together. Fat lotta good that class is doing for us now, huh?"

The man looked up and recognized his old classmate. He nodded to acknowledge that he was indeed Mark Williams.

"Boys, it's our lucky day. This here piece of shit is a Mormon, aren't you, Mark? I'm betting that all of these guys were Mormons, too, and I am betting that they have lots of supplies, ain't that right, Mark?"

Mark looked stunned, betrayed.

"Where is your camp?" the leader of the bikers asked.

Mark did not respond.

"This is how this works," the leader began. "When I ask a question, you answer or I cut off a body part. The first question was free. Now, let me try this again. Where is your camp?"

"There is no camp," Mark stated unconvincingly.

"Wrong answer, cut off an ear."

Mark looked at the man, finding it hard to believe that he was not joking. For a single moment, he looked at the man and recognized humor and warmth in his eyes, but the look transformed into self-satisfaction and malice as one of his minions removed Mark's left ear with a sharp knife and the flick of a wrist.

Mark screamed in pain as terror overwhelmed him. He now realized that Tom was right. He would have been much better off going out on his own terms. These men were going to torture him until he gave them what they wanted and then they would rape and pillage all of his people. Could he be strong enough to resist? He said a prayer, asking for the strength to carry on.

"Where's your camp?" the leader asked for the third time.

There was a long pause.

"Okay, bring me his dick," the man said.

"Wait, wait," Mark called out. "I'll take you to my camp. It's just a few miles away, but you have to promise that you will let me and my family live."

The leader laughed. "What the fuck are you going to do out here? You do realize that unless you are ready to do battle every minute you are going to die a bitter death, right?"

"Those are my terms."

"Fine. Wrap up his ear and let's go get us some Mormon pussy."

CHAPTER 36

When Ethan walked out onto the porch of the commissioner's office, Samantha's back was to him. She was talking to one of the men who was standing in front of her. Cowboy noticed Ethan and came over to him.

"Hey, be careful, I might get the idea that you worry about me," Ethan said as he scratched the dog behind the ears.

Samantha turned around at the sound of his voice. Ethan looked up from where he was petting the dog and locked on to her in the eyes with his. She gave him a genuine smile. Ethan smiled back. They held each other's gaze for a moment longer than they needed to.

"Dinner is started. It should be ready by the time we get to my place," she said with a sheepish grin.

"Great, I can hardly wait," Ethan replied.

Even one of the guards on the porch had a grin on his face. It was a nice human moment. It was like stepping back in time before the virus showed up. Everyone felt it and seemed to recognize it as not many of those moments had been happening lately.

Sam led the way as they headed north away from the dump.

"It's not very far. A little over two miles," she said.

"Ya, okay, no hurries," Ethan said. He was just enjoying walking with her.

Samantha smiled.

"So, what did you and the commissioner talk about?" she asked.

Ethan filled her in. When he got to the commissioner's confession, for lack of a better term, about finding his family, she stopped walking. She never turned around and he could tell that she didn't want him to see her face. Samantha rubbed the sleeve of her shirt across her eyes.

"Can I ask how you two knew each other before all this happened?" Ethan asked.

She started hiking again. A minute or two went by.

"We belonged to Alcoholics Anonymous together," she said. She stopped and turned around. They were going up a slight hill so Ethan was looking up at her.

"Oh," Ethan said. "I wish I wouldn't have been so honest about how much he and I had to drink during our talk."

She kind of chuckled.

"Don't worry, I'm not the AA police."

"No worries," Ethan said with a worried look on his face.

"Shit, they don't have AA police, do they?" he wondered.

"I don't think he's following the rules anymore," he said and then felt stupid for the comment. She stopped and turned around again.

"It's okay, Ethan," she said.

He noticed she used his first name. It sounded nice coming from her.

"It's a long story," she said. "You get close with each other in AA. It's on a different kind of level. Everybody becomes family and you become a part of everyone's family. Good parts and bad. The word friendship doesn't cover it. You're saved from a common peril. Booze being the peril," she paused.

"It's more like being a survivor is a better description, somehow. Like I said, it's hard to explain. But, to survive one virus, sort of, to speak only to… Anyway, it's a long story."

"Someday if you feel like telling it, I've got nothing but time," he said.

"No, you don't, at least not right now," she replied, "but thanks."

"My place is on the other side of this clump of trees. Let's hope Mike has been working on dinner and not his next batch of moonshine."

She had a small place. As they approached, Mike was standing on the porch smoking. He flipped his cigarette out into the yard.

"It's on the table getting cold, waiting for you two." He turned around and walked into the house.

"Somebody is a little put out that we're late for dinner," she said.

They both chuckled and went inside.

When he was finished eating, Ethan slid his plate away.

"I gotta tell ya, that was some of the best fried chicken I've ever eaten and that's no bullshit," he said.

"Thanks," Mike replied. "I kinda take pride in my chicken."

Samantha stifled a chuckle.

"What?"

"Nothing, nothing. Like Ethan said, that was a great dinner. Thanks for making it, Mike."

"Ethan, you promised to tell us why you're walking around outfitted like Ma Bell," she said turning toward him.

"Yes, I did."

"Well, before we get going, I'm going to grab me something to fortify the cup of herbal tea Samantha is going to offer us. I'll grab you some too, Ethan."

"Ah, thanks but no thanks," Ethan replied.

"Suit yourself," Mike said as he walked out.

"Ethan, you don't have to pass up Mike's offer because of me telling you I'm an alcoholic," Sam said.

"I know, it's not that. It's just, I mean, I don't feel like having one."

She looked at him and realized he wasn't having a drink because he was uncomfortable drinking in front of her. It was because he liked her and didn't want to make or do anything that would alter her feelings.

"Okay," she said.

Mike reentered with a cup in his hand.

"Okay, let's have it."

Ethan looked at both of them and told them that everything he was going to tell them was the truth, and he told them he was going to tell them everything.

"There's this guy, his name is Victor Kraus," he started, and he told the whole story.

When he was done, they both stared at him and then looked at each other and then back to him.

"Alright then, let's go get this fucker," Mike said, feeling a little gung-ho because he'd made several more trips to get "cream" for his tea as he put it.

"Glacier is a pretty big place," Samantha replied.

"How well do you know it?" Ethan asked.

"I know it very very well," she said. "I've hiked every part of it and more than once. Every time it's like the first time."

"So, have you got any theories on where you'd hold up if you were a mad scientist?" Ethan asked her.

"Ya, actually I do. And, if we head into the park from the North Fork area, we'll be able to check them out one at a time as we move deeper into the park. But, if the guy is just in a tent someplace, I mean like I said, it's a big park. Need more tea?" she asked.

"I'll have another cup. It's pretty good," Ethan said.

"Bullshit," Mike said. "You drinking the same tea I am? And no, I don't want another cup. Anymore so-called *tea* and I won't be able to stagger home."

"The taste kinda grows on you," Samantha said as she poured Ethan's tea.

"So do warts," Mike replied, "and I don't care for them, either. So, if we are done talking about this Victor asshole, what's the plan? We need a plan. A plan, man."

"You're drunk," Samantha said.

"So, what's your point?" Mike replied.

"He's right, we need a plan," Ethan said.

Mike gave Samantha an "I told you so" look and took another sip out of his cup.

"The first thing we need to do is talk with Bob in Hamilton. I missed our last designated calling time."

"So, call him," Mike said.

"I will, as soon as you give me back the phone," Ethan replied.

"Oh, yeah," Samantha said as she got up and went to the cookie jar by the sink and grabbed the phone.

"Where's the solar charger? The flour jar?" Ethan asked.

"No, it's in an empty Tampax box under the sink in the bathroom," she replied.

Mike let out a snort.

A strange voice answered Bob's phone on the third ring. It was a voice Ethan didn't recognize.

"Where's Bob Watkins?" Ethan asked with a sense of urgency in his voice.

"One moment," came the reply.

After a pause of several minutes, a familiar voice came on the line.

"This is General Short, Edwards."

"General, I need to know where Bob is and I need to know right now!"

"Calm down, he's coming. You missed your last appointed time to call, son. It's not like we're just sitting on our asses waiting on you, understand?" Short replied with a curt voice.

"Fucking generals, how come they always act like generals?" Ethan thought.

"Ethan?" Bob said sounding relieved.

"Hey…"

"You had us worried, kiddo," Bob said. "In fact, somebody else won't wait any longer to talk to you."

"Ethan?"

"Fran. It's good to hear your voice," Ethan said.

"You too, honey. I've been so worried since you missed your last call. I've just been sitting by this damn phone staring at it, waiting for it to ring."

"Really? Sorry to worry you like that, Fran," Ethan said, wishing he could see General Short's face.

"Ethan, you just stay safe and come back to us. We need you to come back to us, okay?"

Before Ethan could respond, he could tell Fran had started crying. And even though she had taken the phone away from her mouth, he heard her say something to Bob.

"I don't give a shit what they're telling you, Bob, I'm not hanging up before I tell this boy I love him."

"Fran?" Ethan said.

"Yes, Ethan?"

"Fran, I love you, and I promise I'm coming back. You can take that to the bank."

"I love you, too, and I'm going to hold you to that promise. I better give the phone back to Bob before somebody has a flipping cow. Be safe."

When Ethan knew Bob was back on the line, he told him about running into Samantha and Mike. And then about the dump and the commissioner.

"Bob, I've told Samantha and Mike pretty much everything," Ethan said when he was done.

"By everything, just what do mean, Edwards?" General Short asked.

"I mean everything, General."

"Are you sure that was—?"

"What's done is done," Bob interjected before Ethan and the general could go at each other.

"If Ethan thought he should tell them, then we back him on it," Bob said.

"Thanks, Bob. In fact, I need their help and they've agreed to provide it. Samantha has hiked Glacier Park extensively. And frankly, obviously I can find Glacier Park, but from that point on, I'm pretty much a tourist," Ethan explained.

There was a short pause.

"Can you put her on the phone?" Bob asked.

Ethan handed Sam the phone.

"He wants to talk to you."

"Hello?" Samantha said tentatively into the phone.

"Hello, this is Doctor Bob Watkins. May I ask if you prefer to go by Samantha or Sam?" he asked.

"Depends on how much trouble I'm in and who's asking."

"Well, I can assure you that you are in no trouble with me. In fact, I would like to thank you for helping my friend Ethan. I'm going to call you Sam, you sound a bit more like a Sam as opposed to a Samantha. Sam, when you and Ethan find Victor Kraus, I need to get to him. For reasons that Ethan can explain, if he hasn't already. I'm pretty sure I've got an airplane and a pilot. All I need is a place to land. That's kinda the extent of my plan. What are your thoughts?"

The phone was quiet for a minute.

"Baab," Samantha said after thinking for a minute, referring to a small Native American hamlet just outside the park.

"There's a landing strip at Baab. Actually, it's kinda between Baab and Saint Mary."

"We believe that Victor is in the Many Glaciers area, either at the lodge there or perhaps at Sperry Chalet. If we can land at Baab, what's the time frame for getting to him?" Bob asked.

"You could get to both places in a day. Many Glaciers is real doable. The chalet would be a really good hump."

"Thank you, Sam, could you please put Ethan on the phone again?"

"Ya, Bob?"

"So for right now, here's the plan. After you find this bastard, we meet up at this airstrip Sam told me about at Baab. Then we go get Dr. Kraus."

"Sounds good. We'll take off tomorrow morning. Hopefully, I'll be in touch in a couple of days. Talk to you then," Ethan said.

"Be careful. Talk to you then," Bob said and hung up.

Bob turned around to see Fran standing there with her arms folded looking at him.

"We touched on my leaving earlier," he said.

"Yes, we did, but how long have you known that you were going to do this?" she asked.

"For a little while," he answered. "There's no other way, Franny. It's really our only hope, and it's a slim one at that. I can tell you're mad and I'm sorry."

"I'm not mad. Okay, I'm mad, but not because you're going. I'm mad because you didn't tell me that you were actually going in after this guy," she said.

"I didn't want to worry you."

"I believe that when you say it, but it's still a chickenshit deal on your part. You go and get this vaccine and get your ass back to me, you understand me, Robert Watkins?" she said as she put her arms around him and squeezed him tight.

"I'll be back," Bob said in a very bad Arnold Schwarzenegger accent. "I love you, Franny. You're the one."

Ethan, Sam, and Mike discussed their route through the park while Mike had a few more of his special teas.

"Well, we better hit the sack, we've got a lot of ground to cover tomorrow," Samantha said.

Mike stood up and staggered backward, the only thing preventing him from falling over was the wall.

"Jesus, Mike," Samantha said.

"Don't fuckin' start, you ain't my mother," Mike responded.

"Ethan, you can get him home, and then I'll see you in the morning."

"Ya, if I knew where to find his home," Ethan replied.

"I can find home, asshole."

"Hey, Mike, back off a little with the mean drunk routine," Ethan said in an 'I'm not putting up with any of your shit' voice.

"Okay, okay, sorry, jeez. I didn't realize you're so sensitive."

"I'll get him home," Ethan said as he took hold of Mike's arm and headed to the door.

"Come on, Cowboy," he said.

Cowboy looked up at Ethan from where he was laying on the floor with an 'I'm pretty comfortable' look. He then looked over at Samantha.

"He can sleep here tonight," she said, as she reached down and patted him.

"Tough luck, Ace," Mike said to Ethan.

"Come on let's go," Ethan said as he led Mike to the door.

"Tough luck, no shit," he thought. Actually, he wasn't sure what he thought.

CHAPTER 37

Victor sat in the courtroom looking around to see who else was present. He couldn't quite figure out how he had been captured. The judge looked forward toward him with glaring eyes that pierced his body. Victor looked at the others at his table, what appeared to be the defendant's table. He saw three unrecognizable faces, all serious looking, and one face that he knew well but could not seem to remember from where. He looked at the prosecutor's table and was shocked to see Jane Bailey sitting there with a team of attorneys.

Did she survive? He wasn't sure how she could possibly have survived such a fall. Then he looked back up at the judge's bench and he noticed that the judge had two people sitting behind him. One was Victor's father, stoically looking forward. Victor could not tell if he was pleased or upset. He never could. On the other side sat Victor's graduate school mentor, Dr. Richard Stockman, a wildlife ecologist. Then, Victor remembered to whom the face he recognized at his own table belonged; it was the face of Lesya.

"This has got to be a dream," he thought. *"I have to wake up."*

Next, George Bailey entered the courtroom, followed by Pappie Anders, and then all of the Glacier Park Rangers. Next, came several members of the Genesis Project. Victor started to squirm in his chair as the judge announced that there was a grizzly bear in the lobby that requested a moment alone with the defendant. Victor jumped in his chair trying to object as his defense team announced to the judge that they would not object to the meeting. Victor looked at Lesya who smiled maliciously.

"That bear is going to kill me," Victor tried to yell, but no words came out of his mouth.

"You have destroyed mankind and you have killed these innocent children," the judge said.

Victor turned to his defense team, begging them to not let him meet with the grizzly bear, and then he realized that his lawyers were Ben and Becca Bailey. Children. Victor tried to scream, he tried to throw himself down on the floor, but he could not move, could not utter a sound. He looked at his father's face, it stared ahead emotionless. He looked at the stream of people entering the courtroom, it was an endless line of anonymous faces. Victor had the sense that the line went on forever.

"I did it to save humanity," Victor tried to scream, but no words came out. He turned to his father's gaze, but there was nothing there, except for the stoic face and now tears.

"You should have taught me right from wrong," Victor yelled at his father. "I never knew the difference. A kid cannot learn that for himself, he needs a father to teach him that."

Suddenly, Victor was standing on the rock overlooking the drop-off from which he had pushed Jane. He looked down and realized that he was completely naked, and he tried to remove himself from the rock's edge. His feet were somehow attached to the rock, and then he looked up and saw the charging bear. It appeared to run in slow motion as is charged toward him, and he was expecting a painful impact when it hit him but instead, both he and the bear were launched painlessly off the ledge and floated slowly downward toward the rocks.

Somehow during the fall, the bear turned into his mother and held him as if he were a small child. The fall seemed to take forever, and Victor felt comforted by his mother's presence, but that comfort soon passed as Victor realized that he had landed on the rocks, but instead of being rocks, they were piles of dead human bodies of all nationalities. Victor tried to scream and run, but the bodies were everywhere, piled on him, horrible grimaces staring at him with bared teeth. Victor scrambled to the top of the pile where he found his mother waiting for him. He climbed into her lap and she held him again as if he were a baby. Victor became calm, and dozed off, only to be abruptly awakened by his mother's tears that were falling from her cheeks onto his face.

The tears changed colors from translucent to crimson red, as Victor realized his mother was crying blood. He looked down at his body and saw that his mother had stabbed him in the heart with a giant golden sword.

"You never cared, only about yourself. You are all you have ever seen," she said, mournfully.

Victor screamed as he realized he was about to die. His mother morphed back into the grizzly bear and began to violently devour his body. Victor screamed and woke himself up.

The room was dark with only the pale light of the moon sneaking in through the back window. Victor took a deep breath as reality came back to him, and he tried to shake the uneasy feeling that overcame him as he realized he was dreaming. There was a sense of relief to know that he was not being judged, and his imagination had gotten the best of him. He carefully removed himself from the bed, being careful not to awaken Ben and Becca, both of whom had been sleeping with him since they learned of their parent's deaths.

Victor got up, went to the table and poured himself a glass of cold water and took a drink. He then rubbed his eyes, and sat in a chair and attempted to make sense of the dream. Dreams had always fascinated him, even though he rarely remembered having them. This one was vivid, and it brought up several things that Victor would ponder. He found it odd that his dream treated his father as the rest of the world had seen him, whereas, Victor had a strong relationship with the man. Victor found him to be warm and generous, kind and loving. Everyone else only saw the stoic face.

Victor wondered if there was any truth to the statement he yelled at his father in the dream regarding knowing right from wrong. Had his father failed to teach him the difference? First of all, Victor never believed in such nonsense as sin or morality. He was a proud naturalist, and he always valued nature above all else. There was no reason or cause to weigh right or wrong except in how something might impact nature. After several minutes of thought, Victor disregarded the dream as unconscious babblings of the mind, and laughed it off. He crawled back into his position in the bed between Ben and Becca and went back to sleep.

The early morning light peeking through the chalet windows woke Victor, and he once again made his exit from the bed without disturbing the two children, who still slept soundly. When he returned with the sad news their parents had died, Ben and Becca at first thought he was playing some kind of practical joke. He told them he found their bodies off the ledge where it looked like their dad had fallen off and their mother had fallen, too, but only after she attempted to climb down to help their father. He thought about taking the kids to see the bodies, but when they began to sob inconsolably, he realized they believed him and proof wasn't necessary.

For the rest of that day, the kids stayed in the chalet and cried, and Victor showed them great compassion and empathy. He held them, and promised them they would be safe. He told them when they were ready, he would take them to their great uncle at the other chalet. However, Victor had his own plans regarding the uncle and the children. First of all, the uncle had to go. It was plain and simple; he was a threat. He could show up at any minute and blow everything. Second, Victor intended to win these kids over and become their father. They were going to become his progeny, the vessels that would carry his plan into the new world if he was unable to do so himself.

Victor had breakfast ready when the children awoke, and they toyed with their oatmeal, eating only a few bites before giving up. They moped around for most of that morning, and Victor knew he had to start his training of them as soon as possible. He encouraged them to get dressed and offered to take them outside to get some fresh air. They were less than enthusiastic, but he pushed for it, and they finally went outside with him. Victor suggested they go to a beautiful spot on the top of a mountain and have a memorial service for their parents, and even though they were not thrilled with the idea, the kids went along with it.

Once on top of the mountain, Victor lay a blanket on the ground and motioned for them to take a seat. Then he began the service.

"Life is precious," he started, "and life is finite. We never know from one moment to the next how much life we have. When it ends tragically, it feels unfair, like we have been robbed of the amount of life that we should have with someone we love, but the universe does not guarantee anyone any amount of time. So, we celebrate the life of George and Jane because we are grateful for the love and compassion they shared with us. We are grateful for the lives they lived and we are grateful for the love they showed to each of us. Would either of you like to say a few words?"

There was a long pause as each child looked at the ground and tried to think of something to say. Ben finally spoke up first.

"I loved Mom and Dad, and I never expected them to die so soon. Dad was so strong, and mom loved us so much. I don't know how we can live without them. But, I know they would want us to be strong and to live good lives. I know they loved me, and I know they are in heaven and they will watch over us always."

"Can we say a prayer?" Becca asked.

"Sure," Victor said. "Would you like to say it?"

Becca nodded.

"Heavenly Father, I don't know why Mom and Dad had to die, and I am afraid. We need them and we miss them and we love them. Please welcome them into heaven and help them to be with us every day as we go through life without them."

Becca began to sob, and Ben grabbed her and held her close to him.

"And help us be strong, Father, because we are just kids and we don't know what to do without them," Ben added.

"Father, we don't understand this tragedy, and we need your guidance to help us through. Please watch over these kids and help them to grow strong knowing their parents loved them and are still with them in spirit. Do you want to add anything else?" Victor asked, looking at Ben and then at Becca.

"And please let them be reunited with our puppy, Brownie, who died when she was just a baby," Becca added.

"And please let them know that we love them and we will do everything we can to make them proud of us," Ben added.

"And as we go forward, help us turn the grief that we feel into a strong sense of love and purpose. Help us to take the things they stood for, love of nature, a sense of adventure, and passion for peace into every day we are alive. Help us celebrate their lives by the way we live our lives," Victor stated.

When everyone was had said all that they could think to say, Victor closed out the prayer.

"In your sweet name we pray, Jesus Christ, Amen."

Afterwards, Victor invited them to take a few minutes and absorb the scenery around them and then tell a few stories about their family.

"I remember when I was just six years old, I got a hold of some matches and I accidentally caught our shed on fire," Ben said. "I was able to get the fire out before it burned the shed down, and then I tried to cover up the burn marks with mud. When Dad went into the shed later that day, he saw it was burned and he asked me about it. I lied to him and told him I didn't know what happened. He could tell that I was lying, but instead of getting mad at me, he just asked me a bunch of questions. When I didn't answer his questions, he knew I did it. I was so afraid he was going to be mad at me. But instead of getting mad, Dad hugged me and told me he was glad I was okay. Afterwards, he took me out behind the shed and taught me how to build a fire the proper way. He told me fire was an important tool and that one should know how to use fire in the proper way so it was useful and did not cause any damage. I am so grateful he was nice to me and taught me how to use fire."

"Mom was also very patient. She would teach me how to play dress up, and she always told me dressing up and makeup were not what made me beautiful. She always said beauty was inside me, not on the outside, and dressing up was not about making me more beautiful, but it was really about looking nice for those around me. Mom always said I was beautiful on the inside and the outside," Becca said.

After the three of them were finished with the memorial service, they hiked back to the chalet and Victor prepared lunch. The kids were a little more hungry and ate their lunches without hesitation. Afterwards, Victor wasted no time in teaching the kids about his doctrine.

Over the next few days, Victor delved right in, teaching the children about nature and ecology. He hoped he would have the entire winter to teach them, but he could not be certain. Even in one of the most remote places on earth, he had already encountered and had to kill more than a half-dozen people. He had to be prepared with Plan B as soon as possible.

One morning, Victor took the children to the spot Pappie had taken him to observe grizzly bears. The three of them sat down on the very spot where Pappie died, and Victor took out Pappie's field glasses and showed the kids the sow grizzly bear and what appeared to be a second-year cub. The kids were really excited to see the animals, and Victor took advantage of their excitement.

"That is nature," he said. "Do you think that your mother loved you more than the grizzly bear sow loves her cub?"

He looked at the kids to see if either of them would provide an answer.

"Yes, because we have souls," Becca finally said, even though the look on her face indicated she was not confident in her answer.

"Well, you are wrong," Victor stated emphatically, "and I'll tell you why. Nobody knows what a soul is or what God is or what love is for that matter. I don't know either, but I do know this. If we have souls, then all living things have souls, so the mother grizzly bear feels as strongly about her cub as your mother did about you. These trees around us have souls and the wisdom to breathe for the planet. The earth has a soul, a giant soul, that encompasses us all. Why do you think that only the human soul matters?" Victor looked at Becca, who appeared to be at the verge of tears.

"I don't know," she stammered.

"I'll tell you why, my dear," Victor said, using a more compassionate tone. "It's what we teach ourselves. We are the only species on the earth that has language and we use language for good purpose and for bad. Are you superior to all other life on this planet? That whole idea is born of language. When you look at the grizzly bear, do you feel superior? No, you feel respect, you feel awe, you feel a primordial connection to it, you do not feel a need to compare yourself to it. Comparison and ranking are ideas in the mind and concepts that make human beings less important and more dangerous than any other species on this planet."

Victor looked first at Becca and then at Ben.

"Do you understand?" he asked.

The kids nodded, but Victor could tell that they were nodding because they were afraid to disagree and not because they were in agreement.

"There is one thing you should know about education," Victor said. "Most people think you get an education so you can get a job and make a lot of money. That is a stupid human idea. First of all, education is not learning. Any damn fool can learn something if you pound it into his head. Education is learning how to learn, how to become your own teacher and teach yourself anything you want to know. Your education will help you see who you are, and only then can you find your true vocation. So, I don't expect you to agree with everything I say, or to absorb it without questioning it. If you disagree, let's talk about it. Silence is the enemy to education, questions are the currency. So, what are you thinking?"

"Why do you think people are so bad?" Ben asked.

"Unconscious and untrained thinking is a disease, and every human being has it. It's not that human beings are intrinsically bad—"

"What does intrinsically mean?" Becca interrupted.

"Good," Victor stated. "It means something that is built inside of you, a part of your internal makeup. So, I don't believe humans are fundamentally bad, I think they are fundamentally selfish. And here is the part that is most interesting. I think every species is fundamentally selfish. Every species has the instincts it needs to take care of itself and thrive.

That is evolution at work, and that is fundamental to what life is all about. Humans have that, too, but the problem is the ability to think and use language give humans two additional vehicles for exploiting their selfishness. They have the advantage because they can think and plan ways to outwit and outcompete other species, and they can use language to organize and to justify. These are dangerous commodities, uhh... dangerous tools if humans are not paying attention to what they are doing."

Ben looked puzzled. "I don't know what you mean when you say humans are not paying attention? How can you do anything without paying attention?"

"Often we focus on the things right in front of us without ever thinking through the consequences," Victor said. "For example, for breakfast, we had oatmeal. Where did the oatmeal come from? We did not grow it or harvest it or process it or box it up or drive it to the grocery store, who did? We don't know, and most of the time, we could care less. All we really care about is that we have food. However, each step in the process of creating oatmeal costs the earth something. Growing the plant takes nutrients and water, harvesting it takes labor which needs food and water, boxing it up requires trees for creating the packages and all manner of machinery to build the boxes and seal them, transporting them requires fossil fuels that were extracted from the earth. We pay a few dollars for a box of oatmeal, but the earth pays a huge price, and yet we never really think about that."

"But, I thought you just said thinking's a disease?" Becca asked.

"Unconscious thinking is a disease," Victor clarified. "Thinking can be very productive and very powerful if it is conscious and trained. However, most of the time, the mind rambles on and we humans stumble along completely mindless of what we are doing. That is the disease. When our instincts clash with our mindless thinking, we become addicts. Humans are addicted to everything their instincts drive them to want. Addicted to sex, addicted to power, addicted to the need for safety, addicted to procreation, addicted to comfort, addicted to safety, addicted to certainty, you name it. And the problem with all of this is we live on a planet that has limited resources. If humans are allowed to go on without limits, without balance, without thoughts about sustainability, then not only will they wipe themselves out, but they will take the planet down with them."

"Does this mean the virus thing that is killing people is a good thing?" Ben asked.

Victor was overwhelmed with a burst of emotion and wiped away a tear as he looked at the boy.

"You're getting it," he said. "That is exactly right."

CHAPTER 38

David's recovery was very slow. He could barely move for several days, and when he finally was able to get to his feet and take a couple of wobbly steps, he had to take a nap afterwards. He was weak and any exertion left him exhausted. Fortunately, Aiden had recovered remarkably well, probably due to his young age, and seemed to have no lingering disabilities. He proved to be a Godsend for David, as he needed lots of help and the young boy was up to the task. Aiden became David's eyes and legs.

"Aiden? Is it daylight outside right now?" he asked.

"Yes, the sun is up," Aiden replied.

"I there anyone else in the house?"

"No."

"Did you look in all of the rooms?"

"I think so," he replied.

"I need you to do something for me, okay?"

"Yes, sir."

"You can call me David, okay? You and me are partners now."

"Okay, David."

"Aiden, I need you to go downstairs and find a flashlight and then open every door and go into every room and tell me what you see, okay?"

"Okay."

"One of those doors will lead you to the basement and there are three rooms down there. I need you to go down there and tell me what you see, okay?"

"Okay, David, I will."

"That's a good boy. I want to know if there is any food or water or anything that looks like tools or medical supplies, okay? If you cannot tell what something is, draw a picture of it in your mind so you can describe it to me, okay?"

"Okay, but are there any ghosts in the basement?"

"I've been down there many times and never saw a ghost. It should be safe, okay?"

"Okay."

"Oh and Aiden, please look at each of the windows and tell me if any of them are broken, okay?"

"Will there be any bad guys down there?"

"No, Aiden, I think this house is safe. But, please be careful and make sure the doors are locked, okay?"

After several minutes, Aiden came back upstairs to where David was resting.

"I couldn't find a flashlight," he said. "It's too dark down there to see if there is a flashlight."

"Was it dark down there the last time you went down there?"

"No, the sun was coming through the windows then."

"That's odd," David said, thinking for a minute. "Did you hear any pounding noises since the last time you were down there?"

"Yes, it sounded like someone was building something on this house."

"I think they boarded us in," David said, wondering if they did it to protect them from intruders or to prevent the virus from leaving the house. Either way, it was clear they were not expecting survivors.

"Aiden, did Sister Anne have a flashlight?"

"Yes, she did, but I don't know where it is."

"Will you look in her pockets?"

"No, she is dead and she has a really scary look on her face."

"Okay, can you help me find her? I will crawl toward her and you lead me, okay?"

"Okay."

David managed to get into crawling position and Aiden grabbed him by both ears and gently pulled him toward Sister Anne's body. As he got closer, the stench was so bad that he was surprised that he hadn't noticed it before now. He guessed that he had become accustomed to the smell, and he knew they had to get the body out of there.

When he arrived at her body, he asked Aiden for some guidance.

"Okay, Aiden, can you take my hand and place it near her pocket?"

Aiden did so. David reached into the pocket and pulled out a rosary. He then asked for help finding the next pocket, and Aiden guided his hand a second time. In that pocket, he found a box of matches, a small candle, and a flashlight.

"Bingo," he said.

He fumbled with the flashlight, and when he clicked the switch, he asked if the light came on.

"Yes, the light is on but it is very weak," Aiden said.

"Okay, your first mission is to use this light to go downstairs and find another light or batteries, okay? Do you know what batteries look like?"

"The kind that shock you when you stick your tongue on them or the ones that are round?"

"Look for any of the round ones."

"Okay," he said and then David could hear his footsteps heading across the floor and to the door.

David felt around Sister Anne's body and realized that she was laying on the throw rug that Aunt Gertie had placed in the meditation nook. He felt around the perimeter of the rug, and noted that she was lying on it diagonally. He moved around the body to get into position and then slowly moved the body to one side of the rug. He then crawled back around and got to the front of the rug where he could roll her body up in the carpet. He worked carefully, placing the rosary on her chest before he wrapped her body tightly in the carpet.

When he was done, he felt exhausted, so he started to crawl back to the area where his bed had been. However, he lost track of which direction that was and as many times as he had meditated in that room, he had not paid close enough attention to know where he was. Therefore, he had to crawl in a couple of different directions before he figured it out and ended up back on his bed. When he did, he collapsed on the bed and fell into a deep sleep.

"There are no flashlights and no batteries anywhere downstairs," Aiden said.

David was barely coherent, but did manage to hear him.

"Okay, what else did you see?"

"This light doesn't work too well," Aiden said. "It is not so bright."

"Okay, Aiden, I think the battery must be running low. Turn it off and let me think for a minute. Are all of the windows downstairs dark?"

"Yes, it looks like day outside when I am up here, but it is really dark in all the rooms downstairs," the boy said. "The basement is really dark."

"What can you see from the window up here?"

"It's way up high so I can't see out of it."

David remembered that the two windows in this room were octagon-shaped designer windows that were about 4 feet up the attic wall on the front and back walls.

"Okay, let me get up and put you on my shoulders so you can see out them."

David attempted to get the boy on his shoulders and then get to his feet, but he was too weak. He could barely get his own body to stand upright, and after doing that, he felt weak enough that he thought he might collapse. So, he managed to get into the crawl position in front of the window on the front side of the house.

"Okay, Aiden, can you climb up on my back and see out the window?"

"Yes."

The boy climbed up on David's back and looked out the window.

"What do you see?"

The boy was silent.

"Aiden, I need you to tell me what you see."

"Uhhh, there is black smoke in the sky, and it looks like a lot of houses have been on fire," he said with his voice shaking. "It looks like someone took an eraser and erased some of the houses across the street."

"Do you see anyone out there?"

Aiden looked as best as he could up and down the street.

"It doesn't look like there is anyone at home in any of the houses. There are some dogs running around. There is an old black man who looks like he is walking in circles at the end of the street."

"What does he look like?"

"He is wearing a hat that has an Indian head on it, and he has gray hair and a lot of hair on his face."

"Can you see his hands?"

"They are in his pockets. He has a backpack on that has a big N on it and it is red."

"Does he have a tattoo on his neck?"

"I can't tell," Aiden said. "His neck is too far away."

"I think his name is Keno," David said. "If it is who I think it is, he is a homeless man who used come here for dinner sometimes. Do you think you could climb out the window and stand on the porch roof and yell to him? He might be able to rip the boards off our front door so we can get out of here and go get some food and water."

"I'm scared, because it's a long way down to the roof."

"No, Aiden, it is the same distance as you just climbed. You will just have to jump down a couple of feet and then you can go to the edge of the porch and yell his name."

"Will he understand me, David? He looks like he is lost and just going round and round."

"Yes, he gets real nervous, but he will understand you and he will be happy to know I am okay."

"How does the window open?"

"There is a latch at the top and bottom that you pull toward you and then push on the top of the window and it will pivot open. There should be just enough room for you to slide out."

Aiden opened the window, and as David predicted, there was just enough space for Aiden to climb through the opening head first. David tried to stand up and grab the boy's legs to prevent him from diving headfirst onto the roof of the porch, but he was too late. By the time he had reached his feet, the boy was uncomfortably laying on the porch roof, crying and holding up his scraped hands that had taken the brunt of the fall.

"Aiden, are you alright?"

"No, I hurt my hands," he said, holding them up for David to see.

"So sorry about that, will you be okay?"

The boy sniffed and shook his head.

"Can you yell to Keno? Yell his name."

Aiden wiped his eyes and got to his feet. He then walked closer to the edge of the porch roof and yelled at the man who was walking in circles at the end of the block about a 100 feet from the boy.

"Keno," the boy yelled. "Hey, Keno, I am up here."

When Keno heard his name being called, he stopped pacing and tilted his head upward. When he heard it the second time, he turned in the direction of the voice and saw the boy standing on the porch roof. He walked toward the boy.

"He's coming."

"Good, Aiden, that is very good. Let me know when he gets here."

"Keno, it's David Gilbert and this is my friend, Aiden. We are trapped in this house and it is boarded up. Can you help us?"

Keno wasn't sure what was going on. He had heard Mr. Gilbert got the Ebola and died, and he was afraid the house was filled with the virus.

"Is he looking up at us?" David asked Aiden.

"No, he is looking at the ground and walking in circles," Aiden said.

"Keno, I need you to break into the front door. We need food and water or we are going to die in here."

Keno was a homeless man who had lived on the streets of Washington, DC for years, maybe decades. He was among a large population of street people who were functionally mentally impaired. He was able to do basic functions and take care of basic problems, but he lacked the capacity to work and manage his life. He was bright and capable, but often seemed to slip off into a different world.

"Aiden, is he coming?"

"No, David, he left. He's walking away from us now."

David sighed. The situation was bleak. There was no food, and no water in the house. David did not know how long it had been since they had consumed the last of the milk jugs full of water that Sister Ann had brought upstairs with her. David tried to remember the last time that he took a drink, but could not remember if it was one or two days ago.

"Aiden, grab my hand and let me bring you back inside, okay?"

David felt Aiden's hand and lifted the small boy back up and through the window. Having been exposed to the fresher air outside provided context for how bad the attic smelled because of Sister Anne's decomposing body. Aiden gagged when the smell hit him. Unfortunately, he had nothing in his stomach to throw up.

Aiden led David by the hand back to his bed and helped him get settled and covered up. The activities of the day had completely exhausted David, and he needed to rest. He wasn't sure how much of his malaise was due to his recovery from the virus and how much was due to a lack of food and water. Regardless, he needed to sleep. When David stirred a couple of hours later, he realized that Aiden was lying right beside him.

CHAPTER 39

The hike to Sula, MT took Lamar and Larry about two days. They spent the first night in a dried-out drainage culvert that was several yards away from the highway. At first light, they were up and walking north, just out of sight of the highway, but using it as a guide. They managed to walk about 15 miles the first day, and knew that they would have a few less miles the next.

"I sure wish I had known we would be walking long distances," Lamar said, as he removed his tennis shoes and looked at the blisters forming on the bottom of his feet.

"I really had no idea that it was this bad out here," Larry said. "I figured things would get crazy with this pandemic going on, but I figured it would mostly be on the east coast, and maybe in the large population areas, like California. I figured we would be pretty safe out here in God's country."

"Me, too," Lamar said. "We had it pretty good back at camp."

The two men ate a few of the rations they had in their pockets, and filled their water bottles in the river. They then scouted out a place to sleep for the night and decided they would sleep in the timber just above the highway, but far enough away that they would not be spotted.

"What does your cousin do in Sula?" Lamar asked.

"Well, he was a logger for many years, but last I heard, he had some type of accident, so he got out of it. He was building log cabins last I heard."

"When did you talk to him last?"

"He and I were never close, but I always kept up with him through my mother. He is her brother's son. Last time I saw him was about three years ago at his dad's funeral."

"I hope he can help us."

"He's the rugged type, so I am betting he will be hunkered down and will be able to help us if he doesn't shoot us first!"

"The way things have been going, we could use a little good luck and a few blessings," Lamar said.

The next morning at first light, the two were up and on the move. The night was uneventful; however, it certainly was not enough time to heal their sore feet. Lamar put on the same socks and shoes, and took a few tender steps as his feet acclimated to walking again.

"Let's start this day with a prayer," Lamar said.

Larry bowed his head and Lamar said a few words, asking for strength and protection as they made their journey, and then the two men set off. Along the way, they encountered a few homesteads from a distance, but only looked at them through a set of binoculars Lamar carried with him. Some of them looked like they had been burned, others seemed to be intact. There was no sign of activity at any of them. They decided it was too risky to investigate any of these. When they finally arrived in the small town of Sula, it was late evening, and they decided that the safe thing to do would be to hike into his cousin's place through the woods so no one would see them coming.

"My cousin lives on the edge of town on a small farm," Larry said. "We should be able to get there and to the house by following the timberline behind his place."

"Are there any other houses in that timber?" Lamar asked.

"No, he owns that land and vowed to never sell it off."

The two men trudged through the trees until they saw the cousin's homestead. Lamar looked through his binoculars, saw no activity, and handed them to Larry.

"Where do you think he would be?" Lamar asked.

"Not sure, but I can pretty much promise you he will be guarding the front entrance. I think our safest move would be to knock at the back door and announce ourselves."

The two men darted quickly from the tree line to the back door and Larry knocked loudly.

"Randy, this is your cousin Larry, are you in there?"

The two men stood on either side of the door, protected by logs that were part of the house.

"Randy, we need your help, I am here with my friend Lamar. Are you there?"

There were no signs of anyone in the house and the grounds were eerily quiet. Just as Lamar and Larry were about to move toward the front of the house, they heard rustling behind them. Larry looked back first, just in time to see his cousin's rifle pointed at them.

"Larry, what the hell are you doing here?" he asked. "And, who is this with you?"

Larry felt instant relief when he recognized his cousin and watched him lower his weapon. Over his cousin's shoulder, he could see the hideout he had emerged from. It was basically a small room that had been buried underground with a thatched lid completely concealing it when it was closed. Randy was protecting his house from the hideout.

"It's been a while," Larry said, "you look good. We came here because we need your help."

"I'm afraid that I don't have much to offer," Randy said. He moved toward the two men with a noticeable limp. When he got close enough to Larry, he reached out an arm and offered a half-hug.

"The name is Randy," he said as he extended his hand toward Lamar. "Nice to meet you. Not been meeting too many new folks, lately."

Lamar took his hand and shook it, feeling relieved the man seemed to be welcoming them.

"So, what brings you to these parts?"

"Well, actually, we are headed to Glacier Park, but have encountered nothing but trouble so far," Larry said. "The world has gone to hell, and we have seen it firsthand."

"It's showed up around here, too. Fear tore through this town and pretty much set the stage for anarchy. It's every man for himself."

"Have you seen signs of the virus here?" Larry asked.

"That's the least of our worries. When the power went down, folks assumed the worst. Fact is, most folks around here believe the virus was released by the US Government to reduce the population. They have gone into combat mode. At least the ones who are trying to protect themselves. It seems others have taken this as an opportunity to do whatever the hell they want."

"It's sad that it has come to this," Lamar said. "Just when we need to band together, everyone seems to have gone completely rogue."

"Why are you going to Glacier Park? Seems like the wrong time for a vacation," Randy said with a chuckle.

"We picked up a signal on the ham radio. It seems that some military types believe that the man who started the pandemic is hiding out up there and he has a vaccine."

"No shit?"

"That's what we heard. We felt that we had to go check it out," Lamar stated, suddenly questioning the wisdom of making the trek under these circumstances.

"Well, that seems like a long shot, and it doesn't look like you have much in the way of supplies," Randy said.

"Well, that's where you come in, if you are willing," Larry said. "We are hoping that you can help set us up for the trip. We started out with a truck full of supplies and several men, but we barely made it out of Salmon before we encountered trouble. There's a motorcycle gang running things down there now, and they are not so nice."

"Fucking Californians, I'll bet you anything," Randy said. "They come in here and buy up our land during the good times and then their thugs come to take everything when the world is coming to an end."

"Probably so," Larry said. "So, if you were going to Glacier these days, how would you go about it?"

"There's really only one way to travel now and that's on horseback. Any vehicle will draw too much attention, and besides that, the pulse knocked out a lot of them. A good horse can get you 30-40 miles a day pretty easily, but even so, that's still gonna take you a week."

"Well, given that it has taken us about three days and two vehicles to get here, that sounds pretty reasonable," Lamar said. "Do you have horses we could use?"

"Thing is, I have a couple of good horses, but that is all I have," Randy said. "How sure are you there will be a vaccine at the end of the rainbow?"

"Well, we are willing to bet our lives on it," Larry said.

"Okay then," Randy said. "I am not planning on going anywhere anyway, so I reckon I could donate a couple of horses to the cause. What is your plan with the vaccines if you find them?"

"To save humanity if we can," Lamar said. "I'm not sure how many there are, but if we can help get them to the right people, then I do believe that will make a difference."

Randy thought for a moment, and then motioned for them to follow him into the house. He unlocked the door and entered and the two men followed him. The inside of the house was completely dark because he had boarded up all of the windows, and he did such a good job of it that even the late evening light outside did not penetrate it. A few steps inside the door, he stopped and lit a kerosene lamp, which illuminated a rustic entryway that led to the kitchen. He motioned for them to have a seat at the kitchen table, while he secured the back door.

"Have you had anyone out here raising trouble?" Larry asked.

"Well, I pretty much have the entire property booby trapped, so there have been a few attempts, but so far, no one has made it to the house. You two were the first to come in from the back. I've been expecting someone to try that, so I set up a patrol out there."

Randy reached into a cabinet a removed a gallon-sized baggie filled with dark rectangles and placed it on the table.

"Venison jerky. I am sure you boys are a little hungry," he said.

"Oh, man, the good stuff!" Larry exclaimed, digging into the bag and then handing it to Lamar who grabbed a couple of pieces.

"How are you set for weapons?" Randy asked.

"We have none. They were all stolen."

"So, what do you expect to find in Glacier Park? Is this guy alone, or is he going to have an army with him?"

"According to the radio report I heard last, he was alone. We are expecting him to be holed up, probably in one of the chalets, waiting for the world to come to an end," Lamar said, as he realized he never really considered the question until Randy had just asked it.

"Well, I'll give it to you guys," Randy said. "You got balls. You are still trekking on with no supplies, no weapons, and no means of transportation."

"We sent a couple of men back to camp to get a new vehicle and some more supplies a couple of days ago. They were going to meet us here, but I am assuming you haven't seen them," Larry said.

"Nope."

"I hope they are okay," Lamar said tentatively, knowing that it was not a good sign they had not made it yet. "Hopefully, they will get here in a day or two."

"Well, for the sake of humankind, and because I am a sucker for relatives," Randy began, "I will set you guys up. I'll give you a couple of horses, enough rations for a couple of weeks, and a couple of guns, but you should leave at first light. Things are so uncertain in this town I am afraid if you wait for your friends, they may come here and find us all dead."

The three men spent the next hour or so mapping out a route to Glacier Park. They agreed that they should avoid all of the towns along the way, so they mapped out a route through Lolo National Forest that took them just west of Highway 93 North.

"The problem is," Randy said, "you are going to have to cross Interstate 90, but I would do so several miles west of Missoula. I heard things are bad there. Hamilton is pretty much locked down by the military, so if you go anywhere near there, you will likely be detained. I would cross west of Missoula and then stay east of Highway 83 until somewhere between Seeley Lake and Condon. That is where I would cross over into the Flathead National Forest and then take it all the way to Glacier Park, staying west of Swan Lake. That's some rugged country through there, so it will take some doing to get through it, but at least you will be fighting the terrain and not hostile humans."

"That sounds like a good plan," Larry said. "Have you ever ridden through there?"

"Oh hell no," Randy said. "I logged up through there a couple of times over the years and hunted elk in some of that country, but never on horseback. You both good with horses?"

Lamar smiled. "I rode them a few times when I was a boy, but I am afraid I haven't had much practice as an adult. Hopefully, it will be like riding a bike... you never forget how?"

Randy laughed and shook his head. "Are you sure you two are up for this?"

Lamar and Larry looked at each other and then both men nodded in unison.

"Alright then," Randy said. "Well, make yourselves comfortable for the night. There's some fresh water in a jug by the sink. You can sleep in the two bedrooms down the hall there. I will keep an eye on things so you two can get good and rested. You are going to need all the strength you can muster, and this may be the last decent night's sleep you see for a while."

The next morning at first light, Randy had them all outfitted and ready to go. He provided each man with a sleeping bag, a rifle, a pistol, and enough food and ammo to get them to the park. He also provided a few other essentials, including matches, a hatchet, bug spray, a couple of jackets, and a pair of heavy duty wire cutters.

"You're gonna have to cut a few fences along the way," he said when he saw the confused look on Lamar's face. "Can you think of anything else?"

When they were certain that they had everything that they needed, the two men climbed on the horses and headed north through the trees leading away from Randy's cabin.

Riding on the back of a horse was a lot harder than Lamar remembered from his childhood days. The constant pounding on his crotch quickly became about as painful as anything he remembered, and it was only about two days into the trip he noticed that the constant friction was rubbing a hole in the Mormon garments that he had received several years earlier at a Nauvoo endowment ceremony he was blessed enough to be able to attend at the main temple in Salt Lake City. When they stopped for the night, he brought the subject up with Larry.

"Are your garments wearing a little thin?" he asked.

"Yeah, and so is the skin they are covering!" Larry exclaimed.

"What do you suppose we should do about that?"

"I have no idea," Larry said, "but I'm not taking them off."

"No, I guess we'll just have to endure it. I guess God will understand under the circumstances."

The trail over the next few days was rugged, and Lamar and Larry moved slowly. They finally decided that it was impossible to stick to the original plan of traveling only in the national forest and opted instead to follow close to the highway where the terrain was a little more favorable. This put them at greater risk of being seen, but they reasoned that they would be better off taking their chances than killing themselves on the side of a steep mountain with a couple of skittish horses.

So, once they made it across Interstate 90 west of Missoula, they stayed in the national forest until they were north of Seeley Lake and then they followed MT 83 N until they were just about to Bigfork. As they traveled through the Swan Valley, the natural beauty was spectacular, and it was eerily quiet. They were fortunate enough to not encounter any traffic on the highway, and they were very careful when they came across any signs of former civilization.

"This valley has got to be the most beautiful place on earth," Lamar said.

"I agree. I have never been here before, and I regret I never spent time here," Larry replied.

"I just can't imagine this place wouldn't be swarming with people. The weather is beautiful, the lake is calm and peaceful, and these mountains are just spectacular."

"I suspect that if folks are around, they are sticking pretty close to their hideouts. That's good for us, given our track record."

They decided to travel through the small town of Swan Lake at first light, hoping that if there was trouble in this town, they would be able to avoid it. The town was small with only a few buildings and a bunch of lake houses. As they rode through, being careful to stay as far into the forest as they could, they noticed that many of the business had been destroyed, probably by looting. Some had been burned, and all had windows broken out. It did not take them long to make it through the town and they made it without seeing anybody.

"I wonder if the virus made it this far?" Lamar asked.

"If I understood the news correctly, I don't think that any place was immune. That guy planned out the attack in every detail."

"There will be a special place in Hell for that man," Lamar stated reassuringly. "Hopefully, he will be taken into custody so anyone who survived will be able to get a little closure on this. The human race needs to be able to heal after this," Lamar said.

It took them two days to get from Swan Lake to just north of Bigfork. They were about five miles due east of Kalispell in the Flathead National Forest when they encountered their first human. They had set up camp there the night before, and Larry started a fire in the morning to boil some water for coffee. After they had breakfast and enjoyed a little coffee, they put the saddles on their horses and were about to mount them for the next leg of their journey when they heard the sound of a human voice.

"What brings you boys to these parts?" a man in a cowboy hat asked. The man speaking looked friendly enough, and he wore a star on his shirt indicating he could be law enforcement. The three men with him did not look so friendly.

The voice startled Larry, who was closest to them, and he turned quickly to see who was speaking. Lamar reached for his pistol and was about to pull it out when the man spoke again.

"No need for guns, gentlemen, I am the sheriff in these parts and I just need to know what you are up to."

Lamar relaxed his grip on the pistol and looked at the man.

"Just passing through," he said.

"The problem is; we have had a lot of folks who were just passing through lately who ended up causing a lot of problems. Seems that you can't really trust folks these days."

"We are headed to Glacier Park," Larry offered.

"Park's closed these days," the sheriff stated. "You may want to find another vacation destination. I hear Hawaii is nice this time of year."

The men with the sheriff laughed.

"We are not breaking any laws, Sheriff, and we really do not intend to stay here for very long. We expect to make it to the park in a day or two."

"What business do you have in the park? Last I heard, the park was closed until further notice and it is a federal crime to enter it," the sheriff said.

Lamar gave Larry a look that indicated they should not disclose why they wanted to go to the park. The look was not missed by the sheriff.

"Okay boys, here is how we will handle this," the Sheriff started. "This county is run by Commissioner Anthony Harms. I will take you two to him and you can negotiate your plans with him."

"And if we refuse?" Larry asked.

"That's simple," the sheriff stated. "These men with me are trained to stop anyone who is a threat to the county, by arrest or otherwise. If you refuse to follow direct orders from the sheriff, that makes you a threat to Flathead County."

Larry looked at Lamar, who was contemplating the situation.

"Well, we are not here to make trouble. We are Mormons and we want to do the right thing," Lamar stated. "So, we would be willing to do whatever is required."

"I'm glad to hear that, gentlemen. I'm going to need your weapons," the Sheriff said.

CHAPTER 40

You might say that Felix Francis Williams was born into the eye of the storm. He was born in the mid-1960s in southern California to a drug-addicted hooker who had little time and absolutely no patience for inconveniences. The only reason that she kept possession of the baby at all was because it afforded her the opportunity to collect a welfare check and a couple hundred dollars each month in food stamps, which she promptly spent on the drugs of her choice. From a very young age, Felix was left to care for himself in whatever rundown hotel room his mother had rented. The boy never knew his father, but then again, neither did his mother. Fortunately, for Felix, he made a friend at one of these cheap rent-by-the-week hotels, a girl about his same age named Sadie. She always called him Felix Francis and he called her Sadie Sue, even though her middle name was Marie.

Sadie was in a similar situation as Felix in that her only caregiver was an alcoholic father who rarely provided even the most basic necessities, leaving the girl to scramble for food and clothes. Felix and Sadie had met at the Royal Court Inn when both of their parents landed there, and became fast friends when they realized they were in the same boat. After the two met for the first time at around age eight, they were inseparable, and they spent nearly all of their time together scavenging for food and committing petty crimes to get goods and occasionally money for the things they needed.

Given the transient lifestyle of the parents, however, it was only a matter of weeks before one of the parents would move on to the next cheap hotel taking their child with them. Fortunately for the two friends, all of the cheap hotels were in the same rundown section of the city, and so the two friends were always able to track each other down and did what they had to in order to hang out together.

Sadly, the friendship ended only a few years later when Sadie's father murdered her while in a drunken stupor. He had come back to the hotel in the early morning hours and demanded she give him all of her money. Sadie and Felix had broken into a paper machine by a bus stop and had stolen about $14.00 in quarters, but Sadie was not about to give the money up to her drunken father. When she refused to hand over the money, her father charged her, grabbed her by the throat, and strangled her to death. Whether he meant to go that far is a mute point, and one that Felix never even thought about.

When Felix arrived at the room the next morning to get Sadie to hang out for the day, he found the door of the room was cracked open. He pushed it all the way open and stepped inside to find Sadie laying on the bed. Her face was pale and her eyes were open and vacant. Felix knew instantly she was dead. Sadie's father was also in the room, on his knees beside her weeping inconsolably.

"I killed her," he mumbled. "I just wanted the money, and she wouldn't give to me."

It is impossible to express in words what Sadie meant to Felix. To say that she was his only friend, the only person on the planet that cared about him, or the only person he ever knew that valued him were inadequate. She was the only sense of hope in Felix's entire life. As he looked at her lifeless form on the bed, that hope died. His heart, which had been opened slightly by her, snapped closed in that moment, and Felix was reborn into a different person.

There was no more hope in his life, no more thoughts of a peaceful or meaningful life, no desire for a happy future. Felix vowed to himself that no one would ever hurt him again. Before he left the hotel room, he stopped and picked up a heavy brass lamp and returned to where Sadie's father was kneeling.

"You are a worthless piece of shit," he screamed.

He then savagely beat the drunk man to death with the lamp. This was the turning point in Felix's life, and he never relied on another soul for anything after that day. For the next several years, he lived on the streets, became involved with a local gang, and rapidly turned into one of the most violent teens on the streets. He was arrested many times over the years for theft and vandalism, and he was sent to foster care on multiple occasions, but usually ran away within a couple of hours or within a few days if the place proved worthy of a little rest. A short stint at a youth detention center helped him realize he needed to be smarter about the crimes he committed, and he quickly learned it was much better to operate within the safety a group. He thrived in the gang where his fighting abilities became revered, and he became known simply as Rage.

At the age of 17, Rage tried to join a local chapter of Hell's Angels, but was unable to make it into the organization because he simply did not play well enough with others. During his probationary period with the organization, he nearly beat to death the man who was sponsoring him. He had no loyalty to anyone, and his male ego could not allow any man to be his leader. He had to be the alpha male. Rage soon formed his own motorcycle group, known as The Devil's Dark Knights. The organization was constantly in flux as the membership included the rowdiest and most violent motorcyclists around, and frequently most of the Dark Knights were in jail or in prison. They spent the better part of two decades wreaking havoc wherever they were, regardless if it was on the streets or behind bars.

When the Typhon virus hit the Los Angeles metropolitan area, Rage was out on parole and rounded up 10 Dark Knights and headed northwest, fleeing from the only thing he felt could stop him. They robbed, murdered, and pillaged their way to Salmon, Idaho, a town that Rage felt was small enough and secluded enough to be safe from the virus but with enough resources to sustain the group. In Salmon, they picked up a couple of additional riders and quickly took over the town, hoarding resources, killing citizens, and taking whatever they wanted.

They established a system for controlling the highway by blocking bridges, and chasing down cars that happened to be driving by. It did not take them long to become an even a greater threat than the virus, and anyone who survived in the area, knew this motorcycle gang was far more dangerous than the Typhon virus itself.

When the Devil's Dark Knights captured Mark in the van and convinced him to take them to his Mormon camp, Rage had only one thing on his mind: comfort. When Rage and the other Dark Knights accepted Tom Haines into the motorcycle club, it was because he had claimed he could find out where the Mormons were hiding, and he could deliver years' worth of supplies, and probably a nice place to live. Rage and the Dark Knights were ready to enjoy some comfort, and were ready to have a home base.

Mark directed the Dark Knights to his group's camp even though he felt a bit like Judas as they pulled into the long gravel road that led to the compound. He wondered if they would kill everyone there, but quickly turned his thoughts to God, saying a silent prayer that his Heavenly Father would intervene and protect them. Unfortunately, no prayers were answered that day.

The Dark Knights rode into the camp with guns a blazing, shooting everyone who came out to greet them and sending the rest of the inhabitants running for cover. When the dust settled, the Dark Knights got off their bikes and went from cabin to cabin, collecting the survivors and bringing them out at gunpoint to face their leader.

"You told me my family and I could leave," Mark said to Rage. "Be a man of your word!"

Rage looked at Mark with a sympathetic look that quickly changed to delight.

"Do I look like a man of my word?"

"Please, I beg of you," Mark said.

"Is that how a man who wants to save his family begs?" Rage asked as he let out a jovial laugh.

Mark got down on his knees before Rage and begged for his family's life.

"This coward sold you all out and now he wants to take his family and leave," Rage said, speaking to the anxious group of Mormons who had been rounded up and who were being held at gunpoint before him.

"Please, I beg of you, let my people live," Mark said.

"Funny, now he wants all of you to live. Well, there ain't nothing for a Mormon to live for in this new world. Your God and all your charity and love have no place left in this world."

Rage removed a pistol from a holster on his side, placed it at point blank range on Mark's forehead, and pulled the trigger.

The crowd gasped and screamed as the gun went off, sending Mark's body to the ground.

"Okay, who wants to tell me where these men were going when they left the camp? I know that you have everything you need right here to survive for months, maybe years. Why would your men leave?"

The crowd was stunned by the murder they just witnessed, and no one spoke out.

"I guess you Jesus-loving-mother-fuckers don't understand the language of violence. Let me explain this to you. I ask a question and you answer. If you don't answer, I kill one of you. The first question was free. Why did the men leave the camp?"

Once again, the crowd remained silent.

"Okay, bring me the youngest one," Rage said.

Two Dark Knights grabbed a small boy, about three years old, tearing him from the grasp of his screaming mother and delivered the crying child to Rage.

"Look what you are doing to this poor child," Rage stated as he executed the little boy.

The crowd was outraged, and several of the men charged toward Rage and the other Dark Knights, who shot them in their tracks. Some of the women began reciting verses from the Bible as Rage continued.

"I am the shadow of death and I am not going to stop until I get what I want. Why did the men leave?"

A woman spoke up. "You are going to kill us all anyway, so why should we give you anything. You are an animal and you are going to take whatever you want. So, just kill us all and do what you do."

Rage looked at the woman, and then to the rest of the crowd.

"You are right," Rage said, "but hope is a funny thing. Bring me the next youngest child."

Two Dark Knights moved to grab a small girl who was hiding her face in her mother's chest. As they wrestled the girl away from her, the woman began to plead.

"Please, not my baby, not my baby, not my baby… They were going to Glacier Park. The men, that is where they were going…"

"Ahh, finally, someone with some common sense. Now technically, you did not answer my question. You told me *where* they were going but not *why* they were going. So, I'll give you one more chance. Why were they going to Glacier Park?"

The woman hesitated, and Rage placed his pistol on her daughter's forehead and looked the woman in the eyes.

"They were going after a man they believed has a vaccine for the Ebola virus."

"Well, now, there is an answer I can appreciate," Rage said. "Because of your honesty, you will suffer the least."

He walked over to the woman and shot her in the head. He then walked back to the little girl who was still being held in position by two Dark Knights and shot her in the head.

"Dark Knights," he bellowed in a deep and powerful voice, "kill all the men and children and let's have some fun with these fine women tonight. Tomorrow morning, we are going to Glacier Park."

CHAPTER 41

Samantha woke up to Cowboy's low growl just before she heard the knock on her door. She told Cowboy to settle down that it was just Ethan, although it was earlier than the time they'd talked about meeting. She slid into her jeans and threw on a Glacier National Park T-shirt.

"Just a sec," she called out.

Cowboy's growl picked up even more.

"Cowboy, settle down," Sam said as she stopped in front of the mirror and ran her fingers through her hair, doing with it what she could.

Then it hit her. Christ, she was acting like, well, like a girl waiting on a boy. It was then that she noticed the T-shirt she'd grabbed. The irony was not lost on her. She smiled. She kind of liked the way she was feeling. That changed when she opened the door.

Delvin Horten and his little brother Raymond were standing outside her door.

"Morning, Counselor," Delvin said and spit in the dirt. "You look good in the morning. *Real* good."

"What do you want?" Sam asked, the contempt and disgust heavy in her voice.

"Now what changed your attitude? Were you expecting somebody else when you opened the door all smiles and what not? You pick up a change in the princess's attitude, Ray, or is it just me?"

"I definitely picked up a change of attitude," Raymond replied.

Samantha didn't respond.

"Your new boyfriend around? He ain't hiding behind you is he? Tell him—"

"Get the fuck out of here, you inbred assholes, and do it now or else," Sam said.

Unfortunately, she'd let the moment of trying to intimidate them slip by when she paused. Instead, her words had the opposite effect. She saw Delvin turn and he saw fear creep into her eyes.

"You got quite the mouth on you, you know that? You think your fuckin' shit don't stink? A virus is killing off mankind and leaving behind lawyers. Guess there's certain things even a virus won't fuck with."

Raymond picked up the dangerous change in his brother. "Delvin," he said.

Delvin didn't respond he just continued to stare at Samantha.

"Delvin," Raymond said again only this time louder.

"WHAT!" he snapped at his brother.

"We ain't supposed to touch her. He made that clear. He said don't be touching her."

"Fuck him. I don't see him around here, do you? I ain't takin orders from a fucking drunk. She just got done telling us that our daddy fucked his own sister. That's what inbred means. Ain't that right, Counselor? What's a matter, you ain't got no more smart ass remarks in that pretty little mouth of yours?"

Sam was silent and she was terrified.

"You know what would look good in that pretty mouth of yours?"

Cowboy nudged Sam as he stepped through the door with his teeth bared. Delvin and his brother both took a couple of steps back. Sam thought she might have a fighting chance of getting to the pistol by her bed. Delvin slowly slid his hand down to his side and pulled out the hunting knife that always hung there.

"Raymond, you with me?" he asked.

"I hear you, bro."

"Snoopy here is going to nail me, and when the fucker does, you grab the bitch and I'm going to gut this fucking dog and then you and I are going to have some fun with the counselor."

"Bad plan," Ethan said from behind Delvin.

Delvin spun around swinging his knife hand in a wide arch.

"Grab the bitch," he yelled.

Raymond lunged at Samantha only to be met head on by over 70 pounds of purebred pissed off German shepherd. Cowboy went for Raymond's throat. Raymond blocked the dog with his forearms. Both went to the ground with Cowboy on top of him.

Ethan had anticipated Delvin spinning around and left enough distance between himself and the knife-wielding man. Delvin was consumed by rage. The two men circled each other, Delvin making slashing motions with his knife. Ethan slowed his movement and almost imperceptibly turned his body sideways. Delvin saw it as a chance. He lunged toward Ethan with his knife. Ethan moved sideways and allowing Delvin's arm to go by him, and then grabbed it and pinned it against his body. He could feel the strength Delvin possessed. Ethan took the palm of his free hand and smashed it down on Delvin's elbow joint, breaking his arm. Delvin cried out in pain. The knife dropped to the ground. Delvin landed on one knee breathing hard through his mouth.

"I'm going to kill you, mother fucker," he screamed at Ethan.

"Not today," Ethan said as he stepped forward and kicked Delvin under his chin breaking his jaw and knocking him cold.

Ethan then turned to Cowboy and Raymond. Raymond was desperately fighting to keep the dog from his throat. Ethan had to pull Cowboy off him. After the dog was out of the way, Ethan turned back to

Raymond who was kicking with his legs, trying to move himself away from them. Ethan grabbed him and drug him to the side of the small house and propped him up against the wall. After slapping him a couple of times across his face, he had his full attention.

"When you wake up, you need to tell your brother what I'm going to tell you. If you or him come close to this woman again, I'm going to kill both of you. Even if only one of you is stupid enough to try something, both of you are going to die. Do you hear me?" he asked.

"Yeah, yeah, I hear you," Raymond said

"Let me ask you this, Raymond, is it?"

Raymond nodded.

"Look at me," Ethan said

Raymond looked up.

"Do you believe me?"

"Yeah, I believe you, man."

"Good," Ethan said, as he threw a massive punch driving Raymond's head into the wall of the house, breaking his nose and knocking out his front teeth. Raymond slumped to his side.

Ethan called Cowboy over and got on one knee. He gave the dog a hug and scratched behind his ears.

"Good job, buddy. Good job," he then stood up and turned to Samantha.

"Sam?" he said.

She rushed into his arms and squeezed him tight. As he wrapped his own arms around her, he could feel her trembling.

"You're okay, you're okay," he said. "I'll never let anything hurt you."

She knew he was telling her the truth and for the very first time in her life, she felt totally safe. She didn't want to leave his arms. She felt his hand on her head as he held her to his chest. She looked up at him, tears running down her cheeks. Ethan cupped her face in his hands, brushing the tears off her cheeks with his thumbs. As he bent toward her, he felt her rise to meet him. When their lips met, he felt her mouth open and her tongue. Neither one could have said how long they kissed.

"We need to leave," Samantha said to him when they finished kissing.

"I suppose we do," Ethan responded and bent and kissed her again.

"Dammit, we really need to leave," she said as she gently pushed herself away from him. As she did, she felt his arms release their grip of her. But instead of letting her go, Ethan spun her around and held her tight to him again. She could feel him press against her. She put her hands on his arm and bent her head down and whispered.

"Ethan, we have to go."

"I know," he said as he kissed the back of her neck.

"Ah, shit," she said as she pressed herself tighter against him.

"Jesus," she heard him say and then felt him let go of her.

"My pack is ready. I'll just be a minute," Sam said as she disappeared into the house.

Ethan looked at Cowboy. He shook his head, bent down and gave the dog another scratch behind the ear. He realized that in spite of everything bad going on, he felt really really good. He looked up as she came out of the house. He knew she was the reason he felt so good, and he knew that something had happened between them he couldn't explain.

As they approached Mike's cabin, Samantha called out his name. A grunt came from inside, and the door opened revealing a disheveled-looking Mike with a cup in his hand. He beckoned them in.

"Morning, sunshine," she said looking at him holding his head as he sat at the table.

"I might be feeling a little rode hard and put away wet. I'll get over it," he responded.

"Well, start now," she said as she told him what had transpired with the Horten brothers.

"Those boys have always been bad news even when they were just little kids," he said, looking at Ethan with an 'I knew there was a lot more to you than what you let on' look.

"We better get going. Once they get word back to the dump, I've got a feeling you and the Commish ain't going to be drinking buddies anymore."

"I can't believe he sent those goons to my place," Samantha said.

"It was the smart thing to do on his part. It was about answering questions he has about me," Ethan replied.

"Ya, well, he got his answer. Let me grab my shit, I'll meet you guys outside," Mike said.

When Mike came out of the cabin with his pack on and a rifle slung over his shoulder, he found Ethan and Samantha standing together with the fingers of each other's hands interwoven and looking in each other's eyes.

"So, the flames of love erupt in the middle of chaos. Looks like you kids are talking about the prom," he said.

They let go of each other's hands and looked at him somewhat embarrassed.

"No worries, boys and girls. In fact, it's kinda nice, somehow. So what's the plan?"

"Apparently, you don't remember our conversation last night. We've got to get to the North Fork Road," Sam said. "Once there, we'll head out to Bowman Lake in the park."

"How far is it?" Ethan asked.

Sam looked at Mike and he shrugged his shoulders.

"Probably a day to the North Fork and a day to the lake. Then up and over Brown's Pass. Stoney Indian Pass drops down from there to Glen Lake. We could spend the night at Elizabeth Lake."

"There's real good Grayling fishing at Elizabeth Lake," Mike added.

"Really? Grayling? So, what are you using for bait?" Ethan asked.

Before he could answer, Sam took a step closer to them.

"Sorry," they both said at about the same time.

"After Elizabeth Lake, we'll head over Ptarmigan Tunnel and drop into Many Glaciers. There are a lot of grizzly bears on that trail, especially this time of year. So, we'll need to watch for them. From there, we're half a day's hike to Sperry Chalet. I guess we should check it out first since that's where your guy Bob thinks Victor might be. And, if we don't find him there, we can head over to Granite Park Chalet. However, I think there is a fire burning in the northern part of the park, so we will have to play that by ear."

"So, it's pretty much the same route we discussed at my table last night. But apparently certain people, do to a self-induced memory loss, have forgotten that."

"I haven't forgotten anything, smart ass," Mike said as he looked at Ethan. "You sure you want to hook up with this?"

Before Ethan could answer, Mike continued, "I'm talking about, like, right now. Like I said, our buddy, Commissioner Harms, is number one going to be plum pissed that young Rambo here took out two of his guys. Which by the way they, weren't his A team."

"What's number two?" Sam asked.

"YOU. And don't get all pissy when I say this. But, you're special to that guy in some way and for some reason. And that's the bottom line. He's going to not only send everybody he's got after Ethan, but he's going to send them to find you once he realizes that you've eloped with our buddy here. So, let me bounce this Plan B off you," he said.

"He's a plan guy," Ethan said to Sam who let out a chuckle.

"Fuck, you two are made for each other. My point being, it's going to be harder than Chinese arithmetic to get from here across the valley floor to the North Fork, and it's going to take twice as long as we think if we have to avoid Harms' people. I've got a set of wheels parked up around Whitefish."

"Really? This is news," Samantha said.

"We've all got our little secrets. Anyway, we grab it and head north on logging roads. That way if we are spotted, they might think that we are heading north to British Columbia and Ethan's cousin. Which by the way, is he a real guy?"

"He is, and I'd bet money he's holed up someplace up there."

"When we hit the Red Gate Road, we'll cut over to the North Fork Road, drop south to Polebridge and then into the park."

They all looked at each other.

"Makes sense to me," Sam said.

Ethan nodded in the affirmative.

"Okay then. We're burning daylight," Mike said as he set off.

After over an hour of nonstop hiking, they stopped inside the tree line on a small ridge overlooking Highway 93 North.

"So, I noticed that you're not packing the Ruger Mini 14 today," Ethan said as he took a drink from his canteen.

"Jesus, getting old ain't for pussies," Mike said wiping the sweat off his face with a bandana. "That and my blood alcohol content is probably a little higher than normal," he paused in thought. "Then again, it's probably about normal. Yeah, I decided to pack the old Winchester 270 today. After you told me about what happened this morning, I thought it might be handy to be able to reach out a little farther than the Mini can."

"Flat shooting gun," Ethan responded. "I'm a Tikka 30-06 guy myself." And he made a mental note to have Bob bring his 30-06 with him if it was possible.

"Can't go wrong with a 30-06," Mike said, "In fact, some people..."

"Hey, somebody is coming down the highway," Sam said pointing north.

A four-wheel-drive pickup with two men in the front and two more standing in the box of the truck hanging onto the roll bar was heading south on the highway at a fairly fast rate of speed. All three of them crouched a little lower. By this time, they were all looking through binoculars.

"Jeez, that guy is driving like he's on a mission or..." Mike said.

"Or like he's meeting someone. Look to the south," Ethan said, finishing Mike's sentence for him.

Another truck approached from the south heading north. It was a four-wheel-drive truck set up identical to the southbound one. Two men in the cab and two standing in the box. They slowed and stopped side by side.

"I guess words out about what happened at Sam's place," Mike said.

"We better double time it to your ride," Ethan said.

"It's not far, about an hour or so if we hustle. Like I said, getting old ain't for pussies," Mike said as he grabbed his pack and headed out at a quick pace.

They stopped at the bottom of a skid trail, which was basically two sets of tire tracks winding steeply through the trees and up the ridge. Mike wiped his face and the inside of his bush hat, took a swallow from his canteen, and then dumped some water on his head.

"Shit, don't want to hump like that again. At least not for a while. Our ride is backed about halfway up this hill." He took another drink of water.

"Help me with this camouflage net, would you?" Mike asked Sam and Ethan.

Once the netting was off, they stood there looking at a 1968 Apache Chevrolet two-wheel-drive pickup truck.

"It's got a little body cancer, but other than, it's in pretty good shape for the shape it's in. Kinda like me," he said with a chuckle.

"She's got a 292 inline 6. I backed her up the hill just in case the battery went dead. We can put it in second gear, give her a push, and bump start her."

"Sounds good to me," Ethan said as he dropped the tailgate. Cowboy jumped in without even being told to.

"Looks like we're not the only ones tired of walking," Mike said. "Throw your shit in and let's fire this baby up."

The truck started after several attempts and with a bit of coaxing. Mostly, it took some precise pumping of the gas pedal and a massive amount of profanity from the driver.

"There we go," Mike said as he gently revved the engine. He slipped it into second gear and eased the clutch out. The truck tried to move but didn't. Sam and Ethan both looked at Mike.

"Fuck, forgot I've got rocks in front of the front wheels. Ethan, I'll keep her running, will you jump out and grab 'em for me? Don't worry, I won't steal your woman, she's way too bossy for me."

Ethan removed the rocks and jumped back in and down the skid trail they went. He couldn't help but think of Carl. He was certain that the old Chevy would have made Carl's good truck list.

"Like I was saying, we should hit the Red Gate Road above Whitefish and then cut over to the North Fork Road," Mike said.

"Sounds good to me. That should put us to Polebridge in about two hours give or take," Sam replied.

They went by several groups of people who appeared to be camping, or perhaps squatting was a better description, on the Red Gate Road above the town of Whitefish. Either way, they didn't seem interested in having visitors. After about an hour, they hit the North Fork Road. Mike pulled over.

"I think it's probably best if we go back to hiking from here."

"I agree," Sam said.

"The Canadian border is about twenty miles up this road. I wouldn't be surprised if Harms doesn't have people watching it."

"You guys get out here, I'll head up the road a bit and find a place to stash the truck as best I can," Mike stated.

"You going to need help with the camouflage netting?" Ethan asked, as he motioned for Cowboy to jump out of the pickup box.

"No. In fact, I was thinking that I'd leave it so that maybe they would find it and think that we're trying to get across the border. I mean, if it looks like it was dropped off recently and in a hurry, who knows?"

"Doesn't hurt to try," Ethan said.

"You're a thinker, that's what I love about ya, Mikey!"

"Bullshit. Anyway, I'll see you guys some time tonight or early tomorrow," Mike replied.

"Okay, be safe," Sam said, the humor in her voice was replaced by concern.

"Safe is my middle name," Mike said with a grin as he slipped the truck into second and drove off.

Ethan and Samantha were about twenty feet inside the tree line when Ethan told Samantha to hold up. She turned to look at him.

"What?" she asked.

He pointed at Cowboy who had stopped and was looking intensely to the south.

"Listen," he said.

"I don't hear anything..."

Ethan held his hand up. She stopped talking and he could tell by the expression on her face that she could hear it now. They both crouched down. It was an engine noise they heard and it was getting louder by the second.

"Stay here," Ethan said to her as he dropped his pack and headed toward the edge of the tree line. He was back to her in less than a minute.

"Whoever it is, is coming north very fast, I can see their dust plume."

"Mike's only a few minutes ahead of them. Ethan, we've got to do something," Sam said, her voice registering a new urgency.

"Shit. Shit, you're right," he said, looking at her.

"We gotta go. We gotta get away from the road."

Sam looked at him and shook her head no.

"He'll be okay, Sam."

Within seconds, the noise from the truck was nearly upon them, so they got lower to the ground. Moments later, the truck sped by them with dust bellowing from beneath it. Sam looked at Ethan with fear in her eyes. He didn't say anything, he just took her hand and led her deeper into the woods.

By chance or by habit, Mike happened to look in his rearview mirror and saw the vehicle heading toward him.

"Ah, shit," he muttered as he dropped from fourth gear into third and punched the gas pedal to the floor.

The 292 engine jumped to life. Mike drove as fast as he could, knowing that he didn't have much chance of outrunning whoever was behind him. He also figured that there was probably a good chance that there was another truck heading south from the border, which gave him about twenty miles and ten minutes to come up with a plan. About the only thing he had going for him was that he could see where he was going, and at the same time, he was raising a hell of a dust plume behind him. He tried to remember which road he was coming up on. On his right was the North Fork River which acted as the border to Glacier National Park. Left on Tamarack Road was the only choice he could come up with.

He passed a forest service sign telling him that he was coming up on the road. He'd have to keep a close eye out for it. Suddenly, there it was. He dropped from fourth to second gear, and at the same time cranked the wheel and stood on the brake. The ass end of the truck broke loose in the gravel. Mike felt it coming around on him and knew that he wasn't going to save it. The truck came to an abrupt stop. His rear tires were in the ditch and his front end was pointing straight at the river. Mike pushed his door open.

He was a little shaken up, but knew he was out of time. He grabbed his rifle from the gun rack and was thankful that it had stayed there. Using the side of the truck box for support, he went around to the back end of the truck. His pack had been thrown out of the box and was laying down in the ditch about thirty feet away. About the time he got to his backpack, his pursuers blew past him in a cloud of dust. Mike saw the red brake light reflection as he stumbled across the road toward the river.

They hadn't seen him with all the dust, but it wouldn't take long for them to figure it out. The river was low as the main run off from the snowpack hadn't happened yet. He slid down the bank and into the water. The cold water helped get the cobwebs out of Mike's head. As he waded out into the river, he could hear men shouting above him. The water rose on him. It got about waist high. He struggled against the current as it caught his backpack. Mike wasn't willing to let it go just yet. The water started to drop and his going got easier the closer he got to the opposite bank. He splashed out of the water and made his way across the river rocks toward the tree line. He was starting to think that maybe they weren't going to see him.

Then the rocks in front of him seemed to erupt in small explosions. Almost simultaneously, the chatter of automatic rifle shots reached his ear. If they were spraying, they weren't aiming or at least he hoped. To his left about fifteen yards, he noticed a pile of driftwood. Mike veered toward it.

"He ain't stopping," one of the men on the road said.

"I can see that."

"Well, what do you want to do, Frank?"

"He gets behind that pile of driftwood, we could pay hell getting him out."

"Put one in him," Frank replied.

"Just a few more steps," Mike thought as he heard the gunshot.

When the bullet hit him, it kind of spun him half way around and threw him off balance. He hit the river rocks hard with his right side but was able to keep his rifle elevated in his left hand stopping it from slamming into the rocks.

The shooter was aiming for Mike's hip. He'd lined up on the center of his lower back. Knowing that if he was off a little, he would still hit his target. What he failed to factor in was that he was shooting down hill, and therefore, his shot was going to be high. The small, fast bullet hit Mike's backpack at a slight angle spinning him around.

"Nailed the fucker," the shooter said.

"He's moving."

"Fuck, get him," Frank yelled.

Mike was crawling toward the driftwood when the rocks around him began to explode.

The gunfire was wild, but it was only a matter of time before they zoned in on him. At that moment, another truck coming from the north slid to a stop. A cloud of dust covered all of them. By the time it cleared, their target had disappeared behind the driftwood.

"Where is he?"

"We had him till you guys blinded us. He's behind that pile of driftwood now and he's armed," Frank said.

"Sorry, man, we didn't know," answered one of the new men.

They heard a rifle shot and crouched as they spun toward the road. One of the three men who had been with Frank dropped to the ground.

"Jesus Christ, get down, you dumb bastards," Frank yelled.

He and another man crawled to the man who crumpled to the road. He was hit in the shoulder and writhing in pain. Frank motioned a third man over.

"Drag him over to the truck and out of this asshole's line of fire. The rest of you bastards put rounds on that wood pile."

The three remaining men and two of the new men opened up on the driftwood pile. They stopped when their clips ran empty.

"Maybe we got him," one of them said.

"Why don't you stand up and find out?" Frank retorted.

Mike knew he'd hit the man by the way he dropped to the ground.

"Jeez, them guys must have a lot of bullets," he thought as he covered his head with his arms and tried to make himself as small as possible behind the wood.

The wood splintered all around him. When the firing had stopped, he took his arms away from his face and looked toward the tree line. It was a good forty to fifty feet of open ground and there was no way he was going to cover it fast enough over river rock and with his right side feeling like someone had beat on him with a baseball bat.

There were eight men on the road all armed with automatic assault rifles, one badly wounded. Frank left the wounded man by the truck and along with another one crawled to the edge of the road.

"Okay, listen up. Jim, you and Harry head about two hundred yards down the road. Pete, you and Charlie do the same up the road. Then work your way down to the river. When you get to the river, Jim, you fire one shot and Pete you do the same. The rest of us will stay here and open up on the wood pile. We'll give you cover fire as you cross the water. Head straight across to the tree line then work your way behind this guy and take him out."

"What if he's already dead?" Charlie asked.

"Then, I guess we're just wastin' bullets."

Charlie thought about it for a second.

"Well, shouldn't one of us stay with Pat?"

Frank looked at him.

"He ain't going anyplace; now, goddammit, get moving."

Fred Benson, his son Ryan, and his nephew Kenny had been watching from the ridge above the road.

"Looks like they got somebody pinned down, Pops," Ryan whispered to his dad.

"It would appear that way."

"We just going to sit here and watch?" asked Kenny.

"Them's the men from the valley. Gotta be the commissioner's men," added Ryan.

"Yeah, most likely. Don't much care for the commissioner or his men," Fred said.

"Care even less for what I've been hearing about what's going on in the valley and about this so called dump setup they got going on."

"They're getting ready to move," Kenny said. "What you want to do, Uncle Fred?"

"I don't want to do anything," Fred answered. "But this is what we're going to do…"

Fred instructed the boys to spread out about twenty feet on each side of him. "Get behind a good-sized tree. When you hear me shoot, the two of you start shooting, too. When them fellows start shooting back, you duck behind the tree and don't look out till they stop. It will be alright, boys, do as I say."

When both boys had found their spots, Fred sighted down his .308 Browning rifle at the guy on the road who had been doing all the motioning with his hands. Fred couldn't shoot him in the back, but when he turned sideways to talk to one of the other men, Fred pulled the trigger. Both the boys armed with 30-30 Winchesters started shooting.

Frank dropped flat on the road and lay motionless and two of the other men were hit. The remaining four scrambled to the truck for protection.

Mike heard the firing from above him, and when he realized that it wasn't directed at him, he struggled to a crouch and peeked over the wood. He didn't know who was shooting at who. Maybe, somehow, Ethan and Sam had gotten to him, but he didn't think so or at least he hoped they weren't that dumb. Whoever it was, it didn't matter. This was his chance. He grabbed his pack and limped his way into the tree line. The firing stopped, but Mike didn't; he continued deeper into the woods.

Up on the road, after spraying the hillside with bullets, the four men crouching behind the truck were scared and disorientated.

"Shit, man, we're shot to shit. Can you see anything up there, Pete?"

Pete was crouched behind the front tire of the truck and he slowly started to raise himself up. When he was high enough, he peeked his head up and looked over the hood of the Ford scanning the ridgeline above them. He turned to tell the other three men that he couldn't see anything, but before he could get the words out of his mouth, the side of his head exploded in a mist of blood. He dropped to the ground, legs twitching as he lay in the dust.

One of the other men screamed "Fuck you" and stood up and started firing blindly at the ridge line. He fell back when a well-aimed bullet hit him in the chest.

The remaining two men stared at each other terrified.

Charlie swallowed hard. "Hey, hey you on the hill, let's talk," Charlie yelled.

No one answered back to him.

"I mean, there ain't no need for further shooting," Charlie yelled.

More silence.

"Shit, Charlie, what are we going to do?" asked Harry, his voice quaking.

Charlie held up his hand signaling Harry to stop talking.

"So, what you want to do here?" he yelled out.

A calm voice came back. "Wonder if that fella you were shooting at has made his way into a firing position behind you boys?"

The two men behind the truck instantly spun around, fear gripping them.

"Throw your guns over the truck and stand up with your hands above your head."

The two men behind the truck looked at each other. Charlie shook his head no to Harry.

"This is a time-limited offer, boys. Do it now," Fred said.

Harry looked at Charlie.

"Don't."

"Charlie, I'm done," Harry said, as he threw his rifle over the truck and stood up hands over his head.

"Tell your partner he's got ten seconds to follow you. Or you're a dead man."

Harry looked to Charlie with pleading eyes. A grimace came across Charlie's face and he tossed his rifle and with raised hands stood up.

"Don't move. We got guns on you," Fred yelled down. He then motioned both boys over to him. He looked the first one and then the other in the eyes.

"If we let these fellas go, they are going to tell their buddies who did this, and then they are going to come after us with a vengeance. And, they will not just come after the three of us, but everybody we know. They'll have to, they got no choice if they want to keep control over people. In order to control people, you've got to keep everybody scared of you. You boys understand what I'm saying?" Fred asked.

Both boys nodded.

"I'm not leaving anyone who can identify us. It's hard times and it takes hard men to…" he let his thought trail off. "You boys stay up here, keep your rifles trained on them two. You got no part in what's going to happen. You remember that. This is on me and me alone." Fred turned and went down the ridge. He leaned his Browning against the front of the truck and unholstered his Ruger 44 magnum revolver.

"Get down on your knees," he told both men.

"Why?" asked Charlie

"Get on your goddamn knees," Fred yelled.

"Ain't doing it."

Fred shot him in the chest.

Harry dropped to his knees, his face looking at the ground. He pleaded for his life.

"Jesus, please. Jesus, don't kill me, I'm sorry. I'm sorry," he sobbed.

"I'm going to kill you. I have to and you know that. I'm giving you a chance to make peace with your maker if you want to."

Through his sobs, Harry simply muttered, "I'm sorry, I'm sorry. Please don't."

Fred re-cocked the single action pistol and shot him. He then went around to each of the other men, shooting each one in turn with the magnum. He, too, was leaving a message.

CHAPTER 42

In the weeks after the virus had hit the Washington, DC area, chaos and mayhem gave way to an eerie dark calm that settled on the ruins of the city as those that survived the virus or somehow avoided infection hid from other survivors. Survivors were even more dangerous than the infected, because at least it was clear that those who were infected would soon be immobilized and then dead. Most survivors, however, wanted everything that you had.

It was shocking how fast a city full of resources could disappear seemingly overnight. Grocery stores were looted and burned, as were hospitals, universities, gas stations, restaurants, houses, etc. Nothing was safe, and once someone gathered up a cache of supplies, they themselves became the next target. It seemed everyone battled not so much for the supplies themselves, but for the right to own them. In fact, there were many instances where a person on the verge of losing his supplies would light them on fire rather than give them up to a thief.

There were rumors on the streets that certain sections of the city had been designated as government sanctioned safe areas where survivors could go, but the rumors were unreliable, and no one had heard any official announcements from the governments since the electricity went out. There was a strong sense the US was at war and was focusing all of its attention on that effort. Those closest to military bases noticed the heightened activity at those sites. However, no one had a clue what was really going on, and the loss of mass media left everyone in the dark, both literally and figuratively.

David and Aiden had been holed up in the Compassionate Neighbors safe house on Girard Street for several days. David was sure that they were close to death. He could not remember the last time they took a drink of water, but he was sure it was more than three days prior. In addition to his own symptoms, which included a swollen tongue, dry mouth, severe headache, and severe lethargy, he also noticed that Aiden was showing signs of severe dehydration. Most notably, the small boy did not have the energy to get out of the makeshift bed they had created on the floor of Aunt Gertie's meditation nook on the third floor.

David pulled the small boy close to him as he readied them both for the impending transition. He thought back to Aunt Gertrude's death a few months earlier. It seemed like a lifetime ago. He fondly remembered how she described her death as a recycling, and he wondered how his own molecules would be re-configured in the universe. His thoughts then turned to a statement that she shared with him.

"What did I do with my one wild and precious life?" he wondered. A sadness came over him as he realized that the work he really truly loved had only just begun.

"David, there is a noise," Aiden said in a small, weak voice.

David was thinking about all of the people who suffer in the world and how their suffering had been so much deeper than his own, when he finally heard Aiden speaking.

"David, I think there is someone breaking into the house."

David wasn't sure if the boy was delusional or if there was someone making a noise he could not hear. He listened carefully for a few seconds before responding.

"Aiden, I don't hear anything, are you sure there is a noise?"

"Yes, it sounds like people are breaking sticks on the door by the porch," Aiden said.

"Okay, well, let's just wait and see what happens, okay? Maybe they are here to help," David said.

The boy did not respond. Soon, the noises grew louder as the sound of breaking wood gave rise to loud thumps.

"I'm scared, David, what if they are coming here to hurt us?"

"It's okay, Aiden," David said. "Everything will be okay."

The loud thumping noise gave way to a loud crashing sound as the front door burst into the house in fragments, followed by loud footsteps. It sounded like a small army was coming in.

"Search the whole house," a strange voice said. "You two check the basement, you two check the main floor, my boy here and I can check the third floor. C'mon now, let's move."

David listened carefully, trying to figure out if he knew these people. The voice did not ring a bell. David and Aiden braced against each other as the footsteps on the stairs grew louder and closer to them. Aiden hid himself under a blanket as the door opened.

"Damn," the voice giving the orders exclaimed, followed by loud retching sounds.

The second person to enter the room also stopped to vomit.

"Damn, I think they are all dead, sure smells like it," the leader said. "Let's get the hell outta here."

"Hey wait, we're alive," David said meekly. "Please help us. We need food and water."

The man in charge turned back to the pile in the middle of the room. David was barely visible in the heap of blankets and clothes that had become completely scattered into an unorganized mass.

"David?" a second voice said.

David searched his memory to see if he could place the voice with a face.

"David, David, David," the excited voice repeated. "Your friend Aiden here still?"

"Keno? Keno, you came back! Oh, thank you. Who did you bring with you?"

"I'm Paul. Keno told us that you were in here, but no one believed him. The only way we could get him to shut up about it was to break down this door and check."

Aiden popped his head above the covers, and Keno let out a loud squeal of delight.

"Aiden! There he is, I told you there was a boy up in there. David is blind, he told me that before," Keno said.

"Yes. Both Aiden and I caught the virus and we both survived. However, I lost my eyesight as a result. Aiden seems to be just fine, isn't that right, Aiden?"

Aiden nodded, but did not take his eyes off the two haggard-looking black men who entered the room.

"His real name ain't Paul," Keno volunteered. "His real name is Boss Man 'cuz he always gotta be in charge of everythin'."

Paul laughed. "No, my real name is Paul and that is what you guys call me. Now, c'mon Keno, let's get these guys outta here. The smell alone up here might be enough to kill us all."

David felt a large, rough hand grab him and help lift him to his feet. However, he was so weak that he could not walk or stand without help. Paul bent down, picked David up, and carried him across the room and down the stairs as if he was his new bride. Keno mimicked Paul's move and carried Aiden in exactly the same way. They delivered the man and the small boy to the front porch.

"Let's get these guys some water," Paul said.

David sat on the front porch, soaking up the late fall sun. From the feel of the sun, he guessed it was early afternoon, and he could tell by the lack of humidity that winter was around the corner. Aiden sat close enough to David he could feel the warmth of his small body on his side. He reached over and put his left arm around him. One of the other men came up to them with water bottles and attempted to hand one to David. When David did not respond, Aiden reached over and grabbed the water bottle and placed it in David's right hand.

"Thank you," David said as he opened the bottle and drank slowly. Aiden did the same.

After they each took several small swallows, the same man offered them some Lance Grilled Cheese Crackers. They tasted stale, but were still delicious. David and Aiden devoured the crackers and sipped water until all of the others who were searching the house came out and gathered on the porch.

"Okay, listen up everyone," Paul said. "Let's get these boys back to the warehouse. They are safe. They already had the virus and lived, so they are not dangerous to us. We have to carry them because they are very weak."

Paul picked up David and started walking down the stairs to the street. Keno lifted up Aiden and followed close behind them. The rest of the group fell in line behind them.

"Where are you taking us?" David asked.

"We got our own place over by 16th avenue. You'll be safe there and you can stay there as long as you like."

"Who is running the place?" David asked.

"We are," Paul said rather rudely. "What, does that surprise you that a bunch of homeless people could take care of themselves?"

"Not at all, I am glad to hear that you are safe."

Paul did not respond, as he seemed to be lost in thought. After several minutes, he continued.

"Before the power went out, they sent the troops around to gather people up, take them to safe areas. They never even noticed us. I was sitting on a fountain wall at the park over by the elementary school when I first saw them. They had a bullhorn and said that folks should come forward 'cuz they was a safe place to go."

Paul paused, swallowing his emotions and perhaps his pride before continuing.

"They stopped in the parking lot of the park, which was right across the street from a large condominium complex. They had a couple of large army trucks. People started coming outta da condos and crossin' the street. Mostly white people, some Asians, a few of Indians. I walked across the park and told them that I wanted to go. They asked me where I lived and where I worked. When I told them I was homeless, the conversation ended. The young white punk told me to fuck off. I told him it wasn't right, and he told me that if I didn't step away, he would shoot me."

"Was this U.S. military?" David asked.

"Far as I could tell."

"That's wrong."

"Don't matter now," Paul said. "There was no place for us homeless in their plans. We was gonna have to take care of our own selves. I tried to tell all the others, but most of them would not listen till it was too late. Hundreds of us are dead, and there are only 15 of us who have survived and stayed together. We been workin' real hard to gather up supplies."

"Have you seen these safe places that the military was taking people to?"

"No. They said over the bullhorn that there would be several safe zones in the city that they could stay in, but we have been all over the city getting stuff and ain't never seen any safe zones or safe houses. Your house was the only place we knew of that was taking care of the sick. We figured that no one would survive there 'cuz this sickness ain't got no mercy in it."

"Have you seen any of my people around?"

"Nah, we only heard about your house, and then Keno saw the little boy on the roof and told us where you were at. He told us you were different than the other white guys, more like the ones that helped us out at the homeless shelter."

David stopped speaking so he could think about what Paul just told him, and rested his head back on Paul's large arm. After several more minutes, Paul stopped and there was the jingling of keys and a loud screech before they started moving again. Paul carried David into the warehouse, and when everyone else was safe inside, the door closed with the same screech followed by a loud clang and the sound of a lock engaging. Paul set David down in an old metal outdoor chair. Keno set Aiden down in a similar chair just a few feet away from David. Aiden scooted his chair over so that it was close enough to touch David's chair.

"We will make you guys a bed. Keno will show you were to use the bathroom. The food and all the stuff we been gathering is along the walls and there is a lot of open space, so you shouldn't have to worry about walking into nothing. We can find you a stick to use as a cane."

"Thank you for coming to get us," David said.

Paul only nodded, but Keno beamed with pride.

For the next few days, the group of homeless people looked after David and Aiden, giving them food and water. It took only a couple of days for Aiden to spring back to life, but David was slower to recover. After about five days, he was finally able to stand and walk short distances. Aiden took him for strolls around the nearly empty warehouse. It was already cold inside this place and David could not imagine how they would survive the winter in there.

During the day, several of the homeless people left the warehouse to go scavenge for things, and either left David and Aiden locked in or with one or two other members of the group who stayed behind to look after some chores. Aiden described the inside of the warehouse to David as best as he could, but there were only so many ways that Aiden could think of to describe gray steel and concrete and wide-open spaces. David asked if they had guns, but Aiden said he wasn't sure. He did not see anything that looked like a gun. Given that guns were outlawed in the district, David would have been surprised if they had any.

During one of these outings, Keno was left behind to keep David and Aiden company. Keno had known David through the help he received from the Compassionate Neighbors Organization, and the two had always been close. Keno was an interesting mixture of sophistication and immaturity. On one level, he had the mentality of a 10-year-old boy. He was afraid of the world but also hopeful, cautious about people but bold about taking risks, fun loving but hated to work. On another level, he had the ability to connect with people in a way that exuded extreme confidence and trust; that is, once he got past his own inhibitions.

"Keno, you never told me how you got your name," David said, after the three had finished eating a breakfast of boiled oatmeal sweetened with Sweet n Low packets.

"My daddy called me Keno 'cuz he said I was one in a million," Keno replied.

"What was your real name?"

"Winston. My daddy loved his cigarettes, I am just glad he didn't name me Pall Mall."

David laughed but Aiden did not catch the humor.

"Where is your momma and daddy?" Keno asked Aiden.

"They died."

"How? Did the virus get them?" Keno pried, but with a curiosity born of true interest.

"My dad came home from a business trip and then we had to go the grocery store. We even went to the one across the street that he hated because they charged too much. We bought so much stuff, I didn't know how we would get it home, but Dad made us push the three carts across the street to take everything up to our house."

Aiden paused for a moment as he tried to recollect all of the details. David listened intently. He had never heard Aiden's story before. He was curious, but did not want to trigger any emotional trauma for the young boy. He figured that the story would emerge when the time was right. It appeared to be the right time.

"Then Mom and Dad got into a huge fight because mom wanted us to fly to my grandma's house. Dad wouldn't let us leave. He locked the door and said that we would stay there until help arrived."

"Help didn't arrive, did it?" Keno asked.

"No. Daddy got sick first, but Mommy wouldn't let me go see him. I saw him, though, when she opened the bedroom door, and his hair was all sweaty and he had a mean look on his face. After he died, everything got really scary. Mommy tried to call Grandma, but the phones stopped working. Then the lights went out. And people kept banging on our door and yelling and there were gunshots. I looked out on the streets from the glass door by our balcony, and I could see people everywhere, running around with things in their arms. Things were on fire. No one was nice like they used to be."

"When did your momma get sick?" Keno asked.

"I don't remember, because the TV wasn't working, but maybe a week after Dad died. When she started getting sick, she took a bunch of food and water into the bedroom and locked the door. She told me to stay away no matter what and do not open the door for anyone but the police, a fireman, or an army guy."

Aiden paused a moment, as tears welled up in his eyes. Keno moved closer to him and put an arm around his shoulders.

"You are so brave," Keno said.

"After Mommy died, I went into the bedroom. First, I had to unlock the door with a toothpick like daddy showed me how to do, and then I went in to see them. It smelled terrible in there, and Mommy looked like she was very unhappy when she died. Do unhappy people go to heaven?"

"Good people go to heaven, and they don't have to be happy when they go," Keno said. "When did you hook up with David?"

"David saw me hiding on our balcony. He tried to get me to talk to him, but he did not have a uniform so I wasn't allowed to."

"Why were you on the balcony?"

"It smelled too bad in the house. I had to get away from it if I could."

"Did anyone else ever come to try to help you?"

"I don't think so. But, I think our neighbor scared some bad guys away so he helped me."

"When did you get sick?"

"After David took me to his house. I was there only a little while and then I got so sick. I don't remember it that much, but when I woke up, David was sick, too. I think I made him sick."

"No, you didn't make me sick, we were probably both already infected when we met. You got really sick, I didn't think you were going to make it, but you are so strong," David said, directing his comments to Aiden.

"Wow," Keno said. "You have been through a lot. I think you're a pretty lucky guy, too. I'm gonna call you Bingo."

David laughed softly as he wiped a couple of tears from his cheeks.

CHAPTER 43

Victor continued his lessons with Ben and Becca daily, bringing in new experiences each day to enliven their learning. He began teaching them basic Ninjutsu moves, and had them repeat exercises that helped them develop the skills necessary to maneuver a knife against an attacker with fluidity and grace.

"In Ninjutsu, the first tenet is you cannot control your enemy or the circumstances leading to a confrontation, however, you can control yourself. Therefore, you must train yourself to be ready to respond in a moment's notice. You must be able to respond the same if you are completely calm or overwhelmed with fear. We will work on developing the muscle memory that will allow you to be free of your sympathetic nervous system."

The kids really enjoyed working with the knives and doing the exercises for the first hour, but the routine became tedious and the kids complained as the practice continued.

"You must become masters of your own intentions, rulers over your own biology. You must learn to be in complete control of yourself, physically, emotionally, and mentally to become a Ninjutsu warrior."

"This is cool and all," Becca said, "but I don't really want to be any warrior."

"That is stupid. You are being a stupid girl. Are you going to rely on everyone else to take care of you? The world has changed, young lady, and unless you can take care of yourself, you will be destroyed by some stupid thug who can do whatever he wants to you."

Becca looked at Victor, quickly decided he wasn't kidding, and picked up the knife she had been working with and continued to do the exercises despite the fact that her hand ached.

"The second tenet of Ninjutsu is there is something to be learned from everything," Victor said. "Now, I don't mean this in the stupidest sense where we make shit up to justify away a bad feeling," he said.

"I don't know what the stuff you just said means," Becca said.

Victor was getting impatient with the little girl.

"For example, when someone dies, we say all kinds of stupid things like, they are now angels, or the sunrise or full moon is more magnificent because the person who died has a hand in making it better. This is pure rubbish. This is not truth, there is no evidence of any afterlife, and we just say this stuff to make ourselves feel better. Beautiful lies. We must go deeper to learn the true lesson in every situation," Victor said.

"But what about God, Victor?" Becca asked.

"Look, child, there is no God." Victor snorted impatiently. "Religion is another beautiful lie that we tell ourselves and teach our children. Your parents lied to you because it was easier to tell you the lie than it was for them to face the harsh truth. The truth is no one knows why man evolved on this planet, or all of the species for that matter. It's a mystery."

"But the Bible says that God created the Heavens and the Earth," Ben said meekly.

"Stupid child, who do you think wrote the Bible? God? Look, I know your parents raised you in a religion, but let me ask you this. Have you ever seen anybody born into a Catholic family who was Jewish or Muslim? No, because religions are not truths, they are fictions that are only passed on by embedding that theology into the minds of children, using frightening concepts to scare them into believing. Children will believe anything their parents tell them. That is how religions work. However, many religions believe homosexuality is an immoral choice, not linked to biology or genetics, but instead to choice and poor moral judgment. Yet, homosexuals are born to all different cultures all across the world. Don't you think that if it were merely a choice or a moral failing one of these cultures would have prevented it? No, homosexuality is a biologic truth. Religion is a fabrication, a beautiful lie that helps believers live as if their lives had context, when in truth, they are founded upon falsehoods and misconceptions."

Victor glanced intensely at the kids, who looked completely confused. He decided this was a lesson for another day.

"The third Ninjutsu tenet is conditioning yourself will help you succeed in stressful environments. You must train your body to move independent from your thinking. You must be just as accurate when you are overwhelmed with fear as you are when you are completely calm. Okay, let's move on to a new exercise."

Victor led the children to a large tree he had carved on to create a clearing of the bark, exposing a one foot by one-foot square target for throwing knives.

"Okay," Victor said, "it's time you learned how to properly throw a knife.

Victor removed one of his throwing knives that was well worn and showed it to the two kids.

"I have had this knife the longest. It was my first knife and I learned to throw with it. It is not the best knife in the world, but if you can learn to throw this one, you will be really good with a good knife. Now, here is how you hold a knife you plan to throw, and then you raise your arm up like this, and then in one fluid movement you bend the arm down rapidly and snap your wrist as you let go."

The knife sailed perfectly to the center of the spot that was cleared on the tree.

"Wow," Ben said, "how did you get so good?"

"You must practice until you can throw a knife in your sleep. It must become instinct. Okay, Ben, you try."

Ben walked over to the tree, removed the knife, and returned to the spot where Victor had thrown it from. He lined up as Victor had shown them, positioned the knife in his hand as he had been instructed, lifted his arm, and then let it fly with the flick of his wrist. The knife sailed smoothly through the air and hit the mark, but did not have enough velocity to stick in the tree.

"That was an excellent first throw," Victor said. "You just have to practice the wrist flick a little more because that will give the knife more speed."

Victor retrieved the knife from the ground and came back to the spot where Ben was standing. He handed the knife to Becca.

"Okay, Becca, now you try."

Becca took the knife and threw it, ignoring all of the instructions Victor had given. The knife sailed toward the tree but was way off the mark. It hit the side of the trunk and bounced off, landing in the brush several feet from the tree. Victor was visibly upset.

"Go get the knife, and this time, throw it like I taught you to," he said through gritted teeth.

"This is stupid, I don't want to throw knives," Becca said.

Before Becca could turn around, Victor was on her. He grabbed her by the neck and lifted her tiny body into the air. He held her at his eye level.

"Listen here, you ungrateful little bitch," he exclaimed. "You are going to do this and do it right, do you understand?"

Ben had retrieved the knife and returned to where Victor was holding his sister. For a brief moment, he thought about stabbing Victor with it.

"Let her go," he screamed.

Victor dropped the girl and she fell hard on the ground. He then grabbed Ben, removed the knife from his hand, and slapped him so hard that he too fell to the ground.

"Were you going to stab me, you ungrateful little jerk?" he screamed.

"No," Ben stated, with tears streaming down his cheeks.

"Then you better never come toward a man with a knife in your hand unless you are prepared to use it, do you hear me?"

Ben nodded meekly.

Victor turned toward Becca who was laying on the ground whimpering. "I wanna go live with my uncle," she said.

Victor looked at the girl and then at Ben. He had lost his temper and things had gotten out of hand. He realized that he was about to lose his two students. The thought crossed his mind that it would be easier to just kill them and be done with them, but he had bigger plans in mind. He decided to change his tone.

"Listen up, guys," he started. "I am sorry that I lost my temper. I did not mean to hurt you. The world is different now. You have got to be able to protect yourself, and I guess I let my fear get the best of me. I just want to make sure you both have every skill I can teach you so you will be safe in this new world."

He looked at the two kids. His words were not making the situation better. They both appeared to be indignant, firmly entrenched in their anger toward him.

"Okay, enough practice for today," he said. "Let's go pick some huckleberries and see if we can see that grizzly bear sow and her cubs, shall we?"

"Really?" Becca asked. "You are going to take us to see the bears?"

"Yes, we are ready for a break. Come on, let's go see if we can spot them."

Ben helped Becca to her feet and the two came toward Victor. As they approached, he kneeled down so that he was eye level with them.

"I am so sorry," he said. "I just want what is best for you two, and I guess I went about it the wrong way today. Can you find it in your heart to forgive me?"

The two kids looked at one another.

"You really scared me," Becca said.

"I know. Can you forgive me?"

"I can forgive you if you promise never to hurt my sister again," Ben said.

Victor swallowed hard. Every part of him wanted to beat this kid for not understanding his intentions, but he held back the rage.

"I can do that," he said. He extended a hand toward Ben.

Ben took his hand in his and shook it, feeling confident Victor was true to his word.

"What about you, young lady, can you forgive me?"

"Yes, but I am still mad at you."

"Fair enough," he said. "I will do better. Now, come on, let's go see the grizzly bears."

The three of them left the tree target area and returned to the chalet to get some water, some containers for collecting huckleberries, and Victor's small daypack. They then hiked up to the huckleberry patch and filled their containers with berries and then continued to the spot where Victor sat to observe the bears. After several minutes of sitting there quietly eating huckleberries, the bears appeared in the small clearing several yards away.

"There they are," Victor whispered, pointing toward the clearing. He handed his binoculars to Becca.

"Wow, the mother bear is huge," she said. "And her babies don't look like babies."

"No, baby bears grow quickly and they usually stay close to their mother for a couple of years. I would guess that these bears are about to go off on their own."

Becca handed the binoculars to Ben who took a turn observing the bears.

"Do you see how the sow looks after the cubs? Love is an instinct that is present everywhere in nature. These bears are perfectly content in their natural environment. In fact, all animals are content in their natural habitats, that is why it is so important we not let human beings destroy the planet and all of the natural habitats animals need to be content."

"They sure are beautiful," Ben agreed. "I would sure hate to see their home destroyed by humans."

The three of them stayed there observing the bears until something sent the bears scurrying off into the thicket. They then gathered up their things and headed back to the chalet.

CHAPTER 44

Tony Harms sat at his desk head bent down eyes closed rubbing both his temples, wishing the guy on the jack hammer in his head would take a break. He hadn't had a drink since his meeting with Edwards, and he was seriously questioning his decision to stop drinking. He knew from past experience that deciding to stop was easy. Staying stopped, on the other hand... He stopped rubbing his temples and looked up at the two men standing in front of his desk.

"Okay, so, one at a time. I can hardly understand you mumbling sonsabitches. And start at the beginning," the commissioner said to the Horten brothers.

When they were done explaining the situation, he shook his head looking at both of them.

"Hell, sounds to me like you boys got lucky they didn't kill you. And, neither one of you recognized the other two fellas' that were with Edwards?" he asked them.

Both shook their heads no. Right then, there was a knock on the door.

"Enter."

In walked the sheriff and with him was a hard-looking man named William "Wild Bill" Clark. Clark had been a Navy Seal at one time and was the person that Harms put in charge of what he called the Rapid Reaction Unit, which had been called out to secure the exits out of the valley when the Horten brothers were discovered.

"You boys go get some well-deserved rest. And, I apologize for sending you men into an ambush. Trust me when I say that I'll see to it that you're very well compensated for what happened. Now, if you'll excuse us."

The Hortens mumbled a thanks and left the room.

"I want those two lying ignorant assholes gone." He looked at Bill.

"They'll be worm food before the day is out, I promise. But, we got other issues," Bill said.

"I'm listening," Harms said in a sarcastic voice.

The other two men shot each other a glance.

"I'm a little on edge at the moment, gentlemen. The only thing worse than a wet drunk is one trying to get dry. It can bring out the prick in you. Anyway, tell me what's going on," Tony said while looking at the sheriff and then shooting Bill a glance.

Wild Bill was the dangerous man in the room, and he was the man that Harms would most likely look to for solving whatever the issue was. However, he didn't want the sheriff to feel slighted.

"We've lost contact with a couple of truck units up the North Fork," Dale reported.

"I've sent another two units to find out what's going on up there. We should hear from them at any moment," Bill stated without emotion.

"Edwards said he had a cousin in British Columbia, maybe that's where they're crossing," Harms said. "Hopefully, we'll know more when your other unit's report. What else?"

"Well, we picked up two men coming into the Valley from the South. Mormons," Dale said.

"How do you know that they're Mormons?"

"That's what they told us. Lamar and Larry."

"Lamar and Larry," Harms repeated.

"Must take more than a deadly virus to keep those boys from knocking on doors to pass the word. Where are these missionaries?"

"We're holding them at the old armory," Dale said.

"These guys are pretty... well, I'm not quite sure how to put it."

"They're a cross between bible thumpers and pussies. In my book, they just can't believe everything's gone to shit. Including man's treatment of his fellow man. As if that hasn't always been shit," Bill retorted.

Harms took a cigar out of the humidor on his desk and rolled it in his fingers.

"Let's go visit these fellows where they're at. I don't want them to see our operations here at the dump," he said as he got up. "I need to get outta here anyway."

When they got to the armory, Harms told Bill it would be best if he waited outside while Dale and himself talked to the Mormons. Then, he told Dale that he needed him to follow his lead and play along with his plan as he outlined it to them.

"Gentlemen," Harms said as he stuck his hand out to Lamar as he entered the room.

Lamar took the commissioner's hand. Harms looked down at the handcuffs on Lamar's wrists.

"Sheriff, these aren't necessary are they?"

"No, sir. Sorry about—"

Harms held up his hand and Dale stopped speaking.

"It's alright, Dale, you were just following procedures," he said in a fatherly voice.

"I'm Commissioner Anthony Harms, and you gentleman are?"

"I'm Lamar Young and this is Larry Keener, sir."

Harms took Larry's hand in both of his after Dale had taken his handcuffs off.

"No need for the 'sir,' although I appreciate the politeness, especially in these troubled times. I believe you gentlemen have already met our sheriff," he said. "Please sit down."

The two men sat.

"When was the last time you gentlemen had anything to eat?" he asked.

Lamar and Larry look at each other, but before they could answer, Harms turned to the sheriff.

"Dale, please get these men something to eat and drink. Make sure it's warm and there's plenty of it. And I'm sure we no longer need a guard in the room."

"Absolutely, Commissioner," Dale said as he motioned for the guard to leave.

After the door was closed behind them, the commissioner continued. "I apologize that you weren't treated better." Harms turned his hands up and spread them apart as if to also apologize for their surroundings.

"We are a Christian community, and sometimes we struggle with reminding ourselves of that. But, these are troubled times in which we live." He paused. "Well, it's not an excuse. Or perhaps it is. How's that old saying go? These are times that try men's souls? To that, my mother would have responded with 'The Lord does not give you a cross to carry that you cannot bear.'"

Lamar and Larry ended Harms statement with an amen.

"And now, if you wouldn't mind telling me of your journey here. Although, each man's business is his own and I certainly don't mean to intrude. However, none of us here have left our little valley since the virus broke out. I simply ask because I have heard rumors and talked with strangers we have aided. We must pray for guidance but prepare for the worst."

Lamar looked at Larry. Larry nodded. With a heavy sigh, Lamar told Harms of their travels and the trouble they encountered, leaving out the reason for their travels north.

"Well, all I can say is how sorry I am for the loss of your bishop, but thank God it was not even more tragic."

There was a knock on the door.

"Enter."

In came the sheriff, carrying a pitcher of what appeared to be some kind of juice followed by two deputies with what appeared to be chicken dinners. After they set the trays on the table, Harms motioned for the two men to begin eating. It looked like a feast to Lamar and Larry. When their mouths were full of chicken, Harms cleared his throat. Both men looked up from their plates.

"Gentlemen, I thought perhaps we'd give thanks first."

Lamar and Larry were overcome with embarrassment and started to apologize profusely.

Harms held up his hand.

"You are both obviously famished. No apologies necessary." Then the commissioner simply bowed his head and prayed. "Heavenly Father, we thank you for this food and ask that it give us nourishment to do your will. Thank you for the safety of our community, and we ask that you also provide safety to these two men. We pray that those in pain seek your comfort. In the name of our savior, Jesus Christ, we pray. Amen."

After saying Amen with Larry, Lamar looked the commissioner in the eyes. He thought he could see tears forming in Harms' eyes.

"Thank you," Lamar said. It was all that he could bring himself to say.

"Yes, now I'll leave you two. Enjoy your meal. If you need to use the restroom or for that matter you need any assistance at all, someone will be right outside the door to help."

"*And keep you from leaving*," he thought to himself, but he didn't say that.

"Perhaps we can talk further after you're done eating," the commissioner finished as he got up and left the room.

In the hallway, the Commissioner saw Bill and Dale walking out of the room right next to where he had just left Lamar and Larry and he held a finger up to his lips signaling them to be quiet. He motioned for them to follow him. The three men went outside the building. Harms pulled the cigar out of his pocket and rolled it in his fingers.

"Between not drinking and starting to run out of cigars, this survival thing could become a real pain in the ass."

"Jesus, Boss, you laid the Holy Roller thing on pretty thick in there," Wild Bill said.

"You think too thick?"

"No. I mean, fuck, you had me wanting to convert. Hell, Commissioner, I think you could sell an ice cream cone machine to an Eskimo. That was an Oscar-type performance, man."

A man stepped outside.

"Mr. Clark?"

Bill turned to him. "Yeah?"

"We've got word out of the North Fork. Team Seven just drove in."

"I better go talk with them, if that's okay."

"Yes, by all means, Bill," Harms replied.

Bill shook his head as he walked away. "An Oscar, I'm telling you, an Oscar."

Harms turned to Dale.

"What did you think, Dale?" he asked.

"It was good, Commissioner, it was really good," he said hesitantly

"I can sense a 'but.'"

"Nothing, it was really good," Dale said, now with a little fear in his voice.

"It's okay, Dale, tell me what's on your mind. You have my word I won't get angry."

Dale kind of sighed and Harms thought perhaps now the sheriff was tearing up a little. Dale cleared his throat.

"Well, sir, I guess I kinda wish it hadn't been an act. That it'd been true," he said and then turned around and walked away.

As Harms watched him walk away, he stuck the cigar in his mouth. "*Me, too,*" he thought. He felt ashamed by the fact that he had thought of his dead family in order to bring tears to his eyes when he was talking to the Mormons. He wondered what kind of man would do that. He wondered if that was the type of man he had always been. Perhaps not. But it was certainly the type of man he was becoming. His thoughts were interrupted once more.

"Excuse me, Commissioner," a voice announced. It was the same guard who had informed them of Team Seven's return.

"Yes."

"Mr. Clark sent me to get you. He asked that you come at once to the front of the armory."

Clark turned from his discussion when the commissioner approached. Harms could see the rage on Clark's face.

"They killed eight of our men just above Polebridge on the North Fork Road. All of them had multiple gunshot wounds and all of them had headshots."

Harms must have looked puzzled by the shocking news and Clark's barely contained rage.

"THEY FUCKING HEAD SHOT THEM AFTER THEY WERE ALREADY DEAD," he screamed. "It's a message. They're sending us a FUCKING message!"

Harms put the cigar in his mouth for a moment. When he took it out and spoke, his voice was cold and he looked at Clark with an intensity in his eyes that made Clark recoil. Aware that the other men were watching his reaction, Harms took steps toward Clark in a way that made everyone wonder if he was going to strike the other man. Clark backed up a step or two from Harms.

"I want you to put together a team of 10 men. Outfit them for the backcountry, be prepared to leave before first light. Make no mistake, we are going to send a response to this message. Do it now." Harms put the unlit cigar back in his mouth.

Clark swallowed hard, and then turned and started to walk away.

"CLARK," Harms called out, not looking at the man but rather studying the end of his cigar.

Clark turned around and with a grudging voice answered, "Sir?"

"Perhaps we should channel some of our rage to the question of how did someone manage to kill eight of our men? Whom, if I'm not mistaken, were personally trained by you. Because it certainly is something that I'll be interested in hearing your take on."

"Sir. Yes, sir. Am I dismissed, Commissioner?"

"You're dismissed, Mr. Clark."

Harms walked back to the armory wondering just what the hell he was going to do in response to the mess this morning. He paused for a minute and tried to clear his head before he knocked on the door and walked in.

"Gentlemen, I trust your meal was alright?"

Both Lamar and Larry assured him that it was very good.

Harms actually smiled and could tell that these men were sincere in their gratitude. It made him feel good.

"I thought perhaps we could stretch our legs a bit if that's alright with you fellows."

Once outside, Harms pulled the cigar out of his pocket.

"I fully respect your beliefs on certain substances. Although, in all honesty, I do not share them. So, with your permission," he held up the cigar.

"Absolutely, by all means, Commissioner," Lamar responded genuinely.

Harms lit the cigar puffed a few times on it and blew on the end of it to make sure it was burning evenly. He then motioned with his hand and started across the lawn. After a few minutes of silence, Harms stopped and turned to Larry and Lamar.

"May I confide in you gentlemen?"

Both of the men nodded.

"We've had..." Harms paused for a moment as if he was searching for the right words, knowing that he was adding to the suspense that he could see building on Lamar and Larry's faces. He continued, "...a tragic incident that took the lives of eight men. These brave men were not only murdered," he paused again and made a point of swallowing hard.

The gesture conveyed a sense of sorrow and resolve.

"The evil that did this to these honest men... After they killed them, they went around and shot each one of them in the face with a high-caliber pistol. I can only assume they did this so the families of these men would suffer and be tortured even more so. As I said earlier, each man's business is his own. But, as I also said earlier, it is my God-given duty to protect what is left of our valley's way of life. Having said that, I'm compelled now to ask the both of you why you're in the Flathead. Because, I'm sure it's not by accident, and I know you won't insult me by telling me it is. Or at least I hope I've earned your respect enough that you won't."

Lamar and Larry exchanged a look.

"Commissioner, I can answer for both of us in saying that you have our utmost respect. Could we have a moment alone please?" Lamar asked.

"I don't see why not. But, in all honesty, gentlemen, you've just told me that my hunch is right. That you do have a purpose for being here, because if you didn't, you wouldn't need anytime to discuss something that didn't exist. Perhaps, I can offer you assistance in what you're doing, perhaps not. I'll be around the corner sitting on the bench finishing my cigar." And with that, Harms walked away.

Larry looked at Lamar. "Lamar..." he started.

"I don't know. Every time that we have trusted someone outside our own people... well, it has not turned out good. At all," Lamar stated.

"That's true and I can't argue that point. However, I believe that this is the first time on our journey that we have encountered a man of God such as ourselves. Perhaps, he is not one of us in the sense that he does not belong to the Church of Latter Day Saints, but he certainly is one of us in Christ," Larry said.

"I want so badly to believe what you say is true, Larry. I do. But it's just this feeling that I have. What about that scary man who was with the sheriff? He looked as bad as anyone we have encountered so far."

"Once again, I can't argue with you there, brother. Ask the commissioner about him. Base your decision on whether or not we share with him what we are after contingent on his answer to that or any other questions you might ask. Because, I will go along with whatever you decide. You started out as our leader and that has not changed. But, Lamar, the fact is we have no supplies left, and even more important, no idea where we need to go from here. I have never been to Glacier Park nor have you. I will end with this last thought. Lamar, before you decide, remember that we prayed with this man. And when that prayer was done, I saw tears form in his eyes. A person can't fake that. I believe it was truly a glimpse into the man's soul."

When they went around the corner, they found Commissioner Anthony Harms in what appeared to be deep thought, which in fact he was. He was considering Clark's foul mood over the loss of his men and probably even fouler mood over the way Harms had spoken to him. The commissioner was wondering just what Wild Bill would do to these Mormons in order to get them to talk and which one would break first. He was betting on Larry. Hearing them approach, he removed the cigar from his mouth and stood up.

"Commissioner, we both believe that you are a man of honor, and like I've said, we both respect you." Lamar paused.

"Please continue."

"Well, sir, I feel that I must ask you about the rather serious man who was with your sheriff when we were first brought here, and what his role might be in your organization."

Harms let out a chuckle.

"Sorry, Lamar, I don't wish to make light of your question. I've just never heard of Mr. Clark, whom you must be talking about, being referred to as a serious-looking man. Which actually, in fact, is an accurate description. I, myself, find him downright scary looking. And, if you know what he has been trained to do, well, Mr. Clark is a very dangerous man; make no mistake about that. I'm trying to think of a way that I can explain his current role here." The commissioner paused in thought.

"Frankly, the only way to explain what he does for us, that comes to my mind, is to compare him to the Archangel Michael. Having said that, I can assure you I'm not putting any of us on par with the Lord or his angels. But, we are all his servants. I am sure you have had the unfortunate experience of encountering persons bent on doing evil. We, too, have had to deal with similar people. Not everyone who has traveled to our valley has turned out to be like you two. I'm afraid a recent group of travelers, whom I chose to trust against the advice of Mr. Clark, is responsible for the murders of our men I mentioned earlier. As you will recall, the Lord asked Michael to lead his armies against Satan and be the guardian of his people. Well, I have asked Bill Clark to do the same. I have come to understand, with each passing day, what a sacrifice he is making for all of us, because he has been the man that goes to bed at night and spends his every waking moment in a struggle with evil. I can only imagine how strong his faith must be. Not only to carry out that role, but also not to succumb to it." When Harms stopped talking, he realized that he had unconsciously raised his voice and that it, in fact, carried a conviction that was not contrived.

"Hopefully, that explains Mr. Clark's role and answers your question. Because, for right now, it is the only explanation I can give you."

Lamar looked to Larry and Larry nodded to him.

"May we join you?" Lamar asked.

"Of course," Harms said, moving to the center of the bench so that he would be in between them.

Once on the bench, Lamar began. When Lamar had finished telling the commissioner what brought them to the Flathead Valley, the three men sat in silence. After formulating a quick plan in his head, Commissioner Harm's finally broke the silence.

"You obviously are going to need supplies. Are either one of you familiar with the park at all?"

Both men shook their heads indicating that they were not familiar with the park.

"Then, in addition to being outfitted for the journey, you'll need a guide. Have you a plan of what to do with the vaccine once it's in your possession?"

"No, we haven't. It is becoming quite apparent that our plans have not been as well thought out as they should have been," Lamar said.

"Don't beat yourself up. You did well to make it as far as you have. God saw fit to bring you here for help, and help is exactly what we are going to give you. Gentlemen, if we want you to leave in the morning, then we have no time to waste," Harms said standing up. Lamar and Larry stood with him.

"Thank you, Commissioner," Larry said.

"Yes, thank you," echoed Lamar.

"No, thank you," Harms responded. "I believe that it is imperative that we keep this information between the three of us. If it got out, well, let's just say it would cause quite an uproar. Everyone would go after it, and that I'm sure would most likely destroy any chance that we have in obtaining it."

It was not lost on Lamar that Harms' conversation had gone from him and Larry to we. He hoped the apprehension that rose in his stomach was ill-founded.

Harms flagged down the first person he saw and gave them instructions to find the sheriff and have him arrange for outfitting Lamar and Larry with packs and supplies for a week-long hike into the backcountry of the park. He also told him to inform the sheriff that the four of them would all be dining together this evening.

After leaving Lamar and Larry, Harms found Clark barking orders to the men he was assembling to take with him in the morning. Clark saw Harms approaching and walked toward him.

"We need to talk in private," Harms said to him.

Clark turned around. When he found the man he was looking for, he yelled.

"Simms, take over," he shouted and then turned back to Harms.

Harms stepped out of his way, indicating that Clark should lead. Clark led them into the men's room. One of the stalls was occupied.

"Who's in there?"

"Goodman," said a tentative voice from the stall.

"Pinch it off, Goodman, and get your fucking ass back out to the assembly area."

"Ah, I'm kinda in the middle of something here."

"NOW, GODDAMIT," screamed Clark.

"What the fuck?" came the response from the stall, but moments later the toilet flushed. Richard Goodman emerged doing up his pants.

"Sorry, I didn't realize it was you, Mr. Clark." He then noticed the commissioner. "Ah, you, too, Commissioner."

"Get," Clark said.

When he was gone, Harms walked over to a sink and started to wash his hands. After drying them off, he turned to Clark.

"I didn't care for the way you addressed me earlier, Bill. Having said that, I realize that you were understandably very upset. Needless to say, my response was based on the need to keep the established command structure clear. I want you to know that I have every confidence in you and your abilities. I can think of no one more important to me than you."

"I was way out of line. We'd all be up a shit creek without you, sir. I mean that." Clark sounded like a son who had been reprimanded by his father and was seeking absolution.

"Then, not only is the matter closed, it is also forgotten. Something has been brought to my attention that is a game changer. Not only for us, but if this information is true, for the whole messed-up world. I found out why our Mormon friends are here."

"HOLY SHIT, HOLY SHIT," Clark said when the commissioner told him why Lamar and Larry were heading through the Flathead Valley.

"Yeah, no kidding."

"Tell me we're not going to let those two Bible thumpers go after this guy."

"Actually, that's exactly what we're going to do, and you're going with them. Before you say anything, hear me out."

Harms told Clark of Lamar's question about him and how he answered it. He then asked Clark if he thought he could guide them where they needed to go. After Clark indicated that he could guide them, the commissioner told him that he would give them a one-day head start and then follow them with the men currently being assembled. He expressed to Clark that his gut told him that somehow Ethan Edwards was involved in all this. He explained that Edwards showing up and the arrival of the Mormons was just too much of a coincidence to not be all related. He also felt that the bloodbath in the North Fork was also tied into it.

"You're going to have to play your part of being my archangel. Do you think you can do that?"

"Hell yes. I always wondered if all that shit they taught me as an altar boy would come in handy."

"I didn't know you were an altar boy," Harms said genuinely surprised.

"Yeah, not many people do. I got kicked out for beating the crap out of the kid who I did mass with. Little bastard ratted me out for skimming out of the collection plate. My old man put a serious beating on me for that." He paused. "Now that I think about it, those Mormon dudes kinda remind me of that kid."

Harms laughed.

"Do you know your way around the park?"

"I found my way through jungles in South America and the mountains of Afghanistan. I'm pretty sure I can negotiate Glacier National Park."

"I have no doubts."

"What happens when I get this guy or vaccine thing?"

"Well, we sure as hell aren't sending it back to Salt Lake City. But, for now, we better go find your new best friends."

CHAPTER 45

Samantha and Ethan froze when they heard the sound of gunfire. She started to head back the way they'd come, but Ethan stood on the trail in front of her.

"I know, but wait a minute," he said.

After what seemed like an eternity, they heard a single rifle shot.

"That's gotta be Mike's 270. The first shots we heard were automatic rifle fire but that last one was a high-powered rifle. That's gotta be Mike," he said.

Ethan no sooner stopped talking and the sound of rapid gunfire filled the air again. Then it stopped as suddenly as it started.

"You think he's alive?" Sam asked with a shaky voice.

"Ya, he's still in the fight."

"Let's go," she said.

"We should angle back toward the river, hopefully, as we get closer we can zero in on his location," Ethan said as he turned and started toward the river moving as fast as the forest would allow him.

It wasn't long before another single shot rang out. Ethan stopped and turned to Samantha but before he could say anything, more rifle shots filled the air. The rifle shots were followed by another angry burst of automatic gunfire. Sam looked at Ethan with a puzzled look on her face.

"I don't know, Sam. I can tell what's automatic rifle fire, but the other stuff sounds like larger caliber rifles. Whatever is going on, a whole lot of lead is getting thrown around, that's for sure." He started through the woods again. There were more gunshots

"Pistol," he said looking over his shoulder at her. "That's a big pistol and they were measured shots."

"What does that mean?" she asked, almost in a panic.

"Hard to tell... Does Mike carry a pistol?"

"I think a Smith 9."

"Well, that sure as hell wasn't a 9 mm. And the way the shots came slow like that... It's almost like..." He stopped, not wanting to finish his thought. He didn't want her to tell her that it sounded like someone was taking their time. Like they were systematically executing people.

"Like what?" she asked.

"Like, I think it's over," he said.

"Over? *Over* like what the hell does that mean?"

"It means number one, I think Mike's alive and the first single shot we heard was him. I also think there were more than him and the commissioner's men involved. Look, I'm guessing at most of this, but I'm positive about that first single shot. And…" He stopped.

"And what?" she asked with a mixture of fear, anxiety, and anger in her voice.

"And, Sam, I'm willing to go absolutely anywhere with you. But, I've got to tell you, I don't think we can help Mike. We haven't heard any more gunfire. Whatever happened is over. He doesn't need our help. But, like I said, if you want to go look for him, then we should go."

She knew what he was really saying to her. Mike either got away or he was dead. Them going to find out wasn't going to accomplish anything. Samantha couldn't bring herself to say what she knew they should do. So, instead, she just turned and started walking back the way they'd come.

Sam led them through the forest at a brisk pace. When they did stop, which wasn't often, they exchanged very few words or, for that matter, it was as if she couldn't look at Ethan for very long. Finally, with the light beginning to fade, they came upon Bowman Lake.

"We better stop here for tonight," Sam said. "Tomorrow, we will make Elizabeth Lake, and then the next day, we can start really looking for this Kraus guy."

"Okay," Ethan replied. "We should run a dark camp inside the tree line on the far side of the lake."

She nodded at him and set out again.

They set up their sleeping area at the bottom of a huge pine tree. After splitting one of Ethan's MREs, they sat sipping a cup of Sam's herbal tea from Ethan's canteen cup, which he'd heated over his little propane camp stove.

"I think there's going to be a storm," Ethan said as he pointed to the eastern sky. "You can smell it in the air."

Sam nodded. They passed the cup between them drinking in silence as the darkness of night enveloped them.

"You think I'm bossy?" Sam asked, not looking at him.

"Um… No. I think you're assertive," he answered.

She gave him a weak smile. Lightning flashed in the distance.

"He's okay, Sam."

"He's my only…"

"Not anymore," Ethan said, as he reached out and pulled her to him.

They held each other tight and he could feel the wetness of her tears on his cheeks. She pulled away from him and guided his hand to her breast while leaning into kiss him. When they stopped kissing, Ethan slowly started to undo the buttons of her shirt. He kissed her neck as he moved his lips to her shoulders and slid her shirt off. Samantha stood up, reached behind her back with both hands and undid her bra and dropped it to the ground. Ethan took his shirt off as he watched her slide her jeans and panties down and step out of them. Lightning flashed and for a brief moment, he saw her standing naked before him. His heart raced.

She came toward him and the two of them fumbled to get his jeans unbuttoned. Ethan raised his hips and hooked his thumbs in the band of his underwear and pushed them down over his hips. Samantha pulled them the rest of the way off as she straddled him. He felt her take him in her hand and guide him inside of her. Ethan heard the air escape from her mouth as he entered her and felt her warmth. He closed his eyes. He felt her start to move her hips against him, picking up speed and intensity. Ethan swallowed hard as he felt himself beginning to lose control. Samantha stopped, bent, and kissed him.

"It's okay," she whispered in his ear and kissed him.

He put his lips to her ear, gently nibbling her ear.

"I just need a moment. My God, you feel so good, go slow for me," Ethan said, wanting this moment to last forever.

He leaned up and cupped her breasts and brought one of them to his mouth. Samantha started to slowly move her hips against him. When she let out a soft moan, Ethan could wait no longer. She lay with her head on his chest and felt him gently push her hair from her face with his fingers. Samantha closed her eyes as she savored his touch and, once again, she felt the safety and security in his arms. She wished he would hold her forever. Lightning lit the sky again and thunder boomed.

"Wow, mood lighting by God," Samantha said.

Ethan had been with other women and wasn't by any means a novice. But this was different; this was not like any other time. He'd had sex, but for the first time in his life, he knew what it was like to make love to a woman. If someone were to ask him how he felt, he realized he would not be able to put his feelings into words. He felt wonderful. So wonderful in fact, for some reason he almost felt like weeping. He was grateful when she spoke.

"You were perfect."

"It's dry lightning," he said, and then felt stupid. He needed, wanted to say so much more. "Sam…" he started to say.

She raised herself from his chest gently kissed his lips, and whispered in his ear.

"I know. I feel the same way." She lay her head back on his chest, closed her eyes, and fell asleep in his arms.

When he awoke, he didn't want to move, but the arm he was holding her with had fallen asleep. That, and he had to pee so bad he would soon have to sandbag his eyeballs. She stirred and opened her eyes.

"Sorry," he said.

Samantha smiled and then leaned up and kissed him.

"No worries," she said. "I've really gotta go pee." She got up and gingerly walked off in her bare feet.

Ethan smiled. God, there was just nothing phony about this woman. He, too, wondered off to do his business. As he was relieving himself, Ethan was overcome with the feeling that they had always known each other. When Ethan got back, Samantha was standing there naked. He stopped and looked at her.

"It would be a shame to waste that," she said, looking down at him.

Ethan was pretty sure he blushed.

"Perhaps, we can go back to saving the world in a few minutes," she said, as she lay back down.

Ethan followed her to the ground, and agreed that the world and its problems could wait.

They hadn't hiked for very long early the next morning when Samantha stopped and pointed at the cloud of smoke rising off in the distance.

"Looks like there's another fire above Granite Park Chalet," Samantha said. "Hard to say which way it's going to go, obviously it will depend a lot on the wind. It will be the shits if it connects up with the other one."

"Had to be a lightning strike from last night. *What*?" he asked as he saw her smile.

"Nothing," she said.

"What?"

"I was just thinking that's not the only place lightning struck last night. I probably shouldn't be making light of the situation. Know what else I'm thinking?"

Before he could answer, she continued.

"I'm thinking if Mr. Kraus is at Granite Park Chalet and he's got half a brain, he's heading to Sperry Chalet and not just hanging around to see which way this fire goes."

"That makes sense. So, we should get to Sperry Chalet tomorrow, right?" Ethan asked.

"Yeah, if we take off just as it's getting light outside, we should get there by mid-afternoon."

After hiking all day, they set up camp and once again shared an MRE and gave a Cowboy his own.

"I don't really know anything about you," Samantha said as she leaned her head against his shoulder.

"There's really not that much to tell," he replied.

She looked up at him.

"You do remember that I'm a lawyer, right? I can always put you on the witness stand..." Her smile faded. "You don't have to tell me anything if you don't want to. But, you can trust me, Ethan. How did you and this Bob guy get to know each other?"

"You are a lawyer," he said smiling.

"And, I'm pretty cute."

"Actually, you're really cute," Ethan said and kissed her.

"Bob and Fran Watkins looked after me when I was younger," he started as his story just seemed to pour right out of him.

Once he started, he told her everything, even things he hadn't planned to. When he finished, she leaned in closer to him and squeezed her tighter.

"What about you, Counselor?" he asked after they'd been silent for a bit.

"It's getting late and we've got a pretty good hike ahead of us tomorrow," she replied.

"By God, you are a lawyer."

"Come on, I'll show you some of my better legal and maybe not so legal moves," she said as she grabbed his hand and led him to bed.

The sky was just starting to lighten to the east the next morning when they headed out. They stopped mid-morning for their first break. Ethan had been in the lead. He stopped next to a tree that had the bark ripped off it about six feet from the ground. There were obvious claw marks in the wood.

"Apparently, we are in some grizzly's neighborhood," he said. "That's a big bear... look at the size of its claw marks."

"So normally, I'd say that we need to make a lot of noise. Like, sing while we hike. But, that's kinda tough when you're trying to sneak up on somebody. That, and you really don't want to hear me sing," Sam said.

"I bet you sound better than you think."

"Stop trying to butter me up. You already got into my pants." She could tell from the moment she said it, that her comment had come across wrong and her intuition was confirmed by the hurt look on his face.

"Sorry, I was trying to be funny. I didn't mean to take anything away from the last two nights."

"That's okay. I'm just... I've never met anyone who makes me feel like you do. And just so you know, I've been known to do a little karaoke at the Antler Bar when the mood strikes me."

"Really? Like who?"

"Willie Nelson."

"Willie Nelson? Are you kidding me?"

"Yeah, Willie Nelson."

She shook her head.

"Okay Willie, it's time to get on the road again," she said as she moved past him on the trail.

"Very funny."

"That was funny."

After getting several hundred yards from the tree that was scratched up by the bear, they paused for lunch, which consisted mainly of some granola. They'd been keeping Cowboy close to them as they hiked. Hiking with a dog in grizzly bear country had its drawbacks. As they sat on the hillside, it was Cowboy who perked up when the wind changed. Cowboy stood looking at the ridge across from them. Both Sam and Ethan grabbed their binoculars and started scanning the ridge.

"There," Sam said.

"Where's *there*?" Ethan asked.

"See that rock out-cropping?"

"Yeah."

"Down and to the left."

"Give me a time."

"What?" Sam asked.

"If the rocks are twelve o'clock, give me a time," Ethan replied.

"Oh, okay. Umm, ten... or between nine and ten... I guess."

"Wow, that's a big bear."

"Yeah, it's already trying to put on weight for winter."

Ethan lowered his Vortex binoculars and looked at Sam, but before he could say anything, he caught a glare of sunlight off of something. He leaned back so he could see around Sam's back and brought his Vortex binoculars back up to his eyes. Sam looked over her shoulder at him.

"Shhh. Slowly, lay back and roll over. We're not alone. Don't bring your glasses up just yet."

When they were both laying on their stomachs Ethan said to Sam, "Let me see your binoculars, we need to make sure your lenses are coated."

"They're coated," she replied.

"Okay, then see the big larch standing by itself? That's twelve, look to six."

"Oh my God, do you think that's him?"

"Look behind him a few feet. That looks like two young kids."

"No doubt about it. Nobody said anything about him having any kids," she said.

"Look around them. I don't see any real backpacks. The guy looks like he's got a daypack on, but that's it. So, if they don't have packs..."

"Then, they must be staying some place close. Like Sperry Chalet?" Sam said, finishing his thought.

"So what do we do?" Sam asked.

"Well, we stay plumb still and move only after they do. I picked up the glare off the lens on his binoculars. We just got lucky he didn't see us first. And we watch. Then we follow them, and call Bob when the opportunity arises."

"I'm just asking, okay? So, don't go all Marine on me."

"I'm listening…"

"What if, like, we have to pee or poop?"

"We ain't moving till they do. So, use your imagination," Ethan said flatly.

"I was afraid you were going to say that."

Thankfully, they didn't have to wait long. The grizzly bear herded her two cubs together and meandered off with them in tow. About fifteen minutes after the grizzlies left, the man stood up and motioned for the children to follow him.

"Something is weird about this guy and those two kids," Samantha said.

"Weird how?"

"Like I don't know, just weird. I'm getting a strange vibe even this far away."

"So what's normal?" Ethan asked.

"Good question. It's not like I'd know normal, but I'll tell ya what, buddy, trust me, I do know weird and something is weird. It's like he's their teacher or something, not their father… it's just…"

"Let me guess, *weird*!" Ethan stated with a smile.

She looked at him. "You being a smart ass?"

"Absolutely not! You learn in combat to trust your gut sometimes more than your eyes. And, if your gut is saying something ain't right then that's good enough for me, darling." He scooched over and gave her a kiss.

"Thanks," she said.

"Still gotta pee?"

"I never had to pee."

Ethan made a face. "That's tough duty."

"When they leave, I'm taking a timeout and we ain't voting on it."

"Hey, that's cool. It will give them a bit of head start on us, I'll see if I can't raise Bob on the satellite phone and you can do what you need to do."

"Take a poop… I need to take a poop."

"Okay, okay, take a poop… you can take a poop."

CHAPTER 46

Bob was in the lab when the call came in. Bob was always in the lab.

"Doctor Watkins?" a young corporal's voice asked shakily.

Bob turned to face the man talking into the mic behind the glass.

"Sir, there's a priority one satellite call for you in the com room. General Short has already been patched in," the corporal said.

Bob nodded and moved toward the decontamination chamber. When he got to the communication room, the same young corporal handed him a headset with a mic on it. Watkins let out a deep sigh before putting it on. If you didn't know Bob Watkins, you might not notice it, and he'd be the last to admit it. He was tired, bone tired; worse than when he was working the Ebola outbreak in Africa in 2014 and 2015. It was after he got home from that outbreak that his heart troubles started.

"Doctor Watkins is coming on line," the corporal said into a table mic. He pushed a button and pointed to Bob.

"Watkins, you there?" he heard General Short ask.

"Yes, sir…" Before he could get anything else out, he heard Ethan's voice. He sighed again and felt as if a little weight had been lifted from his chest.

"Bob, I think we found him," Ethan said, not being able to totally control the excitement in his voice.

"That's… that's great."

"Tell him the rest," Short interjected.

Ethan explained everything starting from the time they left Mike up to the time that they spotted who they assumed was Victor.

"First off, I hope your friend Mike is alright."

It wasn't lost on Ethan that with everything he'd just told this man, his first thoughts were about the safety of someone he'd never met. But, then again, that was the kind of man, the kind of human being, Bob Watkins was.

"I agree with your assessment of the confrontation involving your friend Mike. This commissioner and his gang might not have as tight of a grip on things as they think. As for this thing with the children and who we think is Victor… Well, I'm just not sure what to think. General, have we any intel that might suggest he took these kids with him from the start?"

"None whatsoever. Although, obviously our intelligence assets are practically nonexistent. However, we need to move forward with the assumption that the individual that Edwards and the woman…"

"Samantha," Ethan said.

"Yes, yes, Samantha... observed is Victor Kraus. That means that Doctor Watkins needs to get out there immediately."

Bob smiled. The general was finally convinced that he should go.

"Yes, I do," Bob interjected as the thought crossed his mind he needed to get out of there and away from the lab as much or more than he needed to get there.

"Okay, you said you had a plan, Bob, to have Burt fly you up here in his Cessna."

"That's pretty much the long and the short of it. I was hoping that Samantha could meet me in Baab and that you could—"

"Keep eyes on the target," General Short cut in.

"I was going to say watch this guy. Anyway, once Sam and I find each other, perhaps the two of you can arrange where we should meet up. From that point on, I guess we can wing it."

They could hear General Short moan loudly.

"Sorry, General, I meant to say assess the situation and adjust plans from that point."

"No, you didn't. I know you people think I've got a stick up my ass so far that I've got a lump in my throat, but I can assure you without going into it the world situation is becoming more rather than less precarious. So, let's get on with it."

"Right, Ethan, put Sam on."

"Okay, here she is."

When Sam was done talking to Bob, she handed the phone back to Ethan.

"Yeah," he said into the mic.

"Alright. If it goes the way we're hoping, Edwards, you and Watkins should be seeing each other in a couple days, two and a half at most."

"Sounds good. Hey, Bob, if you get a chance, grab my Teka, it's behind your couch."

"We are on lockdown here. I haven't been back to the house since you left."

"Any other special requests?" General Short asked sarcastically.

The phones were silent. General Short broke it.

"Hey, kid?"

"Yes, sir."

"Get this done and it goes a long way toward pulling that stick out."

"No doubt, it's probably pretty uncomfortable, sir. We'll get it done."

Bob Watkins turned around one more time to see Fran, her arms folded, looking terrified as she stood in the hall just outside the door to their living quarters. He smiled and raised one hand slightly as she did the same and then she walked back into their room. Watkins stood a moment longer now looking down the empty hallway and wondered for the first time since he'd met her if, in fact, this would be the last time he ever saw her.

He walked outside. In front of him was a Humvee with three soldiers standing in level four hazmat suits, all armed. Bob had on an old comfortable pair of Levis, his favorite flannel shirt, and his Filson bush hat.

"Ready, sir."

Bob took a deep breath and filled his lungs with clean, cool Montana air. Being outside and breathing unfiltered air was the best medicine he could have hope for. Throwing his pack over one shoulder, he headed toward the Humvee.

"I am ready to go, boys," Bob said as he climbed in the vehicle and the four of them headed toward Darby.

When they pulled up in front of Burt Long's place, it looked deserted. Bob and the soldiers got out of the Humvee. Bob reached back inside and took out a bullhorn.

"Burt?" He waited a second. "Burt, you in there?"

Bob saw a piece of wood slide back in the front window. After a minute, the front door opened just a crack. Whoever opened it wasn't exposing themselves.

"Bob, that really you?"

"Yeah, it's really me, Burt."

"Who's the Martian-looking fellows with you, Bob? Even more important, how come they are all suited up and you're not? You ain't sick, are you?"

"No, I'm not sick, just tired. These young men are suited up, as you put it, because they're going back to the lab in Hamilton and I'm not."

"Why aren't you going back?" Burt paused. "Oh... my oh my, not Fran, not Franny..."

"No, no, Burt, Fran is just fine, she's still at the lab working."

"Now I'm really kinda confused. What would make you leave Fran? Cause with what you've just said, it doesn't sound like they'll let you back in seeing as how you're not wearing one of those suits."

"Burt, let me ask you... and I know you'll be straight. Has anybody in the house been sick?"

"Goddammit, that kinda hurts, Bob. I've been straight with you from the day I met ya. Oh, there might be one or two clients or properties I fudge on. But all in all, I think—"

"Burt, anybody been sick?"

"NO and NO."

"Then, I've got a favor I need to ask you. I need your help."

"Name it, Bob."

"You best hear what it is before you agree to anything."

"Then come on in and tell us."

Bob spoke with the soldiers for a moment, letting them know that they could head back to the lab and then grabbed his pack and headed into the house. The first thing he noticed, which was actually two things, Phil and Carl in the living room crouched behind recliners with assault rifles. In contrast, Doris, Burt's wife and Ethel, Phil's wife, were sitting at the kitchen table. Both women stood up when Bob walked in.

"Fellows," Bob said to Phil and Carl. "What's the chance of getting you boys to point those things in a different direction?"

Both men lowered their guns.

"Shit, Bob, it's really you," Phil said.

"Yep, it's me. Ladies," he said turning to the women.

"Bob, come sit down let me get you something to eat," Doris said as she walked up to him and gave him a hug.

"Thank you, Doris, but I ate just before we left Hamilton. How are you folks doing on supplies? And, obviously you decided to team up."

"Well, we just thought safety in numbers. That and we combined our supplies, which are holding out pretty good but ain't going to holdout forever. In fact, we better knock down some game real soon or it's going to be a long long winter," Phil said.

"Lots of slow moving elk out there," Carl added.

Everybody knew he meant cows.

"Surviving by yourself gets pretty boring pretty fast. It helped when Carl set us up with CB radios. But after awhile, that kinda lost its glamour. It was Burt who came up with the idea that we team up. After we figured that none of us were sick, it made sense. Burt and Doris have ample room. So, what the hell? So far, seems to be working out okay. We haven't killed each other yet."

"Hasn't been for lack of arguing. Sit down, Bob, let me get you something to drink," Doris moved toward the sink.

"Actually, I thought I might offer you all a little something. I'm assuming, Doris, that you've got something we could make coffee in." His statement made everybody perked up.

"Absolutely," she said. "Coffee? You're a Saint!"

Bob dug around in his pack.

"And, Burt, what's the chance you've got some glasses around here?" he asked, pulling a bottle of Scotch and a bottle of Crown Royal out of his pack.

"Saint my ass, more like an angel."

When Bob had set everyone up with the beverage of their choice, he explained to the group the purpose for his visit. When he was done talking, everyone sat silent for a moment. Phil's wife, Ethel, was the first to speak up.

"I'm sure that there are very good reasons, but I have to ask, why can't the government send somebody out there with you? I mean, I can understand why they feel you need to go but…" She paused.

"I'm sure they've got good reasons, honey," Phil said.

"I'm sure they do, Phil, and that's why I asked. I'd like to hear them," she responded. "I mean, all the tax money and other shit, pardon my language. Well, you'd just think they'd have some military types to do this."

Everybody went silent. Bob stood up and poured everybody a few more sips into their glasses. When he sat down again, everyone was looking at him.

"That, Ethel, is one hell of a good question. And, I wish that I could give you a good answer. But I can't because I am I not allowed to say. What I do know is that this thing got dumped in our lap. This fellow, General Short, I told you about is a man of integrity. And if he thought there was a different way or a better one, I wouldn't be here talking to you. Maybe having ordinary folks do this somehow makes sense because it's ordinary folks who always get asked to step up to the plate." He paused. "If we don't get this vaccine, I'm afraid things are going to get worse, not just here, but all over the world."

"It's why they gave Frodo the ring, maybe." Everyone turned to look at Carl.

"What?" he said looking back at them. "I mean at some point, God's got to enter into the deal, right? Maybe, it's not because they ain't got anybody else, but maybe they don't trust no one else. That's why in Lord of the Rings Frodo and them other guys were the only ones that could do it. It's like those in charge didn't actually chose them. Destiny, or I think more likely God, chose 'em. Way I see it, it's pretty much the same thing here."

"I think I like Carl's explanation better than mine," Bob said.

"He's been reading the books."

"Yeah, I'm 'bout half way done with Return of the King," Carl said.

Bob thought, *"Okay, makes sense now."*

"Well, Ethel?"

"Guess you can't argue with logic like that. Doesn't mean I'm any less scared."

"Hey, I got a quick question."

"Go ahead, Carl."

"What's this thing called?"

"What do you mean?"

"This virus it got a name?"

"Not really, I guess. Some people are calling it the Typhon virus and we've given it a scientific code. Carl, have you got any better suggestions?"

"No. I was just kind of thinking... If it's the measles and the Ebola... Maybe MEBOLA would work."

"Well, if the opportunity comes up, I'll mention it. In the meantime, we need to decide if you are going to help us."

"Hell, Bob, we decided before you asked," Burt said. Everyone else nodded in the affirmative, including Ethel although she started crying.

Phil rubbed her back and told her it was going to be okay.

After much discussion, they decided Burt and Carl would go. Phil was none too happy with staying behind but Ethel looked relieved.

They were up and going before sunrise. Bob made more coffee, which everyone was happy about. Phil had gotten up earlier and baked fresh biscuits that were delicious. Doris and Ethel made use of some of them by making eggs benedict. Burt suggested that due to the mission at hand, a drink for luck was in order. The women argued against it because of the fact it was so early. Burt made the argument that with the current state of things being too early wasn't a worry. Being too late, on the other hand could be a real problem. In the end, they voted on it. The decision to have a drink for luck passed four in favor two against. Then the tears started.

The three of them pulled out of the yard with the blessing of those they left behind, a 'get 'er done' attitude, and what was left of the booze. Just in case.

As they pulled into the airstrip, which was actually just outside of Hamilton, Burt commented that the Cessna 185 should be good to go. He had fuel in the hangar, and there was no doubt that the plane was mechanically sound. They'd do an extra thorough preflight check, make sure the battery had enough juice, which if it didn't, as Carl pointed out, they'd take the one out of the truck. All in all, they should be in the air in under an hour. And then a little over an hour in the air to Baab. Burt had never flown there, but with the GPS Bob had brought with them, they figured the flight should be a piece of cake. They were inside the hanger when a vehicle pulled up outside.

When they looked out to see who was there, three men stood by the hangar door. Monty Weston and two other men had gotten out of the Sheriff's Suburban.

"Just what in the hell do you assholes think you're doing?"

"Where's Sheriff Maxwell?" Bob asked ignoring Monty's question.

"He didn't make it. I'm in charge now," he said with a smirk.

Bob was visibly shaken by the news.

"So, like I was saying..."

"We aren't telling you a goddam thing." Bob's voice was hard.

Both Burt and Carl looked at him. They'd never heard him sound like that.

"We'll see about that. You're all under arrest for violating the curfew and travel restrictions order."

"Curfew? It's not even eight o'clock in the morning yet for Christ's sake," Burt said.

"Monty, I've had triple bypass surgery, a major heart attack, and I'm betting I'd still kick your ass, so I'm not in the mood to fuck around with the likes of you," Bob said taking a step forward.

"Careful, Watkins," Monty said as his hand went to his pistol.

It was then that they heard the roar of engines. They all turned and saw two Humvees flying across the airfield. Both vehicles came to a stop one on each side of the group. Each with a soldier wearing a bio suit standing behind an M-60 machine gun. Two soldiers from each vehicle exited. They were fully armed and also in bio-suits.

"Dr. Watkins," one of them said walking up.

"Colonel Woolard, it's nice to see you," Bob said recognizing the commander of the Hamilton lab.

"Sir, General Short thought that we should check up on you and make sure you got off to a good start on your mission. I assume everything is going as planned."

"It will be now that you're here, Colonel. Colonel, if you'd allow me one thing before we continue, I'd appreciate it very much," Bob said.

"By all means, sir, whatever you need."

"Thank you," Bob said taking two steps forward. He then threw a punch that knocked Monty Weston on his ass.

"Son of a bitch, that hurt," Bob said wringing his hand.

He looked down at Monty.

"You wouldn't have made a pimple on Jim Maxwell's ass. Don't you ever smirk when you mention that man's name." He then turned back to the colonel.

"Colonel Woolard, if you hear of this… this person causing anybody any grief… well, I'd consider it a personal favor if you'd take care of him in whatever way you saw fit."

"It would be my pleasure, Doctor."

Twenty minutes later, they were in the air and headed north.

Everything was a lush green and the summer colors were so vibrant it was breathtaking to see the view from the plane, although there was a thick haze to north where smoke from a forest fire had been accumulating. The view to the south was like being in a picture or a postcard Bob thought as the small aircraft flew through the Two Medicine area on its way to Baab. The small community of Saint Mary passed beneath them. A moment later, Burt put the Cessna into a bank.

"That's gotta be it. It's not like there's going to be more than one," Burt stated.

"What do you think?" Bob asked.

"Looks okay, at least the windsock is still up," he said as they made another pass over the field and then banked into a turn.

"Hey, I see somebody," Carl said.

When the plane leveled out, sure enough, there was a person standing with a dog waving one arm.

"That's got to be Ethan's friend, and Cowboy," Bob said.

"Let's hope so; makes me wonder who else is watching us. I'm going to put us down on the next pass. Carl, sit back."

The plane landed and bounced over the field. Burt slowed it and taxied it over by where Samantha was standing, and came to a stop just a few yards from her.

After hugging Cowboy, Bob stood up with wet eyes.

"Hello, Samantha, I assume? I'm Bob Watkins, this is Burt Long and Carl Gunderson," Bob said sticking his hand out.

"Nice to meet you, Dr. Watkins," Sam said taking his hand. Bob winced when Sam squeezed his hand.

"My friends call me Bob and you, young lady, are one of them."

Burt stuck out his hand.

"Any friend of Ethan Edwards is like family to us. I'm Burt."

"And I'm just Carl. You're the prettiest friend Ethan's got, that's for sure."

"Well, thank you, Carl," Sam said.

"So, now that the introductions are over we need a…"

"Plan," Sam finished Bob's sentence. "We need a plan."

Bob noticed that a sadness had come over her.

"I think that Sam and I should head out to find Ethan as soon as possible. As for you two and the plane…"

"Maybe, we should ask those guys," Burt said pointing at six men on horseback who were rapidly approaching them.

The three men and Samantha waited with their backs to the plane in an attempt to show a non-threatening stance. They didn't have to wait long. The six riders formed a half-moon crescent around them as they came to a stop, with each man spaced about 10 feet from the other. It was pretty obvious that these men were Native Americans and that they had planned their positions. By being spaced out, they expanded their field of fire. The riders were all armed with an assortment of rifles. The man in the center leaned forward in his saddle.

"Samantha?" he asked, with the tone of his voice being as much a statement as a question.

"Walter? I can't tell you how nice it is to see you. How are Mary and the kids?" she said, her voice apprehensive.

All of the riders knew what she was asking.

"They're okay," he replied.

Sam was scared to speak at that moment because she was sure that she would lose it emotionally. It was like, for some reason, it hit her all at once. There were so many dead, so many families that weren't okay and never would be. She nodded to show that the news was good.

"We've been watching you for a while, Sam, we knew you were coming. We didn't know you were meeting anyone."

Sam turned to the three men beside her and introduced them.

"This is my friend, Walter Walks At Night."

They all nodded to each other.

"Why are you here?" one of the other riders asked.

Walter shot him a look. The man went quite but was not happy about the silent reprimand.

Sam shot a glance at Bob and the other two. Then turned back to Walter.

"We're looking for a man." She turned to Bob and kind of motioned to him so that everyone knew who she was talking about.

"This man is a doctor."

The riders exchanged confused glances as if to say, *"Okay, you're looking for a guy and you've got a doctor. Now what?"* Bob stepped forward.

"The truth of the matter is…"

"A white man telling us the truth. That would be a first in over three hundred years," one of the riders said.

Burt muttered, "Jesus Christ."

"You got something to say, buddy?" another rider asked him.

"Burt," Bob said shooting him a glance.

"WHAT? We ain't got time for this shit. I mean fuck the whole goddamn world is falling apart. There isn't room enough to stack the dead. To top it off, there are assholes and groups of assholes out there murdering raping and God knows what else. And, ya know it's the same all over the world. I mean Jesus Christ, if a guy stopped and thought about it, we probably don't deserve to survive. But never mind the current state of affairs. With all that going on, these guys want to argue about how our great great great grandfathers screwed them over. Let me ask you fellows, do we look like we're here to mess with you guys?"

"You done?" Bob asked through a clenched jaw.

"Yeah, I guess. I mean the conversation was heading down the wrong road, Bob."

"Well, I'm sure you did a lot to straighten it out. Mr. Walks At Night, perhaps you and Samantha and I could take a short walk."

"Anything this doctor's got to say, he should say to all of us," said the man who brought up the truth issue.

"Actually, I can't, but, standing around here doing this isn't solving anything. And like my companion, actually that's wrong, like my friend said, we don't have the time for it," Bob replied.

"We ain't here to cause trouble," Carl said in the just plain honest sounding way Carl said things.

"Let's take a walk," Walter said getting off his horse. "And everybody... everybody," he said as he looked between his guy and Burt, "is going to get along while we're gone, right? You all talk about something that... maybe it's best if ya just don't talk."

He motioned to Sam and Bob and the three of them went around the front of the plane. They stopped after a short distance.

"Do you know how your group has weathered this?" Walter asked.

"We lost a few members, not all of them to the virus. Tony Harms lost his entire family. He went back out."

"That's too bad, Tony was always solid."

"Not solid enough."

Bob was looking at them with a puzzled look on his face. They both noticed it. Sam looked at Walter. Walter nodded to her.

"We're members of Alcoholics Anonymous. That's how we know each other."

"Thanks, I was wondering. Now I know. I'm familiar with AA, not in the way you are. It's a great organization."

"Yeah," Walter said. "This guy you're looking for he wouldn't happen to be holed up at Sperry Chalet would he?"

This time, it was Bob and Sam who exchanged a look.

"It just so happens that's exactly where we think he might be."

"You're not an 'I've got a runny nose' type doctor, are you?"

"No, I'm not. I'm a 'world-altering, virus-fighting' type of doctor."

"And this other guy up at the chalet?"

"Is the man we think caused all of this. We also think he's got a vaccine for it."

"*We* is?"

"The government or what's left of it. Which, I'm not sure what is left of it. I've got an Army general telling me that the military is still functioning and I assume that some of the government is as well. This same general is also telling me that we're on the verge of a nuclear holocaust. I'm not sure why, probably because we're humans. Like my friend Burt said, makes ya wonder if we're worth saving."

"Some of us are. I think my kids are."

"I'm sure they are, in fact, so is my wife. And a lot of others," Bob said. "Speaking of kids, does this man who you apparently know is at Sperry Chalet, have any kids with him."

Before Walter could answer, Sam spoke up.

"Me and a friend named Ethan Edwards saw a guy yesterday west of Sperry watching a grizzly sow and two cubs. He had a couple of young kids with him. Nobody was aware that our guy had kids with him."

"The guy at Sperry didn't have kids with him until a little while ago."

"How long have you been watching him?"

"Since we went looking for old Pappie, the caretaker. Most of us have known Pappie since we were kids. We haven't seen him up there, which is very odd."

"You know damn good and well he didn't just get lost. Pappie knows this place better than most," Sam said.

"So, why not approach this guy and ask him about this Pappie?" Bob asked.

"Not real sure to tell you the truth. This guy's got a bad vibe around him. So, we decided to just to watch him. Check up on him every two or three days. We don't have anybody watching him right now. The man we had on him left to tell us about Sam heading this way. He also told us you weren't alone. Anyway, he smells like your guy if you know what I mean."

Back at the plane, the other riders had dismounted. Everybody was standing around looking at each other in an awkward silence. Carl couldn't take it anymore.

"Good ice cream at Saint Mary," he said.

"What?"

"I was just thinking when I was a kid, whenever we'd come to the park, my old man would always get us an ice cream cone at Saint Mary."

"You'd have trouble getting some now," one of the riders said.

"It all melted. Or, at least the stuff we didn't eat melted. Our generator quit running," another man said.

"What was it doing before it quit?" Burt asked.

"Why?"

"Because, Carl here is pretty much the best mechanic in the state of Montana," Burt said jerking a thumb toward Carl.

"Thanks, Burt, that's real nice of you."

"Hell, it's the truth, Carl and I should have said it to you a long time ago."

"Is it gas or diesel?" Carl asked.

"Diesel."

"Bet it's the fuel filter. Probably got moisture in it."

"Well, we ain't got another fuel filter."

"Bet you do and don't know it. Bet there's a diesel tractor around we could rob one off of. Or hell, diesel fuel pumps at a gas station have diesel filters on them. Switch the filters out, crack the injectors to get the air out of the system, and give 'er a try. Bet it'd start."

The other men looked at each other. Bob, Sam, and Walter walked around the front of the plane and returned to where the men were standing.

"Well, everybody still alive?" Walter asked.

"Yeah, we didn't scalp anyone, at least not yet," replied the man who had brought up the comment about white men telling the truth.

Bob walked up to him stuck out his hand. "I never got your name," he said.

"Oliver," the man replied.

"Oliver?" Burt said, with a funny voice.

"NOW what?"

"Nothing," Burt said. "Nothing. Oliver is a nice name."

Everybody couldn't help but let out a chuckle. Walter introduced the rest of his men.

"Okay, so here's the deal. Me, Joe, and Ronald are going to head toward Sperry with the doc here and Samantha."

Bob had a smile that nobody saw. He liked it when people called him Doc. Unfortunately, the only person that used that nickname on a regular basis was Fran, and that was only when they were getting ready to fool around. Bob snapped back around to participate in the conversation.

"Sam needs our help getting a guy out. We're going to put everybody on horseback," he turned to Bob.

"Guess I'm assuming you can ride. I know Sam can."

"I can ride," Bob said, trying not to sound indignant and not fully succeeding.

"Okay, good. Ollie, you and the other men take our other new friends into Baab."

"I'd just as soon stay with the plane. Ollie?" Burt said looking at Oliver.

"Don't go there," Oliver said with a smile conveying he was kidding.

Burt held up his hand.

"Walter, it's as obvious as a diamond in a goat's ass that you're not telling us everything. We elected you our leader at the tribal council meeting and I trust you like a brother. But can ya understand where I'm coming from?" Oliver stated.

"I do. And, you're absolutely right. It might be better if we did leave somebody with the plane. So, Burt is it? You and Oliver can stay here and keep an eye on the plane and work on race relations," he said, deciding to ignore the most important parts of Oliver's question. It didn't go unnoticed.

"I could go to town and see if I could get that generator going for you guys," Carl piped up.

"That would be real helpful. Thanks. Well, let's do this."

"I've got to grab a couple of items and my pack," Bob said.

The last two items that Bob retrieved from the plane were two rifle scabbards. He took his rifle out of one and handed it to Walter as he tied the other scabbard to Sam's horse.

Oliver looked at Walter and walked up to him as he gave him a hug. "Be careful, brother. We need you my friend," he said.

Walter nodded. When they mounted, he spoke a word to them in their native tongue. The other three men and Carl said it back. They all kinda looked at Carl.

Walter smiled, turned his horse, and headed across the field with Bob and Sam following close behind the three Native Americans. They rode at a steady pace for quite awhile. After they'd crossed a small meadow, Walter stopped.

"I think it would be best if we left the horses here. The trail gets pretty narrow and there's no place to go on a horse if something was to happen."

"I agree," said Sam.

They dismounted and continued on foot with Sam packing Ethan's rifle.

CHAPTER 47

Every time Larry and Lamar spoke, the hair on the back of Wild Bill's neck stood up. *"They just make my skin crawl,"* he thought as they hiked. *"And Jesus, they're noisy... the only way they could be louder is if the whole fucking Mormon Tabernacle Choir was with them."*

Finally, when he couldn't take any more, he spun around.

"GOD da..." he caught himself.

Lamar looked at Larry. They could sense hatred spewing from the man.

"God wants us to be quiet," he said, trying to cover himself and control his anger and disgust. It didn't work.

"Sorry," Lamar said. "Have we done something wrong, Mr. Clark?"

"Have you done anything wrong? Seriously! You pious asshole, you haven't done anything right... When the time comes, I'm going to gut you like a fish. I'm not sure why I just don't kill both of you right now," Clark thought.

"We just need to be quiet. It... the noise from our voices will travel farther than you think."

"No problem, Mr. Clark. All you have to do ask. Do you think someone else is close enough to hear us?" Larry asked.

Bill thought he might blow out every blood vessel in his head. It took a supreme effort to control the rage welling up in him.

"We don't know if anyone else is close enough to hear us. But, perhaps we should assume that the possibility exists that there could be. So if it's FUCKING OKAY WITH YOU, LARRY, LET'S BE AS QUIET AS POSSIBLE, OKAY?" Clark's teeth were clenched so tight he thought his jaw might explode into tiny fragments. He turned and started back up the trail.

Lamar and Larry gave each other another look.

Larry mouthed the words, *"I'm sorry, Lamar."*

Lamar reached out and touched Larry's arm, gave him a weak smile, shook his head slightly, and mouthed back, *"It's okay."* They both headed up the path behind Wild Bill, trying desperately to avoid making any noise.

They had been moving along the trail at a pretty good pace, but Clark would stop them every so often by holding up his hand in a fist. He would turn his head from side to side to listen, and then tilt his head back lifting his chin. Larry, who was right behind him, realized that he was smelling the air like an animal would. When he was done, he motioned them forward again. After about an hour of hiking, Wild Bill stopped and motioned for Larry and Lamar to get closer to him.

In a low voice, not quite a whisper, Wild Bill said, "If you have to take a piss, wait until I stop. Stay stopped until I start again." He could tell Lamar had a question.

"What?" he asked, agitated.

"How will you know that we've stopped?"

He leaned in closer to them and in a whisper.

"Because I won't be able to hear you fuckers stumbling down the trail," he said with an evil smirk.

He could see both men were terrified of him. However, he had long since made up his mind. No more pretend bible thumping bullshit. It was just a matter of when he would take out these Mormons. He decided he would make up some story for the commissioner. He figured the bottom line was that it would be one less thing the commissioner would have to worry about anyway.

The commissioner had told him that these two might come in handy when he found this Victor guy, because he might be able to use them as a decoy or something. He smiled as he thought of sending Lamar and Larry in to get killed as he came in from the other side by surprise. He figured that would be okay with the commissioner. Particularly, if he was able to get the vaccine and maybe even take this Victor guy alive. Hell, the commissioner would be plum happy with him he figured. Yeah, he reckoned that would probably be okay.

Lamar cleared his throat, which brought Wild Bill back to the present.

"Wait for me. When I get back to you, I'll motion if it's okay. Piss right on the trail. If you have to shit, that's a different story. I guess point at your ass or something. I'll lead you off the trail. Got it?" Both men nodded.

"Good." Wild Bill turned and started up the trail.

Lamar and Larry were not only tired but both felt a sense of humiliation. Both times they needed to relieve themselves Clark stood and watched them. It was obvious he took pleasure in their discomfort. To top it off, when Lamar made an eating motion, Clark wagged his finger and shook his head 'no' with a broad grin on his face. Lamar made a decision that when they did stop and were allowed to hold a conversation, he intended to tell Clark his treatment of them was unacceptable, and if it continued, he would be left no other choice than to inform the commissioner when they saw him again.

Maybe it happened because Lamar was thinking about their seeming untenable situation or perhaps it was because he was just plain worn out. It didn't really matter why. It happened. He tripped going down a slight hill. Contrary to Clark's instructions about keeping spaced intervals between each other, he had allowed the distance between himself and Larry to close. The trip propelled him forward and into Larry's back. It had the predicted domino effect.

Larry had been careful mostly out of fear, but he had kept his distance from Clark. Both he and Lamar fell to the ground. When Larry struggled onto all fours, he saw boots on the path in front of him. He looked up. Had someone been there to ask him, he would have stated he looked directly into the face of evil. Wild Bill Clark stood above him, his rifle pointing down with the muzzle almost touching Larry's head. Looking into Wild Bill's eyes, Larry was actually struck by the fact that they looked void of emotion. Wild Bill's facial muscles relaxed and he let out a sigh. It sounded as if he had come to a decision. Larry's eyes widened as he realized that Wild Bill was going to kill him.

"IT'S MY FAULT, IT'S MY FAULT. Mr. Clark, please. It's my fault," Lamar pleaded as he clamored to his feet. "Mr. Clark, I apologize, please, it was my fault. I promise we will do better."

Clark didn't move or acknowledge that he even heard Lamar speaking. Larry looked up at him terrified.

"Mr. Clark, I'm going to be sure to tell the commissioner how patient and understanding you have been with us."

It seemed as if the mention of the commissioner broke Clark out of his spell. He finally looked up at Lamar, still holding his gun only inches from Larry's head.

"We need to move, someone might have heard all the noise. We need to move," he said again and yet he didn't move nor did his rifle.

"Yes, yes, I agree with you," Lamar stammered.

Clark looked at him again and nodded as he pulled the rifle up, turned, and started back down the rocky dirt path.

Lamar went to Larry and helped him to his feet.

"Lamar, he was going to kill me. I know it, I could see it," he whispered.

"I know."

"Lamar…"

"He did not kill you. God stood on this path between you and him, Larry. He did not kill you. And, we are not going to give him another chance to kill either one of us. I will come up with a plan, I promise, before this day is out."

When they looked down the trail, Clark had stopped walking and stood there with his back toward them. Larry's legs almost gave out but Lamar steadied him. Clark gave no indication of having heard what the two men had said. He simply motioned for them to move forward with his hand.

CHAPTER 48

Before they split up and Sam went to meet Bob at the plane, Ethan and Sam followed Victor and the kids back to Sperry Chalet. The more they observed them, the more Sam became convinced something was just not right. After they knew Victor was staying at Sperry Chalet and they had talked with Bob and the general, it was time for Samantha to head out and find Bob. It was agreed Ethan would keep an eye on the chalet. Before she left, Ethan insisted that Cowboy go with her. He told her Bob would be anxious to see his dog and vice versa. When she gave him a *"that is total bullshit"* look, he also admitted he would feel better about them splitting up if the dog went with her.

"I knew that," Samantha said.

"Then why'd ya make me say it?"

"Because, a girl likes it when her man is, like, all worried about her." She moved close to him. He put his arms around her and pulled her even closer.

"So, I'm your man?"

She leaned back.

"Aren't you? Although, it's not like I've got a whole lot of competition."

"Darling, I'm all yours. You're so far ahead of the competition, they think they're coming in first."

"Okay... I think I understand that. Either way, I'm taking it as a verbal confirmation that we consider ourselves boyfriend and girlfriend."

"Jesus, you're such a lawyer. Here's more than verbal confirmation," he said as he pushed her hips into him and kissed her.

"Easy, big boy," she said as she pushed herself away from him.

"Let's stay on the task of saving mankind."

Her departure was rapid. She turned back, looked at Ethan, gave him a warm smile, patted her leg, scratched Cowboy's head, turned around, and was gone. Ethan wanted to rush after her. He felt almost sick to his stomach. This whole love thing was a cross between being so happy he could hardly stand it and having the flu or something. He smiled as he realized it was the first time he'd ever thought the word love about a woman. He certainly never said it to one.

"I love you, Samantha," he said out loud.

He didn't think it sounded bad at all. In fact, he liked the way it sounded so much he figured he might try it out on her.

"Well okay," he thought, *"I'll think about trying it out on her. In the meantime, let's see what our buddy Victor or whoever that is with those kids is up to."* He spent the next hour or so focused on learning as much as he could about the guests at Sperry Chalet. It was the only way he could distract himself from worrying about Sam.

As he watched them, Ethan could see the kids moving about outside the cabin. After a few minutes passed, Victor came out and beckoned them into the lodge. He was drying his hands on a towel. Ethan assumed he must have prepared lunch for the three of them. As he chewed some jerky that Mike had given him, Ethan came to a decision. He decided he would backtrack up the trail in the hopes Mike had been on it trying to catch up with them. He knew it was a long shot; in fact, it was even more than a long shot. But, he figured there wasn't much chance Victor would head toward Many Glaciers, and if he did, Cowboy would warn Sam of anybody being around. He knew one thing now that he'd thought about Mike: there was no way he was going to be able to just sit there. He stuffed the rest of the jerky in his mouth, hoisted his pack, and headed back the way he'd came.

Ethan heard a noise and froze on the trail. He immediately crouched down and pointed the Marlin down the trail in front of him. He clicked the safety off. He could hear a man talking. He couldn't quite make out what he was saying, but there was no doubt someone was on the trail. He silently moved off the trail, dropped his pack, and took up an assault position.

It was almost like the man coming at him just appeared on the trail. Ethan looked back up the trail for a split second, and when he turned back, the man was standing right there. As the man moved up the trail toward him, Ethan realized this guy moved like a cat sneaking up on its prey. Two other men appeared behind the first. These men were much more labored in their movements. It was a stark contrast how different they were from the lead man.

Ethan knew Sperry Chalet, the kids, and possibly Victor Kraus were only about thirty minutes from where they were on the trail. Ethan couldn't let these men stumble into them.

Ethan lay his Marlin down and unholstered his .45. After letting all three men go by him, Ethan stepped out onto the trail. It appeared the lead man held up his hand for a stop before his second foot hit the trail.

"Hold up, fellas," Ethan said.

They all froze.

"I've got a .45 on you boys so turn around real slow, okay?"

The three of them slowly turned around.

"You, up front. You're going to want to lay that M4 down."

Clark smiled. "I'm thinking you're going to want to lay yours down too, partner."

"Not sure why you'd think that."

"Because, I'm pretty sure that we aren't far away from Sperry Chalet. And, I'm even more sure that if either one of us starts shooting, the asshole we're after is liable to bolt. And well, it's a big fucking park."

Ethan was silent. Lamar and Larry had been looking back and forth during the conversation between Ethan and Clark.

"I'm betting you're Ethan Edwards, am I right?"

Ethan was silent.

"Yeah, I'm right. And, I'm betting you're after Victor Kraus and the vaccine."

There was still no answer from Ethan.

"Ah, right again. Just so you know, hoss, we ain't going to end up on the same team."

"You seem to know quite a bit," Ethan said, wondering what the hell he was going to do next.

The guy was right about a shootout. No doubt, Kraus would take to the brush and then everything would be for nothing. On the other hand, three against one wasn't very good odds and, he had a pretty solid gut feeling the guy doing the talking wasn't somebody you'd want to fuck with.

"So, what do you say, Edwards? We put down the hardware and see what happens."

"Shit," he thought, realizing he was actually a little bit afraid of this guy.

"Three on one, not sure those are odds I'm willing to take," Ethan said.

Clark put his rifle down and started walking toward Larry and Lamar. Larry watched carefully as Clark approach. Clark made a motion with his head and moved a finger pointing in Ethan's direction. Larry turned to look at Ethan. Clark took four quick steps, and at the same time, he pulled his knife. Larry felt the hand over his mouth and gasped as Bill Clark stabbed him just under the ribcage, twisting the knife, before pulling it out and guiding him to the ground.

"Lamar, you better try and stop your friend from bleeding out."

Lamar rushed to Larry who was laying on his right side and trying to hold his hand to the wound. Lamar put his hand on top of his friends. He could feel the warm blood start to seep between his fingers. He looked up as Clark walked by.

"Don't worry, your time's coming, Lamar. Gotta take care of this Jar Head first. How 'bout it, ace? Odds better now. Don't forget, we don't want to spook anybody."

Ethan tossed his pistol down the trail behind him and pulled his K-Bar from its sheath.

"That's it, that's it," Wild Bill said as he got into a combat crouch.

Doing battle on the trail was like knife fighting in a narrow hallway. The two men made stabbing and slashing motions toward each other as they moved up and down the trail. Clark stabbed toward Ethan and withdrew to avoid Ethan's counter thrust. As he withdrew, Clark went into a slight crouch, putting almost all of his weight on his back foot. Ethan didn't pick it up. Ethan counter thrust and he also withdrew, expecting Clark to jab back. However, as Ethan was backing up, Clark sprang out of his crouch, took one step, and leaped into the air, kicking Ethan in the chest.

Ethan was knocked off balance and propelled backward by the force of the kick. He couldn't get his feet back under him. He went to the ground, his shoulders hitting first, followed by his head snapping back and striking the ground hard. He felt the K-Bar slip from his grip. Ethan tried to buy himself some distance by kicking his legs and feet, ironically, much like Raymond Horten had tried to do to get away from him. Clark pounced on him with both hands on the hilt of his knife. Ethan caught Clark's wrists with his hands, barely stopping the blade from penetrating him.

Clark forcefully positioned himself on top of Ethan, aiming the knife at his throat as he pressed down on it with all his strength and body weight. Ethan tried to hold the knife back, but not only could he see it slowly getting closer to his throat, he knew deep down he didn't have the strength to stop it. So did Clark, who displayed a thin smile when he opened his mouth to breathe a bit. Ethan felt Clark's spit sprinkle on his face as he exhaled.

> Ethan was overcome with sadness, not fear. He knew he would never see her again. *"Please, God, not now, not yet,"* he thought.

All of a sudden, Clark's eyes went wide. Ethan felt the pressure of Clark's force gradually weaken. Then, Clark's face went ashen. Ethan heard him mutter the words "FUCK ME" as he pushed Clark off of him. Ethan looked back to see what caused the sudden change of events and saw Clark lying on the ground with Ethan's K-Bar sticking out of his back. Ethan then noticed Lamar on his knees, tears streaming down his cheeks. Lamar stood up and went back to Larry. He bent down and gently brushed his hair from his forehead. Without looking over his shoulder at Ethan, he spoke.

"He was a good man. He told me to help you. 'Lamar, you must help him,' he said." Lamar stopped for a moment before continuing. "I felt the life go out of him and he was gone."

Ethan reached down and pulled Lamar to his feet and led him back up the trail. The two men sat on a downed log by Ethan's pack. Ethan took a drink from his canteen and handed it to Lamar.

"Ethan Edwards," Ethan said, not sticking out his hand.

"Lamar Young," Lamar replied taking a drink and then handing the canteen back to Ethan.

Ethan just nodded and took another drink of water.

"Pretty obvious you and your friend weren't with that guy."

Lamar looked up from the ground at him.

"I think it was more like that guy was with you. If you know what I mean," Ethan said.

"Clark."

"What?"

"Wild Bill Clark," Lamar said holding his hand out for the canteen. "May I?"

"Ya, sure," Ethan said handing it back to him.

"This Clark guy, he seemed to know who I am." He paused. "And what I'm doing. I'm wondering about that."

Lamar looked at him for a moment. He felt... He didn't know what he felt. Sad, he was just sad and wanted it to all go away. With a heavy sigh, he handed the canteen back to Ethan.

"Clark works, sorry, worked for the commissioner. He was, as he put it, his Archangel Michael."

"Not real familiar with my angels. He the one who went around kicking ass for God?" Ethan asked.

Lamar smiled. "Yeah, pretty much."

"So, this Mr. Clark, he's the guy who kicked ass for Commissioner Tony Harms," Ethan said.

Lamar gave him a questionable look.

"Me and the commish met, in fact, he offered me a job."

"He may reconsider," Lamar said.

"He knew my answer when he asked. How'd he hear about Victor and the vaccine?"

"We told him," Lamar said. "We had been quasi-arrested by his sheriff. But the truth is, we needed help. The truth is, we've needed help from the very start. Apparently, there was some kind of a shootout around the dump. The commissioner said someone killed eight of his men. He told us in order to help him protect his people, he needed to know why we were there. When we told him, he offered to help us. We thought he was a man of God. I'm beginning to wonder just what that is anymore. I do believe that he was telling us the truth about his men being killed. Was it you?" Lamar asked looking at him.

Ethan leaned forward; it was obvious he had become anxious hearing this news.

"No, it wasn't me. Did you hear anyone talk about a man named Mike?"

"No, I don't think anyone mentioned that name. Although I... who knows."

Ethan thought about what Lamar had told him. It made sense. He knew there was more than just Mike shooting. He couldn't explain why, but in his gut, he figured Mike had made it out of the gunfight.

"How'd you hear about Victor and the vaccine?"

"I heard about it on a ham radio transmission from some forest rangers." He paused. "I wish I'd never heard it. If I hadn't heard it, Larry, the bishop, and probably few other brothers would still be alive."

"It is what it is. By the way, thank you," Ethan said, holding out his hand.

Lamar looked at it.

"For what? Killing a man?"

"No," Ethan said, looking down at his hand. "For saving one."

Lamar followed his eyes. It took a second before Lamar grasped Ethan's hand.

"Now what?" Lamar asked, holding Ethan's hand.

"Now we finish what we've both set out to do," Ethan said. "I can always use some help."

"That's a new one. Usually, it's us..." he paused, "I guess it's just me now... asking for help. What about the bodies?"

"We'll hide them."

"I don't—"

"We can come back, Lamar, and take care of them. But, I don't think we have time right now. In fact, I don't think Clark was all of the commissioner's plan. If I know the commissioner as well as I think I do, I'm thinking he'd hedged his bet by sending a posse to back up Wild Bill."

"About the time we left with Clark, the commissioner was getting a group of men ready to go investigate the shootout I mentioned earlier," Lamar stated.

"Shit. Come on, Lamar, we better get moving."

When Ethan and Lamar arrived at the area near the chalet, evening was approaching. They found a good place to watch the chalet and keep an eye on the trail. After they had settled in, Ethan broke out some jerky and trail mix.

"Sam and Bob should be here early in the morning. At least that's what I'm thinking. I was hoping they'd get here tonight," Ethan said somewhat anxious.

Lamar looked at him, studying him carefully for a moment. "It sounds like you know this Bob and Samantha pretty well."

Ethan turned to look at him.

"Ya, you could say that."

"Did you know them before the outbreak?"

"Bob. I've known Bob pretty much my whole life. Him and his wife, Fran. They kinda raised me. I met Samantha and her friend Mike after I got to the Flathead," Ethan replied.

"Did you say Bob and his wife pretty much raised you?"

"That's right." Ethan didn't expand on his answer and Lamar could tell he wasn't going to.

"Do you believe in God?" Lamar asked right out of the blue.

Now it was Ethan's turn to look at him for a moment.

"Kinda an inquisitive fellow, ain't ya?" Ethan asked staring at him.

"I think it's going to be a long night, Mr. Edwards. I am afraid if I don't talk, I'll just sit here and think of my brother dying in my arms. I don't really want to ruminate on that memory." Lamar went silent and looked down.

"It's Ethan, not Mr. Edwards, okay? And Lamar, I don't know what I believe."

"I'm not sure what I believe in anymore. How could a loving God let all this bad stuff happen?" Lamar asked still looking down.

They sat silent. When Ethan started to speak, Lamar looked up at him.

"I wish I knew what to say to you, Lamar, to make today easier. I don't. Some days are just hard and nothing can be said or done to make them easier. I don't know you from Adam, but I think you are a man of faith from what little you've said. And, I think you are questioning that faith today. I've seen men kill each other and I've killed other men. Some needed killing. Hell, I don't know. Guess what I'm trying to say is when bad shit happens, if a guy doesn't question it or wonder what the hell... then you've gone dead inside and you're not part of the rest of us. So much has been lost by so many. If you are a man of faith, I don't think it's a big deal if you question it. I don't think whatever's up there..." he paused and pointed to the sky, "thinks it's a big deal. But, it would be a shame if you lost it."

A weak smile formed on Lamar's face.

"For someone who doesn't know what he believes in..." Lamar started, but then paused as he looked behind Ethan. "Hey, there's a dog standing behind you."

Ethan slowly turned his head as his hand reached for the K-Bar on his hip. He broke into a huge grin.

"Took you long enough," he said and patted his hand on his hip. Cowboy trotted over to where he was sitting.

After explaining things to Lamar, Ethan had Lamar stay and keep an eye on the chalet, and he left with Cowboy to go find Sam and Bob. He hadn't made it very far when he heard something or someone coming toward him. Ethan quietly stepped off the trail with Cowboy by his side. A man with a rifle was in the lead followed by Sam then Bob and three other armed men. Much like he had done when he encountered Lamar, Larry, and Clark, he let everyone pass by him. However, this time, Ethan wasn't going to hesitate or worry about noise. If these three men were a danger to Sam or Bob, he intended to shoot them in the order in which they were aligned. He would shoot the last man first, then the next, yelling for Bob and Sam to duck, then shooting the third. His only concern was getting Sam and Bob to duck.

By the time Walter heard him, he felt the barrel of the .45 on the side of this head.

"Move and die," Ethan said.

Walter froze.

"Tell 'em to stop."

Walter gave a soft whistle. Everyone stopped and turned to look at him. Ethan made sure he was covered by Walter's body. It took Joe a second to actually realize what was going on. He started to raise his rifle.

"Don't…" Ethan said.

"Ethan, Ethan," Sam called out as she started moving toward him. When she realized what was going on, she stopped.

"They're with us. It's okay, they're with us."

Bob also called out Ethan's name. Ethan relaxed his grip on Walter who stepped away from him. Samantha found herself in his arms. He held her tight and kissed her. When they were done, she turned to Walter and the other two men.

"This is my friend, Ethan."

"Yeah, I picked up on that," Walter said.

Bob walked up to him. Ethan and Bob hugged each other. They patted each other's back and made those noises in their throats that men make when they fight back tears. When all the hugging and introductions were done, Ethan told them about Lamar. He glossed over what had happened with Clark on the trail.

Walter looked at Ethan. "You're pretty stealthy for a white guy," he said.

Ethan looked back at him, not quite knowing how to take what he said. "You're pretty noisy for an Indian."

"Bullshit! It wasn't us you heard. More likely, it was your girlfriend or the old man," Walter said.

Ethan had a 'what the fuck is your problem, buddy' look on his face as he looked over at Sam.

She spoke up. "Walter, what the hell?"

His gaze broke from Ethan and somewhat embarrassing he mumbled, "Sorry, didn't mean anything by it."

Bob stepped forward. "Ethan, we should maybe go find this fellow named Lamar and decide what to do from there."

Ethan nodded. "Follow me," he said.

By the time they got back to Lamar, it was dark. After another round of introductions, their discussion turned to how they were planning to capture Victor and, as was pointed out, not injure the children that were in the chalet with him. No one knew for sure why he had these kids or who they were.

"Well, it's not like we can just walk up, knock on the door, and ask the guy to surrender," Ethan said.

"Why not?" Walter asked.

"I mean; I knock on the door. When the guy opens it, I pop him in the nose. Two of you guys are on each side of the door frame and we storm in… problem solved."

"What if he answers the door with a pistol in his hand or swings it open as he steps back and levels a 12 gauge at you? Then, we've lost the element of surprise. What do you tell him then, huh? Cause you ain't exactly Avon calling," Ethan stated snidely.

Before Walter, who looked pissed off, had a chance to say anything, Sam spoke up.

"I agree with Walter," she said.

"What?" Ethan asked as everyone looked at her.

"Well, I kinda agree with him. And, I also kinda don't, so let me explain."

"We're all ears."

"Instead of Walter going up to the door, I do it. I'll tell this guy that I saw his light from the trail," she said and pointed to the cabin.

A faint glow could barely be seen coming from a window that had a blanket hung in front of it to prevent just such a thing from happening.

"That light's going to become more evident as it gets even darker so, we wait for a couple hours. And, with all this smoke from the fire, there's not going to be much light from the moon or stars. So, the 'I saw your light' angle holds water. Then, I'll tell him that I tripped on the trail traveling in the dark and sprained my ankle. I know it's dangerous to be hiking in the dark and normally I wouldn't. I had stopped for the night, but I heard a noise and it frightened me. I thought maybe it was a bear. I've been struggling along for what seems like forever and then thank God I saw the glow from your cabin."

She paused and nobody said anything.

"We'll rub some dirt on my jacket and jeans. I'll leave the front of my jacket open, drop a couple of buttons on my shirt, bat my eyes... All that kinda damsel in distress stuff. While I'm doing that, Ethan, you and Walter will have worked your way around back. I'm sure you'll be able to hear me talking after the door has opened. You guys go in the back and surprise him from behind. If things go bad at the door, I'll drop to the ground and one of the other guys can wing him."

"It's not a bad plan," Walter said.

"I'd let her in," one of Walter's men said.

"Me too," said the other.

Both of them responded with a little too much wishful thinking in their voices for Ethan's liking.

"Shit," Ethan said.

"What now?" Walter asked, his irritation evident.

"Buddy, you and me are going to go around at some point," Ethan thought.

"Shit, because it's a good plan. I just don't like it."

"Then that's what we're going to do," Walter said.

With the plan settled, everybody hunkered down to wait for it to get darker. Sam leaned into Ethan and put her head on his shoulder.

"I'm glad you worry about me so much," she said, looking up at him.

He kissed her forehead.

"I love you, Sam." There he said it.

"I know." She arched up and gently kissed him.

"I love you, too," she said as she squeezed him tight.

"I need to go and talk with Walter and see if he'll tell me what crawled up his ass."

"That's my girl," Ethan thought as he watched her leave.

"Changes everything, doesn't it?" Bob said as he sat down next to Ethan.

"You've got no idea," Ethan said.

"Actually, I do. And I'll tell ya, kid. There's nothing like it. And there's nothing to compare it to. Maybe the only thing that could be greater is the love for a child. This love deal... Well, it's the best deal there is."

Walter approached them.

"It's probably dark enough. We should make our move to the back of the chalet. I told Samantha to give us twenty minutes to get there."

"Yeah, that should work," Ethan said, getting up. He bent down and started to dig in his pack. When he turned around, he had his bolt cutters in his hand.

"Didn't see that coming. Not everybody lugs around bolt cutters," Walter said.

"Old habit I picked up in Iraq."

Walter nodded.

CHAPTER 49

The group of homeless survivors came running back to their warehouse after only a few hours of scavenging and unlocked the door with a clear sense of urgency. As soon as the door clanged shut, the group began shouting and talking over one another.

"OKAY, CALM THE FUCK DOWN," Paul said in a booming voice that echoed through the warehouse.

Aiden, David, and Keno looked at the group with concern.

"What happened out there?"

"It was an ambush. We walked into a large condo building and there were people in there waiting for us. They was not residents, these were rough-looking people, guys and girls. Two of us led the way through the loading dock, and it was dark. As soon as we got our lights on, we could see them. There were maybe 10 or more. They attacked us with metal poles. One of them fuckers had a giant pipe wrench. I think they killed T-man."

"What did they want?" Paul asked.

"I think they was protecting that place. I think it is full of good stuff and they want to keep it for themselves."

"We gotta go back and see if we can get our guys outta there," Paul said. "We are missing four. You say T-man might be dead, what about the others?"

"Not sure, it was crazy in there and I dropped my light as soon as I saw T-man's head explode. We all turned and tried to get outta there, and they kept coming."

"Why did you leave them behind?" Keno asked.

"We didn't; we ran out of there and they were chasing us. They just stopped chasing us a couple of blocks ago."

"Do they know where we live?" Keno asked.

"I don't think so. They seemed to just want to chase us away from the condo, so I don't think they want to hurt us."

At that moment, a large bang echoed through the warehouse, followed by several more bangs and loud screaming. There was a gang of thugs banging on the large warehouse door.

"Shit, they are here," Paul said.

"What we gonna do, Boss Man?" Keno asked.

"We are going to defend our turf."

"Wait, I have a better idea," David said. "Let me go out there. I am blind, they will see that I am not a threat. Let me talk to them."

Paul looked around the room for support, and saw many faces that looked positive.

"Okay," Paul said, "but if there is any trouble, we care going to come out fighting."

"Fair enough," David said.

"Okay, listen up. Everyone grab a pipe, a hammer, any type of weapon and be ready to charge out the main door. David, we are will send you out the side door in case they attempt to charge the main door when we open it to let you out. All you have to do is walk to your left and it will take you to the front of the building where they are."

Paul opened the side door quietly and let David exit. They then gathered around various holes in the side of walls to see how the negotiations turned out. David made his way to the front of the warehouse and reached out to those who were gathered there.

"Hello, friends, my name is David. There is no conflict here. How can we help you?"

"What the fuck is this?" the leader of the group asked aloud.

The crowd responded with loud jeers.

"This is how you roll? You fucking come to our place and disrespect us and then send a blind guy out to greet us? Oh hell no, this is not going to do."

"Look, friends, we are all just trying to survive out here. Our group did not know that the condo building was yours. We were just trying to find some food and water. We do not wish to have any conflict with you and now that we know that you are using that building for a home, we will no longer try to enter it."

There was a long silent pause.

"We are all brothers now, brothers of the new world, and we need to stick together, love one another, help one another. What do you say?" David said. "It's time to stop fighting and starting living in unity."

David was encouraged by the silence, and all of the homeless survivors watched intently as the leader of the gang moved slowly toward David. At first, it looked like the man was going shake David's hand, but as he got closer, he raised his right arm and hit David on the head with a pipe that he held in his right hand.

"Peace out, motherfucker," he said. "LET'S BURN THESE MOTHERFUCKERS OUT!"

Paul watched in disbelief as David crumpled to the ground, and then he let out a loud yell and opened the large warehouse door and led the charge to defend their home. The battle was bloody and even though there were roughly equal numbers of fighters for both groups, it was obvious that the gang was much more experienced with hand-to-hand combat. Moreover, they were ready with Molotov cocktails, which they threw into the warehouse as soon as the main door was opened. Fires flared up as their beds, clothes, and food supply began to burn.

Aiden watched David fall to the ground and let out a small scream. Keno grabbed him and started directing him to the back of the warehouse. They were clear of the main warehouse area by the time the fires started. Keno led Aiden to a small section of the back wall where there was a small opening cut out. It had been secured in place, but it was a small door out of the building. Keno removed the makeshift door that covered the opening.

"C'mon, Bingo, let's get out of here," he said as he pushed the boy through the opening.

When he was out of the building, Keno followed and then leaned the door back into the opening. Keno led Aiden through an area that appeared to be an old junkyard and into an alley. Keno did not stop until they were safely away from the building.

"We can't leave David," Aiden said.

"We will go back and get him when it is safe, we just have to wait till those guys leave."

The gang of thugs made quick and easy work of the homeless survivors, leaving most of them moaning on the ground as all of their supplies burned up behind them. When the leader was satisfied that these thieves would never tread on his territory again, he rounded up his group and they started to leave. David was just coming to when the man walked by him to make his exit. David reached up and felt the wound on his head and winced in pain as he felt the open cut on his head.

"We are all brothers now, there is no need for war," he said weakly.

"This guy is something else," the leader said.

After taking a few steps away from the warehouse, the leader returned to where David lay and reached down to grab his hand and helped him to his feet. He then reached into a sack that he carried on his back and removed a rope that he tied around David's neck. When it was secure, he pulled it tight, leading David on a path behind him.

"Look, everyone, we have a new pet. A blind peacemaker."

David tried to respond, but the rope was too tight. He had to focus all of his attention on his breathing.

CHAPTER 50

When she was at the chalet door, Samantha could hear a man speaking, not necessarily in an angry voice but more of a lecturing tone. She paused for a second before she knocked on the door. The thought crossed her mind that she hoped Ethan and Walter were ready and this plan would work. The voice in the chalet went silent the moment she knocked. There was no response. She knocked again and this time asked for help in a halting, cracking voice that she didn't have to fake.

"HELP, PLEASE?" she said, almost shouting it.

From behind the door, she heard a man's voice answer. "GO AWAY. WE CAN'T HELP YOU."

"PLEASE," she shouted back and then went on to explain her story, ending with another plea for help in a voice that sounded as if it were on the verge of tears.

There was silence from the chalet. Finally, the voice answered.

"Move back from the door far enough so that I can see you from the window."

Samantha limped off the porch and stood back far enough to be seen. She turned slightly toward the window holding her left arm as if to show it was hurt and she also pretended to limp on her left ankle. The light in the house went out. She couldn't tell for sure, but it appeared to have been a kerosene lamp. When the bright light hit her a few moments later, she was surprised because it came from the door not the window, which was exactly what Victor was hoping for. Sam let go of her arm and gingerly turned toward the light holding her hand in front of her eyes in an attempt to block the bright light from shining directly in her eyes.

"I'm hurt, I need help, please," she said.

"Get on the ground," the voice behind the light stated.

She took a limping step toward the light.

"Please I…"

"GET ON THE GROUND NOW! RIGHT NOW!"

"Okay, okay, I'm sorry," she said as she took her backpack off and let it slide to the ground. Once again trying to make her voice sound like she was terrified and on the verge of tears. Once again, there was no need to fake it.

Sam gingerly lowered herself to the ground where she lay face down. The light moved toward her. She turned her head and could see that he was standing over her. The bright light went off and it was replaced by what she thought was sure to be a headlamp.

"Be still and don't move. I have a pistol and I won't hesitate to use it. I'm going to search you," he said as he knelt down beside her.

Victor stuck his pistol in the back of his pants. He ran both his hands down her arms and along the side of her torso. He then pushed her legs apart and reached between them into the crotch of her jeans. Samantha flinched.

"Be still," he commanded as he ran his hands down her right leg to her boot. He then switched to her left side and repeated the process.

"Ow, that hurts," Samantha said.

"Hush. Be still and roll onto your back."

Samantha gingerly rolled onto her right side. While laying on her back all she could see was the light from his headlamp.

"Stretch your arms out like you're on the cross."

For some reason, his reference to the cross terrified her, but she did as she was told. He bent down and ran his hands over her torso again, this time starting from her belt line and slowly moving his hands up to her breasts. As his hands went over her breasts, Victor noticed how beautiful she was and how terrified. His hands slid back to her breasts.

"Please," Sam said as the tears rolled from the corner of her eyes. All she could see was the light from the headlamp.

Victor stood, turned off the headlamp, and turned the bright light on again.

"Get up," he ordered.

Sam rolled onto her right side.

"Can you help me?"

"Get up," he repeated.

Sam struggled to her feet. Once again, she gingerly put weight on her left ankle.

"Go to the cabin," Victor instructed her, as he shown the light in front of her.

Sam limped off toward the cabin. Over her shoulder, she could see him reach down and retrieve her pack.

Ethan and Walter made it to the back door before Sam knocked and they discovered that the door had a Forest Service padlock on it. Because there was very little light back there, Walter couldn't clearly see the look on Ethan's face, but he could feel it. Ethan reached out and held the lock straight out. Walter took the cue and grabbed hold of the solid padlock body. Ethan then put the shackle portion of the lock in the jaws of the bolt cutter and waited. It wasn't long before they heard Sam's first knock on the door.

Walter and Ethan held their breath as the cabin went dark. They heard the front door open and saw a bright light come on. When the bright light moved out of the cabin, they knew they had their chance. Ethan cut the lock, which made a snapping sound. They waited. The bright light out front had been replaced with a smaller glowing one.

The back door of the cabin swung inward, allowing the two men to crawl into the cabin with Ethan in the lead. As they felt their way forward in the dark, Ethan bumped into a counter. He felt along it with his hand. Reaching behind him and finding Walter, he gently pushed on Walter to guide him up next to him. Ethan knew that they were behind a counter most likely the one between the kitchen and the living room of the cabin. Both Walter and Sam had been in Sperry Chalet on numerous occasions and had described the interior to him. The two men took up position behind the counter. After a short wait that seemed like an eternity, they could see a light coming back into the cabin.

"Stop," Victor said from behind her. He shut the door behind them and locked it.

Sam stood with her back toward him. He shut the bright flashlight off and turned on his headlamp again. She could hear him behind her, and soon the room was lit with the light from a Coleman lantern. Ethan looked at Walter and brought a finger to his lips and then held it up and pointed to himself as a signal to wait, indicating that he would make the first move. Walter nodded. He could tell that Ethan knew what he was doing. Samantha turned around to face Victor.

"You don't need to point that gun at me," Sam said, hoping Ethan and Walter could hear her.

"Sit down," Victor said, motioning toward a chair.

Sam sat down.

"Take your left boot off," he ordered.

Sam paused as Victor motioned with his pistol for her to proceed. Sam bent down and removed her boot.

"Remove your sock, also, and pull up your pant leg."

She did as she was told.

"It doesn't look swollen to me."

"I can tell you it certainly hurts, especially, when I put weight on it. My whole left side feels bruised."

Victor looked at her. He couldn't help but notice that she was a very attractive woman.

"Show me the side of your leg."

"What?"

"Stand up, remove your pants, and show me the side of your leg."

Sam slowly stood up, and winced in pain as she did.

"My left arm is injured. I don't think I can undo my jeans."

Victor looked at her, with his eyes going up and down the full length of her body. Victor swallowed hard as he realized he was becoming aroused. He swallowed hard again.

"Turn around," he instructed her.

She felt him come up behind her. She also felt the nose of his pistol in her side. Victor reached around her and tried to undo her jeans. As he did, he pressed himself against her. Sam could feel that he had an erection. She fought back a shudder as a revolting feeling overcame her. She stood perfectly still as he pressed himself harder against her. After a few moments of pressing against her, he bent to the floor and set the gun down. Then, Sam felt both of his hands on her as he undid her jeans and started to slide them over her hips.

"My God," she thought, "where are Ethan and Walter. What if..." She fought back the urge to call out to them.

Victor spun around quickly in response to the sudden noise, only to be met by Ethan's fist as it slammed into his face, knocking him backwards and to the floor.

"FUCKER," Ethan said as he bent down and grabbed Victor.

Just as he was about to punch him again, Sam went to Ethan and grabbed his arm and told him to stop. Ethan rolled Victor over onto his stomach and wrenched his hands behind his back. Victor grunted in pain. Ethan looked at Walter.

"Handcuff this asshole," he said as he turned his attention to Sam.

"The children..." she said, as she looked at Victor who was now sitting with his hands behind his back and leaning against the chair she had used.

"Where are the children?"

He smiled at her with blood dripping from the side of his mouth, his teeth smeared with it. He motioned with his head and spit blood on the floor. He wondered how she knew about the children and what else these people might know about him.

"They're in the bedroom hiding," he said. He saw no point in not telling them. They would have found them soon enough.

After securing Victor with a pair of handcuffs Bob had brought for the occasion, Walter went to the front doorway and called to the others. As everyone entered the cabin, each one of them paused and looked at Victor who was now sitting in the chair with his hands bound behind his back. Bob was the last one into the cabin. He looked at Victor.

"Dr. Kraus. I'm Bob Watkins."

Victor smiled again and spit more blood onto the floor.

"Dr. Watkins. You'll have to excuse my rudeness for not standing but as you can clearly see I'm at a disadvantage."

Sam and Ethan came out of the bedroom with Ben and Becca. Victor looked up at them.

"Children, I'm afraid that we will not be continuing our lessons. However, you both know what I have taught you. Be strong, and stand up for what you believe."

"Perhaps, someone could take the children back to the bedroom so they can pack their things up," Bob said. "But first, let me suggest we find something to eat."

"Our food is in the kitchen," the boy said.

"Good, good," Bob said. "Are you hungry?"

The boy shrugged his shoulders.

"How about you?" Bob asked, speaking to Becca.

She gave him no response.

"Well, I know I certainly am," he said. "You gentlemen keep an eye on Dr. Kraus while Ethan, Sam, Lamar, and I go prepare some food."

"What the hell are you doing, Watkins?" asked Walter.

"I'm hungry, Walter, as I'm sure everyone else is. None of us has eaten all night. So, I'm going to find some food," Bob said as he went into the kitchen followed by the others.

While they were in the kitchen looking for things to eat, Bob pulled Ethan aside and spoke to him in a whisper. "We have him, but we must be careful in how we handle him. The man is a mass murder on a scale never seen before. However, he is also extremely intelligent and the only person who knows where the vaccine is. When the food is prepared, we will eat and then switch places with Walter and his men."

Ethan gave Bob a questioning look.

"I only trust two people in this cabin one hundred percent. This vaccine..." He paused. "Well I'm not sure how other people will react, but I do know that it needs to go with me back to Hamilton."

Ethan nodded to let Bob know that he understood.

The group prepared a smorgasbord of foods containing a variety of dried fruits, nuts, grains, and canned goods. While they prepared the meal, Bob explained to the kids that they were taking Victor in for questioning because he had broken the law, but he assured them they would be safe and protected from him. Bob couldn't tell if this pleased the kids, frightened them, or pissed them off. They were pretty guarded with their emotions. As planned, when the four of them and the children had finished eating, Bob went back into the living room.

"Walter, you, Joe, and Ronald should go eat."

Walter looked at Bob and nodded, but he didn't move.

"Go ahead, Walter. When you get back, we'll come up with a plan. Okay?"

Walter turned his eyes toward his two men. Both nodded and the three of them went into the kitchen.

Bob turned to Victor and spoke to him in a low voice. "Dr. Kraus, I know that there is a vaccine."

Victor smiled, exposing his still bloody teeth.

"I knew that Lesya told someone, I guess that was you?"

"Lesya was a colleague of mine. I followed her work very closely, she was a good scientist," Bob said. He didn't bother mentioning that the U.S. government had suspected that she might be involved in bioweapons research.

Victor let out a little laugh.

"Your colleague, your colleague," he said, struggling to control his voice and keep its volume under control. "I loved her. I loved her for years, ever since we were children not much older that those two in the bedroom."

"What happened to Lesya?" Bob asked softly.

"Lesya is gone. She was lost on the battlefield," he said as his eyes clouded over with tears.

Bob struggled to control his emotions.

"Victor, may I call you Victor?" Bob asked.

"I'd prefer to keep it formal, Dr. Watkins."

Bob smiled.

"Very well then," he said.

"Dr. Kraus, will you tell me where the vaccines are?"

Victor smiled back at him. "First of all, by what authority do you detain me? Last time I checked your credentials online, you were a Ph.D. that worked for the National Institutes of Health. You do not have the authority to arrest me, therefore, I consider this a hostile kidnapping. Furthermore, if I had access to a vaccine, which I do not, I certainly would not turn it over to the likes of you. Perhaps you haven't been paying attention, Dr. Watkins, but the U.S. government has been the greatest government on the planet for the last 200 plus years, so I would say that they have not only perpetuated the problems that are destroying this planet, they have led the charge. Why would I be willing to cooperate with that entity? Why should I…?"

As Victor ranted on, Cowboy walked up next to Bob. Victor stopped suddenly when he noticed the dog.

"What a beautiful canine," Victor said as he watched Cowboy. "You know, the earth needed to be preserved for creatures like him and for all the other species who have no defense against man. This virus may have been bad for mankind, but it provides a new environment that gives every other species a much greater chance at survival."

Cowboy wandered over to the window and lay down.

"You of all people, Dr. Watkins, surely know that this viral pandemic just sped up the process that nature itself would have eventually brought about. It was just a matter of time before some new plague thinned the herd of mankind. This virus just happened to accelerate things so that there would be something worth saving."

"You speak of this virus as if you had no idea where it came from. C'mon, Dr. Kraus, be a man and admit what you did. Lesya told me everything. You played God is what you and the others did, Dr. Kraus. Everything you say as a scientist is true. The planet could not sustain the recent human growth explosion, but your group had no right to intervene in the natural evolution of things. By doing so, you have interrupted the natural process, and that is not what we do. You cannot correct the injustice that you have done." He paused. "However, you can help the situation by turning over the vaccine. You can help mankind rebuild."

Victor laughed. "That has been my goal all along, Dr. Watkins."

Bob noticed that Cowboy had stood up and was standing on his hind legs pawing at some books on the shelf. Bob walked over to the shelf and looked at the books. He grabbed the one that seemed to be of most interest to the dog; it was the Bible. He patted Cowboy on the head.

"What is it, boy?" he asked, taking the Bible down from the shelf. He opened the front cover and turned to the first chapter. The book of Genesis.

"Your group was called the Genesis Project was it not?" he asked.

As he thumbed through the pages, he discovered that a square had been cut out of the pages in the middle of the Bible and inside the cutout space were four vials. Bob turned to Victor who had been watching him closely. Bob took the vials out of the book and put them inside his jacket pocket. Victor's face went dark with rage.

"Be careful with those, Dr. Watkins, you have no idea what might be inside those vials. You may unwittingly release the next great pandemic on the world," Victor stated snidely.

Bob could not get a read on whether or not he was being honest. He studied his face, but Victor was a seasoned actor. It was difficult to determine if he was telling the truth. As Bob was pondering the possibility that the vials contained a different deadly virus, Victor yelled out.

"You Native American gentlemen in the kitchen might be interested to know that these white people just offered me a deal for a vaccine. And, oh yes, I almost forgot to mention it but they left you three out of the equation. Looks like you will be royally screwed by the white man yet again."

Bob felt himself go from zero to a hundred on the rage scale in a nanosecond.

"YOU BASTARD KRAUS, YOU ARE NOT A SCIENTIST, YOU ARE NOT EVEN A MAN FOR THAT MATTER, I'M NOT SURE YOU'RE HUMAN."

In his rage, Bob took a step forward toward Victor. Suddenly, Bob felt like someone hit him in the chest at full force with a giant sledgehammer. He clutched at his chest as he tumbled to the floor. Victor's high-pitched laugh was the last conscious thing he heard.

CHAPTER 51

Victor assessed the situation as he watched the scene unfold. The old scientist crumbled to the ground mid-sentence, and everyone ran to his aid. Everyone, that is, except for the two men who were guarding him. They stayed close to his side. For a moment, Victor thought about trying to escape, but decided that the time was not right. There were still too many guns and several yards of cleared field that he would have to run through with his hands behind his back. He would be an easy target. He decided to wait until his chances of escape improved.

In the chaos that ensued as a result of Bob's sudden collapse, Ethan assumed command of the group while Sam began performing cardiopulmonary resuscitation on the old man.

"Walter, I need you and your guys to take Victor to Baab. Tell Burt and Carl to get the plane ready, we will need to transport Bob to Hamilton ASAP."

"I'll be right here with ya. Those two men are the best I have; they can get that prick to Baab and make sure that he does not escape."

Ethan looked at Walter, sizing him up. "I don't need you here."

"I don't remember anyone putting you in charge…"

Ethan thought about getting in this guy's face, but decided against it. "Fine, send your guys down to Baab with the prisoner. Lamar?"

"Yes, Ethan?"

"I need you to go with them and take care of these kids, okay?"

"That would be my pleasure. I will also be praying for your friend."

Ethan was glad to see that although Lamar's faith may be wavering, he was not giving it up completely. He nodded and then turned back to watch Sam work on Bob.

Lamar walked over to the kids and noticed the look of terror on their faces. He stooped down so that he would be at their level when he spoke.

"My name is Lamar," he started. "Can you tell me your names?"

The kids sheepishly offered their names to the man.

"That should be easy to remember. Bold Ben and Brave Becca. I want the two of you to know something about me. I am a dad. I have five kids, and I love kids. I will do whatever I can to protect you, okay?"

The kids nodded in unison and then Becca spoke up.

"Are you guys bad? Are you going to hurt us?"

Lamar paused a moment before responding.

"I know whatever I say is going to mean very little because you do not know if you can trust me. So, I am not going try to convince you one way or another. But here are a few facts about me that I hope will help."

He removed a family photo from his wallet and showed it to the kids.

"This is my family and they mean the world to me. I will protect you like I would protect one of my own. Second, I am a Mormon, which means I am a very religious man. I believe we should love one another just like Jesus loves all of us. And third, I have been hurt by many people since the virus came, and I do not want to be one of those people that causes pain. I don't know these people we are with, but they tell me that they are good and this Victor guy is bad. I believe them."

"He is very bad," Becca said, pointing to Victor. "He told me that God is stupid."

Victor glared at her.

"Well, he is wrong, and he is going to be punished for his crimes, in this life and in the next," Lamar stated.

"We need to get down the trail," one of Walter's men spoke, as he took the handcuff keys from Walter.

Lamar helped the two kids gather up a few things, and when everyone was ready, they fell in line behind the two men leading Victor down the trail. The early morning light was bright enough to see the trail.

It wasn't long after the group left with Victor and the kids, when the glass in the window of the chalet shattered suddenly, and Ethan and Walter fell to the floor to take cover. Sam crouched lower, covering Bob who lay laboring for breath and wavering in and out of consciousness. More bullets struck the cabin. After about a minute, the firing stopped.

"YOU IN THE CABIN, YOU'RE SURROUNDED," a familiar voice yelled.

Ethan, Sam, and Walter exchanged looks.

"How's it going, Commissioner?" Ethan yelled back.

"A hell of a lot better for me than it's going to be for you in about two minutes, Edwards," Harms yelled back.

"Tony, stop being such an asshole," Sam yelled.

There was a pause.

"Who else is in there?" the commissioner asked.

"Walter W. from East Glacier," Walter said.

"Walter, I'm glad to hear you made it. How's your...?" He stopped short.

"They are fine, Tony, I'm sorry about yours. I truly am."

There was a silent pause before the commissioner spoke.

"Me too. Thanks, Walter, I know you mean it. Walter, I've got the cabin surrounded. If you give up, I give you my word no one will be harmed."

Before Walter could answer, Ethan yelled back.

"Have you seen your buddy Mr. Clark around, Commissioner?"

"I take it you have, Edwards. I'm impressed. I thought there was more to you than met the eye, but I didn't think you'd be good enough to take out Wild Bill."

"I wasn't. He killed Larry and he would have killed me if not for Lamar. Bottom line, though, is your buddy is probably grizzly bear shit by now."

"I'm sorry to hear about the Mormon," Harms said. "But, all that doesn't change the situation we currently find ourselves in now does it?"

About forty yards from the Chalet, two additional men lay in the brush listening to the exchange.

"He's right, it doesn't change the situation," Mike said as he lowered his binoculars. He then turned to Fred Benson who was crouched down next to him. "But, maybe we will."

"There ain't no doubt about that," Fred said.

After the group transporting Victor and the kids had walked a couple of miles down the trail, Victor began to complain that he had to use the bathroom. When one of the guards volunteered to hold his dick for him, Victor refused.

"I have to take a shit, are you going to wipe my white ass for me, too?" he asked snidely.

The two guards looked at each other.

"You'd like that," one of them said. "I got this."

The guard led Victor off the trail and up the hill to a flat spot in the trees.

"Make it snappy."

"How am I supposed to take a shit and wipe with my hands cuffed behind my back?"

The guard rolled his eyes and approached Victor. After fumbling in his pocket for a few seconds, he retrieved the key and unlocked the cuff on Victor's right wrist. He then bent Victor's right arm painfully behind his back until he had safely locked the right handcuff tightly around a small tree that was about three inches in diameter. Victor barely had enough room to squat down and could barely touch the ground with his right hand.

"What about toilet paper?" Victor asked.

The guard laughed. "This is an organic toilet, you're gonna have ta use dried leaves off the ground. Ya got five minutes. Do your thing. Oh and, just fer the record, I'm just waiting for the first excuse to shoot yer ass, so go ahead an' try something... you'll make my day."

Victor looked at the guard but saw no room for mercy in his eyes. He waited until the guard took a couple of steps up the hill and turned his back toward him. Then he made his move. First, he dropped his pants and underwear so that it would appear that he really had to go. Next, he quickly removed the ring on his left-hand ring finger. It was a custom-designed titanium escape ring that came apart and contained a handcuff shim pick and a small tungsten-titanium carbide saw blade.

Victor looked at the handcuffs, and his heart sank as he realized the cuffs contained double locks, making them impossible for him to pick. He removed the blade and sawed furiously on the first link on the left cuff. After a couple of minutes, Victor had managed to cut through one side of one link. He then put all of his weight on the cuff and pulled on the cut link until there was enough space to remove the left cuff from the chain, which was still attached to the right cuff that was still attached to the tree. Victor left his hand loosely attached to the link so that it would appear that he was still connected.

"Time's up, pinch a loaf and let's get moving," the guard said, as he turned and headed back toward Victor, his rifle pointing toward the ground but ready to use in an instant.

Victor reached down with his free right hand and removed a custom-made throwing knife that was hidden in the sole of his hiking boot. He had one knife in each boot, but only retrieved the knife from his right boot.

"False alarm," Victor said. "I have the damnedest time taking a shit when I am stressed out."

The guard looked at Victor in disgust.

"Can you help me pull these pants up? It's harder to do than you might think with one hand tied up."

The guard shifted the rifle up, and slung it over his shoulder. He then turned and started to walk toward Victor to help him with his pants. Victor threw the knife as soon as the man looked up and caught him in the left eye, burying the knife deep into the man's brain. He fell to the ground dead. Victor retrieved the knife and thought about taking the rifle but decided that it would just be a liability. He moved toward the trail as he evaluated how he would escape. Unfortunately, they had stopped on a section of the trail that was steep. He could try to escape by running up the hill further, but he would not make it far and he would be easy to track.

The steepness of the trail also made it difficult to travel forward to get around the other guard who was waiting for them. The only way down this mountain was on the trail, which meant through the guard and the Mormon. He crouched down and assessed the situation. Lamar and the kids had sat down on the uphill side of the trail and appeared to be praying.

Victor shook his head and muttered under his breath. The other guard was standing about 15 feet down the trail, looking down the side of the mountain. Suddenly, he turned and looked up to the side of the mountain where Victor and the other man had gone.

"Let's get movin'. Is everything good?" he shouted up the hill.

Victor determined that he would have to take out the other guard first, but the man was a little out of his range. Therefore, he decided that he would drop down the trail just uphill of Lamar and the kids, taking them by surprise. Victor quietly climbed down onto the trail, hit Lamar in the back of the head with a large section of a tree branch, and grabbed the two children, using them as a shield. Lamar fell to the ground, rolled several feet down the trail in front of them, and grabbed his head. He had no idea what happened. When the guard turned to see the commotion, he immediately noticed Victor crouching behind the two kids. He lifted his rifle and took careful aim at Victor, who moved Becca in front of his head.

"You don't want to kill one of these kids, do you?" Victor asked.

"Not particularly, but you don't seem to mind."

Without warning, Victor used the knife that he held in his hand to cut Becca's throat. As her body fell to the ground, the guard gasped in disbelief. The momentary pause cost him. Victor then threw his knife accurately and forcefully, burying the knife deeply into the bridge of the man's nose right between his eyes. He fell to the ground.

Ben screamed out as his sister's body fell to the ground and he removed the knife that Victor had given him and stabbed Victor deeply in the left thigh, only a second after Victor had thrown the knife at the second guard. Victor screamed out in pain as Ben ran down the trail. Victor reached into the sole of his left boot and retrieved a second knife. In one fluid movement, he aimed it at the back of Ben's head and let it fly.

Lamar had been watching the whole scene unfold, and when he saw Victor take aim at Ben, he jumped up without a moment's hesitation and got between the knife and Ben just as Victor released it. Ben had just gotten to where Lamar was lying and the sudden jump from Lamar knocked him off balance. The knife caught Lamar on the back of his right side in the kidney, and he let out a scream as he and Ben tumbled together off the trail and down the steep embankment. Lamar and Ben plummeted down the hill for several yards before they landed on a small rock outcropping, hidden from the view of the trail above.

Lamar was unconscious and the knife in his side was barely visible as it had been forced deeper into his side by all of the tumbling. Ben was badly broken up and barely coherent. Ben looked around. He could see nothing but steep mountainside above and a steep drop off below. They had landed on a pile of black and gray rocks with nothing growing anywhere near them. Ben tried to shake Lamar, but Lamar did not wake up. Ben noticed that he was breathing very short breaths and blood was oozing from several large gashes, including one on his forehead.

Ben tried to move into a more comfortable position but finally gave up when he realized that he could not move in any way without increasing his pain. He looked out over the fantastically beautiful park below. The view was stunning. Above, he noticed a large black bird sailing comfortably on the wind currents. He wondered briefly if they would end up being that bird's lunch. His thoughts turned to his sister and tears poured freely down his cheeks as he remembered her small body falling onto the trail. He whispered a silent prayer and then closed his eyes, ready to join her.

Meanwhile, Victor jumped up, winced as the pain in his left thigh registered, and limped to the edge of the trail to see what had become of Lamar and the boy. He could not see them below, which he took as a good sign. He figured they must have fallen to their certain deaths. He could see for several feet in all direction, and it was clear they did not stop on their way down. He felt sad for a moment. He had invested a lot of time and energy in Plan B, and now it was gone. It was time for Plan C, whatever that turned out to be.

He removed the knife from his leg, cleaned it on Becca's shirt, and placed it in his shirt pocket. He then retrieved his knife from the guard's head and returned it to its sheath in the sole of his right boot. It pissed him off that he lost the second knife and he considered climbing down the mountain to retrieve it, but finally decided to let it go. He examined his wound carefully, and when he was certain that no major blood vessels were cut, he sliced the back of Becca's pant leg off of her body and fashioned it into a bandage that he wrapped tightly around his leg. He then cleared the trail of all signs of foul play by rolling the bodies off the steep edge and covering any blood spots with loose dirt.

When he was satisfied that the trail looked undisturbed, he headed down the trail toward the trailhead. After several hundred yards, the trail entered into a very long switchback, which went straight for at least a half mile before turning back in the same direction and heading down the hill. Victor was concerned that the group that was still at Sperry Chalet could be coming along anytime, and he wanted to get to his Land Rover as soon as possible. Therefore, he decided to forgo the trail and head directly down the hill, which was not nearly as steep as it had been earlier. The shortcut shaved about a half an hour off the hike and put Victor at the Sperry Chalet trailhead just as the sun was at its highest point for the day.

He quickly made his way to the Many Lakes Lodge and found his Land Rover. He had disconnected the battery before he left it, so after he was certain no one was around and no one had messed with his vehicle, he retrieved the keys from under the rock where he had hidden them, unlocked and popped the hood, and reconnected the battery cables with the tools he had left hidden beside the battery. He then closed the hood, unlocked the cab, and climbed in. The Land Rover started on the first try.

"I love my Land Rover," Victor said out loud as he checked his gas tank. It was half full. He checked the reserve tank and it was sitting at three-quarters. Victor did a quick calculation and figured that he had about 400 miles' worth of fuel.

He remembered hearing the other men at the chalet talking about going to Baab, but he knew very little about that town and he wasn't equipped to take down that many men at once. He decided his best course was to get out of the park and start heading east. If he could get to South Dakota, he would be able to hide out for as long as necessary, and he had another cache of supplies hidden there. However, he didn't want to get too far away from the park just yet, because he wanted to get his supply of vaccines before he left.

Victor knew the Typhon virus would behave much like the measles virus after the initial pandemic. There would be very few survivors, but there would be pockets of people who never encountered the virus and who would be at risk. In addition, every child born in the future would need a vaccine because, like measles virus, this virus was so contagious it would be nearly impossible to eradicate it. There were only three options for dealing with this virus. You could catch it and die, which most had already. You could catch it and live, but there were severe consequences for most survivors, or you could get the vaccine and be protected from it.

As Victor thought about it, it occurred to him there was at least one other possibility; a person could be resistant to the virus, meaning they could have some unique genetic factor that prevented them from getting the infection. That would be a rare occurrence, but there would certainly be those who were unable to be infected. Regardless, the virus would continue to percolate in the human population just waiting for the next opportunity to cause an epidemic.

Victor left the park through the West Glacier entry point and then headed east on Highway 2. He had made it only a few miles when he encountered a group of motorcycles headed in the opposite direction. There were about 10-12 of them and the men riding these bikes looked rough. Victor slowed down as they passed and smiled as a thought went across his mind. He quickly turned around and headed back in the direction the motorcycles had gone. He barely got the Land Rover turned around when he noticed the motorcycles had also turned around and were upon him.

Victor smiled as he stepped out of his vehicle.

"This must be fate," he said. "We both turned back to meet each other."

Rage and the Devil's Dark Knights glared at the odd man who appeared to have forgotten what fear was. It was at that moment that Rage recognized who was standing before him.

"Hey, Ethan," Mike yelled. "I was wondering if Sam and you all could use a little help? Just so happens I brought some."

Ethan and Sam stared at each other. Ethan smiled.

"Told you he was alright." He could see the tears welling up in her eyes.

"Mike," Samantha cried out.

"Yeah, yeah," he said before she could continue.

"So now what, Commissioner?" Ethan yelled. "You really want a bloodbath?"

Harms turned and looked at some of his men and thought for a moment.

"We need to talk, Commissioner, just you and me," Ethan said.

Walter looked at Ethan. "Why just you and him?"

"Because, if they shoot me, somebody's got to help Sam and Bob if that's you okay with you, Walter."

Walter nodded.

"How about it, Commissioner, we talking or shooting?"

"Maybe both," Harms yelled back. "But, we'll talk first I suppose. Come out, and I'll meet you halfway."

"I'll have you in my crosshairs, Commissioner," Mike yelled.

"I bet you will, Mike," he shouted back. "I bet you will," he said again under his breath.

The two men stopped in front of the chalet with about 7 feet between them.

"I'm sorry about…" Harms stopped in mid-sentence. "Have you got it?"

Ethan nodded in the affirmative; there wasn't time or any point in denying it.

"You won't get it. I'll destroy it first. And, let's face it, Commissioner, what would you do with it if you had it?"

Harms looked at him. "So, what's your plan?"

"I've got a doctor in there who knows what to do with the vaccine, but he's had a heart attack. I've got to get both him and the vaccine to Saint Mary. We've got a small plane there that can get them back to the Rocky Mountain Labs at Hamilton, hopefully, in time to help the doctor and I guess all of us. You know it's our only hope, Harms. What would your family have wanted you to do?"

"Don't even bring my…" Harms stopped.

"You're right, I'm sorry, it was a bad call on my part."

Harms nodded at him. After looking hard at Ethan for a moment, he held his hands up and showed them, then he slowly moved them toward his neck and removed a chain that he had been wearing. "There's nitro in this bottle, hopefully, it will help your doctor. Get him and the vaccine to that lab."

He turned and walked away, but after a few feet, he turned back. "I'll be seeing you again, Edwards."

Ethan just nodded turned and walked quickly back to the cabin.

THE END

Eric Donaldson lives in the Washington, DC area where he works as a virologist. He is married to Shawna, the love of his life, and is the proud stepfather of Callie and Tristan. He enjoys writing, meditating, hiking and backpacking when he is not worrying about the next viral outbreak.

Tim Harmon lives in Kalispell, Montana with his wife, Tammy, who he knows without a doubt is his soul mate. He considers himself to be a student of life and readily admits he's had to repeat several classes more than once. If asked, he'll tell you he doesn't expect to be graduating anytime soon.

CHECK OUT OTHER GREAT APOCALYPSE BOOKS

XY
by D.S. Lillico

An iron fortress protected by automated gun turrets is the only world Elsie has ever known.

When tragedy strikes, Elsie is forced to leave the sanctuary of her home and out into a brutal new world. A post-apocalyptic wasteland filled with savage mutants.

Hunted and alone Elsie stumbles into the care of a giant named Punch, but the world is now full of worse things than giants. Cannibals are starving, bandits are roaming and war is coming.

Elsie's arrival plunges the new-world further into darkness... and is there really something hidden inside of her?

SANCTUARY
by Ian Page

Deeta Nakshband, a Connecticut physician is attacked by a local surgeon while on duty in the hospital. Her friend, Janelle Jefferson, has similar experiences in Miami. Both of them become aware of an increasingly violent world as acts of isolated brutality escalate into civil unrest. They grapple with their paranoia as family members and coworkers become dangerously unpredictable. Worldwide, military units go rogue, war begins in Korea and cities implode as people slaughter each other in the streets. Martial law is declared in an attempt to maintain order. People are arrested, detainment camps are set up and interrogations end with tragic consequences as modern civilization crumbles. Deeta and Janelle band together with family friends and coworkers to save each other and find sanctuary.

CHECK OUT OTHER GREAT
APOCALYPSE BOOKS

THE DEAD FAMILIAR
by J.D. McKenna

In the twilight hours of a failing world, one man seeks to bring his loved ones to safety. Jack Hightower: Marine, bar-keep, and doomsday prepper. He knows of the coming calamity, and on the final night of an old world he seeks a new beginning.
This is the story of that night, the tale of how Jack and his survivor's colony in the north came to be.

DOMINION
by Doug Goodman

Dominion has been taken from man. Now, six friends must cross an apocalyptic wasteland dominated by a hell's me-nagerie of mega-fauna. Their middle-class suburban skills are no longer applicable to the world they live in. To find a safe haven in this world they will need to develop a new set of survival skills and fight the mutated denizens of the animal kingdom for every step of their terrifying journey.

CHECK OUT OTHER GREAT APOCALYPSE BOOKS

WHITE OUT
by Eric Dimbleby

An apocalyptic snowstorm sweeps the globe. Experts predict this freak storm will be "The New Ice Age." Electricity is gone, as are all forms of communication and road travel. As each member of a divided family tries to survive in their own way, they must deal with a snow-driven madness that has gripped the underlying evil in the hearts of men. In an epic struggle to get home and reunite, they will find that terror lies around every snow drift... and even in their very own backyard.

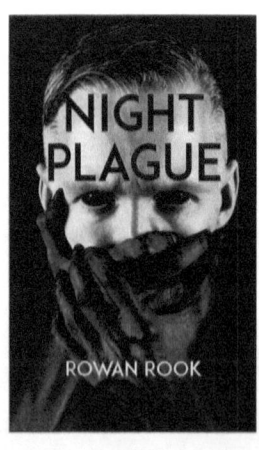

NIGHT PLAGUE
by Rowan Rook

Humankind will soon be extinct. A mysterious pandemic cut through two-thirds of the population in just four short years, and within another four, it will decimate everything – and everyone – left.

The last days are ticking by, relentless and ruthless, and the reclusive Mason Mild finds himself torn between a peaceful end and a brutal immortality. Between his hopeless, but comfortable days with his family, and something new...something violent and wild.

Have the fang marks above his heel dealt him an early demise or a second birth?

www.ingramcontent.com/pod-product-compliance
Lightning Source LLC
Chambersburg PA
CBHW030644260626

47157CB00007B/2475